Also by Jan Springer

Club Rendezvous
Shy Girl

Cowboys Online : Moose Ranch
Cowboys for Christmas
Cowboys In Her Pocket
Loving Her Cowboys
Cowboys in Her Heart
Always Her Cowboys

Intimate Secrets
Intimate Lover
Intimate Kisses
Intimate Stranger

Kidnap Fantasies
Jade's Fantasy
Zero To Sexy

Christmas Lovers

Pleasure Bound
A Hero's Welcome
A Hero Escapes
A Hero Betrayed
A Hero's Kiss
A Hero Wanted
Captive Heroes

Pleasure Bound Boxed Set
Pleasure Bound : COMPLETE SERIES SciFi Erotic Romance
Boxed Set

Tentacles Shifter Erotic Romance
Taken by Him

The Key Club
A Merry Menage Christmas
Sophie's Menage
Jewel's Menage
Jaxie's Menage

The Outlaw Lovers

Jude Outlaw
The Claiming
Colter's Revenge
Tyler's Woman
Resistance
The Outlaw Lovers
Alpha Outlaws Boxed Set

Vampira
Sweet Heat
Dark Heat
Wet Heat
Crimson Heat

Standalone
A Touch of Menage Boxed Set
Shades of Menage Boxed Set
Naughty Girl Desires Boxed Set
Nice Girl Naughty
Sinderella Sexy
The Biker and The Bride
The Fire Within
Bared to Him
Pleasure Bound : A Futuristic Adult Romance Boxed Set
Merry Menage Kisses Boxed Set
Inner Girl Rising
Stripped Naked
Risqué Girl Delights Boxed Set
A Holiday Menage
Ménage À Trois

A Hitman for Hannah
Billionaire Boyfriend
Edible Delights
Vampira
Toygasm
The Dark Side

Watch for more at www.janspringer.com.

Intimate Stranger

Jan Springer

Investigative journalist, Steve McCullen, has returned home with a new face, a new identity, and a burning desire for revenge. His wife, Emily, is about to marry his best friend; the man Steve suspects is behind his faked death and nightmare imprisonment for the past few years.

The minute Emily catches the sexy stranger stealing food from her lighthouse kitchen, she feels a strong attraction to him. Resisting the urge to send him away, she decides to hire him as her handyman. But soon he's making her feel so hot that she's surrendering herself to her naughty intimate needs.

Can she break through the painful walls surrounding this mysterious man? Why does he remind her so much of her dead husband? And why does his welcome touch make her forget the man she's about to marry? When shocking secrets are revealed, Emily must put aside her feelings of betrayal to stop someone who is bent on destroying her second chance at love.

Intimate Stranger
Published by Spunky Girl Publishing
Copyright 2019 by Jan Springer
2nd edition
Cover art by Talina Perkins ~ Bookin' It Designs
Eroded beach cliff and lighthouse Prince Edward Island, Canada ~
photo by Vlad Podkhlebnik / Alamy Stock Photo (licensed)
Models ~ The Killion Group (licensed)

Trademarks Acknowledgement

The author acknowledges the trademark status and trademark owners of the following wordmarks mentioned in this work of fiction:

Coca-Cola: The Coca-Cola Company

Cyclosporin: G&S Pharmaceutical

Mack Truck: subsidiary of AB Volvo, Volvo Group

Prednisone: Central Pharmaceuticals Inc

The New York Times: New York Times Company

The Twilight Zone: CBS

Wizard of Oz: Turner Entertainment Co.

Prologue

"So? Exactly how many kids do you want?" Steve suddenly asked with a serious tone that shocked twenty-year old Emily Montgomery McCullen. She wasn't prepared to show him her reaction. Not too long ago her new husband had said he wanted to wait in starting a family. Now a couple of weeks after that conversation, he was bringing up the subject.

In the bathroom of all places, while he stood here watching her in the shower, his green eyes studying her every movement with a hungry desire she found quite arousing.

"As many kids as you can give me whenever you want, hunky hubby," she answered.

She kept her voice free of the desperation searing through her. Desperation for a family of her own. She didn't want the subject to go away even before it got started. Damned if she was going to get her hopes up if he was just curious. He said nothing as she reached for the showerhead and rinsed off the soap suds from her breasts.

Lately, it was happening more and more often. Him coming in while she was in the shower. Not that she minded him being so interested in her.

In fact, she enjoyed the lusty way his gaze traveled over her body, his eyes hot with desire as he shed his t-shirt revealing nicely toned muscles that laced his chest and biceps.

She swallowed as he lowered the zipper of his jeans and drew his pants and underwear over his lean hips.

Heat billowed through her and her knees weakened as the thick length of Steve's cock erupted.

Oh boy, he certainly was in the mood this morning. Her pussy clenched as she watched his penis swell and lengthen. She liked the power she had in turning him on so easily. Enjoyed the helpless pleasure sparking along her nerve endings, making her excited.

"I've been thinking," he said as he slipped out of his jeans and underwear and then stepped into the shower.

He smelled captivating. The scent of sexy man. Her man.

"Is that why I smell burning rubber?" she teased as she moved over to make room for him.

They were always kidding each other when one of them said what the other was thinking. Sometimes they pretended they smelled smoke and other times burning rubber as in the spinning of one's wheels.

Amusement flashed in his eyes then quickly disappeared as his hands slipped over the curve of her hips, his fingers burning her flesh as he held her.

"There won't be any more rubbers burning the midnight oil when I make love to you from here on out, Emily."

Surprise washed over her. What *was* he saying?

She wasn't on any kind of birth control because the pills didn't agree with her. Instead, they used condoms whenever they had sex. He always had one or two nearby, but she didn't see any within sight tonight.

Understanding zipped through her and she began to tremble.

"I know I said I wanted to wait. But I changed my mind."

Oh my God!

"Are you sure?" she asked, trying hard to keep the quiver of disbelief out of her voice.

Goodness, he had to be sure or he wouldn't be saying it. He knew a baby was a lifelong commitment. He also knew she really wanted a family, so he would never tease her about something this serious.

He nodded as he took the showerhead from her hand and let it drop to the ceramic floor. The expression in his eyes was a look that seared right to her very soul. A look like that told her he was doing this for both of them, not just for her.

Oh my God, he is ready.

There was no question in her mind about wanting babies with the man she loved. And what a beautiful way to create them—by making love in the shower.

She moaned as his palms slid off her waist, over her tummy and up to cup her breasts, his thumbs stroking her nipples. Fire lanced through her at his tender touches and she creamed, readying for him. He held her breasts, lifting them as he lowered his head. Excitement rocked her as his teeth raked her right nipple before taking her rigid flesh into his hot mouth.

"Why did you change your mind?" she gasped, enjoying the heat of his lips. She curled her hands over his strong shoulders loving the way his muscles flexed beneath her fingers. She watched the sexy way he sucked her nipple, his pink mouth, moving erotically.

She almost moaned out loud when he stopped and looked up at her. Seriousness shone in his eyes as he spoke.

"Life is too short, baby. You don't know from one day to the next when you're going to drop dead of a heart attack or a stroke or all those other diseases that are floating around out there. Shit happens no matter how old you are. We may as well get started. We've got this nice little lighthouse from your uncle and it's a great place to raise kids. You said so yourself. No babysitters, no day school. We'll bring them up the old-fashioned way with homeschooling, fresh air and sunshine and a huge vegetable garden out back were we can grow organic food and—"

Emily cut him off by clasping the back of his corded neck and pushing his mouth against her nipple again.

"Open," she demanded.

He grinned and did her bidding. His mouth was once again a brand of heat. More warm wetness moistened her pussy as his lips tugged.

"That feels good, Steve. Just keep doing what you're doing and I'll keep talking for you. My pussy is creaming up a storm and we're going to need all the lube we can get from here on out."

She giggled, not believing he was actually talking about putting a garden out back of the lighthouse. He'd made no bones about not truly liking this place, but she'd assured him the island would grow on him.

She hadn't thought it would grow on him so fast!

"I thought you said you wanted to wait until you decided whether or not you could handle your chapped lips problem?" she teased.

He made a move to remove his mouth from her nipple, but she kept a firm hand against the back of his neck.

"Keep sucking, big boy. Obviously, you've come to the conclusion you can handle chapped lips for the next fifty or so years."

At her remark, his lips twitched in humor. Gently he bit into her flesh, the sharp pain made her gasp and she loosened her grip on his head. He used the opportunity to switch breasts, taking her left nipple into his mouth.

Sweet sensations lashed through her. Her left nipple had always been more sensitive than her right. She didn't know why but that's the way it was. Steve knew it too and didn't give the firm sucking pressure as he'd done to the other one.

Reaching down with her free hand, she wrapped her fingers around the base of his shaft. He was having fun with her, so she would have fun with him too. Beneath her palm, his cock jerked as she squeezed. Quickly she followed by trailing her fingers up and down his shaft. She knew he liked it this way and he groaned his approval.

"After digging up that garden you'll be nice and sweaty. You'll be wanting more showers and I'll be here waiting for you every time."

He groaned again as she slid his cock into her vagina, his thickness invading her. Some of her control shattered. Letting go of his neck, she grabbed him by his shoulders and allowed her fingers to explore the smoothness of his back. Releasing her nipple, he raised his head and swiftly kissed her. His mouth felt hot and fierce against hers and his tongue prodded between her lips like a miniature cock, shattering more of her control.

When his finger slid over her moist clit and he began to massage her with such possession, she hissed her appreciation as the thick waves of pleasure began its wicked ascent. He had her perched on the edge within seconds.

Letting her go, he cupped her ass, lifted her so she could wrap her legs around his hips, allowing him to sink deeper into her.

Oh yes, very nice fit, she thought as wonder cascaded through her. Wonder that maybe on their first try she would get pregnant. She felt dazed too by the intensity of how much pleasure she felt beneath his touches.

"Nice and tight," he moaned against her mouth. Easing her away, he moved her against him again, plunging his cock back into her. She cried out at the exquisite pressure as he pumped and moaned at the pleasure threatening to drag her under.

She could hear the slurping sounds every time he entered her and the scent of their sex mingled in the hot shower steam.

Gosh, she loved the ferocious way he fucked her. Confident and bold. Fierce and passionate.

He knew the perfect angle to hit her sensitive G-spot every time he entered. His swollen cock always stretched her so beautifully. Always with the right pressure. He did everything perfect and his rhythm drove her quickly toward climax. The stirring of an orgasm built fast as he continued his thrusts. Her fingers dug into solid muscle and she tensed, her thighs tightening with anticipation.

Heat seared through her and she couldn't stop the frantic gasps into his mouth as the fierce explosion hit, tearing her apart, mind, body and soul. The exquisite release made her moan over and over again, and a moment later she heard his answering moans as he quickly joined her.

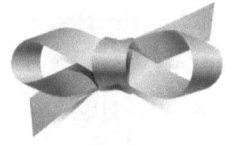

Chapter One

Eight years later

E mily Montgomery McCullen peered through the darkness to the illuminated bedroom clock and smiled nervously.

Midnight. Halloween had arrived. It was now the witching hour. Time to put the romance ritual to the test.

Since she was a young teenager, she'd heard the locals speak of the romance ritual. If a girl or woman of marrying age was bold enough, all she had to do was wait for the Halloween witching hour, sit in front of a mirror, brush her hair and at the same time eat an apple. If the image of a coffin appeared over her shoulder, she would not live another year. If the image of a man appeared, he would be her future husband.

An involuntary shiver scrambled up her spine and she turned her attention to the mirror. A pathetic sparkle of hope flashed in her brown eyes and it brought a harsh chuckle from her lips.

She was twenty-eight years old and she still believed in romance. She should have her head examined. Her one true knight in shining armor had died eight years ago and no amount of superstitious nonsense would change the fact she was destined not to have another wild romance in this lifetime.

Besides, who needed romance? She was getting married in a few weeks to a nice guy. He was a man who used to be good friends with her late husband, Steve. Skip wanted to get started on a family as soon as possible. She'd always wanted her own family, but she'd wanted it with Steve.

She cared for Skip and he liked her, and she knew they would learn to love each other as their marriage progressed. Besides, she wasn't getting any marriage offers by living alone out here on an island in the ocean, so she'd decided to accept the first proposal she'd gotten. Soon she would have the family she'd always craved and her own children to love. At least that part of her dream could come true.

Okay, so the ritual was just folklore and she was being silly tonight. Despite her future finally being mapped out, she still couldn't resist acting out the ancient romance ritual.

Besides, whom would it hurt? No one knew what she was doing tonight. No one knew she was sitting in her lighthouse bedroom unable to sleep, bored stiff, or that she'd totally flipped out in doing this silly ritual.

Emily inhaled a deep breath.

"Here goes," she whispered.

Feeling giddy, she picked up the apple with one hand and her late mother's smooth ivory-handled brush in the other hand. Then she drew the brush through her shoulder-length hair. At the same time, she took a giant bite out of her apple and kept her eyes glued to the mirror.

To her disappointment nothing happened.

Oh well, at least the apple tasted good and her hair would get a nice brushing. She closed her eyes, sank back against the chair and continued to nibble on the sweet treat.

Everything was unusually quiet tonight outside her Shipwreck Island home. No waves pounded the nearby cliffs and the wind didn't so much as whisper against her windowpanes. The only sounds she heard were the brush skimming through her hair, the crush of her teeth against her delicious victim and the faint tick of the clock.

Under the slow ministrations of her brush strokes she thought of her future with the man she would marry. Skip Cole was a journalist like her husband had been. Steve had liked him. Skip was also good father material from what she'd seen in the times he'd taken her to visit his brother and sister's homes. He played easily with his nieces and nephews and they worshipped him.

There was a big problem though. Lately he'd been asking her to leave her snug Canadian island and move back to New York City to live with him in his penthouse.

She hated the big city, the noise and crowded streets, and he hated being away from the city. In order to marry Skip, she had to give up her dream of living in this cozy lighthouse for her other dream of having children come true.

She frowned. Yes, she was settling for a man she didn't love. But lots of people settled and they had successful marriages. They would be a good match. Their marriage would work. She would make sure it would.

Finishing her apple, she ran a final sweep through her hair and tried to ignore the lonely ache clutching her heart. When she opened her eyes, she gasped in disbelief.

In the mirror, over her shoulder, hovered an image of her dead husband, Steve. He smiled that wonderful crooked grin of his.

Her heart crashed against her chest and a cold knot of uneasiness scrambled into her belly.

Whirling around, she realized it was just a fluke.

A moonbeam had zipped through the window and lit up Steve's side of their wedding portrait that hung on the wall.

Emily rolled her eyes and placed the brush on the vanity.

For crying out loud! It was midnight and it was officially October thirty-first. Spooky things were supposed to happen, right? Besides, everyone deserved a good scare on Halloween. It wouldn't be the same if it were treated as just another normal day.

She stood and headed to her open bedroom window. Looking out, she spied the trails of white mist swirl amongst the rocky cliffs below and over the glasslike ocean. The only indication of an approaching storm was the wrinkled gray clouds stalking ever closer to the full moon.

A cool breeze suddenly drifted in and whispered against her bare arms, making her shiver. She reached up to close the window and froze.

An odd noise erupted from somewhere inside her keeper house. *Okay. Don't freak out. It's just a weird sound. Probably nothing.*

From all the years of living alone she'd learned one very important thing. She had to meet her fears head-on and right away. Hiding in her bedroom and scaring the shit out of herself with every little noise only heightened the fear of whatever it might be out there.

She'd do a quick investigation and then she'd get to sleep.

Slowly, she reached for the can of mace her fiancé had brought from the States and insisted she keep beside her bed.

She began to tremble as she tiptoed to her open bedroom doorway and peered out and across the hall into her living room. Delicate moonbeams dusted her furniture with an eerie blue glaze.

For what seemed like an eternity she stood there and listened. Despite not hearing that mysterious sound again she had a horrible feeling she wasn't alone in the lighthouse.

Her tummy hollowed out in a sick feeling as she stared down the hallway and spied a pale-yellow glow splashing from beneath her closed kitchen door. Had she left the light on in that room? No, the light would be brighter than that. Maybe it was from the moon?

Um no. Wrong color.

Resisting the urge to escape out the back door and hide in the bushes, Emily shakily pointed the mace in front of her. Her legs wobbled as she stepped forward. She reached the doorway and rested her hand on the doorknob and listened.

She couldn't hear anything, so she held her breath, turned the doorknob ever-so quietly and pushed the door inward just enough to peek inside.

Someone was leaning into her refrigerator and eating her food! From the size of his shoulders and narrow, lean hips, she knew it was a man. He was dressed in dark pants and a dark jacket.

He seemed so engrossed in devouring her fried chicken that he didn't even notice he'd been caught. To her horror, he stuck his head deeper into her fridge and reached for another one of the drumsticks she'd slaved over in special preparation for tomorrow's fall fair.

A volley of shivers slammed into her. She wished she had cell phone access, so she could call the cops from a safe area. But what could they do? It was a half an hour boat ride from the main island to here. It was on occasions like this she wished she lived in civilization. Wished her only land-line phone wasn't in the kitchen with the intruder.

She tried to ignore the horrible pounding of her heart as it beat against her chest and inside her ears.

She needed to calm down. Needed to get out of here.

She took a step backward and a loose wooden plank creaked beneath her foot.

Oh darn!

The intruder heard the sound and his head snapped up so fast that it crashed against the inside top of the fridge. A quick curse followed.

Shit.

She wasn't going to make it out of here without him being on her.

Fear almost paralyzed her mouth and it was hard to form words.

"No sudden moves," she mumbled jerkily.

The air in her lungs, as well as her nerve, was quickly vanishing.

"I have a gun and I'll blow a hole right through you."

Oh Lord, she sounded like a Texas Ranger in a spaghetti western, but her threat was working, the intruder didn't flinch a muscle. Hopefully she could usher him out of her home before he noticed her weapon of choice wasn't a gun as she said.

"Don't shoot. I'm unarmed," he called out.

He had an odd whispery voice that made him sound as if he had a touch of laryngitis.

"That's your first mistake!" she said, trying to inject toughness into her voice. It was hard. She could barely speak she was so scared, and her breaths were coming so fast she swore she just might pass out.

Stupid! Why don't you run? Get outside and hide somewhere!

The best defense is a good offense so use the element of surprise to your advantage, her late husband used to say and his words rang like a warning bell in her head now.

The mace! She'd forgotten the mace in her hand. If he tried something, she wouldn't hesitate to use it and then she'd run for her life.

"My husband is in the next room. All I have to do is scream, so you better get out!"

"Okay. Okay. Take it easy. I think I'd better explain," he said.

His head was still stuck in the fridge. But he'd returned the chicken he'd been eating to the plate.

Was he getting ready to rush her? She tensed her finger on the can of mace.

"Get out." Her voice was getting stronger now.

"But—"

"Get out! Now!"

Slowly he started moving away from the fridge. Finally, he straightened, and put his arms in the air. His back was still toward her, so she wasn't sure if she knew him. His scent swarmed out of the darkness and she couldn't help but inhale. He smelled of the fresh ocean breeze, wave-crashed beach and to her surprise a deep loneliness suddenly tugged at her heart.

When he reached the door, he hesitated. "I'm sorry, I didn't mean to frighten you."

What was his problem? What was taking him so long to get out of here!

"Leave!" *Please go!*

He lowered his arms and she tensed when his hand snaked out to flick on the light switch. The harsh light burned into her eyes, making her blink. Was he trying to blind her so he could grab her?

Thankfully he remained by the door, raised his arms again and slowly turned around to face her.

She readied to shoot.

He was at least one foot taller than her. Sprinkles of gray dusted his collar-length, golden-brown hair.

He had a strong, straight nose. A tiny cleft in his chin. No lines around his mouth. A mouth that suddenly dropped open in surprise at the sight of the mace.

His skin was too smooth and too pale as if he'd been sick. But it was his eyes that captured her full attention. The color of sparkling ocean blue, they were filled with layers of emotions she couldn't understand. It seemed as if he were overwhelmed by those emotions and she suddenly was too. The most prominent being a haunted sadness that ripped at her insides.

His intense gaze unsettled her. It was an oddly familiar gaze and yet she knew she'd never seen those eyes before. It was an intimate look that said they knew each other, and they shared many secrets, but she'd never met him before.

He seemed to expect her to say something, and when she didn't, he smiled a crooked grin that zapped a powerful jolt of *déjà vu* straight through her.

The spooky feeling urged her not to let this man walk out of her life. Then she saw something around his neck that shot surprise through her. A glittering gold medallion hung from a gold chain that was wrapped around his neck. She could barely make out the image, but instincts told her it was a portrait of a man carrying a child on his shoulders. A Saint Christopher medallion. A medal signifying safety to travelers.

She'd given her husband Steve one like it many years ago, just before he'd been killed.

She watched helplessly as the stranger's large hand twisted the doorknob of the door that would lead him onto the back deck and ultimately the wharf and ocean and far away from her.

Let him go! *He could be dangerous*, a voice inside her shouted.

A loud, hungry growl escaped his stomach and a pang of guilt slithered through her. He turned and stepped across the threshold, toward the dark.

Don't let him leave, her heart begged. Anyone who wore a Saint Christopher medallion couldn't be all bad. Besides, she had her mace. He wouldn't hurt her as long as she had that.

"Wait!"

Her meek squeak stopped him cold and his shoulders tensed. He raised his hands over his head again, clamped his fingers behind his neck and waited. He probably figured she was going to call the police and press charges against him for trespassing.

"The least I can do is feed you. You can put your arms down but stay right there."

She noticed some of the tenseness seep out of his shoulders and he did as she instructed.

Keeping her mace ready and her eyes glued to the tall stranger, Emily moved toward the open refrigerator. She tried to keep calm, but it didn't work.

Her hands shook as she tugged out the food she'd made for the fair. To make matters worse, she could barely scoop the food onto a plate, all the while her jumbled mind chastised her for not getting rid of the stranger.

Such a stupid woman. Send him away!

As she topped the heaping plate of food with more fried chicken, her emotions were all jumbled. Why did he seem so familiar? Why was he here? Why did she care?

It was a mistake encouraging him to linger. The sooner she fed him, the faster she could send him on his way. With plate in hand, she turned to the door and froze.

The stranger was gone, and her emergency house key dangled in the door lock.

·· ❦ ··

HE STEPPED ONTO THE wooden deck just outside the keeper house and thoroughly enjoyed the crisp autumn wind that sliced painfully into his face.

Man! He could not believe he'd talked to Emily! The mere sight of her made him feel so alive. So free.

On impulse he'd flicked on the light switch, eager that she might recognize him. Hoping she would wrap her arms around his neck and welcome him home with a mind-blowing kiss.

Deep down he'd know it wouldn't happen. The extensive plastic surgery to his face had totally changed his appearance and the damage done to his voice box made sure she would never recognize his voice.

But she looked fantastic. Her once long hair was now fashioned into a new shoulder-length wavy do and her bangs were gone in favor of the no-bang hippie look. It suited her better, he had to admit, and she looked so healthy, so fresh, so innocent.

Just looking at her brought back the familiar warmth he'd always gotten when being near her. Brought back the searing memories of their brief time together. Her ultimatum of him giving up his dangerous journalist job if he expected her to stay with him.

Dammit!

He should have stuck to his plan of simply breaking into the lighthouse, grabbing what he needed and leaving. Yet, when he'd checked the hiding place for the keeper house key and found the key still there, an overwhelming urge had gripped him. He'd wanted to go inside his home. Wanted to pretend he had never left. To pretend what could have been, if only for a few short minutes. When he'd smelled the delicious aromas of her fried chicken floating through the air, his stomach had clenched with hunger. It was a gentle reminder he hadn't eaten a meal cooked by his wife in years.

He'd made a big mistake breaking in while she was home. It still wasn't too late to make it right again. He could simply slip away and break in another time. She would never have to see him again. Never have to be afraid of him again.

Indecision screamed at him as he lifted his head to look at the wooden octagonal lighthouse tower attached to the keeper house. This place had been home for such a short, sweet time. Perhaps it had never been meant to be?

Above the lighthouse tower, dark gray clouds threatened to blanket the moon directly overhead.

A storm was coming. In order to keep her safe, he needed to leave this instant before the bad weather hit, but now that he'd seen her, how could he leave?

A soft noise behind him made him whirl around to find her nervously sliding a plate of food onto the deck's railing a few feet away from him. His mouth watered and his stomach growled again.

The tantalizing aromas did the food justice. Without hesitation he reached out and took the plate.

Like a starving wolf, he downed the crispy fried chicken, the onion-drenched potato salad and the arrangement of other goodies she'd stacked on the large plate.

It wasn't until his plate was nearly empty that he noticed her watching him, her face pale and her eyes wide with shock.

He knew fear. Had lived with it for years. Smelled it. Seen it in other people's eyes and he saw it in hers now. He hated himself for bringing terror into her life. But there was something sparkling in those brown depths too.

Curiosity.

When she held up the rusty key that he'd used to gain access to her home, he stopped chewing. The last bite of food suddenly tasted like sawdust and it took a great deal of effort to swallow it.

Shit! In his hurry to get inside the house he'd forgotten to remove her emergency key from the lock.

"Lucky guess?" she asked coldly as she let the key dangle from her fingertips.

"Doesn't everyone keep an extra key behind a loose brick in their outside wall near their back door?"

"Sorry, I'm not buying that one."

"Okay you got me. Your in-laws told me about you."

"Which in-laws?"

"Your husband's brother Daniel, and his wife, Jo."

Relief splashed across her face, but he could tell in the way she held her mace, her finger on the trigger, ready to use, that she still did not trust him.

"I knew your husband Steve too."

"Steve is dead," she said quietly.

The sadness in her voice twisted his insides with painful reality. Yes, Steve was dead. To both of them.

"I know," he replied just as quietly, noting the raw pain shining in her eyes.

Her gaze drifted to his Saint Christopher medallion and he held his breath as a shiver of unease screamed through him. He couldn't let her see it. Couldn't allow that to happen. If she saw the inscription on the back, she'd start asking questions that he wasn't prepared to answer.

He pulled up the collar of his coat in a show that he was cold so she wouldn't get a good look at the medallion she'd given him years ago. His movement made her stiffen into alert mode.

"Why would they tell you about my spare key?" she asked and lifted her gaze to confront him with questions.

"They said you're out on the ocean quite often harvesting seaweed and I should let myself in if you weren't around when I came for a visit."

Let myself in? Now that was a hollow excuse if he ever heard one. He didn't expect her to believe him, but that's all he could come up with on such short notice.

"It's midnight, mister. Obviously, my boat is docked. I'm here. Why didn't you knock?"

"Didn't want to wake you."

Boy, his answers were making him look like a fool.

"And so, what? You thought you'd make yourself cozy until I woke up and found a stranger in my house? You didn't think you'd scare me?" Hot anger tinged her words and bright pink flushed her cheeks, pushing away the sickly paleness.

Man, did she ever look sexy when she was mad.

He shrugged. "I figured I was harmless."

"I'm glad one of us thinks so. Why didn't anyone tell me you were coming?"

"You'd have to ask them."

"Don't think I won't," she snapped.

"Perhaps I should come back another time?"

At his words, she visibly relaxed. Good, she wasn't so afraid of him anymore.

"It might be best," she answered.

Disappointment rocked him and he swore he read disappointment in her eyes too. Did she maybe want him to stay? Was he being naïve to even think she might want him here?

Oh, man. He really better get out of here and fast.

"I really am sorry for being so rude, Mrs. McCullen. I should have come during the day. It's just that your in-laws spoke so much about you. I feel as if I already know you."

"Since you know so much about me, how about telling me *your* name?"

The question floored him, and he hesitated. Here was his chance to spill the whole truth, but he couldn't bring himself to do it. It would only tear her world apart. He wasn't ready to do that. He probably never would be ready.

Before he knew what he was doing, he gave her the fake name he'd been forced to use over the past few years instead of the new one he was now using.

"Chance. Chance Donovan."

She nodded slightly and he waited for recognition to flare in her eyes. But nothing happened. Not that he expected her to recognize the name. Maybe he'd just hoped that she would guess his true identity?

"I don't think my husband ever mentioned you."

That's because I am your husband, he wanted to yell.

"We go way back," he said. "Childhood friends in Montana."

Emily nodded as a spattering of cold raindrops began to trickle down on them. He noticed her shiver. Hell, who wouldn't be cold wearing a pretty peach nightgown on the last day of October.

"I'd better let you get back inside. You're getting all wet," he said.

His gut clenched in anxiety at the thought of heading toward the stairs that would lead him away from her and leave her vulnerable to the threat that she had no idea was lurking nearby.

"It'll be too dangerous to go back out on the ocean now. A storm is coming. You may as well come in, Mr. Donovan."

Inside? Had he heard right? He hadn't expected her to ask him into the lighthouse. A great deal of mistrust flooded her eyes and she still looked very uncomfortable, and that's the last thing he wanted.

"I really should go."

"No, please come inside. I'll put on some hot tea. I can't let a friend of my husband's stay out in the chilly rain and get sick."

He noted the flash of tenderness spark her eyes, a direct contrast to the mace she still pointed at him. The sight of the can made him uneasy and he wished he could wrench it away from her on the odd chance she decided to use it. But he suspected she'd give him a good shot of the fiery stuff before he even made a wrong move.

Over the past years, when everyone thought he was dead and he'd been rotting in prison, he'd experienced the harsh fact of being pepper sprayed. He wasn't anxious to relive those memories.

Keeping a safe distance from her and the mace, he stepped back into the keeper house. She closed the door and headed down the short hallway. He followed her and found her in the kitchen at the sink.

Standing in the kitchen doorway, he suddenly felt awkward.

Earlier, when he'd broken in, he hadn't noticed the changes. First, it had been dark and then when he'd switched on the lights, he'd focused his attention on Emily. Now he realized she'd totally redecorated the kitchen.

The ancient, creaking gray floorboards were now a varnished oak. The plain brown cedar cabinets had been painted a crisp vanilla and the upper doors contained glass panels that proudly showed off an array of fancy dinnerware. Smart brass and ceramic pulls complemented the look.

An elegant island counter included shelves containing more dishes, drawers, an empty wine rack and a black, marble countertop laden with a giant glass bowl filled with a variety of fresh fruit. A new stove had replaced the old one. The only things she'd kept the same were the 1960s refrigerator and the intimate oak table for two.

She'd always had good taste in decor. Not to mention great taste in nightgowns.

Her feminine peach-colored nightgown was painfully thin and the raindrops made parts of it virtually invisible. Try as he might, he couldn't pull his attention away from the erotic sight. Through the sheer fabric he had no trouble making out her lush shape.

No longer a rail-thin young lady of twenty, she'd bloomed into a woman with generous curves. Long legs. Shapely hips. An exquisite waist he ached to touch and perky looking breasts with peaked nipples that pressed boldly against her nightgown.

He closed his eyes as a strong, hot wave of desire washed through him, leaving him totally tense.

She still had the same overpowering effect on him. Hell, it was even more powerful than he remembered. Being without Emily for so many years probably had something to do with his reaction. But he needed to leave here before his body and his heart caved in on him.

"You can have a seat in the living room, Mr. Donovan." Her sweet voice made him open his eyes.

Thankfully she hadn't noticed his intense reaction as her face was turned away from him while she searched for something in an upper cabinet. She dragged down a carton, which he assumed was the tea, filled water into an old-fashioned metal kettle, which he remembered belonging to her late uncle, and plugged it in.

She turned around and nodded to behind him.

"Living room is right next door. I'll bring the tea to you."

Obviously she wanted him out of the room and he had a pretty good idea why. He threw a knowing glance at the wall telephone before he walked into the hall and down into the living room where he stepped straight into his past.

The kitchen had been redone but the living room looked as if he'd never left. The same white-painted wood walls. There were electric baseboard heaters he'd installed under the giant gable windows. The same green overstuffed leather sofa strewn with the same buttery yellow pillows they'd fought with on several occasions.

He smiled as the memories rushed over him like a warm blanket.

There was a new addition though. The braided oval rug that covered most of the living room floor gave the room a bright, informal atmosphere that welcomed Chance and he found himself relaxing for the first time in years.

Chapter Two

The moment the stranger slipped into the next room Emily headed straight for her kitchen phone. Dialing quickly, she inhaled a breath of thanks when her sister-in-law's sleepy voice answered after the first ring.

"Hi, Jo! It's me," she kept her voice a low whisper so the stranger wouldn't hear.

"What's wrong, Emily?" Jo was instantly alert.

"Can't pull one over on you, can I?"

"Not at this hour. What's up?"

"Chance Donovan is here."

"Chance?"

Silence followed and Emily's stomach hollowed out as a shot of terror zipped through her. Did Jo not know who she was talking about? Had Emily been too naïve in believing the stranger when he said he knew Daniel and Jo? Had she fallen prey to him and let him back into her home so he could sneak up on her and kill her while she was on the phone?

She cringed as she imagined the stranger's hand clamping over her mouth and dragging her away into the bedroom.

"Chance is there? Oh, thank God." Surprise and relief etched Jo's voice and Emily once again found herself relaxing. Okay, everything was good.

"I gather you know him."

"Yes. We do. He's actually right there? With you?"

"Bold as life. In the living room. I caught him sneaking around in my house!"

"Oh my goodness. That's great news."

Great news that a strange man was lurking around her house? Emily blinked in stunned disbelief, her heart picking up a mad beat as she had the feeling she'd just been dropped into *The Twilight Zone* or something.

Jo continued. "We were wondering where he'd gotten off to. Hold on. Daniel wants to talk to you."

"Emily, it's me. You said Chance is there? How's he doing?"

Emily frowned into the receiver at her brother-in-law's concerned and frantic voice.

"He seems fine to me. Pretty hungry."

Daniel laughed. "Well, I'll be damned. That's a good sign."

A good sign? The man had let himself into her house with her emergency key for God's sake. That was a good sign? Definitely *Twilight Zone* night here. Emily struggled to keep the anger out of her voice as she continued.

"He said you told him about me and he decided to drop in for a visit."

"You sound rattled. Why don't you tell me what happened, Emily?"

Quickly she explained how Chance had used the emergency key to access her home at midnight and how she'd discovered him stealing her food.

"He's harmless," Daniel said warmly. "Just down on his luck and looking for a place to stay."

"He says he knew Steve."

A slight hesitation before Daniel spoke.

"Oh yes, he knows Steve. I mean he knew Steve, and the rest of the McCullens. He knows us very well. He's been staying with us for a while. I mentioned you were living all alone in that big empty lighthouse and suggested he come over and you'd put him up."

Shit! So Daniel really was behind all this.

"You what?"

"I invited him to stay with you for a while."

Emily blinked, not believing what she was hearing.

"It'll be great," Daniel continued. "He can help you fix up the lighthouse before you put it up for sale."

"Daniel! I don't even know him!" she hissed into the phone.

"Actually, he is a very shy fellow. Like I said, down on his luck. I'm sure your home cooking will cheer him right up. He's nothing to worry about, Emily. Seriously. Truly. You know you can trust me, right? You know I would never put you in harm's way. You won't even know he's there. Listen, I have to go. Sweet dreams."

A split second later the line went dead.

Frig! Was this for real? Had Daniel just hung up on her?

Emily frowned into the receiver. What in the world was going on? She'd just told her usually overprotective brother-in-law that a total stranger let himself into her home and all Daniel said could say was "sweet dreams"?

Ever since he'd gotten married, Daniel had been in seventh heaven. Maybe all his newfound happiness had clouded his judgment?

She remembered all too well that euphoric feeling of being in love.

Twenty years old and innocent, she'd been swept off her feet by the handsome twenty-five-year-old investigative journalist Steve McCullen. He'd moved into her New York apartment days after they met and they were married a few weeks later, coming to her uncle's Shipwreck Island lighthouse for their honeymoon.

At first, Steve didn't like it here. He'd complained about the smell of rotting seaweed and the chapped lips the ocean breeze constantly created. The island was far too isolated for him, being a half an hour boat ride from Prince Edward Island.

On top of that Steve's mind had been tormented over the recent death of his mother, a woman Emily had known for only a few short weeks and the closest she'd had to a mother since her own had died when Emily was young.

When the honeymoon was over, they'd returned to New York and Steve had immersed himself in his work. She'd been too lenient with her new husband, allowing him to leave on those overseas assignments. He was gone for weeks on end and when he came back home, their time together was intense, romantic and too short.

Finally, she'd put her foot down, demanding he stay home more often. To her surprise, he agreed. They'd only recently moved into the tiny lighthouse, after her uncle died and she'd inherited it, when they'd decided to start a family. Shortly after, tragedy struck, and Steve died and her dreams of having a family with the man she loved had been crushed.

She should never have married Steve McCullen. She'd been too deeply in love. A love that had clouded her thinking. Love was nothing but pain and she'd vowed never to fall in love again.

"Do I pass the test?" The stranger's hoarse voice made Emily's breath catch.

God, she loved his raspy voice.

Whirling around, she found him standing in the doorway, his arms casually folded across his wide chest. He'd removed his jacket and was wearing a wrinkled blue turtleneck that fit over his broad shoulders like a second skin.

The blueness of his clothing enhanced the blue in his eyes and Emily found herself mesmerized by his strong gaze. His cute mouth, which was inching upward into that heart-wrenching crooked grin, made her insides quiver with excitement.

No man had made her feel this feminine or sexy since her husband, and damned if she would let this stranger make her feel this good.

"Do you make it a habit of listening in on other people's telephone conversations?" she snapped.

His eyebrows lifted in surprise. Obviously, he hadn't expected her to be so rude. Well, tough. She was pissed off. Pissed because Daniel had set her up with this guy in such a horrible way. Ticked because this guy reminded her of how Steve had made her feel and at how she should be feeling when a guy interested her.

No! She was not interested in him. No frigging way!

"Just wanted to let you know your kettle is whistling Dixie."

"My kettle?" What was he talking about?

"For the tea." He nodded toward the kettle she'd plugged in earlier.

She grimaced at the shrill whistle piercing the air.

"Oh for heaven's sake. I didn't even hear it."

Angrily she reached out to pull the plug and inadvertently breezed her inner wrist right against the hot metal at the side of the kettle. Scorching pain blasted her skin, making her scream as she pulled her arm away.

God that hurts!

Before she knew what was happening, the stranger's hand splayed across the small of her back and he led her toward the kitchen sink. Remaining silent, he maneuvered her burned wrist underneath the tap. Cold water splashed against the painful red welt, bringing an almost instant relief. With the relief came some unbelievable fiery tingles where his fingers held her wrist.

When she looked up at him, she spotted a soft tenderness in his eyes, which made her breath back up into her lungs and had her shifting uneasily at his concern. If he noticed her uneasiness, he didn't let on. Instead, he focused his attention on the water blisters forming on the burned area.

"Could have been worse. I'll get a bowl and fill it with cold water so you can soak it while you sit, it'll be more comfortable for you."

So, he had noticed her move away from him. Did he think she was still scared of him, or did he know she was suddenly totally aware of him as a man? Oddly enough since the telephone conversation with her in-laws, her fear of him had mysteriously vanished, leaving her with this sudden...quite nice attraction.

A moment later he had her situated snugly on the living room couch, her wrist soaking in the cold water, her mind and body sparring over him while he moved around in the next room. Making tea. For her!

She'd always had a weakness for tall, lean, sexy-looking men and Chance Donovan was all of those and much more. His perfectly shaped lips were so kissable-looking, not to mention what she'd like to do to that cleft in his chin. His long fingers where he'd touched her still tingled very nicely. But it was a pleasant feeling compared to the burn screaming through her skin.

Goodness this man excited her.

A noise from the kitchen forced Emily to steady her erratic heartbeat by taking some deep breaths. Heaven knew she didn't want Chance to find her all flustered because he'd know why. A man always knew when a woman was thinking about him. At least it had been that way with Steve.

When she heard Chance's heavy footsteps approaching, she straightened to attention. He placed a tray laden with two steaming mugs of chamomile tea on the coffee table and her heart sank when she spotted the chocolate-potato brownies she'd made for the Halloween fair's bake sale. All cut up and ready to eat.

"I hope you don't mind. I found the brownies stashed at the back of the fridge. I thought it would go perfectly with the tea," he said.

"That's fine," Emily replied tightly. Thank God he hadn't found the pie.

When he sat down on the couch beside her, she became fully aware of his dangerous scent as it swarmed all around her. Suddenly she was trembling with excitement like a young teenage girl who suddenly realized why guys existed.

"How's your wrist?"

Before she could answer, he reached out and lifted her hand from the cold water. A wonderful sizzle of pure heat shot through her again as his fingers carefully turned her wrist around so he could get a better look at her injury.

His cute lips turned down into a concerned frown. "Looks worse than before."

"Doesn't feel so bad. Just stings a little," she lied.

"Do you have something to put on it?"

"I've got some ointment I can put on later." The last thing she needed was for him to start applying slippery ointment on her with his fingers.

"Burns need moisture to heal. Don't let the air get at it. Keep it in the water for a while longer it'll help ease the burning. Then lather lots of ointment on it. Do you have gauze?"

"Yes."

"Tape the gauze over the ointment. It'll prevent the burn from getting dried out or dirty."

His concern touched Emily, making her feel guilty at the way she'd yelled at him earlier.

"I'm sorry I snapped at you before when I was on the phone. It's just..."

What could she say? His crooked grin and fantastic scent got to her? Not to mention she felt angry because she shouldn't be feeling this excited about this man, especially since she was getting married to another man in a few weeks.

"No need for apologies, Mrs. McCullen. Like I said earlier, I'm the one who was rude for barging in on you. If I might ask, who vouched for me on the phone?"

"Jo and Daniel."

"Ah yes. The newlyweds. Daniel said something nice on my behalf?" His luscious lips turned upward into an amused smile, and she found herself fascinated at how pleasantly he smiled.

"Daniel speaks very highly of you and you seem to have made quite an impression on Jo."

"Jo is a very nice woman. A perfect match for my...friend."

"I don't recall seeing you at their wedding this past summer."

"I couldn't make it. Other commitments."

He took a giant sip of tea and Emily noticed how his large hands dwarfed her delicate teacup. She needed to rummage around and produce one of those big mugs Steve loved.

She watched him pick up a giant brownie and shove the entire thing into his mouth. He grinned and said between bites, "This is fantastic!"

"Glad you like it. Um, Daniel mentioned you were looking for some work?"

"He did?"

"You sound surprised."

Shoot. Had she misunderstood Daniel? Was her brother-in-law matchmaking?

An angry burst of wind shook the glass panes in the south windows and Emily noticed him tense at the harsh sound. He sure was a jumpy fellow. He'd reacted the same way earlier when she'd brought food to him outside on the deck.

Her curiosity about this stranger notched up a few degrees.

"I do have some work that needs to be done. If you are interested?"

Indecision flashed in his eyes.

She continued.

"I need someone to repair my dock. I need some help with the seaweeding too. It's just a few days of work."

"I don't want to intrude."

"You already have," she teased, suddenly wanting this guy to hang around and help her fix the place up. It would mean her fiancé wouldn't come over and she would have just a little bit more alone time before remarrying.

Okay, so alone time wasn't quite the word if he stayed. But at least she didn't feel obligated to kiss him hello and goodbye like she did with Skip.

"You can use the room upstairs. Sheets are clean and there's a bunch of quilts and blankets up there in case you get cold. Room and board. Breakfast is usually at six a.m. sharp. Are you interested?"

He bit his lower lip and when she got the impression he might say no, her heart sank. Then he nodded yes, and she was surprised at the waves of happiness shooting through her.

He drained the rest of his tea, then stood.

"I thank you very much for your offer. It's getting late. I think I'd better let you get some sleep, Mrs. McCullen. Don't forget about the ointment and the gauze to keep the burn moist."

"Thanks for the advice, Doctor Donovan."

He smiled and reached for a couple more large brownies.

"Two more for when I go upstairs," he said with a wink.

Emily laughed. "I'm glad you like my cooking. Good night, Mr. Donovan."

"Good night."

She listened to his footsteps as he walked up the steep staircase to the spare bedroom. A moment later the quiet click of the door closing echoed down the stairs. In a flash her thoughts returned to the very interesting telephone conversation she'd had with Jo and Daniel.

Daniel had been thrilled to hear Chance was hungry. The newcomer was a bit on the thin side, but he certainly didn't have a problem with his appetite. Daniel also mentioned Chance was down on his luck. Had he been in some sort of accident? Lost his job? Or maybe he'd lost someone he loved? Maybe that explained why she sensed an overwhelming loneliness coming from him.

And why were Jo and Daniel so concerned about him? Clearly they cared deeply for him. But if he was so close to the McCullen family, then why hadn't anyone ever mentioned him?

They'd been very relieved to discover he was here with her. Had they sent him over as some sort of matchmaking ploy? Daniel made it no secret that he believed Skip wasn't right for her. But lately she'd grown closer to Skip. A few weeks ago he'd stated he wasn't getting any younger. He wanted kids just like she did, so why not get married?

It wasn't a romantic proposal. More like a business deal. But she'd said yes. Oddly enough the thought of getting married didn't hold too much appeal as it had when he'd first mentioned it. Skip Cole didn't whirl up the intense feelings of wild desire or even the love she'd experienced with her late husband. On the other hand, Chance oozed masculinity and he'd gotten her motor running again.

"Who are you, Chance Donovan? And why does your crooked smile and your touch make my insides jump like a live wire?" she whispered beneath her breath as she headed to the bedroom to get the supplies to tend to her burn.

• • ↬ • •

CHANCE SUCKED IN A surprised gasp as he stepped into the cozy upstairs bedroom. Immediately he fell in love with the room's casual nature and the delicious aroma of pine.

When he'd left, this room had been Emily's pink walled frilly room with a white princess bed and white furniture when she'd grown up here. But now it was decorated in a bower of blue shades. The small room was anchored by a beige iron double bed pushed against the wall beneath the sloping ceiling. An old ladder leaned against a nearby wall with an assortment of colorful quilts layering its rungs. Covering the entire length of another wall hung a rope fishing net decorated sporadically with hand-sized pieces of odd-shaped driftwood ornaments and crusty seashells.

Crossing the pine-planked floor, he headed straight for the night-blackened window and looked out. Aside from the silvery rain dropping like sheets, all he could see was his reflection staring back at him.

A stranger's face. A stranger's eyes. He didn't think he'd ever get used to the shocking blueness of those eyes. Eyes that had once belonged to someone else. To whom? He didn't want to know. They had belonged to someone who'd died a tragic death in order for him to be able to see again. But now they were a part of him, just as his new face was a part of him.

Chance frowned and felt the muscles tighten around his mouth. Something else he'd have to get used to was the way his muscles felt when he smiled, frowned or even laughed, but the doctors said he'd get used to it. It just took time. Time wasn't what he had with Emily's marriage swooping down on him.

Reaching into his shirt pocket, he drew out the lip balm and smeared some onto his lips. He hadn't been out here for more than a couple of hours and his lips were already feeling dry. He found himself laughing at that discovery. Shit, at least this time he'd come prepared.

His soft laugh was cut short when he caught the glint of his Saint Christopher medallion in the window. Immediately he reached up behind his neck to unlatch the necklace. He'd have to hide it so she wouldn't find it. Slipping it into his back pocket, he moved away from the window and stretched out on the soft mattress. The truth about his real identity would remain a secret to spare Emily a lot of hurt. He tried to convince himself it was better this way, but why did it feel as if his heart were being crushed to smithereens?

Chapter Three

E mily's eyes slowly opened, and she noticed him standing there right beside her bed. It was the stranger named Chance Donovan and she realized she wasn't the least bit afraid of his being in her bedroom. She knew she'd locked her door before going to sleep and numbly realized she didn't care in the least he'd managed to gain entrance while she'd slept. The only thing she cared about was his nakedness and how hot she felt as she gazed at him.

His long, thick erection made her whimper as he drew closer. He held his cock in one hand and with his other hand he leisurely stroked his swollen length. His blue eyes were half closed, his dark lashes lowering, heavy with lust.

Need screamed through her. A need so sharp and so raw, she cried out at its intensity. She wanted Chance Donovan laying on top of her. Wanted him thrusting into her. Pistoning into her hard and fast, heating her blood and releasing the sexual tension sizzling between them.

Oh mercy! She needed him between her thighs. She could feel the weight of his body move the mattress as he sat down on her bed. Could feel his body heat splash against her naked flesh as he lifted the covers and slid in beside her.

She remained lying on her back, stunned at how wonderful she felt having him here beside her.

"I wanted to make love to you the instant I laid my eyes on you, Emily."

His hoarse whisper sounded rough in the dark, but his words melted over her senses like honey, bringing all her nerve endings sizzling to awareness mode.

"Do you want me, baby?" he asked her. Her breath halted in her throat as he stretched beside her, turning so he was facing her. His eyes held hers captive as he awaited an answer. Such dark, lusty eyes. So dark she could drown in them.

"Oh yes, I want you inside me, Chance. So bad."

He reached out and caressed her cheek, his touch burning her with desire. He drew his gaze to her mouth, and she parted her lips in anticipation. Her blood pounded heat as he dipped his head toward her. The instant his warm moist lips touched hers, longing rocked her. It was shocking, powerful and searing.

As he kissed her, his gentle fingers stroked the length of her throat. Ripples of excitement fanned through her as his kiss deepened. His fingers brushed over her collarbone, seared along the side of her breast and skimmed leisurely over her belly. She sucked in a gasp as she felt his shaft pressing against her left thigh. Arched against his hand as he slipped it between her throbbing thighs.

A finger moved slowly and surely over her clitoris. The small bundle of nerves burst with pleasure so fast and so hard, Emily cried out her excitement.

"Shh, sweet baby. I'll take care of you down here," he whispered against her mouth. And then he was kissing her chin, the length of her neck and across her collarbone.

The finger smoothed back and forth over her clit and her thighs shivered from the exotic tension. When his hot mouth latched over her nipple, she wanted to reach down and run her fingers through his hair, only to discover he'd bound her wrists to the bed while she'd slept.

Again, she felt no fear. Only a consuming desire for her stranger to be intimate with her. A need for him to pleasure her and use her body for his own desires. As he continued to massage her and suck her nipple with erotic intensity, her body tightened with tension.

Two of his fingers dipped inside her pussy, making her arch her hips and moan at the sensual invasion.

"That's it, sweet baby. Let yourself go into the pleasure."

He moved his fingers slowly inside her, stretching her vagina, stroking into her until she heard herself breathing harshly. He withdrew suddenly and thrust into her again, bringing her closer to the pleasure she yearned.

"I can feel your release coming, baby," he whispered.

She could hear the tightness in his voice. The thick tension of arousal pressing against her thigh. Then he was removing his fingers and coming over her, just the way she wanted him to.

She ached bad for him. Wanted to scream her need to him. Her breasts heaved against his chest as he pressed down on her, his warm breath cascading against her cheeks. His lips were set tight with want, his eyes heavy with lust.

Her thighs were trembling with need, her vaginal muscles clenching in anticipation of his entry, the fire of need racing through her in torturous bursts. As he entered her, she inhaled sharply, feeling the stretch. He felt beautiful and intoxicating. Hot. His swollen erection spearing into her.

"You want this, baby?" he teased, and entered deeper.

She yanked against her restraints, craving to pull him into her.

"Yes," she hissed.

And then he slid into her, deep and strong, and she found herself thinking he felt so right inside her. Found herself realizing she hadn't had a man make love to her since Steve. Yet Chance felt so perfect, just as Steve had.

He began pistoning into her. At first slow and gentle as if giving her time to accommodate his thickness and length and then faster, harder, rougher. With every thrust he pulled her deeper into her needs. Drew her deeper into her wants and desires.

"What do you want from me, sweet baby?" he murmured against her ear.

"I want you to fuck me, Chance," she cried out, feeling the desperation begin to overwhelm her senses. Feeling the sexual tension inside her begin to spiral out of control.

And then she was exploding. Her body releasing into a pleasure ball, her pussy spasming around his hard length as she gave in to the chasm of beauty. Surrendered to the sharpest, most erotic orgasm she'd ever had.

Gray slabs of daylight crept into Emily's bedroom as she opened her eyes on a soft moan. She felt tight, tense, aroused, her breaths hurried with sharp little gasps, escaping between her parted lips.

Oh man, she'd been masturbating in her sleep. She realized it the instant she discovered her hand trapped between her damp thighs and her hard nipple beneath the palm of her other hand as it cupped her right breast.

Now *that* was what she called an orgasm, she thought as she began touching her sensitized clit, realizing that it felt almost painful to the touch. How hard had she been rubbing herself in her sleep? How long had she been dream fantasizing about the stranger? And had he heard her moans?

Heat flamed into her cheeks at the thought of him being on the other side of the door and listening to her masturbating. Blowing out a tense breath, she stilled her quick breaths and remained quiet for several moments.

She heard nothing.

He was either still asleep or, maybe if she was lucky, he'd taken off and she wouldn't see him again. But that second thought didn't make her feel good at all. She realized she looked forward to seeing him again.

She'd been awake off and on the entire night and he'd been on her mind the whole time. Every time she fell asleep, she'd dreamed of Chance. God, help her, she didn't even feel a bit guilty about dreaming about him either.

She should though, shouldn't she? At least just a little. Sure, her husband was dead, but shouldn't she feel guilty like she did when she was with Skip?

Tossing those thoughts aside, she focused on her late husband. He'd died only a few short months after they'd married and only a couple of days after they'd started trying for a family. Although she'd been heartbroken at his death, she'd hoped and prayed she might be pregnant from the couple of times they'd had unprotected sex. But her period came and it felt like another death.

She shivered in remembrance and soothed herself by telling herself it was all in the past now and she needed to keep it there or she might become depressed and that's the last thing she wanted. Distracting her thoughts from Steve, she returned to thinking about the mysterious Chance Donovan. Numerous times when she'd awoken from those hot fantasy dreams, she'd wanted to pick up the phone, call her in-laws again and get answers to all those nagging questions she had about him.

Who was he? Where did he come from? What kind of work did he do? Did he have a wife? A girlfriend? Kids? A dog?

Knowing Daniel and Jo, they'd tease her endlessly if she called them again, especially this early in the morning. They would tell her to give up on getting married if the first sexy stranger who came around her place after she'd gotten engaged interested her so much.

Of course, they would be right. She should be concentrating on her fiancé and their upcoming nuptials. At the thought of Skip, apprehension shot through her and she forced herself to whip aside the snug blankets and get out of bed. To her surprise, she felt more alive this morning than she had in years. And her pussy ached wonderfully too. Almost as if she'd truly had a night of hot sex with a well-hung stranger.

After a quick shower, she applied more ointment to the sore burn on her wrist, taped it with clean gauze then dressed in a pink wool sweater and a pair of gray wool slacks and headed into the living room. No sound came from the upstairs bedroom, and since they hadn't gone to bed until well after midnight, she opted to think that he was probably still there and fast asleep.

While the coffee brewed, she searched the back of some of the lower cupboards until her hands fell upon the smooth ceramic of the giant mugs she wanted. She couldn't help but smile at the pleasant memories of the last time her husband and she had sat at their cozy intimate table for two, giant mugs clasped in their hands as they planned on how many children they'd have together. They'd joked about who would change the diapers and get up for the midnight feedings. Unfortunately, their dreams had never been realized.

Emily frowned as she poured the hot coffee and headed outdoors.

The crisp, salty ocean air almost took her breath away as she stepped onto the deck overlooking the cliffs. The rain from last night had given way to a beautiful breezy morning. The sky was turning a cool blue and bright sunshine shot sparkles of diamonds off the ocean's white-capped waves.

Down below, she saw her tugboat tied securely to the wharf, as well as the aluminum boat Chance had arrived in. Strange that she hadn't heard the putter of the boat's engine last night. Probably because she'd been so busy doing that romance ritual she hadn't paid attention to anything else.

Sighing, she sipped the hot coffee and turned to gaze at her small home. It was a white clapboard two-story house with red shutters. It contained a kitchen, two bedrooms and one full bathroom on the main floor and one-half bathroom adjoining the upstairs bedroom

Chance slept in. The house was heated by electric baseboard heaters and steam radiators that kept the entire building nice and toasty during the frigid winter months.

She found her gaze straying to the upstairs window, hoping that Mr. Donovan might be standing there looking down at her. But she saw nothing. Just the reflection of the blue sky on the pane. Attached to the house was the white octagonal wooden lighthouse with the red cap, which towered forty feet into the air. Every time she looked at the lighthouse, she remembered the first time she saw it.

She'd loved it at first sight. The rocky island with red cliffs and red sandy beaches as well as the lonely little lighthouse with the small house had clutched at her heart, reminding her of herself. Alone, her life shipwrecked when at the age of thirteen her parents had died in a car crash and her mother's much older brother, Jeb, a bachelor and her only close living relative, brought her here to stay with him.

At the time she'd been furious at her parents for dying and mad as hell at her uncle for forcing her to leave all her friends in Toronto. Thankfully he had been a patient and gentle man, if not very old and set in his ways. He'd given her only one simple rule. She was in charge of the meals. Before long she'd begged him to give her more chores, and he taught her how to clean the lamps in the lighthouse tower and the surrounding windows so the light would shine brightly through the foggy nights. He showed her how to maneuver his tugboat *Sweet Lies* around the dangerous craggy reefs.

By her fourteenth birthday, Emily knew everything there was to know about running the lighthouse. Then when she turned seventeen a bomb dropped on them.

Uncle Jeb's tiny little lighthouse was no longer needed. A better location had been found a mile down the coast and the new lighthouse would be fully automated and run by the Canadian Coast Guard.

Emily and her uncle were officially out of a job. Thankfully though, they were allowed to remain living in the house, which Uncle Jeb eventually was able to purchase from the income he generated with his tugboat and by raking seaweed and catching lobsters for a living. Emily also helped to pay off the house by getting a seasonal job on nearby Prince Edward Island.

In the town of Cavendish, she helped run a souvenir shop for the many tourists who swept onto the island to savor its beauty, and who came to seek out the birthplace of Lucy Maud Montgomery, the famous author of the book *Anne of Green Gables*.

While working there, Emily took the opportunity to read Lucy Maud Montgomery's books and was soon bitten by the writing bug. She trudged off to do a two-year stint at a college in Toronto where she took journalism and broadcasting. During holidays she visited her uncle at every opportunity and learned the tricks to seaweeding. Shortly after graduating, she got a job as a reporter in New York and shortly after that she caught the eye of world-renowned journalist Steve McCullen.

A sudden burst of anger burned through her at the thought of her late husband. She hadn't been this angry at him since he'd been alive. Why in the world was she mad now? But Emily knew why. Because Chance Donovan made her remember what it felt like to be a woman. Something her fiancé seemed to be unable to do. Abruptly she tossed the remains of her now-cold coffee over the deck railing into the ocean and headed back inside.

• • ∼ɧɔ • •

EMILY PEEKED INTO THE bedroom and smiled. Chance still lay in the same position as when she'd checked on him over six hours ago, just after seven this morning when she'd come inside and had breakfast. Without him.

Fully clothed, his hands were clasped over his stomach as if in prayer and his chest rose and fell in quiet rhythm.

She couldn't help but tiptoe into the room and peer down at him. Sleep softened his features. His lips were parted and tilted slightly as if he were smiling up at her. Luscious black lashes hid his startling blue eyes and he wore a day's worth of whiskers. The shadow gave his face a sexy bad-boy look she found quite appealing.

She noticed he didn't wear the necklace anymore and her gaze strayed around the room in search for it. She didn't see it. He'd probably removed it and she was sure she'd get a chance to take a look at it later when he put it back on again.

On the wicker chair beside Chance's bed she placed a pair of hardly used jeans, a cotton undershirt and a thick denim shirt and a few other items of clothing that had once belonged to her husband. Personal items she'd saved. Clothing she'd touched and smelled and clutched to her heart during the first couple of dark years following Steve's death. When she had finally accepted he wasn't coming home, she'd laundered and folded them and stuffed them into a closet. Now they would come in handy for Chance.

She returned her attention to the stranger. This time as she looked at the casual way he lay on the bed, something powerful stirred inside her chest and two words echoed in her mind.

Déjà vu. He looks like Steve.

She shook her head and tried to get rid of the uneasy feeling slithering through her, but it just wouldn't go away.

•• ❧ ••

THE SWIFT AUTUMN BREEZE was blowing her long hair around her head. She looked so sexy standing there wearing the gray knitted cardigan and jeans. He didn't know why she looked so hot in everything she wore. She just did.

He couldn't believe how swollen his cock was getting either when he saw her wave to him while she stood on the wobbly wharf waiting for him. It was dark and cool and he could see the white mist flowing out her nose and mouth as she breathed.

Behind her, the dark silhouette of the lighthouse was a spooky black fixture jutting out of the cliffs and for a brief instant he felt a spear of fear flow through him for leaving her alone out here. The ocean waves in front of the tugboat swelled and roared as they rolled over each other and crashed against the sandy beach and the rotting wharf.

He'd fix that dock as soon as possible before it fell apart with her on it.

When the tugboat snapped against the protective rubber tires lining the wooden wharf, Emily sprang into action, catching the lines he threw out to her and tying the boat securely to the dock. He couldn't get off the tugboat fast enough. Couldn't get her into his arms fast enough.

"Miss me?" she asked, her dark eyes glittering with a mixture of playfulness and love. Before she could utter another word, his mouth melted over hers. He felt her hands slide up his back and clasp over his shoulder blades like they always did when he kissed her. Her palms were hot, her nails sharp as she dug into his muscles. His body hummed and his mind whirled with happiness as she kissed him back.

He'd been away. Left her here alone for one week. He'd expected her to still be pissed off. She had been when he'd left. Of course she had every right to be. After all he had promised no more long assignments.

He had tried to keep his promise, but sometimes while working undercover promises had to be broken. But he'd make it up to her. He truly would. Soon the undercover work would come to an end and he could downplay the seriousness when it all came out.

Working undercover was why he hadn't wanted to start a family yet. It was dangerous work to expose an illegal transplant organization. But once his part of the assignment was over and the head of the group nailed, he would only have to testify. Then they would be free to go on with their lives.

Suddenly she broke the kiss, grabbed him by his hand and boldly pulled him down the length of the wharf, onto the sandy beach and into the tall blades of grass that grew beneath the towering wooden deck. In here they were out of the wind. In here a bunch of fat candles were nestled along the crisscross of beams and on the grass lay one of her puffy quilts. A thermos with two mugs and an arrangement of cheese and fruit sat in the middle of the quilt.

"I took the liberty of assuming you might want some hot chocolate and a batch of food to give you energy before you make love to me."

"Wow, you sure are getting demanding for my services aren't you, baby? I haven't even got my land legs and you want me performing for you."

"Performing inside me," she laughed.

She pulled him down on the quilt beside her.

In the flickering candlelight her face was flushed, her nose red from the cold, and he didn't miss the open box of condoms nearby.

His breath became erratic as she started taking off his jacket.

"Looks like I'll have quite a bit of performing to do tonight in order to get through that box."

She grinned. "They're flavored. We'll start with the chocolate ones first."

"Are you sure I can perform? It's pretty nippy out here," he teased, inhaling at the lust searing through his body like an untamed animal. Hell, he could be thrown into a bathtub full of ice and he'd still be hot for her.

"I'll warm you up," she whispered.

Her eyes glowed with love and she leaned into him, her sweet, warm lips melting over his, her soft, warm body stretching over him, bringing him quickly down onto the quilt with her right on top of him.

Wow! She usually let him take the lead. This was different. He liked this side of her. She was aroused tonight. Very aroused.

He needed to rein her in. Just a little. Nice and teasingly. Get her frustrated enough so her climax would be that much sweeter.

He slowed the kiss and sipped on her bottom lip. She followed suit, but he could feel the pent-up passion lacing the length of her body in the tight, barely controlled way she held herself back. He shifted his legs a little. Just enough so one of her thighs dropped against his hard erection. He grinned into her mouth as she moaned her approval.

Lips that tasted of sweet wine, he found himself thinking as he concentrated on tasting her mouth. He loved kissing her. Enjoyed the soft press of her lips against his. The taste of woman. The velvety slide of her moist tongue against his. The throb of heat pulsing through her mouth and body. He slid his hands beneath her thick cardigan, finding a soft blouse. Lifting it, he touched feminine flesh. She sucked in her tummy as he flattened his palms on her breasts. Her fingers dug into his shoulders as the kiss became frenzied again.

One of these days he'd suggest they do oral. But for now he would stick to vaginal penetration, just the way she liked it.

There was no hurry. They had all the time in the world to explore each other. All the time in the world. He loved her so much. So much, he literally ached inside his heart every time he thought about her.

Suddenly she broke the kiss and her hands flew to his jean button.

"Your mind is drifting. Am I not kissing good enough?" Her eyes were literally glowing as she pulled down the zipper.

"I'm thinking of ways to please you," he hissed.

"Mmm, I love the sound of that. Lift your hips, stud." He did as she instructed, raising his hips. She giggled and moved off him just enough so he could get his pants and underwear off, swallowing when he realized her face was mere inches from his cock. There was an odd sparkle in her eyes as she studied the length of his shaft. Was she thinking of going down on him? Should he suggest it? Should he reach out and

clasp the back of her neck and angle her head down and see if she would take him?

A split second of disappointment slipped through him when she didn't take him. The disappointment vanished the instant her hands grabbed the base of his shaft and her fingers dropped down to knead his scrotum.

Oh yeah, this felt good.

"You like?" she whispered, her eyes locking with his.

He groaned his approval as lightning raced through his balls.

She wiggled her eyebrows and said, "I've been reading erotic romances. Downloaded them off the net. They've given me some ideas."

Erotic romance?

"What kind of ideas?" He could barely speak as her fingers created ultimate pleasure in his swollen balls.

"Ideas on how to pleasure my man."

"Does it have any ideas on how to please my woman too?"

For the briefest moment her fingers stilled and surprise flashed in her eyes. Obviously the idea of him reading and learning how to please her hadn't occurred to her.

Then a slow, shy smile lifted the tips of her cute lips and it seemed as if a whole new world of understanding opened up to her. He swore he saw her tremble with excitement. Those erotic romances must be some books, he mused.

"If you want to read them, I can give you my electronic book reader. I ordered it a while ago and never had the chance to use it until you left and I got bored."

"You're making up for it fast, babe," he chuckled.

She smiled and continued to squeeze his sac, but this time just a bit harder with one of her thumbs pressing against the sensitive spot between his anus and testicles.

Fuck! That really felt incredible! He almost lost control as his body tightened with arousal. Almost ripped her clothes off and started making love to her.

He fought for the control, found it. Okay, so he would let her have free rein. Wouldn't tease her into slowing down. Wouldn't sexually frustrate her and then bring her to climax. It would be all about her pleasing him tonight.

She pressed a little harder on that sensitive spot, and holy shit his hips flew right up off the quilt as fire seared through him. She giggled. He cursed as she let go of him and concentrated on opening the thermos.

It was a hell of a bad time for a drink, he thought, and almost reached out and stopped her, but then she grabbed one of those chocolate-flavored condoms and he realized she had something else up her sleeve.

He cursed under his breath as she ripped open the foil package with her teeth. Teeth he wished would nip at his cockhead. In the past he'd broached the subject about oral, but she'd looked disgusted at his suggestion and he hadn't brought it up since.

"A little hot chocolate will keep your mind off what's going on down there between your legs." She smiled and handed him a cup. He took a sip. It was warm and sweet.

Come on! To hell with hot chocolate. To hell with her book ideas. He wanted her now.

It was as if she knew what he was thinking for she suddenly moved faster. Taking the condom, she slid it over his plum-shaped, purple-flushed cockhead. Her fingers shook slightly, and he realized this was the first time she was doing the honors to him. He'd always taken care of this business. He'd always been in charge because he knew she was sexually shy. Hell she'd been a virgin when he taken her on their first date.

He'd been surprised when she confided that fact to him after they'd had sex. But he really shouldn't have been amazed that she'd still been a virgin at twenty. During her teenage years she'd lived pretty much in seclusion with her uncle on this island. In the morning he would boat her to school and in the afternoon he would be waiting for her when she came out. During journalism classes she said she was a book worm, concentrating totally on her studies and not on guys, preferring to limit her dates to kisses. If things heated up, she gave the guy the boot.

Thankfully she hadn't given him the boot.

Happiness and lust gushed through him.

What a nice combination, he thought as she returned to that erotic rub beneath his sac. She'd picked up something new in those books she'd been reading, that's for sure. Keep reading them, girl, he mused, and growled at the agonizing joy her touches created.

"Hmm, I don't think you've ever been so hard," she chuckled. She was breathing harshly while she fumbled with rolling on his condom. Definitely inexperienced with a condom, he thought, but she had plenty of time to learn. For an instant he wanted to tell her to forget the safe sex. Wanted to tell her he'd changed his mind and he didn't want to wait for them to have babies. But the protection was suddenly on his cock and he craved her big-time.

"I want you now, Em," he growled.

Relief splashed through her face at his words and he knew she was thankful to relinquish control back to him. He noticed her lips were plump and moist from his kisses. Her eyes sparkling with lust and love. Felt the warmth of being so loved flow through him like a roaring wave.

"Me too. I want you inside me. Make love to me, Steve. Love me."

Shit. How could he resist when she asked so desperately? He couldn't. He had her out of her clothing in record time.

To hell with any more foreplay, he thought as he slid his hand between her legs. She was already aroused. Her eyes were glazed and her face flushed. The tip of her pink tongue peeked out from between her lips. She always did that when she was ready for him.

One slip of his finger into her pussy proved it. She was wet with heat. Being aggressive and bold with him had turned her on.

Wetting his finger with her cream, he rubbed her engorged clit until she moaned her appreciation. Until she was writhing and panting. Her breasts heaving with her every breath. He had her at the edge within seconds.

Urging her onto her back, she spread her legs, lifted her knees and dropped them sideways. He came over her, between her legs, his arms holding him up as he brought his lower half onto her. His cock easily slid into her channel and her velvety muscles clenched around him with welcome.

She moaned as he entered, and he groaned at her ultra-tightness.

Have mercy but she felt fantastic! Hot and moist and tight. And he felt so hard he wanted to scream from the suffering. Coming down on her, he found her mouth and kissed her. She tasted so sweet and found his senses drowning, felt his heart pound from the intensity of his love for her.

Lifting his hips, he thrust his cock into her vagina again, making her gasp at the quickness and the roughness. Usually he was gentle with her, but tonight she had him aching as he'd never ached before. It brought out his roughness. Brought out his need for relief and release.

What they had together was powerful. A strong love. Good sex. A relatively easygoing relationship, except for her shyness. But she'd get over that with time.

Gripping her hips, he held her steady and began the erotic plunging he knew would bring them satisfaction. He strained into her. Plunging and groaning as the pleasure crescendoed. His body ached for release, but he waited until he felt her pussy tighten around him. Waited until she moaned and shuddered with an orgasm.

Seconds later, he joined her, enjoying the pleasure and love and warmth that raced through him as he made love to her. A love so deep and so strong he knew it would last forever.

"Hello? Open your eyes."

The sweet voice seemed to come from somewhere far away, and yet Chance knew she was close. Her ocean scent wrapped snugly around him and he inhaled deeply, allowing her wonderful smell to cascade into every pore. He savored it. Memorized it. Something special for him to hold.

"Are you still alive?" Emily whispered.

Those words sent a chill up his back, forcing him to pop open his eyes and his heart smashed painfully against his chest as he discovered Emily sitting on the edge of the bed, beside him, her teasing gaze piercing through the lingering mist of his sleep.

"You were dead to the world, Mr. Donovan. I came up a couple of times, but you were sleeping like a log. I thought maybe you'd died or something when you didn't answer."

She smiled at him and perfect dimples caved in her lovely cheeks, making Chance's heart do an unbelievable number of flip-flops.

"I hope you don't mind my coming up?" She suddenly looked worried that maybe she'd offended him by invading his privacy.

"Not at all," he answered, wanting to put her at ease but finding himself far from it as he became very aware of the way her warm body heat scrambled through his jeans and flirted with his skin.

"Are you up for some lunch?"

"Lunch?"

She was kidding, wasn't she?

"It's already past one."

Disbelief roared through him. How the hell could it be this late?

"Oh! Wow! I'm sorry. I haven't slept like this in years."

Emily laughed a hearty laugh that clutched at Chance's soul.

"It's the ocean air. You'll get used to it."

He stretched his arms lazily and caught her watching him. In the past, she'd told him she loved his sleepy look when he first woke up in the morning. Was he only imagining that hungry gaze now? That

sexy look that told him she wanted him to make love to her? Of
course it had to be only wishful thinking because she didn't know his
true identity.

He was someone else now. A Humpty Dumpty who'd been put
together after falling apart. Only this time around he had a few
screws missing because he must be insane to accept the handyman
job his wife had offered him last night.

"I've already slept half the working day away. Not a good way to
impress the boss," he replied, not eager to move off the bed with her
sitting so close to him.

He wondered what she would do if he reached up and caressed
her cheek the way he used to do. Would she realize it was him? Or
would she think he was some sex-crazed maniac? Of which he was if
that hot dreaming he'd been doing was an indication. All she had to
do was look between his thighs and she'd know he was hot for her.

He found himself willing her to do that. Instead, she was looking
away from him and that's when he noticed she'd brought in his duffel
bag from the boat he'd come in.

Shit!

"I brought your bag up from your boat."

Chance blinked. Had she gone through the bag? Did she see
what he had in there?

"Don't look so shocked, Mr. Donovan. I didn't snoop. But I
think everything in your duffel might be soaked so I left you some of
my husband's clothes. They should fit you. The clothes you're wearing
are quite wrinkled."

He glanced down at his rumpled appearance.

"I guess I fell asleep in them." *While I was waiting for you to go to
sleep so I could get what I came for and leave*, he added silently.

"I'll go and make some lunch. Oh, and as you probably noticed,
the bathroom up here has no shower, so you'll have to use the one
downstairs in the hallway between the kitchen and living room."

She stood from the bed and turned to leave.

"Um, Mrs. McCullen?"

"Please call me Emily, Mr. Donovan."

"And you can call me Chance. Thanks, Emily, for putting up with my bad sleeping habits. It won't happen again. I'll get straight to work."

"That's something I'd like to discuss with you over lunch. See you in a bit."

He listened to her light footsteps as she descended the steep wooden stairs. What did she want to talk to him about? He peered at the duffel bag she'd set beneath the east window. If she'd gone through his belongings, she wouldn't be acting so bright and cheerful. She'd be firing questions right, left and center.

Had she changed her mind about hiring him? Did his sleeping in ruin his chances of sticking around? He shook the questions aside. What the heck was he thinking? He couldn't hang around Emily. It was too dangerous. Especially for him because she was already interfering with his survival instincts. He hadn't even heard her tiptoeing around up here, and to make matters worse, he'd slept through his best opportunity for getting what he'd come here for and then leaving her forever.

Chapter Four

Emily was placing the burgers onto the buns when she heard the shower taps shut off. While he'd slept, she'd been cooking and baking, replacing the food Chance had eaten last night. During that time she'd been trying to figure out who he was. Why did he seem familiar and why did he use her emergency key to gain access to her home in the middle of the night?

A shy man, as Daniel had described him, wouldn't show up in the middle of the night unannounced. He would have called, and he certainly would have knocked, in daylight. Which led her to the conclusion Daniel hadn't told her the truth about this guy. And she would get to the truth as sure as her name was Emily McCullen.

Closing her eyes, she remembered the sleepy, sexy look on Chance's face early this afternoon when she'd woke him up. *Déjà vu* had splashed through her yet again when he'd stretched those long, muscular arms.

She'd found herself imagining his arms wrapped around her waist as he pulled her against his hard erection. That's another thing she'd noticed seconds before he opened his eyes. The thick bulge between his thighs and the intoxicating heat sweeping through her as she wondered exactly how big he might be. Truth be told, she hadn't seen a man's cock since her husband. And his cock had been big and long and oh-so thick.

Skip certainly didn't parade around here naked. Actually, he never slept over either. Was she making a mistake in marrying a man she'd never had sex with? What if he wasn't a good lover?

Emily frowned.

Heck, who was she kidding? No one would live up to Steve's lovemaking skills. Maybe Mr. Donovan...correct that...Chance's cock might be as big as Steve's, but unless she found a way to get him out of his pants to see—

She nearly gasped out loud when the door to the bathroom squeaked open and a second later Chance Donovan stepped into the kitchen, barefoot and clad only in a snug pair of jeans and the thick denim shirt that had once belonged to her husband.

It fit him perfectly.

She drank in his wet, tousled hair and clean-shaven face and felt her throat go dry. The man looked even better after a shower!

Realizing he was watching her, she refocused her attention on the burgers.

"How do you like your burgers dressed—I mean done?" she corrected herself, feeling her face warm.

"Tons of relish, loaded with mustard, easy on the ketchup and mayo and a slice of lettuce if you have it."

When he suddenly moved closer, her body tingled with excitement. She felt his warm breath dance across the back of her neck, and boy, he smelled very yummy.

"Looks fantastic," he said. "I'm starved. Want me to set the table?"

"Sure. Plates are—"

"In this cupboard."

Emily held her breath as he stretched his arms like a tomcat. Muscles bulged in his shoulder area, and for a moment, she thought the material might actually split as he reached up and dragged out a couple of plates and two glasses. Have mercy! The man certainly was built. And it seemed awfully warm in here.

"Um," she began, trying hard to keep her voice as professional as one would speak to an employee. "I'm short on time today so I couldn't whip up something fancier than burgers, fries and a salad.

I have to get over to Prince Edward Island. There's a Halloween fair today on the main island near the North Cape. That's what I wanted to talk to you about."

He didn't say anything as he placed the plates and glasses on the tiny kitchen table.

Grabbing the plate of burgers and utensils, she asked him to sit. When he did, she swallowed to clear her suddenly dry throat and plunged ahead with her question.

"I wanted to know if you could give me a hand and bring the food over to the fair?"

He shifted uncomfortably, and said rather quietly, "I'm not much for dressing up in costumes...or for crowds."

Ah, this must be the shy side Daniel was talking about.

"I have to tell you I'm not much for fairs either," she lied. "Costumes are optional. I'm not wearing one. Besides, I promised to help out at a food booth for an hour or so and then there is something else I need to do. I noticed your boat is a rental from town. We can tie your rental on to the back of my fishing boat, drop it off and you can wander around the fairgrounds until ten. I'll give you an advance and you can ride on some of the roller coasters."

"Roller coasters and a fair? Is this chore part of the job description?" The tips of his mouth curved upward in amusement.

She wanted to say no. Unfortunately, if she did, he would stay here while she was gone. The last thing she wanted was a total stranger among her things.

"Yes, actually it is."

He shrugged his shoulders and frowned.

"Okay, you're the boss and your wish is my command."

By the tightness around his mouth though, Emily could tell he wasn't too happy about accompanying her to the fair.

• • ❧ • •

THE SMELL OF HOT DOGS and frying onions assaulted Chance's senses as he wandered away from the giant red tent where he'd left the last armload of food he'd trudged in for Emily. They'd been swarmed by a bunch of gray-haired elderly ladies whose eyes sparkled with curiosity as they examined Emily's entries for the bake sale. When their attention focused on him, he'd quickly excused himself, but not before Emily slipped some money into his palm and secured a promise from him to meet her back here in an hour for something called the Pie Sell-Off Contest.

As he walked up the midway, the smells grew stronger and the crowds grew denser. He tried to tune out the steady cry of the barkers as they lured victims into their booths and grimaced at the popping sounds of the air rifles in the nearby shooting galleries. Shouts and screams from the people dressed as vampires, witches and the walking dead zombies made Chance edgy.

The sounds of the guns and shouts churned up the memories he didn't care to remember. Images of intense heat, metal bars, chain-link fences as well as gray cinder-block walls topped with rolls of sharp, shiny barbed wire.

All of it reminded him of stolen freedom. Fear. Anger. Pain.

Automatically his hands slipped to his neck, to the tiny Saint Christopher medallion. His uneasiness slipped up a notch. It wasn't there!

Then he remembered stuffing it under the bed after Emily had woken him earlier today. There was no way he could allow her to get a close look at the medallion because if she read the inscription on the back of it, she'd freak out.

A familiar chopping sound captured his attention and Chance's spirits soared as he recognized what was going on just up ahead. Maneuvering himself through the thick crowd, he found the Timber Sports competition in full swing.

Sweat glistened off the bare backs of the burly men and muscles bulged along arms as they swung double-edged axes into giant chunks of pinewood. A roar of cheers went up as a giant fellow, wearing a black witch's hat, chopped through his block first. A few seconds later another ear-splitting roar erupted as two more men split through their logs.

"Well done, men!" a voice yelled.

Immediately Chance recognized the short, plump, white-haired man screeching into his bullhorn and found himself grinning from ear to ear. Buzz, nicknamed for his short army buzz haircut, had been the fair's Timber Sports caller since Emily had first introduced Chance to the fair years ago.

"Next up is the Double Block Cut. We still have one opening for anyone interested in going up against our current champion." Buzz hesitated then looked into the crowd. "Where is my current champion? Where are you, boy? Show yourself. Ah, here he is. Let's hear a round of applause for our current champion. All the way from the Big Apple USA to defend his title, Skip Cole!"

Chance inhaled sharply at the name. The cheering crowd in front of him wavered slightly and his heart thudded in his ears. His fists tightened into knots and he felt his control slip as he watched the tall, dark-haired man he'd once called best friend step into the opening. What the hell was Skip doing here? The man was more comfortable following up a story in the war-ravaged streets of some foreign country than playing to a fair crowd.

The caller broke into Chance's whirling thoughts. "Still an opening. Who wants it?"

"I'll take it!" Chance yelled.

The cheers died and he hunched deeper into the crowd as all eyes locked on to him.

"Well, c'mon forward, boy. Don't be shy," the caller coaxed cheerfully, and before Chance could change his mind, gentle hands from nearby spectators ushered him toward the competition's opening.

Toward Skip!

Chance's first impulse was to start swinging his fists at Skip's face and ask questions later. His second impulse was to dive into the crowd, leave the island and forget the past few years being held hostage in a prison had ever happened. Running away, however, wouldn't solve anything.

Since regaining his freedom he'd thought about asking Skip why the hell he was going after his wife and why the hell he'd stabbed him in the back by exposing his undercover work to the bad guys the way he had. But Chance's brothers had talked him out of any confrontations until he was fully healed from all his surgeries. Well, he was healed physically if not mentally.

Finding the son of a bitch here at the fair totally surprised him. Fortunately, all his uneasiness flowed away when Buzz handed him a heavy ax. Pain rippled through his shoulders as its weight caught him by surprise and the ax slipped from his hands narrowly missing his feet. The crowd laughed.

"Looks like you're out of shape, mister. You sure you want to go up against the defender?"

"It'll be a pleasure," Chance replied.

"Suit yourself," Buzz said, his white bushy eyebrows knitting together with concern. "What size boots?"

"Eleven." Chance avoided Skip's curious look as he sized him up. Chance grabbed a pair of damp, dirty work gloves from a nearby table.

"Here's your boots. Slip 'em on. What's your name, son? Where're you from?" Buzz whispered.

Chance slipped a sideways glance at Skip, who'd turned his attention to pulling on his own work gloves supplied by Buzz. The thought of revealing his true identity slammed into him. It would be nice to see Skip's reaction. To see how horrified his once best friend would be when he found out that Steve McCullen was in fact alive.

But that wouldn't help Chance. He needed to find out if Skip was behind his incarceration and the only way to do that was give the name he'd been forced to use during his imprisonment. If Skip was behind it, Chance should be able to tell by the look on his face when he announced the name and the state where he'd been kept as a prisoner.

"Donovan. Chance Donovan. State of Texas. US of A."

If Skip recognized the name, he gave no hint of it. He was busy waving to his ever-frantic fans.

Chance frowned as he slid his feet into his safety boots. A perfect fit.

"Our newcomer hails all the way from Texas," Buzz shouted into his bullhorn. "Let's give Chance Donovan a hand for being brave enough to go after Skip Cole, our defending champion for the past six years."

Chance started. Six years! The fucking bastard hadn't wasted any time in taking over his old position as champion of the Double Block Cut version of the Lumberjack Competition. Which led him to the question of exactly how long had Emily being seeing Skip? His brother Daniel had said the relationship and marriage proposal had come out of the blue a few weeks ago. Had he lied? Or not been told the truth by Emily?

"All right men! Get ready!" The caller's shout drew his attention from his thoughts.

Chance stepped onto the huge chunk of pine he was about to chop into, nestled his feet comfortably at the edges of the blocks of wood, held the heavy ax firmly over his head and concentrated with all his might on the scratch marks where he was to chop. When the announcer shot off the signal gun, Chance began his downward swing. The blade of the ax slammed into the thick block, sending jarring vibrations through his arms and straight into his neck. He ignored the discomfort.

His concentration deepened and he kept swinging. Soon he couldn't hear anything but his steady breathing and the blood roaring through his veins. Rivers of sweat cooled his body, and the next thing he knew, burly men with cheerful smiles were slapping his back as cheers flew into the air.

"Congratulations to our new champion, Chance Donovan. All the way from Texas. Winner of one thousand dollars."

Chance gasped at the sum he'd won. The prize had increased in his absence. Cheers flew into the air.

"C'mon, Chance. C'mon get your prize money!" the caller shouted into the bullhorn.

Excited hands pushed him toward Buzz, who slapped ten crisp brand-new hundred-dollar Canadian bills into his shaking hand.

"Don't worry, they aren't counterfeit," the caller chuckled, and Chance answered with a smile.

The cheers and claps shot into Chance again, and to his surprise, he realized he was enjoying all this attention. He smiled sheepishly, rolled up the bills and shoved the wad into his front jeans pocket. The crowd quickly forgot about him as the next lumberjack competition got underway.

A hand slapped painfully onto Chance's back and he froze at Skip Cole's warm voice. "I've been trying to get rid of that title for years."

"Why's that?" Chance managed to croak, his throat clogging up with mixed emotions at seeing his old friend. At wondering yet again how had Skip managed to betray him the way he had?

"The title belonged to a good buddy of mine. I tried to hold on to it in his memory but—" Skip frowned and shrugged his shoulders. "Things change, y'know. Life's getting too busy to fly here to defend the title. My fiancée's moving back with me at the end of next month.

We probably won't have the time to come to next year's fair, so I can't defend the title. Might have a kid by then. She's always wanted a whole bunch of them."

Reality rocked Chance as he remembered Emily's dreams of having a houseful of kids. Being an only child herself, she'd always craved the company of brothers and sisters and wanted their kids to have lots of them.

Why the hell was Skip telling him all this personal stuff, anyway? Was this his way of informing Chance he knew his true identity?

Skip's voice cut into Chance's thoughts.

"You don't sound like a Texan. Lost your accent somewhere?" He slapped his knee and burst into uncontrollable laughter.

Chance didn't know how to react so he stood there inspecting his former best friend.

Skip laughed the same way he always had. Free and easy. Straight up from his chest. When they'd both begun working for the same newbie New York newspaper as investigative journalists, both men had bonded instantly. Chance had sensed immediately that Skip shared the same passion for adrenaline-rush adventures he enjoyed. They'd saved each other's butts on more than one harried occasion while smuggling out stories from war-torn countries. At the same time Skip's easy-going nature and flair for humor had livened up the tension that accompanied their dangerous treks.

When Skip finished laughing at his Texas-accent joke, his dark brown eyes held no hint of hatred or betrayal, only wit.

"I suppose you must hear that line all the time?"

Amusement tinged Skip's voice and his eyes laughed with humor. It seeped beneath Chance's hate and began to nibble away at it, putting doubts into his ironclad idea that Skip was the man who had tipped off the bad guys that Steve was working undercover and had received a disc from an anonymous source. A disc containing important names of people involved in the illegal transplant network.

Chance quickly brushed away the newfound feelings.

"Actually, no I haven't," he replied, injecting coldness into his voice.

Skip sensed his hostility and immediately sobered.

"Well, I can see you must be tired after whacking away at the wood with that heavy ax, so—" Abruptly he stopped talking and his eyes brightened as he peered over Chance's shoulder.

He jumped as Skip suddenly started waving and shouting to someone in the crowd. "Hey, honey! Over here!"

Whirling around, Chance spotted Emily stumbling through the dense crowd toward them. The last thing he wanted was to socialize with the happy couple. He turned to leave, but Skip's hand curled around his elbow, stopping him cold. Before he could yank himself free, Emily's surprised voice captured his attention.

"Skip! I'm surprised to see you here. I thought you couldn't make it in?"

"What? Miss the fall fair?" Skip chuckled. "Not see you? Not on your life."

Chance's teeth slammed painfully together, and his jaw clenched tight with anger as he witnessed Skip kiss Emily on the cheek.

"Mr. Donovan!" Emily's cheerful voice shot through his rising anger.

Chance threw Emily a watery smile.

"You two know each other?" Skip asked.

"We've...met," she said with a warm smile that lifted Chance's spirits.

She glanced at her watch and gasped. "Oh my! Look at the time! I have to get over to the pie contest. It starts in five minutes. Are you two coming?"

Skip linked his arm with Emily's and threw Chance a somewhat pouty scowl. Chance flipped him a smirk and would have flipped him his middle finger if Skip hadn't already turned away. Skip seemed jealous, but then again so was Chance.

• • ❧ • •

"OUR LAST CONTESTANT is Emily McCullen!"

Emily's cheeks flushed hot from embarrassment as the announcer called her name through the microphone. She wiped the perspiration from her damp palms, lifted her pie and headed on to the stage.

"This Pie Sell-Off Contest was Emily's idea and all the money will go toward providing food and shelter for the homeless this winter on Prince Edward Island," the caller hollered.

Loud claps and earsplitting whistles rippled through the huge, warm tent housing what Emily would guess to be over three hundred spectators. People who sat in rows of chairs, staring at her and her pie. Nineteen women and one man had gone before her, entering their pies into the contest, and so far they had tallied a good amount for the cause. More than she had imagined.

"Emily has made her late uncle Jeb's famous seaweed-apple-blueberry pie. Who wants to start the bidding for an evening date with Emily and a chance to eat her delicious pie?"

When Skip's hand shot up, Emily breathed a sigh of relief. She'd much prefer to go on a date with someone she knew.

"Twenty dollars," he called out cheerfully.

"Twenty-two dollars," Dr. Baker shouted.

Emily winked at the physician to thank him for his bid.

"Twenty-five dollars," Skip said with a grin, and Emily found herself answering his smile.

She hadn't expected him to show. She'd received an email from him only two days ago saying he probably wouldn't make it because he was very busy with work. When she heard nothing today, she assumed he wasn't coming. Obviously, he had decided to leave his job to crash the fair. She hated when he dropped in unexpectedly. It made her change her plans at the last minute to accommodate him. God help her when they got married.

"Fifty dollars?" the caller shouted. "How about fifty dollars for a date with Emily and a taste of her delicious seaweed-apple-blueberry pie?"

No one lifted a hand.

So far no one was crazy enough to pay fifty dollars for a pie. The highest bid had been forty-five dollars from a husband of one of the women who'd entered.

"Oh c'mon, folks. It is for a good cause. No one?" He peered anxiously into the crowd. "Looks like she might go to Skip Cole. Going once! Going twice!"

"One thousand dollars! Cash!" a man shouted.

Emily blinked in disbelief. The announcer looked shocked. A deadly quiet floated across the crowd. All heads turned toward the back of the tent where the voice had erupted.

"I said one thousand dollars."

Emily's breath locked in her throat as Chance stepped into the aisle. He flashed a pile of bills in the air.

"Sold! To the gentleman with the bills!" the announcer spat in a flurry of excitement.

Oh my God. Chance was using his winnings to buy her pie and get a date with her? Was he nuts?

She didn't miss the scowl on Skip's face or the stunned silence of the people as Chance strolled casually up to the stage. He handed the one thousand dollars to the announcer, and then asked Emily politely, "The pie and a date with you, right?"

She nodded, still reeling from what had just happened. Shifting the pie off the table into his large hand, he placed his other hand against the back of her waist. His palm burned heat through her, making her breath hitch. He spoke in a low voice so only she could hear.

"The date starts now. We'll eat the pie when we get home."

Her heart pounded a mile a minute as he smiled at her, and amidst hushed whispers, he ushered her off the stage, past the startled onlookers, past a shocked Skip and straight into the dusky evening.

• • ↬ • •

"HOW ABOUT THE HAUNTED House?" Emily shouted with excitement and pointed to the two-story spooky building complete with outside displays of realistic white-boned skeletons whose eyes glowed blood-red and jaws opened and closed to the beat of the earsplitting screams floating from inside.

A familiar icy shiver scrambled up Chance's spine. He sure as heck didn't want to go in there. The screams sounded too real and reminded him of the screams he'd heard in his past. Some of them his own.

When a chain-driven roller coaster rumbled out of the creepy building, he jumped. The vehicle was loaded with wide-eyed, ashen-faced adults and excited children who imitated the screams from the house. Emily touched his arm and he jumped again.

"Whoa there! You're not one for haunted houses, are you?"

Chance's breath caught at the concern slicing across her face. Was he that obvious? He'd better keep a tighter lid on his emotions or she'd start asking serious questions.

"Let me see. If I remember this correctly," Emily giggled, "for someone who doesn't like roller coasters, you've insisted we hit every roller coaster except this one at least once, the Ferris wheel twice, not to mention how you took over the shooting galleries like a man possessed until you won this—" She held up the giant, furry red lobster and he was glad they'd brought the pie back to the boat before returning to the fair to browse around. As she looked at him, her pretty smile widened to the point where he could barely control himself from reaching out and brushing aside the stray wisp of a curl covering her right sweet dimple.

His mind whirled for a plausible answer for not going onto that particular ride.

"I've discovered coasters are fun, but we've just eaten hot dogs, candy apples and cotton candy and look at those people coming off the Haunted House coaster." He pointed to the stragglers stumbling down the wooden ramp. "I think I'll sit this ride out."

"I'm beginning to think you're right," she said cheerfully. "I've never been too good at handling roller coasters with a full stomach. I do, however, have another idea."

Her eyes twinkled mischievously, and at the same time Chance heard soft music float out of a nearby tent. He knew instantly what she wanted.

Before he could protest, she grabbed his wrist. Her hand was a soft, sizzling handcuff he didn't want to escape from and he allowed her to pull him toward the giant tent.

• • ⚓ • •

"I'M A BIT OUT OF PRACTICE," Chance apologized.

Another slice of pain ripped through Emily's toes as he stepped on her right foot for the third time in as many dances.

"You're doing fine," she encouraged as she moved with him to the gentle rhythm of Shania Twain's "You've Got a Way". There was something hauntingly familiar about the way his body glided with hers, and she tried her darnedest to figure out why she'd think she'd ever danced with him before. Another burst of pain sliced across her toes.

He frowned. "Sorry. In all the excitement I forgot to ditch the safety boots from the contest and I'm afraid I forgot to pick up my shoes too."

"Don't worry. Buzz will bring them to the lost and found. We can head over there later and trade them in."

He stepped on her toes again, making her wince.

He swore softly. "Sorry, again. I guess I'm going to have to buy you some steel-toed dance shoes."

"Then I can join in with you at next year's lumberjack contest?"

She warmed when he smiled with amusement. "You think you got the muscles to take me on?"

"I can take you on any time, Chance Donovan. You name the place and the time, I'll be there."

"You're on."

His eyes darkened and she swore his look of amusement turned to a look of fierce desire. He would be a wild lover, she could see that in his hot eyes. In the way he looked at her with sexual intent. In the bold way he pressed his cock against her lower abdomen, the hot knot of his cock feeling steel-hard and very big. The possessive way he held her.

She found herself responding. Found herself licking her lips, wetting them for him. His gaze drew to her motion, to her mouth and she could read the intent in his eyes. Could feel the whimper of need yearning through her body with the same kind of desperation she'd felt last night during her fantasy dreams about him.

She held her breath as his head began to lower toward her.

Oh God! He was going to kiss her? No, way! He couldn't be about to kiss her? Not here. Not on the dance floor. Suddenly she felt overheated. Tense.

She knew his lips would be hot and rough. Knew he would kiss her as if she belonged to him. How? She had no idea, but she just knew it.

Amidst the whirling disbelief that yes, indeed, it really looked as if he might do just that, right here, on the dance floor, a total stranger, kiss her, she couldn't stop the excitement as it flared through her like an explosion. In eager anticipation, she parted her lips.

"May I cut in?" Her fiancé's deep voice intruded into their dance. Oh no! Skip!

Chance's body tensed like a coiled spring against her and she just about jumped out of her skin. The fierce sexual look Chance held for her turned into ice as he glared at Skip. It was the same cold stare he'd thrown at him when Skip had kissed her earlier at the Timber Sports competition.

Oh my goodness, was Chance jealous? How could he be? They'd just met, for heaven's sake. Despite him being a stranger, she wished Chance would say no to Skip's request. She ached to stay in his arms, needed to be kissed by him. Craved to be touched by him. Fucked by him.

The naughty thoughts rocked her and made her step on Chance's foot. He threw her a smile that shot sparkles of enjoyment through her. It was as if he were sending secret signals that he'd meet up with her in just a bit. When he slipped out of her arms and backed away from her, she almost groaned out loud at the loss.

"Go ahead," he said to Skip. His words were calm, a total contrast to the turmoil she read in Chance's eyes.

Before Emily could stop him, Chance had disappeared into the nearby crowd of dancers.

Chapter Five

"I see the way he looks at you, Emily," Skip said as he took her into his arms for the dance.

She noted immediately there were no sparks between them, no body chemistry. He seemed to hold her more as if he were a concerned brother rather than a fiancé. The realization angered her.

"Oh Skip! For heaven's sake. You're overreacting."

"I'm not." His sharp reply captured Emily's entire attention. "There's something about him. I don't know what it is, but I don't trust him. I want you to get rid of him and come back to New York City with me, tonight."

"Good grief, Skip. I don't think so."

"Emily, I'm simply warning you."

"He paid a thousand dollars for my pie and a date with me. I'm not cutting out on a date because you don't trust him."

"C'mon Emily. One thousand dollars? Who in their right mind pays a thousand dollars for a pie or a date? I was so floored I couldn't even come up with a counteroffer."

As he spoke, a shiver of unease scrambled up her spine. She'd sensed something about Chance Donovan last night, and now Skip was telling her he sensed something too. She tried to ignore the worry in his eyes and gave him a quick peck on his warm cheek.

"You're so sweet to worry."

He shifted uneasily and she almost laughed at the hint of a blush crossing his cheeks as he quickly glanced at his watch.

"I get the feeling you have somewhere you need to be," she said. "You don't want to miss your plane. I'll see you at the end of the month."

"In your wedding gown?"

"In my wedding gown," she said, realizing she had way too many doubts about marrying Skip Cole. She should tell him she was getting cold feet. Tell him right now. But he looked excited. She couldn't tell him she wasn't sure of anything. Not at the moment. Not right here in front of so many people. And she couldn't take him back to her place because she had Chance staying with her.

Okay, she wouldn't do anything right now. She would talk to him again when things calmed down and she could think straight again. Maybe then she'd feel differently?

"The dress is almost finished. Did you know? Just needs that final fitting," he said.

She found it hard to smile at what should have been welcome news.

"I didn't know it had come in," she replied. They'd purchased the dress at the wedding shop on the main island and the saleslady had said it would be tight getting the dress ordered and into the store at such short notice.

"Helena's going to surprise you by taking you into town for that final fitting. Act surprised when she shows up, okay?"

Emily nodded.

Helena. Steve's old boss and still Skip's boss. She was a nice older lady. Over the years they'd kept in touch and lately she'd been pushing Emily and Skip together. She even insisted on footing the bill for their wedding.

"I still can't believe she's paying for the wedding planner and this whole wedding. She's extremely generous, don't you think?" Skip asked and awaited her answer. God! He was way too excited about this wedding. It made her nervous.

Again, Emily nodded.

His face fell into a concerned frown. "Email me tonight when you get in. I need to know you made it home safe."

"I will and I'll fill you in all the gory details about what happened tonight on my date." She thought her little attempt at humor would bring a smile to his lips, but Skip remained serious.

"I hope you know what you're doing," he said, and gave her a quick brotherly peck on the cheek.

So do I, Emily thought as mixed emotions began running over her like a Mack truck. Should she follow Skip's instincts and ask Chance to leave? Immediately she caught herself.

Why should she?

Aside from the way he entered her home in the middle of the night, he hadn't done anything else wrong. She was reacting to Skip's suspicions not her own. Chance was okay. She sensed it and she always went with her instincts.

Well, actually almost always. If she went with her instincts, she would tell Skip about her sudden wedding jitters. At that moment the dance ended and before she could gather her nerve to talk to him, Skip made his excuses and left.

The minute he vanished; Chance appeared at her side.

"Miss me?" he teased, and her breath hitched as his masculine scent warmed her.

Before she could answer, a spear of sadness clutched her heart as the next song sliced through the air. "The Power of Love" by Celine Dion. It was *their* song. Steve's and hers.

Tears stung her eyes and she blinked them back. She was about to tell Chance she preferred to sit this one out, but his large hand splayed across the back of her waist and he gently pulled her against his hard length. Heat radiated off him and to her surprise, he didn't grind himself against her as he'd done earlier. He held her gently, tenderly, almost as if sensing she needed space this time around.

"This dance is ours," he whispered as his other hand nestled along the curve of her hip.

Ours?

Stunned disbelief screamed through her. How could he pick the same song as Steve's and hers? Confusion made her stiffen in his arms, but her confusion only lasted a few seconds as she began to react to how nicely his body fit against hers.

Her knees grew weak with the erotic sensations of his warm body pressing so agreeably against hers. She barely noticed the curious glances the other dancers threw their way as Chance held her close. As she stared into his eyes, the music faded into the distance.

They were shadowed, uncertain eyes and an unsmiling mouth. Yet everywhere he touched, the searing heat caressed her body. She wanted to reach up and run her fingers along his strong jaw and trace the dark shadows beneath his haunted eyes.

His sweet, cotton-candy-scented breath flowed softly against her cheeks and, God help her, she ached to curl her arms around his neck and kiss him. As if he knew exactly what she was thinking, his head began to lower once again, his mouth opened, and she felt his warm breath caress her lips.

"Emily!" a familiar man's voice hailed her.

Chance cursed softly, quickly putting distance between them. Emily turned away from Chance's heated look to find Dr. Baker peering curiously at them. He stood not more than two feet away and had a concerned look on his face.

"What happened to your wrist?" the doctor asked.

"My wrist?"

"I couldn't help but notice you have a nice-sized gauze on your wrist. Thought I'd better check if everything is okay."

"She burned herself on the metal of her teakettle," Chance explained.

The doctor's green eyes slid to Chance and she noted curiosity in his gaze before he returned his attention back to Emily.

"Perhaps I should take a look."

"I'm fine. Chance told me to keep it moist with ointment and covered."

"He's quite correct." He turned to Chance and smiled. "I don't think we've met."

"Oh, please accept my apologies," Emily said as she quickly made introductions. Both men shook hands.

"Pleased to meet you, Mr. Donovan. I couldn't help but notice you paid a thousand dollars for a date with Emily and a go at her pie. Do you two know each other well?"

"Actually, we've just met," Chance replied with a friendly grin.

"You in town for very long?"

"No. Not long."

A jolt of sadness speared through Emily at Chance's answer. The thought of maybe never seeing him again never entered her mind. But of course, he wouldn't be here long. He'd only hired on for a few days. Somehow, she'd forgotten that fact. Chance was temporary. Skip was permanent. She didn't know this guy. He was a stranger and she was only using him as an excuse not to marry Skip because she had cold feet. Right?

"Don't let me keep you two from your dance." The doctor returned his attention to her. "Emily, if you think your burn needs attention, please drop into my office anytime, or I can come for a visit. Mr. Donovan, it was a pleasure meeting you. I hope you enjoy your stay and your date with Emily."

Chance nodded politely and Dr. Baker quickly slipped into the crowd. When the doctor was gone, Chance threw her a curious look that read "What's going on with the nosy doctor?"

"Small town." Emily shrugged. "He's been here about a year and already he's just as nosy as the rest. He's not the first who asked about you."

Chance frowned and she wondered if that was worry lurking in his eyes? No, he was probably shy, just like Daniel had said.

"You were quite a hit with the older ladies over at the baked goods tent," she teased.

His frown only deepened. "We should go check the lost and found for my shoes and go home. It's getting crowded in here."

She scanned the smoky interior of the warm tent and realized that, sure enough, the dance floor had gained quite a few more dancers. Gosh, she hadn't even noticed. She'd been too busy staring into Chance Donovan's gorgeous eyes. Hopefully, she hadn't made a fool out of herself. By the way the onlookers were watching them, Emily knew she had given people something to talk about for days. If Doc Baker hadn't interrupted when he did, she would have added even more fuel to their gossip. She bit her lower lip and nodded. "You're right. Let's get out of here."

• • ⁓✿⁓ • •

HUGGING THE CUDDLY stuffed animal lobster Chance had won for her, Emily stood at the stern of her fishing boat *Sweet Lies*. She pretended to study the flickering, colorful harbor lights of the main island as they disappeared into the steel blue horizon behind her, but her thoughts were on him. While they'd been at the lost and found getting his shoes, she'd seen a pair of red slippers some child had lost and it had struck a chord through her, reminding her of the *Wizard of Oz* movie and the theme of the story about there being no place like home. It reminded her of what Chance had said earlier.

When he'd purchased a date with her, he'd said they'd eat the pie at "home" and then after they'd chatted with Dr. Baker, Chance had once again said "let's go home".

Why would he consider her lighthouse his home?

Her tummy hollowed in disbelief at her next thought. Unless...he planned on buying it? Was that the reason her in-laws had sent Chance over here? To buy her little lighthouse? The familiar sadness wrapped around her whenever she thought about leaving. She knew she'd have to let go of her place because she'd be married and living in New York City and having the babies she'd always wanted.

So, why wasn't she thinking happy thoughts about her future husband? Instead she was reliving how Chance's body moved so perfectly against hers on the dance floor. Missteps not included of course. Why would she react so intimately to a stranger? Only one other man had made her react with such ecstasy and she'd married him without a second thought.

Emily frowned. A lot of good that had done her.

She needed to concentrate on Skip, her fiancé. A safe, reliable man who didn't shoot her insides into a tangled blossom of lust. All she had to do was keep Chance at a comfortable distance, and she could do that by supplying him with loads of work. It would keep them both busy and her mind off her attraction to him. That was all it was, a mere attraction. Just like it had been with her husband, Steve.

Then why had his death left her nursing a broken heart? There was no way she'd ever let another man control her emotions like Steve McCullen had. Never in a million years. And that's why she would marry Skip Cole. At least if something happened to him, she wouldn't have her heart broken again.

· · ⚮ · ·

CHANCE STEERED THE boat through the thin wisps of white mist toward the dark silhouette of Shipwreck Island. Giant, frothing ocean waves crashed against the sides of *Sweet Lies* and he braced his feet farther apart as the boat swayed under the onslaught.

Far up ahead in the north sky white blades of lightning forked through the air. There was a storm out on the ocean. That would account for the swollen waves tonight. But that didn't account for the stormy anger brewing inside him.

His jaw clenched painfully, and a bad kind of black rage slammed through him as he thought about Skip kissing Emily back at the fair. Out of all the men in the world why did she have to pick him? She'd never had any romantic feelings for him in the past. Then again, he had been gone for years. Plenty of time for Skip to get something going with his wife.

So why wasn't she happy about the upcoming nuptials like when they'd planned their own wedding? Their apartment had been littered with Vegas brochures on chapels, hotels and restaurants as well as bridal magazines, florist shop brochures, catering menus, samples of bouquets, anything that had to do with a wedding.

He'd seen no evidence of an upcoming wedding back at the lighthouse. He'd seen no love brewing between Emily and Skip. Heck, they didn't even kiss like lovers. Mere pecks on the cheek sure wouldn't make their marriage last or bring on the kids.

Unless... Chance inhaled at an exhilarating thought. Unless she wasn't in love with Skip?

When his ex-best friend had intruded into their dance, Chance sensed her disappointment at the intrusion and she'd even stiffened in his arms. Why? Why would she react that way to the man she was about to marry? Okay, so at first he'd stepped on her toes, but when he remembered how to dance, she'd melted against him. Did she suspect who he was?

No. If she did, she would ask him point-blank.

He was so deep in thought he didn't hear her climb the bridge ladder to the wheelhouse where he stood at the helm until her sexy scent wafted through the cool, salty breeze and a wave of heated desire swept through him. He remembered almost kissing her on the dance floor. Knew her lips would be warm and welcoming. Felt his cock hardening and the blood racing through him in heated anticipation. Just as he was doing now.

"Why do you dislike Skip?" she asked.

Curiosity laced her voice and Chance's grip tightened around the steering wheel. Keeping his eyes glued to the looming silhouette of the lighthouse, he tried to appear nonchalant.

"What gives you that idea?"

"The way you tense up whenever he's around. The way you tensed just now when I mentioned his name."

"I've got nothing against your fiancé," he lied.

She didn't say anything.

"What does he think about you letting me stay out here at your place?" he found himself asking. He wondered how Skip would react with his fiancée inviting him to live at the lighthouse. If Emily were *his* fiancée he'd never allow it. Not that he didn't trust her, it was men in general he wouldn't trust around his beautiful wife.

There was a long silence and then she sighed. "I didn't tell him."

Chance laughed. "Why not?"

"He didn't ask and I didn't tell. No harm done. Besides he's gone."

He grinned inwardly. Skip Cole had deserted his fiancée. What a jerk.

"Sore loser."

"He had business to attend to."

"He's engaged to the most beautiful woman in the country and he'd rather do business?"

He heard her draw in a sharp breath at his comment. It was a sensual sound he remembered well and suddenly he wanted her. Ached to have her sweet lips on his mouth. Craved to have her legs clasp around his hips while he made love to her. He wanted to feel like a man again and he wanted to hear her sexy little gasps when he brought her to climax.

Her sudden frightened cry ripped him back to reality. He saw the tension on her face as she pointed to the silhouette of her lighthouse set on the high dark cliffs.

"Someone's in the lighthouse tower!"

Dread shot through Chance as he scanned the rocky shoreline ahead. He barely made out the black silhouette of the buildings partially hidden behind the white swirls of fog. Nothing appeared out of the ordinary.

"Are you sure?"

"Look up in the lamp room," Emily hissed.

No sooner had she said the words than he spotted the tiny flicker of light flash in the glass windows.

Lightning? No, it looked more like a flashlight beam bouncing off the windows inside. She was right. Someone was in the lighthouse.

Fuck!

"We have to hurry," she urged.

Chance didn't hesitate. Shoving the throttle forward into a faster speed, his heart cracked against his chest like a jackhammer as he kept his gaze glued to the lighthouse. Obviously, Skip had recognized him and that's why he'd left the dance early and come here for the same thing Chance had come for. Hell, he shouldn't have waited so long. Should have sent one of his brothers to the lighthouse the minute he remembered his laptop possibly still being up there in its hiding place.

Shit! He should have gone straight up there last night and checked to see if it was there, taken it and gotten the hell out of here. Now his selfish need to be with her had put her into danger. Within minutes he maneuvered *Sweet Lies* to the dock and cursed when she hopped out of the boat and raced into the misty glow.

· · ~∞~ · ·

EMILY STOOD JUST INSIDE the open doorway of the lighthouse tower and stared up the gloomy interior to the dim light shining at the top. The intruder had left the door open up there. Too bad for him. All she had to do was close this bottom door and slide the bolt into place then call the cops. She was just about to do that when Chance's rushed footsteps crossed the wood deck behind her, and she breathed a sigh of relief. However, her relief was short-lived when she saw the anger splashing across his face.

"Don't ever pull a stupid stunt like that again." He spoke in a harsh whisper, but the undertone of admonishment and anger came through loud and clear.

"Don't move from here," he commanded in quite the authoritative voice she didn't care for. Brushing past her, he stepped into the open doorway and disappeared up the curling stairs, the darkness swallowing him.

His brisk remarks pushed aside her fear and shot a jolt of hot fury into her veins. She wasn't about to let some man tell her what to do or fight her battles for her!

Ignoring his order to stay here, she followed behind him. Darkness closed in around her as she entered the octagonal structure. Using the walls to keep her balance, she practically ran up the narrow curling stairs to catch up to Chance. When he realized she was following him, he emitted a gentle curse, grabbed her hand and began pulling her along behind him. He moved at a very fast pace and she had a hard time keeping up to his long stride. By the time they reached the top step, Emily was huffing and puffing, her lungs frantic for air.

The instant they stepped into the watchtower, the dim light flicked off and a shadowy figure crashed into Chance, knocking him off his feet. Emily screamed as the intruder brushed past her and disappeared through the doorway they had just entered. Footsteps echoed down the narrow staircase as the person escaped.

"Chance?" Emily called out as she gazed into the darkness, her heart pounding with fear for him. She tried to find the light switch but couldn't. A moment later when she heard his heavy breathing from somewhere nearby, she sighed her relief. Then his voice floated out of the darkness.

"I'm here. Just had the wind knocked out of me. Are you okay?"

"I'm fine."

At her confirmation, Chance's shadowy figure rose up in front of her a few feet away, his silhouette tall and menacing against the dark blue night sky behind the glass windows. From somewhere down below the sound of an engine captured their attention.

"He's docked a boat on the north shore," Chance said. "C'mon!" Grabbing her hand, he pushed open the nearby door. Crisp, cool salty air blew against her face as he led her onto the observation deck of her lighthouse.

"Down there!" He pointed down to the ocean where a lone figure sat hunched low in a speedboat that left mist-streaked white waves in its wake as it quickly disappeared around the point.

"You recognize the boat?" Chance asked.

"No," Emily whispered hoarsely. Her legs were shaking and she suddenly felt like crying. Who would come here to her island and invade her lighthouse?

"I'd better go downstairs and see if he stole anything," she said.

Heading toward the stairs, she cried out when her foot cracked painfully into something lying on the floor.

"What's wrong?" Chance asked.

"I don't know. Hit something."

She made her way to the nearby wall, tried to orient herself in the darkness, thankfully found the light switch and turned it on.

When she spotted the black lump on the wooden floor, she gasped in shock. For a moment she thought she was dreaming. Slowly the disbelief made way to joy.

"It's my husband's old laptop computer. I haven't seen it in years. After he died, I looked for it and couldn't find it. Why would someone bring back his laptop? And leave it here?"

The bittersweet happiness felt like that of finding a wrapped Christmas present in a closet after someone had died.

"Is it damaged?" Chance's voice sounded strangled as he came up behind her.

Swooping, she picked up the computer and rapped her knuckles on the lid. "It's as solid as concrete. They don't make them like this anymore. And it sure is heavy."

"I'll carry it down for you."

He made a move to take the laptop, but she didn't want to let go of it.

"No, I'll take it. Let's go downstairs."

· · ໓ · ·

HALF AN HOUR LATER, Chance had retrieved both Emily's furry red lobster he'd won for her at the fair and the seaweed pie from the boat.

She brewed some coffee and they sat in silence as he dug into his second helping of the deliciously sweet seaweed-apple-blueberry pie. She watched him eat. Her eyes were bright with excitement over finding the laptop, her cheeks were flushed and her hair was all mussed from the wind they'd encountered on the way home. Despite her strong outer appearance, he knew by the way her eyes darted about at every little noise that she was still jittery about the break-in.

He was uneasy too. Whoever the hell had been up in the lighthouse had found his laptop. Yet the person hadn't tried to harm him or Emily. They'd been too much in a hurry to get out of here and that kind of behavior was not what he would expect from someone associated with the violence he'd incurred over the years.

Despite that fact, he should put in a call to his brothers, Mathew and Daniel, and let them know what happened. He would do that later. He would get them to come here and pick up the laptop and analyze the contents. That was the only way to keep Emily safe. At least he hoped so. He couldn't help but cast quick glances at the laptop computer as it sat sentry between them on the tiny kitchen table for two.

It was *his* laptop. Loaded with the information that had gotten him tossed into jail, his death faked, his being forced to use a false name and a life of living hell on death row in a Texas prison. His gaze dropped to the disc slot and he breathed a sigh of relief. The disc was still stuffed in there. He wondered if Emily had noticed it yet. Even if she did, he'd password protected the disc. So if she tried it on her other computer, it wouldn't work unless she inputted the correct password.

"Did my brother-in-law tell you what happened to my husband?"

Her soft question pleased Chance. She was testing him. The information she gathered from him would show her exactly how much Daniel trusted him and in turn how much trust she should place in him.

He thought for a moment before answering.

"He said Steve had just quit his job in New York and caught a flight out to Charlottetown. A friend of yours picked him up and drove him to where he had *Sweet Lies* docked near the North Cape. After he boarded the boat, he was arrested because a substantial amount of heroin was found onboard. Within hours of his arrest he apparently committed suicide in jail."

"That's a lie!"

Her angry outburst startled him. For the first time he caught a glimpse of the hell he'd put her through all these years. Correction, the hell they'd both endured because of Skip. Skip, who Steve had trusted with a copy of the information that sat in that disc in his laptop.

"I said apparently," he soothed, yet her eyes continued to blaze with unbelievable fierceness.

"Did he tell you we all had doubts?" she asked.

Chance nodded. "Especially when you demanded to see your husband's body and were given his ashes instead."

"Convenient wasn't it? A mix-up in paperwork they said. Did Daniel tell you what a stupid thing I did after I got my husband's ashes?"

"You scattered them in the ocean. He also told me you were very distraught at the time. It's understandable, Emily."

"My mourning screwed everything up. Throwing his remains in the ocean prevented any sophisticated forensic tests to be done."

"Don't you think they were his ashes?" He held his breath and anxiously waited for her answer. Did she think he was still alive?

"It's not that. My main concern is they probably cremated Steve to prevent us from finding out he was murdered."

"They?"

"If I knew that answer, I'd have put them behind bars a long time ago." She gazed down at the laptop. "Why would someone bring Steve's laptop back after all these years?"

A shiver of dread shot through Chance. He might as well tell her the truth. At least some of it.

"It wasn't brought back," he admitted.

Emily frowned at his words.

"I saw a wall tile missing near the doorway that led up to the lamp room. I think Steve hid the laptop in the wall."

Which was the truth. He had hidden the laptop that morning before he had left to quit his New York job.

Emily frowned as she stared at the computer.

"Why would he do that?"

"Maybe he used to go up there and write his articles? It's a great view for inspiration, and instead of lugging it up and down he just put it up there."

Liar. He put it up there because he was expecting trouble. Stupid idiot that he was, he thought he could handle it himself. He'd been sorely mistaken and paid dearly for being a fool.

Chance forced himself to jab at another piece of the seaweed pie.

"Is this the first time you've had a break-in since Steve died?" he asked, thinking it was highly unlikely someone would come here and look for the original disc after all this time. Besides, Daniel had mentioned there had been break-ins.

"I had a couple incidents shortly after he died."

"Anything stolen?"

"They ripped everything apart as if they were looking for something. They took our computer, printer, fax, other office items and that was it. No jewelry or other expensive items. The second break-in came a few days later. Things were moved around but nothing stolen. Someone was looking for something in the drawers, behind picture frames even the carpets had been lifted. Steve's two brothers made me go into hiding until they could figure out who killed Steve. Then after a couple of years, Daniel took me down to Mexico with him. He was depressed about something but never told me what. I figured it had to do with Steve. We lived with my father-in-law. He was such a nice man, but I was homesick for this place and picked up one day and just had to come back home. Despite their protests. They were so overprotective."

Steve was glad his dad and brother had taken such good care of Emily. If she'd stayed here and been in the line of fire, they would have used her against him in some way. He was surprised they hadn't kidnapped her when they'd kidnapped him and done just that.

"Better safe than sorry," he muttered.

At his comment, she looked at him and smiled, and he couldn't help but inhale as her dimples caved in her cheeks. She looked fantastic in dimples.

"You've got a piece of pie on your lip," she whispered.

To his surprise, she reached over and dabbed her warm finger against his upper lip. Her touch was soft and tender. A direct contrast to how his life had been over the past few years.

Suddenly he wanted to take her hand and kiss her delicate fingers, one by one, and that was just for starters. After that he'd take her fingers into his mouth. One at a time. Seducing each perfect digit until lust flared in her eyes.

As if sensing what he must be thinking, her gentle caress slowed and she drew her finger away. Her gaze quickly followed, dropping from his face back to his laptop, an uneasy smile curling her pink lips.

God, she was so cute when she became nervous. He wished he could lean over and kiss her pretty mouth. Ached to have her lips wrapped around his cock. Taking him deep inside her right down her throat.

Stop it! he chastised himself. *If you try anything she'll think you're a sex maniac.*

Clearing his throat, he looked down at his half-eaten second helping of pie, trying to pretend he didn't notice her anxiety.

"I've been meaning to ask you. Why on earth did you pay one thousand dollars for a date with me?" she asked.

"It wasn't you I was after," he replied, trying to keep his voice causal.

Disappointment swept across her face. It was good to know she was interested in him. Very good to know. Despite that though, nothing could come of it. He needed to remember that.

"It was your pie I wanted," he lied.

A bright smile lit up her face and he felt his cock tighten with need as her dimples splashed across her cheeks again. Oh man, he wanted her so bad. Just like the old days. Heck, even more than the old days.

She laughed, and then said, "Okay, you better eat that piece you have on the plate because you are going to need all your energy tomorrow."

"What's on the agenda for tomorrow? Or should I ask?"

For a moment she looked shy, just like the old days, and it brought such a tender ache to his heart he almost groaned out loud.

"Well," she said slowly, "tomorrow we are going on a seaweed harvest."

Seaweed harvest? He'd never gone on one before. Should be interesting.

"Excellent. Then you can bake me more pies."

Using his fork, he chopped off another piece of the heavenly smelling desert.

"Can you afford the price?" She smirked.

"I'm sure we can come to some sort of suitable arrangement."

He shoved a forkful of the sweet treat into his mouth, and when he looked at her, he didn't miss the tinge of pink that swept across her cheeks before she stood and hurried away to retrieve another cup of coffee.

Chapter Six

"Lucas," Emily whispered. Lucas was the name Steve and she had planned on naming their firstborn son.

She quickly typed the name into Steve's laptop computer and hit the enter key.

The green screen produced two white words, *Access Denied*. She frowned for a moment and then her face lit up with a smile.

"Elizabeth." She typed in the name they'd picked for their firstborn daughter.

The machine whirred and the same two words flashed across the screen. *Access Denied*. She added the two names to the piece of paper containing the growing list of names she'd already tried as a password.

"What else could he have used?" She scrunched her brows together and concentrated for the hundredth time on what had been going on in their lives at the time Steve died.

Steve's boss at the time, Helena Whitney, had told her Steve hadn't been working on any dangerous assignments. Back then, Emily hadn't prodded Helena any further on what assignments he had actually been working on because Emily had been grieving over his death and then she'd gone to Mexico with Daniel. When she'd come back home, she'd been preoccupied in earning a living now that most of her savings had been used up.

Perhaps Steve had used a password from one of the stories he'd been working on at the time?

Emily sighed and shook her head. No, the passwords in those areas were endless. She was positive he would have used a personal password. Something near and dear to his heart. She'd already used everyone she knew and their birthdays.

Absently she twisted her finger through a few strands of hair that fell over her face and remembered the last time Steve had twisted his fingers through her hair.

They'd been standing on their dock, right below the lighthouse, saying goodbye on the day he'd gone off to quit his job...

"Are you sure you're going to be all right here all alone for one night?" he whispered softly against her ear as his fingers sifted through her hair to cup the back of her head.

"It'll be torture tonight, but it'll be twice as sweet when you come home tomorrow."

"Coming home. Mmmmm. I like the sound of that." He smiled, revealing a flash of white teeth.

She didn't smile back at him. An eerie uneasiness dogged her every waking hour since having a nightmare a couple of nights ago that he was going to die. But knowing he was safe hadn't diminished the feeling she was going to lose him. The nightmare or perhaps it had been a premonition had been so violent in its emotions. So devoid of any visions. So intense and vivid she'd awoken in a sweat, totally convinced she was alone and he was dead. She'd been surprised and then relieved to find him sleeping soundly beside her.

The unnerving nervousness tracking her every waving hour since she'd had that nightmare hadn't faded. If anything, her fear for his safety was growing by the minute. Everything in the past few weeks had been too perfect. She'd finally convinced him to quit his dangerous job as an investigative journalist and move permanently here to Shipwreck Island. He'd finally agreed two nights ago in the shower that they wouldn't use condoms anymore. He finally wanted kids.

She was too happy when he told her that. From past experience when things went along too smoothly, something tragic always happened to ruin her happiness.

Steve's hand loosened from her hair and curled gently around her shoulder. He frowned at her.

"Emmie? You've been too quiet this morning. What's wrong?"

"Nothing. I'm just going to miss you like crazy," she admitted. She really should tell him about her premonition. Tell him to stay home. But she wanted him to quit and understood he had to do that in person. After giving his resignation to Helena, he promised to bring back a whole bunch of wool so she could get started on knitting clothes for their cute babies.

Steve's lips tilted upward again and those generous lines around his mouth popped up, making Emily catch her breath.

"I'll be back before you can even blink with that knitting wool." God, how did he always know what she was thinking? His right hand lifted from her shoulder and he brushed his warm thumb against the side of her mouth. "Smile for me so I can see those cute dimples one more time."

She forced herself to smile.

"That's better. Now hold that smile because I want to see it there when I get back tomorrow. We can make love again under the wharf like the other night. Keep the candles burning for me so I can find my way in the fog." His hand dropped away from where he'd been caressing her mouth and he made a move toward *Sweet Lies*.

"Wait!"

At her shout he turned back around.

"Are you wearing that Saint Christopher medallion I gave you last week for luck?"

"You're all the luck I need, babe," he said, and moved closer. His masculine smell wrapped around her senses, sparking all those arousal centers in her body.

"I'm serious, Steve."

His eyebrows burrowed into a concerned frown.

"Why so glum? Yes, I'm wearing it. You told me its good luck and gives safety to travelers."

He pulled down his turtleneck and relief splashed through her as he drew out the old gold medallion that had once belonged to her uncle, turned it over and read the inscription.

"To Steve. Your Endearment Always. Love, Emily. Don't worry, sweetness. I'll keep it on me for as long as you want." He leaned close to her, their lips inches from each other. His eyes sparkled warmly and suddenly all she wanted to do was kiss him and lose herself in the welcome warmth of his strong, hard body. To forget this other creepy feeling she had of him dying.

"I know I shouldn't say anything and I know you're going to think I'm probably a nutcase and overreacting, but I have a bad feeling about you going off this time. I want you to be careful."

"Hey, I'm only quitting my job. Nothing is going to happen to me. And you aren't a nutcase. Maybe you're already pregnant and your hormones are kicking in?"

Emily laughed shakily at his suggestion.

"I don't think hormones click in that quickly."

A roaring wave crashed against the pier, making them both stumble.

"I guess I'll have to fix the dock when I get back."

"You can fix other things too," she said softly.

"We'll continue our plans on making a baby when I get back, okay?"

"Promise?"

"Promise," he vowed, and planted a mind-busting kiss on her mouth, making her knees literally feel weak and her body so hot for him she almost grabbed him by the pants, insisting they have a quickie right here on the dock.

But he pulled away.

"Have those candles waiting on me when I get back. And lots of food too. I'm going to need all the energy I can get in making that baby."

He winked and she almost cried when she watched him hop onto the tugboat her uncle had named *Sweet Lies*. A moment later the boat's engine rumbled to life. From the wheelhouse he threw her a quick wave out the salt-crusted window. She waved back to him and kept waving until he disappeared around the point.

It was the last time she ever saw him.

Emily sighed as sadness swept through her. Now was not the time to think about Steve, she chastised herself. Now was the time to think of the right password.

Leaning back against her chair, she gazed thoughtfully at the blinking cursor. An idea hit her like a ton of bricks.

"Of course. *Sweet Lies*," she whispered beneath her breath. "The password is *Sweet Lies*, the tugboat. How could I have been so stupid?"

Excitement surged and she quickly typed in her boat's name then hit the enter key. The computer whirred a few seconds then stopped.

Access Denied.

Dammit! It was going to be a long night.

• • ⚓ • •

CHANCE STARED AT THE dim light escaping beneath Emily's bedroom door. No one had to tell him what she was still doing up at this ungodly hour of one a.m. She was trying to crack the password.

Unless...

A shiver of unease slipped down his back. Unless she'd already guessed it and gained access to the information? Chance leaned forward and pressed his ear against the door. The distant sound of Emily's fingertips busily pounding away at the keyboard sounded like music to his ears. She was still trying to crack it. He would have been worried if she'd been quiet.

He ran a hand over his bristly chin as he remembered tonight's intrusion up in the lighthouse tower. When he'd seen his laptop computer lying on the floor of the observation room, he'd just about passed out from the shock. All the horrible years of prison life, of being thought dead, of being forced to use a false name faded away and he remembered when he'd slid aside the wall tile, slipped his heavy laptop up onto the thick log support beam and slid the tile back into place.

He hadn't meant for the wall to be a hiding place. He'd placed the computer up there so he wouldn't have to lug it down the long flight of stairs back into the house. He'd made a duplicate of the disc someone had dropped on the doorstep that morning then left the original in the slot, hoping to get a look at it when he came back. He thought he'd only be gone twenty-four hours. Instead he'd been gone for years.

Everything from that day was a blur due to the head injury he'd received complements of a fist-happy jail guard. He did remember the spot where he'd put the laptop. Remembered the urgency to get the disc to Skip. Emily's nervousness that morning. But after that, things remained hazy from that day until he woke up in a prison infirmary weeks later.

He'd had years to try to figure out what in the world the people who held him prisoner wanted, and it always led back to the mysterious disc he'd found on the front doorstep of the lighthouse. The disc had piqued his interest the way it had shown up.

He'd password protected the disc and backed it up onto his laptop then made another backup disc. He'd pocketed the backup, left the original in the drive and stashed the laptop in the secret wall compartment.

His gaze dropped to the light still seeping out from beneath Emily's bedroom door. Damn it. He wanted the laptop and that disc. But it looked as if he were in for a long wait.

·· ◦❧◦ ··

SHE WAS IN CHANCE'S arms again. They were dancing. And he was whirling her around as if they were both floating on air. Instead of being on the dance floor in the fair tent, they were here in her home, in the living room.

Their song, hers and Steve's, hers and Chance's, blared from the radio. Chance held her so perfectly, his embrace so strong and safe that her heart was suspended in her chest, making it hard for her to breathe from the excitement.

"Your dancing steps have improved."

He smiled at her compliment and it was the most genuine smile she'd ever seen. It seemed to come from somewhere deep inside him, from an area in his soul he reserved specifically for her. It was a sexy, teasing smile that melted into her such contentment, such happiness that she wondered why she felt so comfortable in his arms. So welcome. As if she should know who he was. As if she'd danced with him many times in the past. But that was crazy. She'd only met him.

"I want to dance and make love to you at the same time."

His soft whisper caressed her ear and she blinked with surprise at what he'd just said. He wanted to make love to her? Right here in her living room? While dancing?

Erotic tingles swept through her as he chuckled and nibbled on her right earlobe. His hands left her waist and slid up her sides to cup against the outsides of her breasts.

"Hmm, that feels good," she whispered as the heat seeped into her from his palms. She arched closer to him, loving his touch. Trailing her hands off his powerful shoulders, she splayed her palms across his

steel-muscled chest. She didn't seem surprised to discover he wore no shirt. As a matter of fact, he wore no clothing and neither did she.

And it felt so right to be naked with him, a perfect stranger.

His flesh seared against hers. His body felt like an intoxicating flame, a scorching heat, and she suddenly couldn't get enough of him. Something deep inside her pussy awakened and an uncontrollable shiver of lust shifted through her, consuming her, driving her toward a goal she knew she had no control over.

And that goal was Chance. She wanted him. Now. Wanted his cock pumping into her while they danced.

She hissed as his rock-hard cock head pressed against her sensitive clit. He used it as if it were a finger, massaging her clit with sensual assault, up and down, until she was undulating and moaning against his mouth. She wanted to lose herself in his touch. Lose herself in these flames of lust as they burst through her with lightning speed.

His hands left her breasts and skimmed down her sides like two fiery blades of sensations.

Reaching behind her, he cupped her ass.

"I want you now, baby," he groaned.

He kissed her. His mouth a hot, restless brand on her lips. His kiss sizzling her nerve endings to life and sending a deep, gnawing hunger straight through her. His blue eyes darkened as he moved his head away from her. His nostrils were flaring, as if he couldn't get enough of her scent.

"You smell good. Like sex."

"Interesting choice of words. Considering that's what we're doing." She giggled as his hands held her ass cheeks tighter and he increased the tension on her clitoris.

Breathing harshly, she shuddered as swells of pleasure swept around her.

"Straddle me," he moaned against her mouth.

Straddle him? Just as she'd sometimes done with Steve? She'd always gotten a deeper penetration in that position. Always got a better climax.

Cupping her ass, he lifted her. She grabbed him by his biceps, and she inhaled at the powerful flex of muscles beneath her fingertips. Wrapping her legs around his hips, she inhaled as his cock entered her, stretching her, impaling her.

"You like it, don't you, Emily," he growled.

She couldn't answer. She felt hot. Feverish as he withdrew and stroked into her again, his cock filling her to perfection. Pulsing and thick inside her.

They danced this way. Both melded at the hips to each other. His steps were sure and confident as he carried her with him, twirling them around as if they were dancing on a cloud. She took his mouth, savoring the softness of his lips. Enjoying the hardness of his thrusts from his cock.

With each strong stroke, she felt the tension build between them. With every thrust, her body tightened. And then a killing arousal speared into her, making her moan at its intensity. Everything was ripping apart and she was exploding.

Falling into a frenzy of arousal and then suddenly Chance wasn't there. Instead it was Steve. Alive and well and healthy. His green eyes glittering with love.

She welcomed him. Loved him. Lost herself in the pleasure.

Her climax was long and drawn-out.

Perspiration drenched them as they danced and made love under a breathtaking shower of streaking silver stars. She kept kissing him. Moaned into his mouth as he buried himself into her over and over again. Tremors of lust mixed with sensations of love. She felt his body tighten as he neared his orgasm.

He let out a cry, pumped harder, faster, deeper, spilling his seed into her.

And then it was Chance again. They were dancing and loving each other and she'd never felt happier in her life. The happiness gushed through her like a tonic, strong and pure and so beautiful, she swore she would die if it stopped.

Emily came awake on a strangled gasp, her body heated like a furnace and drenched in perspiration, her pussy moist with arousal and her finger buried in her wet vagina.

Oh my, obviously, she'd been masturbating in her sleep again.

She felt on edge. Needed that awesome release from her dream to become reality. Needed that happiness.

Alternating between massaging her ultrasensitive clit and thrusting her finger into her pussy, she sucked in a breath as her velvety muscles clenched and she flowed into the beautiful arousal she'd been dreaming about.

She moved her finger faster, more desperate, yearning to reach that high. In and out like a cock she pumped until she was capturing the mind-numbing pleasure. Demanding the release she craved. Her thighs tightened and her nostrils filled with the scent of her sex, her erotic moans splitting through the quiet of her bedroom.

She rode her hand, allowing the storm to claim her, embrace her and love her. All too soon though, the beauty of her orgasm washed away, thrusting her back to reality and she lay gasping in her bed.

Inside her chest, her heart thudded with maddening speed and soon she heard another sound. A strange knocking, which nibbled through her many layers of satisfaction. When her eyes finally fluttered open, she fully expected the knocking to be Chance tapping on her bedroom door in an effort to wake her and find out what the hell was going on in here with all her moaning.

Her face flamed with embarrassment, but she realized the noise sifted in from somewhere outside and she realized it was someone hammering. What the heck? Who in the world would be hammering at this hour? Her six o'clock alarm hadn't even gone off yet.

When she gazed at the clock, she bolted. It was past nine!

Mercy! With all the excitement of finding Steve's laptop and staying up late last night, she'd forgotten to set the alarm and had slept in!

Within minutes she donned her long johns, jeans, turtleneck and a cozy sweater coat then headed outdoors. A blast of cold wind almost blew her right back into the house and she realized today would be too dangerous to go seaweeding.

Obviously, Chance had realized the same thing and decided to start working on something else. As she picked her way down the steep, rickety rock steps that meandered along the red cliffs, Emily inhaled the bracing wind and wished she was back under her warm covers and masturbating again. Better yet, under the covers with Chance! Her face warmed at that thought and she was glad he'd been outside while she'd been moaning her brains out while finger-fucking herself.

The air was drenched with the smell of rotting fish and sea salt, and she could feel the grittiness of the sand blowing against her face as she stepped off the last stair and walked several feet on to the boardwalk. Glancing around, she realized the hammering had stopped and Chance was nowhere in sight. But on the sandy beach beside the wharf she spotted the neatly piled lumber. Beams that Steve had purchased days before he died. Chance must have found them where Steve had stored them in the shed and carried them down there.

The hammering started again, and this time immediately beneath her feet, making her jump. She grinned. So that's where he'd gotten off to. Quietly she walked off the dock and down the grassy slope to the beach.

She found him.

Eight feet up.

He sat proudly on a brace between the pilings. Several long nails protruded from his cute mouth and he was positioning a two-by-four with his large hands. In the other, a hammer was poised, ready to strike a nail. He hadn't seen her, and she couldn't resist watching him work.

He wore her husband's jeans and the jacket Chance had arrived in the other night. The zipper of his jacket was open, showing off a moss green sweater with a light green turtleneck, and she had to admit Steve's clothes fit Chance very well.

Bright rays of sunshine zipped between the planks of the dock and washed over him, enhancing the contours of his broad shoulders and the powerful muscles in his legs. Even his hands looked large in the light. Strong fingers clasped the hammer, and yet the gentle way he held the wood made Emily remember how his hot hands had rested along the curve of her hips during last night's dance. How tenderly his hands had cupped her ass and how she'd straddled his hips while they'd danced in her dreams.

She blinked those hot thoughts away only to be surprised when a memory from the past floated up from the depths of her brain. Her husband perched beneath this same dock years earlier, sitting almost exactly the same way as Chance was sitting right now. Steve had already begun nailing up some of the braces the day before he left. She'd come down to call him in for supper. When he climbed off the pilings, he'd taken her into his arms and kissed her.

Steve had always been a spur-of-the-moment kind of guy. Impulsive. Without warning he'd reach out and take her into his arms. Hug her. Kiss her. Tell her how much he loved her.

She missed those strong hugs and passionate kisses. Missed them with all her heart.

They'd stripped and made love in the tall grass beside the beach. She could still feel how the cool grass had cradled her body, could still smell the faint scent of Steve's salt-tinged skin as he pressed his cock into her. The sounds of their lovemaking had intermingled with the cries of the seagulls circling overhead. Late evening sunshine had brought out the golden highlights in Steve's sandy brown hair too. Just like the morning sun was doing to Chance's hair.

An icy shiver of *déjà vu* rammed through her veins as the sun slipped behind the gray clouds and the golden highlights vanished.

Trick of the light? Yes, that's all. Besides, lots of men had golden highlights in their hair. Didn't they?

"Emily?"

He'd seen her and was studying her with a curious expression that read *What are you thinking, Emily?* Before he could ask, she forced a cheery note into her voice.

"Good morning! Looks like it was my turn to sleep in!" she called out and headed under the wharf.

"Happens to the best of us," he said between the nails still hanging from his lips as he looked down at her. "I heard on the radio there was a high wind warning in effect. Supposed to calm down later this morning. Figured you wouldn't go out in this weather. I thought I'd start bracing up the dock before she sets out to sea. That is if it's okay with the boss?" he asked, giving her that curious look again.

A luscious smile curled up the corners of his delicious-looking mouth and his piercing eyes held hers for a long moment. Her heart began to pound wildly in her ears and a wonderful warmth splashed through her. Sweet mercy she really did like his smile. There were no lines around his mouth like's Steve's mouth had, but he sure did have a similar curve of the lips, and she had the same kind of breathtaking reaction to him as she'd had to her husband.

She really should keep her distance from him, but how could she when he made her feel so alive?

"Of course, it's okay. Do you need a hand? Or are you hungry?"

"Sure. I could use a hand for a few minutes. Unless you think your muscles aren't up to the task?"

He was teasing her just as he'd done last night during their dance when he'd joked about her taking him on in next year's axe-chopping contest. Her mouth suddenly went dry at the thought of what had almost transpired between them while dancing. If the doctor hadn't interrupted them when he had, she knew without a doubt they would have kissed. At that thought, Emily tried to stifle the warm flush heating her face.

Gosh, she'd been doing a lot of that this morning, hadn't she? Blushing up a storm.

"C'mon, I'll give you a lift up." Chance held out his large hand.

Without hesitation she placed her hand in his and started at the shocking heat as his strong fingers curled around hers. In an instant her brain was sending messages of awareness down to her parts south. Her internal temperature increased as he hoisted her up to sit next to him on the beam.

Suddenly he was looking at her oddly and she instinctively sensed he'd felt something too. Reluctantly he let go of her hand.

She inhaled a few breaths in an effort to calm herself. It didn't work. Especially since she could feel the burn of his thigh pressed intimately against her hip. His ocean blue eyes were mere inches from hers and they seemed...sexual looking.

When he turned away and repositioned himself on the beam, he broke the spell and the searing touch between them. Maybe she'd just imagined the sensual heat glowing in his eyes? Maybe she was reacting this way because she'd been too long without a man?

Yes, that had to be it. She'd been too long without and that problem would be resolved when she got married. To another man. She needed to keep that one thought squarely in her mind and she'd have no problems with Chance.

"I noticed some old candles along a couple of the beams down here," Chance said with softness lacing his voice. Her head snapped around to where a couple dozen votive candles were scattered along the beams.

Oh my God! She'd totally forgotten about them down here. She'd set a new batch of them beside the old melted ones, anticipating Steve's return years ago. Some were missing, obviously blown away in the winds, some had tumbled over, but most were still sitting sentry.

Her face flamed as she remembered the one night she and Steve spent beneath the pier. That night she'd wanted to take her husband's cock into her mouth for the first time after reading a sexy scene in an erotic romance novel. But she'd chickened out. She'd missed out on so much because of her shyness.

"The candles helped Steve find the wharf easier," she lied.

That was a lame excuse if ever she came up with one. Ever hear of the lighthouse? his amused look asked.

Thankfully he didn't mention it any further.

"Can you hold the two-by-four up, like this?" he said between the nails as he held up the eight-foot-long piece of wood.

His gorgeous gaze locked onto her eyes again, regarding her with that sexual look again. She noticed his Adam's apple bob nervously as he swallowed and then cleared his throat. "I'll start hammering at the other end."

She reached up and, taking great care not to touch his hot fingers, placed her hands on the board.

"Got it?"

She nodded again and he maneuvered along the awkward brace like a sure-footed panther, stopping at the other end of the piling then lifted the wood up over his head. He removed a nail from his mouth, set it against the piling, and with a concentrated twist to his oh-so-sexy lips, he began to hammer.

Emily stared as his sweater hiked up to reveal a flat belly and thin crisp-looking hair that ventured beneath the waist of his jeans to the well-endowed bulge. Her pulse quickened and her face grew hot as she fantasized what it might be like for Chance to make love to her. Would he be gentle? Savage? Or a wild combination of both, like Steve had been?

The sound of hammering ripped through her fantasy and she sucked in a hot breath. Her eyes drifted up to his sleek arm muscles, straining against the sweater. The hammering stopped. He reached for another nail and in a moment, he began to hammer again.

Strange how a few minutes earlier she'd thought she'd spied those McCullen golden highlights shimmering in his hair. Last night while they'd danced, she'd experienced the eerie *déjà vu* of having danced with him before.

When Chance's fingers settled onto the piece of wood beside her hand, Emily jumped, not realizing he'd scuttled back already.

"Sorry, didn't mean to spook you. You can let go now. I've got it."

Reluctantly, she withdrew her hand and watched him pry another nail from his mouth.

"Daniel mentioned you were getting married soon."

His casual question almost knocked Emily off the beam where she was perched.

"I haven't noticed any wedding stuff lying around. Ordinarily," Chance said as he positioned the nail against the wood, "when a couple is getting married, they have wedding things lying around the house."

"We have a wedding planner."

"I see." He began hammering again.

When he finished, he removed the last nail from his mouth and frowned as he looked at her.

"Isn't a wedding planner a little...formal? I mean, shouldn't planning your own wedding be more...intimate? With the couple and their wedding party involved?"

"We don't have the time to do it ourselves," Emily said, suddenly feeling defensive.

"A couple should make the time for each other."

She noted the disapproval in his voice and wondered why his opinion suddenly mattered to her.

"If a couple doesn't make the time to plan their own wedding, they sure won't make the time for each other during their marriage." He pounded another nail into the brace.

She had to admit he had a point. "And what about you, Mr. Donovan? Are you speaking from experience? Are you married?" The question slipped out of her mouth before she even knew what she was saying. The hammering stopped. She looked up to find his warm gaze studying her.

"I was married. A long time ago."

She noted the excruciating sadness in his voice and a vast array of emotions stinging his eyes. Love. Pain. Sadness and guilt.

"What happened?"

Oops. Another nosy question. But she couldn't seem to help it.

"Unforeseen circumstances ripped us apart."

Emily expected him to expand on the "unforeseen circumstances", but he didn't.

"Before we got married, my wife had all kinds of wedding things strewn around our apartment and she encouraged me to participate in helping her to plan."

Emily smiled as she remembered all the wedding items littering the apartment before her wedding. "I had to encourage Steve to help me too."

"I expect he enjoyed it in the end, like I did."

"As a matter of fact, yes he did. Especially the food aspects. He hit all the catering businesses and brought home dozens of brochures outlining the menus. Steve always had a ravenous appetite." For more than food, Emily silently added.

"Speaking of ravenous appetite..." He smiled that heart-flipping smile again.

Ravenous appetite? Did he mean food or sex? Oh dear, she needed to get away from him and straighten her thoughts.

"I get the hint, Mr. Donovan. I'll get breakfast going. That is unless you still need me?"

Please say no.

Chance didn't reply. Instead, his lips curled upward into a seductive smile and Emily couldn't help but look at his mouth, which hovered dangerously close to hers.

Oh, please say yes.

"Mushroom omelet," he said after a moment. There was unmistakable passion in his rough voice, and it didn't have anything to do with a passion for food.

"Is that a request?" she asked, totally aware at how husky her voice sounded.

He drew in a ragged breath and nodded.

"I'll call you when it's ready." She made a move to get up and her throat went unbelievably dry as his hot hands spanned possessively around her waist.

"Let me help you down." His warm whisper was mere inches from her ear, and when she caught a whiff of his seductive masculine scent, she felt flushed and tipsy.

He hoisted her to her feet, and she grabbed his shoulders in an effort to steady herself. Warm muscles flexed beneath her fingers and his breath caressed her lips. In a split second she was bombarded by visions of his hot, moist mouth upon hers, his long fingers touching her in the most intimate of ways. Twisting her nipples until the pleasure-pain burn seared through her. Rubbing her clit. Sliding his fingers inside her vagina.

"I'll be up in a few minutes." His words snapped her to attention.

Reluctantly she slid her hands from his shoulders. "I'll get the omelet going."

On trembling legs, she hit the sandy beach and almost toppled.

"Steady as she goes," he chuckled, yet when she looked up at him there was no laughter shining in his eyes. Just heat and desire.

Oh boy, what had she gotten herself into by having him stay here with her?

She felt his heated gaze upon her as she climbed the grassy knoll and onto the stone path that led her up the stone staircase lacing the cliffs to her lighthouse. It took all her strength not to look back, for if she did, she knew she wouldn't be able to stop herself from inviting him to make love to her right there and then on the beach.

Chapter Seven

C hance fought agonizing arousal as he watched her head up the incline. It had been a mistake accepting her invitation to stay here and another mistake to allow her to get so close to him up here on the beams.

The instant he'd touched her, his senses awakened like an explosion. The familiar hum of arousal slammed through him like lightning bolts and he had to fight to keep his hands off her. When his thigh brushed against her hip, he'd noticed her reaction. He'd always been able to read her emotions in her eyes. And he could see she was as hot for him as he was for her.

Need flashed brilliantly in her eyes and suddenly he knew without a doubt she hadn't been with any other man since he'd died. Okay bad choice of words.

Clearly, Skip hadn't sexually pursued her yet. If he had, Emily would have slept with the man. When Skip wanted a woman, he let her know it and then he bedded her. So why hadn't he slept with Emily? And why was he getting married to her? He'd always said he would never marry. Something wasn't right with this picture.

His thoughts drew back to Emily again.

Being under the wharf with her brought back the memories of them together down here. The hot feel of her naked skin beneath him. The rippling muscles clamping around his cock as he thrust in and out. Her soft gasps as he brought her to climax and then let her go into the exquisite world of pleasure.

Moments ago, when he hauled her to her feet, her scorching hands had curled around his shoulders like they'd done in the past.

He'd just about given in to the hot desire racing like wildfire through his veins. He wanted to kiss her so bad it hurt.

The sizzling looks in her eyes was unmistakable. Desire. Raw hunger. Lust.

His guts tightened up in frustration and anger. Yes, he could take her. Just as he'd taken her years earlier, when he'd come home that night and she'd had those candles flickering down here. That night her cheeks had been flushed from the salty air, her long hair tousled by the cold autumn wind and the look of desire she always held for him had made him the happiest man in the world.

Their coupling had always been intense. Sometimes he'd been scared he'd hurt her and yet every time he made love to her; she always matched his savage thrusts. A few days later his life had ended, and Chance Donovan's began.

This morning the look of need on her face was unmistakable. She wanted him. But it was too early. Hell, who was he kidding? He could never stay. He could never tell her what had happened to him in prison.

Chance cursed beneath his breath, jumped off the beam onto the beach and yanked up another board.

Sure, he'd picked up where he'd left off, reinforcing the braces so the dock wouldn't collapse, but he doubted his marriage would hold up under the strain of Emily knowing the truth. That he'd been out of prison for almost a year now and hadn't let her know he was alive. He really should get the laptop and leave. But, how could he?

Skip was the only one who Steve had given a copy of that disc to and Emily had a copy in his laptop. She just didn't know it. Yet.

And he didn't want her involved either. Didn't want her to know he'd been working undercover even after he'd promised her he'd never pursue another dangerous assignment again. She was better off with the warm memories of their marriage, and if he got his way, she'd be better off hating him for doing her a favor and getting rid of her fiancé, the man Chance suspected of violently ripping Emily and himself apart.

· · ⚓ · ·

EMILY HOPED SHE HADN'T made a complete and utter fool of herself. Blushing and making such a silly excuse for having candles under the wharf. Grabbing on to his shoulders the way she had. Jumping when he came near her.

Shaking her head in disgust, she whipped the ingredients of the omelet with renewed frenzy. The man hadn't been here forty-eight hours and she'd almost been kissed twice. More times than Skip had ever tried. No wonder she wanted Chance's kisses! Why did her body have to betray her with such blistering, yummy yearnings she couldn't seem to control?

Just thinking about him made her heat with want. He was a stranger. A handsome, stranger who should be forbidden fruit to her.

Their brief chat under the boardwalk spilled into her thoughts. *A couple should make the time for each other.* His exact words. Boy, he certainly had zeroed in on Skip and her relationship quickly, hadn't he? Skip and she hadn't even talked about the wedding arrangements, leaving everything to his boss. Helena was a dear friend to both of them, she'd even hired private investigators to search into Steve's death. The inquiries had come up empty.

Pointing out his charming gentleman qualities, she'd pushed Emily to accept Skip's proposal. He had a sweet sense of humor, a handsome salary, good looks and he wanted to settle down with a good woman and have babies.

Whenever he stayed over, which was quite often in the past few weeks, he never once approached her in a sexual nature, stating he was an old-fashioned guy and wanted to save himself for the honeymoon. She'd almost laughed out loud at that one when he'd told her that excuse. Wasn't that usually what a woman said to her intended instead of the other way around?

He was romantic though, wining and dining her at the most exclusive restaurants on Prince Edward Island. On several occasions he'd even chartered an airplane to New York for them to catch an elegant dinner and Broadway play or a baseball game.

Other than brotherly pecks on her cheek and an occasional display of affection by surprising her with a bouquet of fresh flowers, he was a perfect gentleman. The total opposite of her husband. Not that Steve hadn't been a gentleman. He was. But he'd been romantic in his touches, not in material things.

He'd always placed a protective hand against the small of her back when he led her into a restaurant. Held her hand while they walked down city streets or along red sandy beaches. No pecks on the cheek from Steve! Only fierce, passionate kisses that made her blood boil and her hair curl as if she were being electrified.

Chance seemed to be the same type of man like her late husband. After he bought a date with her at the fair last night, he'd placed a possessive hand against the small of her back. When they'd toured the fairgrounds, he held her hand. Only when he shot those rifles with fierce determination had he let go of her hand. Then he won the stuffed lobster that now sat on her bed. At the dance he looked at her with those seductive eyes, dark with desire. Just as he'd looked at her today under the boardwalk. On both occasions her body had reacted with violent need.

Chance reminded her of how it felt to be a woman. To want a man to caress her breasts. To want his muscular legs intertwined with hers. To want him to fulfill her every sexual desire.

Instincts told her Chance would make her scream when she orgasmed. He wouldn't hold back on arousing himself either. He seemed to be the kind of man who wouldn't deny himself sexual pleasure. Daniel had said Chance was a shy man. Daniel was full of it. The son of a bitch must have sent Chance here because he was a lot like Steve.

Oh dear! What was she going to do about her attraction to him? The only way she could think to solve the problem was to ask him to leave. Yet it wouldn't be very nice to kick out an old friend of her late husband and his family.

She reached for the frying pan and shook her head as she looked at it. That's exactly how her life was at this point. In the frying pan. If she wasn't careful, she'd soon be jumping straight into the fire.

· · ⤶ · ·

CHANCE SMELLED THE mouthwatering scent of mushroom omelet the instant he stepped onto the deck. The aroma shot memories through his system of late nights, working on deadlines and Emily prodding him awake in the mornings by making his favorite mushroom omelet. More times than not, it ended up burning in the frying pan and he'd be late for work because he dragged her right back into bed with him so he could make love to her.

He groaned softly and closed his eyes, taking deep breaths of the mushroom scent. He enjoyed sex with her, particularly in the mornings. He liked her sleepy look. Tousled hair, dark brown eyes and always a warm, loving smile for him when she woke up to find him leaning over her, ready to kiss her awake.

Then she'd stretch her arms out over her head, jutting her breasts out so perfectly he couldn't keep his hands off them. They'd always slept in the nude. It had been easier that way when they would reach for each other in the middle of the night and have sex because one or the other felt like it.

Opening his eyes, he took several deep breathes of the cool salty air, trying to still the sudden wild racing of his heart.

Shit, if she'd known who he was he'd be taking her right on that intimate table for two. Wouldn't be the first time, either. Or maybe on the kitchen counter. Now that would be a first time.

Okay, chill, man. Don't touch her and you'll be fine, he chastised himself.

Nodding, he opened the door and stepped into the kitchen. He found Emily at the stove, her back turned toward him. Rolling up his sleeves, he headed for the kitchen sink to wash his hands.

"I'm starving like a dog and the omelet smells fantastic," he said casually, acting as if he weren't so hard for her he could start making love to her right here and now. She remained silent, and when he finished, he wiped his hands on a towel and sidled in next to her to take a peek at breakfast. She stiffened. A sick heaviness wrapped around his guts, and he moved away from her. Obviously, she was upset about something.

"Omelet will be done in a minute," she said, tightness edging her voice. "Why don't you grab yourself a mug of coffee."

Yes, definitely upset. He hoped he hadn't gone too far with his comment about her wedding planner and the couple who didn't take the time to plan a wedding wouldn't take the time for each other during the marriage. True those were his personal feelings, but maybe she saw things differently after all the years they'd been apart.

He reached for the mug from the dish rack and poured himself a cup. He didn't offer to get hers because he knew she preferred to drink it steaming hot instead of it sitting on the table, cooling while she prepared breakfast.

Grabbing the cream from the fridge, he dumped in a hefty dose and shoveled in three spoons of sugar. He loved his coffee extra sweet and creamy, and Emily had always kidded him he should cut down on the sugar and cream before he got fat.

He took a giant sip and savored the roasted flavor.

"Tastes great!" he commented, and alarm slithered up his spine when he noticed her watching him, her face pale.

"What's wrong?"

"Nothing." She turned away and picked up the spatula.

"Don't tell me nothing's wrong. Your hands are shaking. Is it me? The way I behaved under the boardwalk? I'm sorry. I came on too strong. Especially since you're engaged. I should have kept my mouth shut about the wedding planner."

"No, it's not that. I didn't mind... I mean, it just brought back memories of Steve and me...down there. And I just realized you take coffee the same way he did."

Chance swallowed the lump of uneasiness knotting up his throat.

"And mushroom omelets were a favorite of Steve's."

"The McCullens always made them when I went to visit their ranch," Chance lied. "I guess smelling it reminds me of those days and how Steve made the coffee for us."

Her face lost some of its paleness and he exhaled a sigh of relief. Hopefully she accepted the explanation and wouldn't think anything more about it.

"Omelet's finished. Take a seat. I'll bring it over."

He pulled out a chair at the table for two and tried really hard not to let the sexy images of him stripping Emily, cupping her ass and hoisting her onto the table.

Oh man, she had such a nice tight pussy and—

Chill! He scolded himself as his cock hardened so much he swore he'd groaned out loud. Thankfully she hadn't heard. Or if she had, she pretended otherwise.

He focused his attention on watching her work.

She'd always been beautiful, but suddenly she seemed even more so. Maybe because he knew he couldn't have her, or maybe because of what she'd said of how he reminded her of Steve.

The magical connection between them was still there. Unbroken after all these years of separation and stronger than ever. What happened under the dock this morning proved it. The hot, needy way she looked at him. The fantastic way her looks made him feel.

He studied the shape of her body as he'd always loved doing. This morning though, it was more than enjoyment that seared through him as he watched the seductive way her breasts pushed out against the thick turtleneck she wore.

He remembered how soft and warm she'd felt this morning against his body when she'd held his shoulders.

Shit! He should have kissed her. Should have followed through on his instincts and his urges. But if he kissed her, then everything would be different. He'd want her even more than he wanted her now.

He shifted uncomfortably, his cock pressing painfully against his tight jeans when she leaned over him to place the steaming omelet onto his plate. Straining for control, he shoved himself and his chair farther beneath the table so she wouldn't see his arousal. He forced himself to pick up the knife and fork and proceeded to dig into the heavenly smelling food.

Just then the phone rang and Emily quickly picked it up. "Hello."

"Daniel! Hi! Yes, he's here."

She smiled into the receiver then listened for a moment. "He's eating breakfast."

She turned to Chance and waved him to come over. Reluctantly he left his delicious-smelling omelet.

"Hi!" was all he could think to say when he pressed the receiver to his ear.

"You dirty dog!" Daniel chuckled in a teasing tone. "Obviously you've worked up quite an appetite. Hope you aren't doing anything you shouldn't be doing."

Chance grinned. "Wouldn't you like to know?"

"Sorry for intruding, but the wife was worried about you, so she told me to phone and see how it's going."

"Quit hiding behind your wife. It was your idea to call or she would have done it herself. You're too nosy for your own good."

Daniel chuckled then continued. "Speaking of wives, I get the feeling you haven't told Emily yet?"

Chance's grip on the telephone tightened and he snuck a peek at Emily, who was watching him curiously from the stove where she was pouring the egg mixture into the frying pan to make another omelet.

"That won't come up," he warned.

"I thought I'd better remind you about your check-up appointment next week."

"I hear you."

"It's important, kiddo. Keep an eye on your health. Watch yourself."

"Yes, Mother."

"I'm serious."

"Okay," Chance replied, knowing full well if he didn't make that check-up Daniel would come and get him.

"Now there's another reason I called," his brother said. The seriousness in his tone vanished, replaced with something that sounded like stunned happiness.

"Another reason besides checking up on me?"

Daniel chuckled softly. "Put Emily on the phone with you."

Chance waved to Emily to join him. When she melted against him, he just about came in his pants. He held the out the phone so they could both listen.

"She's here," Chance said, his voice sounded strangled. He tried like hell to avoid inhaling her sexy scent, but hey, a guy had to breathe, right?

"Jo's pregnant," Daniel replied.

A nice fluttery feeling scampered around in the pit of his stomach at the news. A soft gasp from Emily made him put his arm around her waist.

"Daniel! This is so wonderful." Emily laughed. "It is the best news."

"That's not all. Brother Mathew and his wife Sara are expecting too. I just talked to them on the phone and they told me. Don't tell them I spilled the beans. They want to call you themselves."

"You boys sure have been busy." Chance chuckled into the receiver.

"How far along are they?" Emily asked.

"Jo's three months and Sara's two," Daniel replied. "I'm not even supposed to be telling you this about Jo either. Not over the phone. Jo wants to visit and tell you in person, and Mathew and Sara want to tell you in person too, but I couldn't wait. The minute she was out of sight I had to call." His voice suddenly softened with disbelief. "Oh God! I'm going to be a dad! Hold on. I have to sit down."

"Easy there, man." Chance laughed. "Got smelling salts handy?"

There was silence on the other end. Concern shot through him. The guy hadn't fainted, had he?

"Danny?"

"I'm here. I think reality just hit me. I've got to open up a college fund for the kid. Find out where he or... God! What if he's a girl? How am I going to keep the guys away from her?"

"Daniel," Emily broke in, "first you need to get the baby a room to sleep in. A nursery. With a crib. A mobile with some relaxing music so the baby can fall asleep. And the baby's going to need some clothes..."

"Right. You're right. A bed, clothes, mobile."

"Are you by any chance writing this down?" Chance smiled at Emily. Her brown eyes were beginning to fill with huge watery tears.

Oh man. She'd better not cry or he'd kiss her for sure.

"Write it down? Good idea. Oh darnit! I hear Jo coming. Don't tell her I called you. Gotta go. Bye!"

The instant they were disconnected Chance became very aware of the tears trickling down Emily's cheeks.

Ah shit. He knew why she was crying, and he suddenly experienced the same agonizing pain of loss. Of what could have been. Of what would never be.

"Don't cry, Emily," he said softly. His arms ached so bad to hold her. To comfort her.

"I'm sorry. I can't help it," she sobbed. More tears spurted from her beautiful eyes and she quickly brushed them away.

He reached out and touched his trembling fingertips to the corners of her eyes in a desperate effort to wipe away the continuous stream of hot tears. Damn she smelled good. A tinge of fresh air, delicate baby shampoo and mushrooms. Very appetizing indeed.

"I'm so happy for Jo and her sister Sara. And for the McCullen brothers," Emily whispered as she stared up at him. "It's just...Steve and I never had the chance."

She gasped down a gulp of air then continued. "We were married only a few short months before we decided to move in here. I'd already quit my job and wanted to get into a seaweeding business. Steve wanted to freelance and went to quit his job. When he came back, we were going to start a family...but...he never came back."

I am back! Chance wanted to yell. Instead he said, "Now Steve's brothers' wives are having babies and you're not."

"Neither is Steve. He should be here experiencing the same joys of fatherhood."

"Daniel didn't sound too joyful once reality hit," he teased.

She looked up at him and her face broke into a breathtaking smile. He'd never wanted to kiss her as much as he yearned to kiss her right now. He was so close to doing it. So damn close. But then she turned away and headed back to the stove.

"All his insecurities will fade into the background," she said. "He'll be a wonderful father. The McCullen men will make wonderful fathers."

A surge of pride flowed through him at her confident words. She turned from the stove and headed back to the table, grabbing his plate.

"Anyway, I don't know why I'm telling you all this. Your omelet needs to be reheated and I've got to pick up some baby wool the next time I'm in town so I can get started on some clothes."

Chance inhaled a big gulp of relief as Emily's smile grew stronger.

"They'll both be spring babies. One month apart," she said, nodding as she put the plate into the microwave.

All traces of sadness were gone, replaced with happiness for the women. She literally glowed and he could see the wheels grinding in her head about the clothes she would make with the knitting wool. Wool he'd promised to buy her just before he'd been kidnapped.

A burst of anger swept across him at that thought, but he brushed it away, keeping his thoughts focused on the present and on what she was saying.

"Sara and Mathew's son is a year old now. He's going to have a new brother or sister." Emily laughed and pressed the required buttons to nuke his breakfast. "Sara's going to have her hands full when the new one arrives. She might need a babysitter and so will Jo."

Chance smiled as she continued to chatter cheerfully about the new arrivals. Typical Emily. She wore her emotions on her sleeve. When she cried, she always managed to pull herself together and look on the bright side of things.

He always admired her strength. She never leaned on anyone. When life threw her a punch, she ducked right under it and came up smiling twice as hard. He had no doubt she'd be babysitting her heart out within a few months' time. She'd go on like a trooper once he removed her fiancé from her life.

Chapter Eight

For the remainder of the morning Chance worked himself half to death nailing the braces into place beneath the wharf. His emotions about his brothers' news were seesawing all over the place.

He remembered the last time he saw his only nephew on the Fourth of July when his oldest brother Mathew and his wife Sara dropped in unexpectedly for the fireworks festivities. The baby had just been eight months old and Chance's face had been covered in bandages.

The baby's emerald green eyes were wide with wonder as he stared at him. J.D. had examined the bandages covering Chance's nose and chin from his most recent reconstructive surgery. A distant smile hovered on the baby's pursed rosebud lips and then recognition flared across his chubby face. The robust baby had then held out his pudgy arms to Chance.

"He remembers you from our last visit," Sara had laughed.

Overwhelming love burst inside his heart as he'd accepted the warm, soft bundle who promptly kissed his cheek and began poking curious chubby fingers at the white bandages. Chance chuckled at the warm memory. Now two more McCullen kids were on the way and he would have to put his uncle skills to work.

Suddenly he heard the smooth sound of an approaching motor out on the ocean. Chance's heart picked up the beat and uneasiness slammed through him. What if it was Skip? Or his henchmen? Lifting his head, he spied a large motorboat heading directly toward the wharf.

Toward him!

He was vulnerable out here by the ocean under the wharf. Maybe he hadn't been spotted yet. Maybe he could get up into the lighthouse without being seen. He could get his weapon from his duffel bag.

A split second before he jumped from his perch beneath the rustic wharf he froze and gasped when he spotted a familiar face. His ex-boss Helena Whitney stood at the bow of the boat and she was staring straight at him!

In the past, he'd always been glad to see Helena. Her charming, easygoing smile never failed to make him feel welcome and at ease. She wasn't smiling now and he sure wasn't feeling welcome. Her tightly pursed lips and narrowed icy eyes bore right into him, making him shiver involuntarily. Automatically his fingers tightened around the hammer in his hand.

Helena was not happy to see him. Then again, why would she be? To her he was a stranger dangling beneath Emily's dock.

On suddenly trembling legs Chance jumped into the soft sand and headed up the incline to meet the woman he hadn't seen in eight years. When his feet hit the creaking planks on the wharf, Helena was already being helped out of the boat by a man Chance recognized as the fellow who'd rented him a boat days earlier. The man nodded politely, and Chance nodded back.

"Good afternoon," Helena called out cheerfully as Chance approached her.

The frown on her face had been replaced by the familiar warm smile he remembered so well. Unfortunately, her smile didn't quite reach her gray eyes. Intense eyes that examined his face to the point of making him feel uncomfortable.

"I'm Helena Whitney," she finally said, and extended her hand.

"Chance Donovan." He hoped the shakiness he felt didn't appear too evident in his voice. He accepted her hand. It was small and bony but still held a strong grip. Chance felt the eight years of not seeing her begin to dissolve.

She raised an eyebrow. "The man who paid one thousand dollars for Emily's pie?"

"That's me." He studied her face. She hadn't changed much. Not a gray hair flew out of place in the decreasing wind. Every strand coiffured neatly into the same 1960s baby-doll style she always wore. She had a few more wrinkles on her otherwise immaculately cosmetic-plastered face and the same overwhelming scent of magnolia perfume that he remembered sifted through the air.

She glanced down at the hammer he still held clasped in his other hand. "And I see you are doing some handiwork for Emily too."

He noted the thinly disguised disapproval in her otherwise courteous voice. He didn't know why he suddenly felt so defensive.

"Where is Emily?" she asked.

"By now she's probably browsing through some patterns for knitting baby clothes."

The utter look of shock on Helena's face almost made him laugh out loud.

"Skip and Emily must have decided not to wait for the honeymoon. My goodness, I hope this doesn't mean the wedding gown won't fit."

A spear of anger shot through him at her comment. "Emily's not pregnant."

"But you just said—"

"Her two sisters-in-law are expecting. We just heard the news this morning."

"This is marvelous news, Mr. Donovan. I'm sure it will give Emily and Skip incentive to get working on a family of their own. They do make such an adorable couple, don't they?"

Chance fought down intense anger as she studied his face, obviously awaiting an answer. She sure as hell wasn't going to get one.

"You do know she's engaged to be married?"

"I've heard."

"How long do you plan on staying?"

"Until Emily asks me to leave."

"I'm sure it won't be too long. She's putting her lighthouse on the market. Perhaps you'd be interested in purchasing it?"

Her gray eyes swept across his face again and he shifted uneasily under her obvious stare. What the heck was her problem anyway? Staring at him as if he were some two-headed creature, not to mention throwing Emily's upcoming nuptials in his face.

He shouldn't be blaming her for being so curious. She didn't have a clue to his true identity, and she was most likely concerned about Emily being out here alone with a stranger. It hurt nonetheless at being reminded his wife was going to give up her dream of living here on Shipwreck Island so she could have kids with a man whose idea of a kiss was a peck on the cheek. Emily was a passionate woman. She deserved to be kissed properly.

"Mr. Donovan?"

"What?"

"I asked you if you had any plans of where you'll be working when you leave here?"

"Plans?"

"I could use a handyman at my newspaper branch in Toronto. It's a bustling city in Ontario, Canada. Emily went to journalism school there."

"I know."

Her eyes widened. "You know?"

"She mentioned it," Chance said quickly, realizing his mistake.

"As I was saying, I noticed your marvelous handiwork beneath the shabby wharf as we were sailing in. Are you interested?"

"No thanks."

"Then you must already have plans?"

"I don't have plans, Miss Whitney. I'm just drifting."

"I see. How about experience in journalism? I'm always looking for excellent journalists to send overseas to cover wars. Emily's late husband was my best investigative journalist, but obviously he had emotional problems I wasn't aware of. He hanged himself in jail after being caught with drugs." Helena shook her head in apparent disgust.

Chance found it difficult to remain calm. She obviously believed the lies the authorities had spawned.

"Miss Whitney, why don't you go on up and visit with Emily. I've got work to do." Chance turned away from her, but Helena's hand snaked around his elbow, stopping him cold.

"Mr. Donovan. You haven't given me an answer."

Her smile was fake now. He could clearly see that. And he suddenly had an inkling she suspected he was Steve. Why else would she ask him if he was experienced in journalism?

"Which question haven't I answered?"

"Do you have any experience in journalism?" she asked, her gray eyes assessing his face again.

"I appreciate the job offers, Helena. I'll think about it." The thought of getting back into journalism certainly did give him a certain degree of excitement.

"Splendid! I'll look forward to hearing from you." Suddenly her head snapped up, and as she looked over his shoulder, a huge smile slipped across her face. "Emily! Darling!"

Chance swung around to find Emily waving to them as she skipped down the rickety rock steps on to the dock. In a flash the two women were hugging each other.

"Helena! I'm so happy to see you." Emily chuckled as she withdrew from Helena's embrace.

"You look absolutely lovely, Emily. Your engagement must agree with you."

Chance noticed Emily's smile drop a degree at Helena's comment.

"Doesn't she look lovely, Mr. Donovan?"

"She's beautiful," Chance answered, and his insides brightened as Emily's smile widened at his comment.

"I've come to get you for your final fitting, darling," Helena said.

Chance gritted his teeth and his fingers tightened around the hammer as Emily said rather meekly, "Of course. It sounds wonderful."

She did not sound like an excited bride.

A surge of protectiveness ripped through him. "Maybe you should pick up that baby wool while you're in town. Didn't you say you needed some?"

"What a good idea, Chance," Helena said. "It'll give Emily some incentive."

He wished he could deck Helena. Instead he smiled and continued speaking in as casual a voice as he could muster.

"I could use more wood to replace some of the planks on the dock," he lied. He had more than enough, but the thought of Emily being out there all alone without him to protect her made him uncomfortable. She seemed almost relieved that he was inviting himself to join them. Helena, on the other hand, looked far from happy.

"I'll go and lock up," Chance said. Without waiting for any objections, Chance headed toward the towering lighthouse.

•• ∽ ••

"THE WEDDING DRESS LOOKS absolutely magnificent on you, Emily. A perfect fit. Twirl around so I can see the back."

Emily did as Helena instructed and tried to keep the smile plastered on her face as the sales lady also nodded approval.

"The scalloped v-neck certainly does suit you, Mrs. McCullen," the saleslady said.

Helena's head snapped up and down with obvious impression. Emily found herself thinking that if Helena loved the dress so much, then why didn't she get married to Skip? Not that she didn't like the dress. It was the most beautiful, breathtaking one she'd ever seen. She'd picked it from the catalogue herself. But it just seemed too beautiful for her. It should be for a woman who was madly in love with her man. Not her.

"Now step up on the footstool and I'll pin the length for the hem."

Emily stepped up on the stool and brushed a stray strand of her wind-whipped hair out of her face. If she blurted out she wasn't so sure about marrying Skip, what would Helena say? Emily knew the answer to that. After these last few weeks of planning and even paying for the wedding, Helena would be horrified and most likely faint right here in the bridal boutique.

"The bare back is absolutely gorgeous, Emily," Helena said. "It will pique the male onlookers' interest. They will be so jealous Skip caught you first. Oh, and I've already ordered the flowers for the church and the reception. Yellow roses and miniature red roses with baby's breath. Such a beautiful combination. Darling, why are you frowning so?"

Emily looked up to find Helena scrutinizing her in the mirror.

"Oh Helena! I don't know what to do," Emily burst out, unable to keep her thoughts a secret anymore.

"But those are the flowers you wanted. Have you changed your mind?"

The look of horror on Helena's face made Emily feel even worse.

Yes! she wanted to scream. *I've changed my mind about the wedding. I don't want to get married.*

Instead she bit her lip and steadied herself against blurting out more. She wouldn't disappoint Helena...or Skip. She wouldn't let her dream of having a family dissolve just because she had cold feet.

"My matron of honor is three months pregnant. My bridesmaid is pregnant too."

Helena seemed relieved at that announcement. Well, she certainly hadn't expected that reaction from the elderly woman.

"Your Mr. Donovan already informed me. I will get in touch with our mothers-to-be and see about getting their dresses refitted. Is that what has you so concerned?"

"Yes," Emily lied. "And...do you think I could get lupines added to the flower arrangements?"

"I'll call the florist right away." Helena flipped open her cell phone and began to dial.

Lupines were Steve's favorite flowers. When Emily walked down the aisle, she'd look at the flowers and think of him. She could do anything if his spirit was with her. But if that were true, why did she feel, with each passing day, that another nail was being driven into her coffin?

· · ❧ · ·

CHANCE COULDN'T SHAKE the feeling he was being followed. The tiny hairs on the back of his neck had sizzled a warning the instant the hardware store employee and he had finished stacking the pile of lumber he'd ordered onto the deck of *Sweet Lies*.

He'd been glad Emily suggested they return to the island in the tugboat. Helena seemed thrilled too, paying off the man who'd brought her over, saying the boat she'd hired had been a terribly choppy ride in the high waves. Hopefully it meant Helena wouldn't be coming back with them when they returned to the island.

He'd prefer to be alone with Emily. Maybe try to get into his laptop and see if the incriminating evidence was still intact in the hard drive and on the disc.

Shit. He really should have come earlier or sent one of his brothers to get the laptop. Truth would have it though, when his brothers told him about the break-ins happening shortly after his kidnapping and that his computer and other items had been stolen, the entire place searched, he'd assumed they had found the laptop and taken it.

At that point in time turmoil had racked his life. His dad had come up from Mexico and stayed with him through the painful surgeries to reconstruct his face. Because of the damage to his facial bones, the surgeons were unable to give him his face back without extensive bone grafts, which would have taken him longer to heal and longer for him to regain his freedom. Therefore, he'd opted for a new face, free of scars. It hadn't turned out so bad, he thought as he glanced into the store windows to see if maybe he could glimpse someone following him as he suspected. He'd been doing that for the past hour. Window shopping up and down Main Street of the quaint little town near the North Cape of the main island. But he saw no one suspicious.

Over the years his instincts had been finely honed for trouble. And he sensed trouble the minute they got to town.

Checking his watch, he realized he still had a few more minutes left before meeting Emily and Helena back at the boutique directly across the street.

Helena had tried to persuade him to join them inside earlier, but he noticed Emily squirm uneasily at the invitation. It sure wasn't high on his list of things to do either. Last thing he needed was to see her decked out in a fancy, silky white wedding dress. Especially since he wasn't the groom.

What he needed at the moment was a stiff drink to shake off the spooky feelings of being followed. Since Jake's Bar and Grill hovered right in front of him, he might as well take advantage of the situation.

Inside the narrow hallway, he allowed his eyes to adjust to the dimly lit interior. Things sure hadn't changed much since he'd been here last. A thick cloud of blue cigarette smoke hovered amidst the thin spattering of rough-spoken fishermen hunched on barstools. A fifties tune reverberated from the same ancient jukebox situated in the middle of the dining area off to the left of the bar. The red Coca-Cola refrigerator still held its prestigious place beside the jukebox. Everything looked the same as it had years ago.

He wandered into the room and noticed all eyes turn on him. The small town was a tight-knit community, and he remembered all too well how he'd received curious stares the first few times he walked into Jake's establishment a little over eight years ago.

"If it ain't the pie lover." The ribbing remark came from the young bartender who stood behind the bar, casually wiping a beer glass with a dirty white cloth.

Chance plopped himself onto one of the available barstools immediately in front of him. At first sight, Chance didn't recognize him, but as his gaze roved over the scruffy blond hair tied back into a ponytail, the little scar on his chin and the trademark chocolate brown eyes, recognition dawned.

Holy shit. He was Garrett Rustico.

An eerie sadness embraced him at the loss of missing the bar owner's youngest son grow up from the gangly pimple-faced teenage boy Chance had sometimes helped with his English homework over a bowl of his dad's homemade chocolate-covered pretzels. Not to mention helping Garrett work through his immense crush on Emily.

"Was the pie worth the grand?" One side of Garrett's mouth tilted upward in the all-too-familiar amused smirk.

"You should know, Garrett. You've had your share of her pies."

The young man's smile disintegrated at Chance's comment. Puzzlement shot across his face.

"Do I know you?" he asked.

"I don't know, do you?"

Garrett's Adam's apple bobbed as he swallowed. He studied Chance's face but no recognition showed.

"I'll have a bottle of Jake's home brew," Chance said. "With lots of ice. And a bowl of chocolate-covered pretzels if you still make them."

"Ice in your beer?"

Chance nodded.

"And those chocolate-covered pretzels."

For a split-second recognition flared in Garrett's eyes and then it was quickly extinguished as reality set in. He grabbed a beer bottle from under the counter from the cooler he knew they kept the bottles in and snapped off the lid. Thick white foam bubbled from the mouth of the bottle. He kept his eyes on Chance as he filled the mug with ice. After gently placing the mug and beer bottle onto the counter in front of Chance, Garrett disappeared through a doorway.

Chance chuckled to himself. He knew he shouldn't be fooling around with the sensitive kid this way, but it was one way to keep the kid from asking him more questions about Emily and her pie.

Ah hell. The kid wasn't a kid anymore. He was all grown up. How old would he be now? Twenty-one? No, around twenty-three.

He poured the beer over the thick ice cubes. Then he lifted his mug to the curious fishermen who continued to stare at him with their squinty eyes and sun-beaten faces, said a quick cheers to them and proceeded to drink. The ice-cold beer hit the spot. Smooth, sweet with a tinge of salt fish. Just the way he remembered it.

"Damn good beer," he complimented between a couple of lip-tingling smacks. The old men grumbled their approval and they all set back to chatting amongst themselves or reading their newspapers.

Garrett set a heaping bowl full of chocolate-covered twisted pretzels in front of Chance.

"Anything else?"

"This'll do for now."

Garrett nodded, the puzzled expression now firmly in place as he grabbed the dirty towel and a cloudy-looking beer mug from a half-full dish tray. He resettled himself by leaning his hip against the sparkling mirror that lined the entire back wall and watched Chance.

He knew from previous experience the kid was now working hard to figure out something. It sure wasn't his homework.

"So, where's your old man?" he asked the kid.

"Retired. Moved to Florida." He nodded his head as if he finally figured it all out.

"You know my dad."

"I met him a few times. Long time ago. How's he doing?"

"He's as happy as a clam dropping out of a net. Found himself a woman. They're living together in a retirement village in some trailer park south of Homestead."

A warm feeling slithered through Chance hearing Jake had finally settled down again. Jake Rustico's wife had died tragically when a vicious storm capsized the fishing boat they owned. He hadn't been able to save her and watched her drown. In an instant he'd turned into a widower with four kids to feed. The oldest Jake Jr. had been fifteen.

Garrett, the youngest, had been seven. Jake took out a loan, started up Jake's Bar & Grill and raised his kids, making each one promise they would never work the sea. From the looks of Garrett acting as barkeep, at least the youngest had kept his word.

"How do you know my dad?"

"Lived around here for a short time. Way back." Chance helped himself to a handful of the tiny pretzels. It wasn't a lie. Emily and he had flown from New York for many weekends before they moved to Shipwreck Island.

Garrett nodded then his eyes casually glanced over Chance's shoulder. He knew instinctively Garrett had spotted something awry.

"You've got yourself a tail," Garrett said matter-of-factly.

"How do you know he's tailing me?"

"Hey, man, I'm a barkeep during the day. At night I'm a cop. I know a tail when I see one." Garrett casually placed the mug he'd been cleaning onto a nearby shelf and threw the dirty towel over his shoulder. "Besides, came in right after you. He's just inside the hallway. Hasn't taken his eyes off you since you arrived. Want me to get rid of him?"

"I'll handle it. How much do I owe you?"

Garrett grinned and shook his head.

"On the house. For old times' sake."

Chance nodded his thanks. "Mind if I use your bathroom?"

"All yours. While you're at it, the exit is that way too."

"Thanks, Captain."

The puzzled expression sauntered back onto Garrett's face. Chance had always called the kid "Captain" because of his dream of captaining his own fishing boat one day. Obviously, he'd listened to his old man instead of following his heart.

Chance eased himself off the barstool. Without looking at the door or the shadowy silhouette, he ignored the old cronies' curious glances as they watched him saunter toward the back hallway.

The instant he slipped out of sight; Chance eased himself into another hallway that he knew led to outside. He resisted the urge to head for the exit. Resisted the urge to run. Instead, he stopped.

Cautiously he slid out the gun he'd brought along. He'd secured it into the waistband of his jeans when he'd gone back to the lighthouse to lock up. In quick unison he slid off the safety catch, checked to make sure the clip was full and then held the gun firmly in his right hand while he got ready to reach out to grab the culprit with his left.

He didn't have long to wait. The old floorboards creaked a warning as one set of fast-paced footsteps headed down the hallway.

His fingers tightened on the trigger, and the instant he sensed the intruder within reach, his reflexes, honed from many years of fighting to survive, went into action. Jerking the person right into the hallway with him, he shoved the intruder smack up against the wall. Before he could even blink, Chance had the gun pressed against a soft temple. Wide dark brown eyes blinked in shock at him.

"Emily! What the hell are you doing here?"

She didn't answer. As a matter of fact, her face had turned as pale as a ghost and her entire body trembled with terror against him.

He dropped the gun from her head and closed his eyes as a massive wall of fear threatened to knock him over. "I almost blew your head off."

"What's with the gun?" she whispered.

"I thought you were somebody else."

She shook her head in disbelief, sending a few wisps of hair straying onto her left cheek.

"I'm glad I'm not," she replied, blowing out a breath of relief.

"I'm so sorry. I thought I was being followed."

"What do you mean followed?"

Alertness swept into her face and Chance ignored her question. "Did you see someone lurking in the doorway when you came in?"

"No."

"He must have slipped out when he saw you coming."

"Who?"

"What are you doing here? I thought we were meeting at the boutique?"

Now that the danger was over, he felt the warmth of her body begin to seep through his clothes, making him fully aware he was pressing Emily into the wall.

"I saw you come in here after I said goodbye to Helena."

"She's gone?"

"Yes, she had an appointment."

Chance sighed with relief. Helena and her nosy questions were gone.

Color seeped back into her face and suddenly her eyes flashed with anger as she looked at his gun.

"For heaven's sake put that gun away. Canadians don't own fancy handguns like that. I hope you have a permit for carrying it in this country."

Chance grinned despite himself. Emily had always hated guns. Another reason she'd left the States and come back to her homeland of Canada. He slid the safety catch into place and shoved the weapon back into the waistband of his jeans, making sure to pull his shirt and jacket over it to conceal it.

"Well? Do you?" she asked.

"What?"

"Have a permit to carry it here?"

"No."

Her eyes widened at his admission.

"I do have it registered in the States. I snuck it through customs while I hitchhiked over."

"My God, Chance. You live too dangerously. Hitchhiking and smuggling illegal weapons are not good habits to have."

"Maybe you can try to break me of these bad habits." He chuckled. "Although...us being so close is a habit I'd like to keep. Thank you very much."

At his soft-spoken words her heart pounded frantically against his chest and he knew instinctively the fear had slid from her body, replaced by something else. Awareness. Of him.

He sure as hell was aware of her too. Wide, sparkling eyes stared back at him. A man could drown in those bottomless eyes and never find his way back out. If he were smart, he'd stop staring into them before she pulled him under her magnetic spell and he lost all common sense.

And self-control.

Then again, he figured it was already too late to regain common sense. Especially since Emily's luscious, warm curves snuggled against his muscles, making his body remember all those times he'd made love to her. And all those naughty things he'd wanted to do to her but never got the chance. He found himself growing hard.

She must have felt his growing erection because a shiver trembled through her. Her sweet, feminine scent swarmed all around him. Captured him. Prevented him from releasing his grip on her.

Examining her silky-looking mouth, he wondered if she still tasted as heavenly as he remembered.

"I'm going to kiss you," he found himself whispering.

Oh yeah, he was definitely going to kiss her.

The succulent heat of her mouth melting beneath his lips shocked his senses, sending pleasure straight down into his toes and right up into his brain. It was an intense pleasure. Drugging. Raw and untamed, it was almost painful at how sweet she tasted.

He kissed her. Hard.

And damned if she didn't answer back just as hard. He could barely breathe as her hands dropped to his hips. Could barely think as her tongue pressed against his lips and his senses went into overload. Opening his mouth, he let her in and he just about exploded. Her tongue tasted so good, just like he always remembered. Hell, she tasted even better.

Need shifted through him like a tidal wave. Strong and violent. He pressed his cock against her lower abdomen. Heard her answer with an erotic moan of approval.

Jesus. She sounded so good.

Lifting her sweater, he splayed his palms against her breasts. Momentary disappointment shot through him as he felt the lacy bra meet his hands. Hell, why was she wearing one?

The distorted thought disintegrated as she pushed her lower half against his cock, wanting a harder contact. Ripping his mouth from hers, he came up for air. Kissing her neck, he felt the frantic pulse hammering there.

"I want to make love to you, Emily," he whispered as he kissed her delicate earlobe.

She shivered against him, enjoying what he was saying.

"I want to fuck you so deeply and so hard. I want to taste your pussy and I want my cock in your mouth. I shouldn't be saying this," he murmured as a sharp blade of reality sliced through him.

To his surprise she smiled and Chance's heart filled with love.

"I want that too," she said breathlessly.

Jesus. Had he imagined her saying that?

Her eyes closed and her beautiful rosebud lips parted, and he found himself lowering his head for another taste of her.

"Should take that to the hotel next door."

Chance jerked at the familiar voice from beside them and looked over to find Garrett Rustico watching them. Emily swore softly and struggled to move away from Chance, but he held her still with his body.

"And I'm assuming you have a good reason for interrupting us?" Chance asked, trying to act casual at having been found kissing Emily.

"That fellow who was following you just slipped out the front door," Garrett said, obviously trying like hell from keeping an amused smile off his face.

This time it was Chance's turn to swear. Stepping away from the seductive warmth of Emily, he turned to leave, but her firm grip on his elbow stopped him cold.

"Don't go," she said. Alarm sliced across her ashen face and Garrett moved to block him from leaving too.

"She's right," Garrett replied, his dark brows drawn downward with concern. "The guy is long gone. I do have a description, if you're interested?"

"Shoot," Chance said.

"Six foot two. Black hair. Crew cut. Well-trimmed black moustache. Thin slit of a mouth. Wearing a black suit. Smells like a cop, but more likely a government lawyer of some kind."

An icy shiver shifted aside all his heated desire as he immediately guessed who it could be. If his suspicions were right, it meant someone had recognized the name he'd given in prison and so easily shared when he'd been at the Timber Sports competition for the mere reason of looking for a reaction from Skip. Hell, if the break-in the other night hadn't convinced him that Skip knew his identity, then this man who'd been following him sure made him realize he'd brought danger down on Emily. Big-time danger.

"You know him?" Emily asked.

"No," Chance lied.

"I can get a sketch artist to draw up the face," Garrett said.

"I'm sure it's nothing. Case of mistaken identity."

"Seems to be a lot of that going around today." Another shot of uneasiness zapped him as Garrett threw Chance a wink.

"What do you mean?" Emily asked.

"Inside joke, Emily." Garrett replied as he stared softly at the woman who'd been his first teenage crush.

"Listen, I have to get back to the bar. The dinner hour group is starting to come in."

"Thanks, Garrett." Chance extended his hand and they shook.

"Anytime, Skipper." Skipper was Garrett's nickname for Steve and he didn't miss the way the young man studied him for a reaction. Despite his uneasiness Chance forced himself to remain stoic. He'd definitely played this game too far.

"What in the world is going on between you two? Do you know each other?" Emily asked.

"Chance and I were just gabbing about old times with Steve a bit earlier. So anyways, I gotta go. Like I said before, take it to the hotel next time around. One of the old fishermen might come back and get a heart attack if they see what's going on here."

"Why a hotel when we have a lighthouse?" Chance whispered after Garrett left. Her face flushed pink at his suggestion but she said nothing.

He slid his hand in hers and ushered her toward the back door.

"Come on. Let's go home."

Chapter Nine

"So? What was with the jumpy routine back at Jake's?" Emily had waited until they were halfway back to Shipwreck Island before asking the question so he wouldn't be able to run away and not answer her.

Her emotions were all over the place at what had just happened back at Jake's Bar. She really didn't want to deal with how easily she'd allowed herself to be kissed. Let alone for agreeing to those hot things he'd said to her about wanting to go down on her and wanting her to go down on him and, oh God, she was engaged to another man.

She had to be calm it down between Chance and herself.

"You talking about my cock? Or the nice way you were pushing up against me when I kissed you?"

She stifled a surprised gasp at his words.

"Obviously you're trying to embarrass me into silence with those remarks, but it won't work. It's not every day someone sticks a gun at my head, Chance. I deserve an explanation."

He kept his eyes glued to the salt-encrusted front window of *Sweet Lies* as he expertly guided the boat along the generous ocean swells.

Silence.

"I want an answer. It's obvious by the stunned surprise on your face that you recognized that man Garrett was talking about. Who is he? Why does he frighten you so much?"

"Mistaken identity, Em. That's all," he replied coolly. Too coolly.

"Sorry, but I'm not buying it."

"I'm not selling."

"Why are you afraid?"

"Garrett thought the guy was tailing me so he gave me a description. That's it."

"Bullshit!"

He glanced at her. His look of stone-cold warned her to back off the subject. A shiver of unease sliced through her when she realized he wasn't afraid for himself but for her.

Her heart scrambled into her chest. "So, there is a story. Someone *is* following you. What about the break-in? It had to do with you, didn't it?"

"The subject is off limits, Em."

"When you're living under my roof, the subject is open for discussion."

"The living arrangements can easily be changed," he said.

"You mean you'd move out before telling me what's going on?"

He didn't answer, but the firm set to his jaw and his tense stance told her he would.

"Typical man."

His head snapped around and he glared at her.

"What's that supposed to mean?"

"It means you'd rather keep all your emotions bottled up inside instead of telling me what's going on." She tried to rein in her anger by inhaling a deep breath. It didn't work. "I have a right to know if you're in danger."

"Since when? We're not a couple."

"Could have fooled me by that kiss in Jake's Bar," Emily muttered beneath her breath.

"It was the adrenaline rushing through my system. I was saying things I shouldn't have. Especially to an engaged woman. I was wrong. It won't happen again. Another bad habit I need to break."

His confession made an eerie sadness clutch at her heart.

"Fine. You're still not off the hook, Chance. Are you in danger?"

"Everything is under control. You don't need to worry."

"I won't worry if you don't."

He threw her a disgruntled glance then focused his attention back to the ocean ahead. The waves were still too choppy to do seaweeding today. She'd make them some lunch and leave Chance to do what he wanted. It would give her some time to try to crack the password preventing her from getting into Steve's computer. Chance and the break-in were connected. But how? And damned if she would ask him since he wasn't answering her questions anyway.

Emily bit her lower lip. Someone was after Chance and he was scared. She could smell the raw fear lurking all around him. Keeping quiet never solved problems. She'd always tried to knock that phrase into Steve's thick skull too. He never listened to her, either.

She hugged herself as another icy chill bit through her insides. No one was going to harm Chance Donovan. Not if she had anything to say about it.

.. ᘛᘚ ..

EMILY SHOOK HER HEAD in puzzlement as she tried to think up yet another password to enter into the laptop. The hammering she heard drifting up from the beach made her thoughts return to the mysterious Chance Donovan and their conversation as they'd returned from town.

The subject was off limits he'd said. Like hell. He had thrown her against the wall and poked a gun against her temple for a reason. Someone was following him. Who? Why?

Garrett had mentioned the man looked like a cop or some kind of lawyer. What kind of trouble was following Chance?

Why hadn't he denied the lighthouse break-in had to do with him? The person who'd broken into her tower had been looking for something, but what? How had they known the laptop was in that wall after all these years?

Emily closed her eyes and rubbed the tense muscles cramping painfully throughout her neck. Another question nagged at her. Why had Chance once again said "Let's go home" before leaving Jake's Bar and Grill?

He said those words as if he already owned her place. Why didn't he just come right out and tell her he wanted to buy her home?

How could he afford it? The man had admitted he'd hitchhiked up here for heaven's sake. If he had money, then surely he would have found a safer form of transportation.

What was with the gun? She'd always disliked guns. Probably because she'd grown up in a country where guns just weren't readily used except for hunting. Maybe if she'd grown up south of the border, she wouldn't be so frightened of them.

Nothing to fear but fear itself, her uncle Jeb had always told her when he'd captured her disapproving glances while he'd cleaned his hunting rifle. With grave patience he'd explain to her how people feared guns only because they weren't familiar with them or educated about how to use them. When people knew how to handle them and how to store them safely, the fear subsided into a sensible respect for the weapon, he'd said.

She didn't believe it.

In her reporter days she'd seen the damage a bullet did to a body. Gangland shootings in which the back of a teenager's head had been blown away or a child who'd accidentally shot himself or someone else because a parent hadn't stored the gun properly.

Now Chance, the man who'd so effectively kissed her as she'd never been kissed before, a man who looked at her with such tenderness in his eyes, a man who admitted he wanted to make love to her, also carried a deadly weapon. But, boy oh boy, did he know how to kiss.

She moaned as her pussy throbbed with the need to have Chance's cock sliding into her. Wow, did she ever want him to fuck her. She wanted his mouth on her pussy. His cock in her mouth.

Her breath hitched at the thoughts. She hadn't thought this way since Steve. Hadn't felt this intense and aroused for years. With Chance being a stranger, she found herself being bold as to what she wanted. Kissing him back just as fiercely as he kissed her. She'd pushed her tongue into his mouth, letting him know she wanted their tongues to mate. She wanted to mate with him. Had wanted to take him right there up against the wall where anyone could have come in.

Thankfully it had been Garrett who'd found them. Any other person would have gossiped about the intense kiss to the whole province. She didn't want Skip to hear that she'd been unfaithful. At least not through local gossip. She would have to tell him in person.

She would have to acknowledge she had doubts about marrying him. Maybe tell him she was sexually attracted to Chance. No, she couldn't do that. She couldn't hurt Skip that way. It wasn't as if she were in love with Chance. It was more like lust, right?

Lust. Yes, that's it. It was the same kind of raw, powerful feelings she'd had for Steve right off the bat. And look where that had gotten her. A broken heart.

No, she didn't want to go through that intense love again.

The sound of hammering stopped the route her thoughts were going and she smiled despite her anger at him. He certainly did have a way with his hands. He'd worked straight through dinner. Then he'd switched on the floodlights, claiming he wanted to get the job done tonight so they could go seaweeding tomorrow without worrying about the dock heading out to sea. As if it would. The dock had been falling apart for years, bit by bit, and still it stayed.

She knew there was another reason he stayed outdoors and away from her. He didn't want to pick up where they'd left off when

Garrett Rustico had interrupted them at Jake's Bar and Grill. She couldn't blame him for staying away. He probably thought she was a loose woman, allowing him to kiss her. Especially since she'd already allowed another man to lay claim to her by agreeing to marry him.

·· ↝ ··

WHEN HE FINALLY LAID the hammer to rest inside the toolbox, Chance's muscles were aching. Night had dropped a few hours ago and a cold chill sifted through the misty air. From his perch inside the tilted woodshed where he kept all the tools and building supplies, he peered through the open door up at the towering octagonal lighthouse and the white clapboard keeper's house nestled snugly beneath the tower's shadow. To his disappointment a buttery glow shone from Emily's bedroom windows.

No doubt she'd be pecking away at the keyboard, trying out some new passwords. Too bad with all the excitement today they'd forgotten to pick up the knit wool. He'd been hoping knitting baby clothes for the upcoming arrivals would keep her off the computer.

It wouldn't have kept her anger at bay during their return trip from town. She had every right to be red-hot mad at him. He'd pulled a gun on her. He'd pressed himself against her. Kissed her. Threatened to make love to her.

On the boat back here, he lied like hell when he'd told her she was merely a bad habit to him. A bad habit he had to break.

She'd tried to conceal her hurt by keeping a stiff, calm voice, but he'd always been able to see her true emotions. It was now quite obvious to him she didn't love Skip. For God's sake she had just finished trying on the wedding dress she'd be wearing down the aisle for another man when he'd told her he was going to kiss her. She'd merely accepted her fate with a lovely smile on her lips and kissed him back with such a fierce passion he knew she was having doubts about the upcoming nuptials.

If she was in love with another man, she would never behave this way. Instead, she would be kicking and scratching out Chance's eyes.

Hell, he should march right up there and take what was rightfully his. And Emily belonged to him. He wanted her so bad his entire body ached with a maddening craving to make love to her. He'd blown any chance of keeping her out of the line of fire by announcing his prison name to the entire fairgrounds the other day. If Skip was behind his incarceration, then he would know that name. He would know Chance was Steve. He would know Steve would want his wife back.

So why had he sent a lowly henchman to the lighthouse to search the place? How would they know he kept his laptop in the wall up there? Why hadn't they found it when they'd broken in years ago? He sure hadn't told anyone. Even the beatings and threats he'd received behind bars hadn't made him spill the truth.

For if he had, they would have killed him early on in his incarceration. At least that's what he'd been betting on. Until they decided he was better off being killed for his body parts and placed into a private transplant hospital after getting shot in prison last year. That's where his brothers had found him.

And he hadn't been happier. Until he saw Emily the other night. His sweet wife, who had no idea who he was. He'd hoped to keep it that way. Now, however, after kissing her, after feeling her soft curves press against him, he wasn't sure he could keep his secret.

He stepped through the open shed doorway and shivered as the cold ocean air sliced through him. The clang of a buoy out in the water made him peer across the calm dark blue ocean for anything suspicious.

The feeling of being watched had disintegrated upon leaving town, but it didn't mean they weren't out there. Watching. Waiting.

An icy sensation crept up his spine as he remembered Garrett's description of the man he'd spotted following Chance into Jake's Bar and Grill. The man could have been anyone. If Chance had paid attention to his finely tuned survival instincts, instincts that had kept him alive through the brutal horrors he'd experienced over the past few years, he might have actually caught the culprit following him. Instead, he'd been thinking about Emily, the darn wedding dress and reminiscing about the past.

Clearly being around her wasn't in either of their best interests. He needed to figure out a way to persuade Emily to go and stay with Daniel and Jo before these people made their next move. He could trust his brothers to protect her, and it was up to him to get rid of the danger.

Chance leaned over and picked up the gun from the picnic table where he'd left it for easy access. Checking to make sure the safety was on, he shoved it into the waistband of his jeans. Jeans that had once belonged to him. He'd been surprised to discover Emily had kept them. Another indication she hadn't totally forgotten him.

A white twinkle far out to sea captured Chance's attention and he automatically stiffened.

A boat?

He narrowed his eyes and squinted through the thin trails of mist forming over the water. He couldn't take any chances. Settling himself on the picnic table, he watched and waited, all the while thinking about Garrett's description of the man he'd seen. If the identification was correct, then the break-in and the guy following him in town was just the tip of a fast-approaching tidal wave with more bad things on the way.

• • ᥫᩭ • •

"YOU SURE YOU'RE UP to this?" Emily laughed as she watched Chance pull the long-handled seaweed rake through the shallow ocean waters from his perch at the stern of *Sweet Lies*. At her question, the frown of concentration he toted vanished and he lifted his head. To her surprise his eyes shone with excitement.

"This is great!" he replied.

Immediately he returned to his job of raking the seaweed, the cute frown of concentration back on his face, the exquisite muscles in his arms bulging very nicely beneath his turtleneck stealing her breath clean out of her lungs. Within a few seconds he slapped his first haul onto the deck.

"Hey, not bad for the first time." Emily chuckled as she leaned over and ran her fingers through the slippery brown sea plants. "Still good quality for this late in the season. Probably because of the excess of sunny days and the unusually warm ocean temperatures this time of the year."

"Now what do we do with it?" Chance asked.

"Haul it into the middle of the net I've laid out here on the deck and then when there's a huge heap at the end of the day, I use the winch and hoist it up. Then we bring it into town."

"Sounds like a simple enough way to earn a living."

Emily grinned. "You won't be saying that after ten hours of work."

"Ten hours?" He gaped in disbelief.

"That's not including an hour lunch break and two fifteen minute breaks or the ride back to town."

He grinned and eyes sparkled now with amusement.

"I think I catch your drift."

"Not to worry. Since it's your first day out, I'll only work you eight hours. How's that?"

"You're a slave driver," he grumbled beneath the teasing look he threw her way.

She inhaled when his muscles strained against his turtleneck again as he hoisted the seaweed-laden rake into the air and maneuvered the seaweed into the middle of the net where he dumped it.

He'd come in late last night. Her heart had thumped a mile a minute as she'd listened to his footsteps pad around the kitchen. The sound of the microwave whirring had quickly followed and she knew he'd found the supper she'd prepared for him and left in the refrigerator.

In the darkness of the bedroom, she'd lain in bed listening to Chance's footsteps as he hesitated at her bedroom door. Part of her had hoped he would come in and make love to her, follow through on those words he'd murmured while they'd kissed in Jake's Bar.

Telling her he wanted to make love to her. Wanted to fuck her hard and deep. And that he wanted his cock in her mouth. She'd never done oral with Steve. Had come close that one night under the wharf but she'd chickened out.

Both disappointment and relief slammed through her when she heard him go in for a shower and then upstairs to bed. After he'd gone up, she'd stared at the wedding portrait, remembering the other night when she'd been playing that Halloween romance ritual and spied Steve's face over her shoulder in the mirror because of the moonlight splashing on his side of the wedding photo.

In a way the ritual had come true, hadn't it? Chance seemed so much like Steve. In the foods he liked. The way he touched her back when he led her somewhere. He'd even picked her and Steve's song during the dance. How uncanny was that?

And the way he kissed. Oh yes, he definitely kissed like Steve. Maybe even more powerfully. More passionately. Demanding in the way he pressed his erection against her. Not really the way she'd think a shy man would behave with a woman he'd just met.

Damned if she'd awoken all hot and tense again this morning. Scorching dreams of Chance doing wicked things to her had her masturbating again under the covers. She didn't know how much more of this tension she could take either. Every time she looked at Chance she wanted to touch him. Wanted to relive her scorching dreams, especially the dance dream where they were both naked and dancing beneath the silver stars. She'd had that dream again last night, except Steve hadn't taken over Chance's place. This time it had been just Chance and his gorgeous cock, pumping into her pussy over and over again.

"I hear seaweed is pretty good fertilizer for farmers. Is that where this is going?"

Oh God, she had to stop thinking sex. Stop!

Taking a deep breath of the cool air to steady her nerves, she continued raking the seaweed and cleared her throat.

"Some of it goes to farmers so they can replenish the trace minerals they lose due to the conventional over-fertilization with chemicals. The rest depends on what orders are waiting in town at my seaweed factory."

"Your seaweed factory?"

"Actually I own half of it."

"The McCullens didn't tell me you owned a factory."

"They don't know. I haven't told them yet. I wasn't sure it was going to fly."

"But it is, isn't it?"

"This summer has been fabulous; we've got tons of orders. That's why we're out here so late in the season. I'm trying to make profits look good so my partner Jen and I can get a bank loan and purchase a second fishing boat next spring. We're going to hire someone to look after the factory and Jen wants to captain *Sweet Lies*. Garrett Rustico, you met him at Jake's yesterday, has expressed interest in captaining the new boat if we get one."

"You're kidding? I thought he was a cop?"

"He is. I might add you two appeared quite chummy yesterday. Hit it off quickly, didn't you?"

"He's a likable fellow. What else can they use this stuff for?" Chance eyed the seaweed in the net. He was changing the subject. Okay, she'd let him off the hook this time.

"Oh, Mr. Donovan, haven't you heard?"

Chance shook his head.

"Times have changed. Seaweed is not only good for the farmers, it's good for your body. Now we harvest seaweed as sea vegetables."

"Sea vegetables?" He twisted his face into a sour grimace and Emily had to laugh.

"Sea vegetables are an excellent source of iron, Vitamin A and Vitamin B12, all of which are found in our fruits and vegetables. It's also high in fiber and is a good source of protein."

Chance looked doubtfully at the clump of seaweed in the net.

"This ugly stuff? Hardly looks appetizing."

"I didn't get any complaints from you the other night or at breakfast this morning when you devoured more of the pie."

He smiled sheepishly. "I hope you brought some of it along?"

"I did."

He rubbed his hands together with appreciation. "Yum. Let's break into it now."

Emily grinned.

"News flash. The vitamins you ingested at breakfast will get you through to lunch."

Chance laughed a hearty laugh that made her insides sing.

"A guy can try, can't he? What else is it good for?"

"Are you asking for a lesson in the uses of seaweed?"

"It might give me an incentive to work harder." He wiggled his eyebrows.

Emily's heart slammed up against her chest at that eyebrow wiggle. So much like Steve. He used to do that too. God, she simply had to stop comparing the two. They were separate men. She needed to remember that fact because it wasn't healthy to relieve the past through Chance. The reason he was so much like Steve was why she felt so attracted to him. If she could remember that fact, she'd be okay.

"Well, it's used as a thickener in soaps, shampoos, ice cream and other foods. It's a million-dollar-plus industry on Prince Edward Island and other coastal provinces and states. And it's also used in cosmetics and skin-care products. Did you know that a Japanese conglomerate invented a way of extracting algin molecules that bind tightly to water and they'll be used to create longer-lasting lipstick?"

"I don't know what you said about the Japanese scientific jargon, although I do know you don't need any lipstick."

She glanced up at his gentle voice. His eyes suddenly seemed a richer blue and she felt his warm breath sear her lips. Only a cool ocean breeze fought the sizzling sparks blazing between them. Despite her earlier self-argument to remind herself he wasn't Steve, she found herself anticipating another kiss like yesterday. Maybe it would even go further?

"You look pretty damn good the natural way." Without saying another word, he broke the intense gaze and disappointment shot through her as he returned to the stern where he sliced the long-handled rake back into the shallow water where she'd anchored the boat.

Emily sighed heavily at the interaction that had just taken place between them. What in the world was she going to do? She was so attracted to Chance that she was willing to put her future with Skip in jeopardy.

She lifted her rake over the port side and found it difficult to concentrate on scanning the rocky bottom of the ocean with him around. Whenever he moved, she couldn't help but watch his muscular arms or long legs or his cute frown of concentration. She wished it was summer and hotter than blazes. Then he'd remove his shirt and she could enjoy the scenery even more.

Warmth blushed across her face and it sure wasn't from the autumn sun. Her fingers tightened on her rake. She had better keep her mind and her eyes on the job and her thoughts on whether she truly wanted that wedding in a few weeks' time.

Chapter Ten

Cold wind snapped against Chance as he took a momentary break from rearranging the morning's catch of seaweed to allow it to bake on the deck in the hot glow of the early afternoon sun.

Today the sky was a wild, sharp blue with dots of black clouds hovering in the northeastern horizon. Bright sunshine shot silver sparks off tips of the ocean waves, making him blink in awe at the beauty of Shipwreck Island.

In his years of captivity, he'd dreamed of this secluded island many times. His desperate mind spit out memories of this sun-drenched coastline like a drowning man frantically grabbing onto a life preserver. His mind's eye had scanned every craggy crevice of the red rocky cliffs that stretched down to the equally rusty red sandy beach. In all those dreams, Emily had been with him, just like she was with him now.

A momentary tinge of panic nudged away the shaky calm that had enveloped him since he'd arrived on the island. Was he dreaming? Was he still being held prisoner? Had his mind snapped and crossed over into lunatic land so he could mentally be with his wife? Or was he really physically here?

One look over his shoulder confirmed he was indeed sane. Emily stood at the helm, her eyes squinting into the sunshine, her brown hair tucked into a black woolen fishing cap. She looked so cute as she tapped her fingers on the steering wheel to the catchy melody of the song "Will You Remember Me?" that blared out of the radio as she started the engine of the tugboat.

He lifted the heavy seaweed-laden rake and tried hard not to wince as his sore muscles pulled and tightened with these new movements as he slapped the stuff onto the deck.

Cripes! And she did this for a living? She had to have some pretty powerful muscles in her arms. She'd no doubt beat him at next year's fair in the Timber Sports contest. A low chuckle erupted from behind and he lifted his head. Emily stood smiling at him.

"Sore?"

"Nothing I can't handle," he lied. He needed a break. Big-time. And he was hungry too. Besides hauling in seaweed, he'd been keeping an eye out for anyone suspicious but hadn't seen a thing. In turn he felt calm and starving and eager to spend more time with her. Preferably without all this seaweed between them.

"Good. What do you say we forget about lunch and get straight into this afternoon's catch?"

His mouth dropped open in shock and Emily burst out laughing. "You should see your face! Thought you said you could handle it?"

"I lied."

"I thought so," she giggled and then pointed to his right. "There's a great spot for lunch just over there."

His breath burst from his lungs to where she pointed. It was a tiny peninsula jutting out of a cove. The cove had always been one of her favorite spots to picnic. He nodded his approval and excitement rammed into him. Tossing the rake aside, he cast out the anchor.

He couldn't wait until they got there!

. . ❧ . .

EMILY SAT DOWN ON THE warm piece of driftwood. She was tired but it was a healthy tired. She could only imagine how Chance must feel on his first day out.

She remembered the uncomfortable achy feelings very well. Every spring, after a winter's long break, her muscles ached in places she'd forgotten she had muscles. The aches only lasted the first few days until the body became re-accustomed to the new movements. And by the way Chance winced every now and then when he picked up a piece of driftwood for the fire, she knew he experienced those same aches.

She was surprised he'd even volunteered to build a fire after all the work he'd put in this morning. To keep away the chill of the day, he'd said.

When he had an armload of dry wood gathered, he tramped over to where she sat dishing out the food-filled containers. The black remnants of an old fire were barely visible and that was the spot he picked to set up the campfire.

She hid a smile when he grimaced once again as he squatted down, struck a match and lit the newspaper under the kindling house he'd erected. The edges of the paper curled into black. Gray plumes of smoke billowed momentarily then the paper burst into flames that eagerly licked the dry pieces of twigs and driftwood. When the fire crackled to life, he heaved a huge sigh of relief and promptly crashed butt first upon the rusty-colored sand close to the fire.

"Be warned. I've worked up a serious appetite," Chance chuckled heartily as he rubbed his hands over the warmth of the flames. Taking that as her cue, she unscrewed the thermos lid and poured him a healthy dose. "Hot coffee with plenty of sugar and cream."

"And caffeine," he added cheerfully. "To keep me revved up so I can work all afternoon."

Emily had to laugh. "I knew your tough-guy attitude was just an act, so I came prepared."

He grunted, took a swallow of his coffee, nodded his approval and leaned his back against the log on which she sat. She handed him a lobster sandwich, a tuna sandwich, potato salad, an orange and a banana.

He cocked a curious eyebrow at her. "You feeding an army?"

"If you eat it all, then I'll treat you to some chocolate potato brownies and a slice of pie."

In answer he took a huge bite of the lobster sandwich and once again nodded his approval. They ate in a comfortable silence, but she didn't miss his wary gaze thread across to the opening of the cove.

The waves were getting higher, but she'd maneuvered her tugboat through much worse.

"Wind's picking up. Might be a storm coming," he mumbled fifteen minutes later as he greedily worked away at his slice of pie.

"It'll come ashore in a couple of days."

He threw her a curious grin.

"I heard it on the radio this morning," she confessed.

"Ah yes. I forgot about the modern conveniences in this rustic setting." Once again he glanced out across the ocean.

"Don't worry about the storm, Chance."

"Huh?" He snapped his gaze back to her and she could tell he was indeed worried about those dark clouds in the eastern horizon.

"The lighthouse has survived many hurricanes and wild storms. I'm sure it'll survive more even after I've gone."

"Daniel told me you were selling."

"Are you interested in buying the lighthouse? Is that why you're here?" she blurted, suddenly wanting to know if he might want to be the new owner.

"Actually...I do love it here."

"You want to buy it?"

He frowned and shook his head. "Unfortunately, I can't afford to."

"So? Why are you here then?"

Yesterday he'd clammed up when she'd asked him, but hopefully today with a full belly and being tired he might give her a clue as to why he had let himself into her home in the middle of the night. And grabbing food from her fridge wasn't the real reason.

He placed his empty plate down on the sandy beach beside him and rubbed his hands high over the crackling fire. It seemed as if he would ignore her question. Irritation snapped through her patience.

"I want the truth, Chance. Are you hiding from the law? Is that why Daniel sent you here? Was that a lawman following you yesterday?"

"Daniel didn't send me here, Emily," he said softly. "I came here of my own free will. Just to say hi to an old buddy's wife."

Bullshit.

"Then why haven't you mentioned Steve anymore?"

"Figured you'd bring him up when you wanted to talk about him. Since you've brought him up, why are you selling the lighthouse? Are the memories you two had together here bad ones?"

Emily sighed as his words bit painfully into her.

"I'd rather not be reminded of what this place means to me when I get married."

"You aren't selling because he wants you to, are you?"

She shrugged and took a delicate sip of her coffee. "He's never really asked me to sell. I could keep the place. Maybe rent it out or come visit. But he doesn't want to live here."

"But you do, and he's never talked you out of selling it, has he."

"No. It's my idea. It's taken me a long time to decide to sell. Now I just want to go on with life. Put the memories behind me and start living again."

"So, the memories here are bad?"

His soft question made her look at him. Sweet tenderness glowed in his eyes, a tenderness she ached to experience.

The breeze ruffled his hair and the crisp sun played with the faint lines of silver as well as those shimmering golden highlights she thought were just like Steve's the other day when they'd been under the wharf.

Odd, but she swore if she stared hard enough at this man, she could almost see Steve's face staring back at her. She felt uncomfortable with that thought and at the way this conversation was going.

"Are the memories bad?" he asked again, his voice still soft but now etched with a tinge of desperation.

"They are wonderful memories," she admitted, unable to unlock her gaze from his face.

He approved of her answer with a gentle nod of his head, yet his voice turned hard. "Then it means you are selling out to break your connection with your husband. You shouldn't get rid of a place you obviously love. The memories are good so you should keep the place. Don't turn your back on what you love."

An icy chill swept through Emily at the truth in his words. Chance was right. The only reason she was selling her lighthouse was because of good memories and to finally break with her past.

Every ounce of Shipwreck Island and the lighthouse contained some memory of Steve and their dreams. This tiny peninsula had been a favorite picnic spot of theirs. A place she'd avoided coming to because of those painful memories, and yet for some odd reason today she'd just naturally steered *Sweet Lies* into this cove without even a second thought.

Chance remained silent for a long time as he studied her. The more he looked at her, the more uneasy she felt. His intense gaze pierced her heart and seemed to be searching her soul. It seemed as if he could read her mind. As if he knew her secret about Skip. That she truly didn't love him. Sure enough, his next words confirmed he could read her like a book, just as Steve had always been able to do.

"You're just settling for this Cole fellow." It was a statement not a question. "You probably figure you aren't getting any younger and it's time to start that family you've always wanted."

"I don't see how that is any of your business," she snapped, anger breaking her uneasiness.

"Did I strike a nerve?" He casually placed another piece of driftwood on the fire.

"Why are you being so nosy?"

"I guess I did touch a nerve." His soft whisper unraveled her and suddenly she wanted to tell him the truth. If only to unburden herself of her doubts.

"Okay! I'm not in love with him. I do care for him though. That's good enough for me." *And just because your kiss almost had me dropping my pants so you could fuck me, doesn't mean a thing*, she added silently.

Chance looked up from the fire with obvious disapproval flaring in his eyes. A shiver of guilt speared through her. Guilt at having such a wonderful sexual attraction to this man when she was supposed to marry another.

"Cold?" he asked.

"I guess so."

Without warning he stood and lifted the knit wool blanket she'd brought along from the boat. He unfolded it, slipped it over her shoulders and then to her horror slid onto the log beside her and wrapped the other end of the blanket over his shoulders. Immense body heat sizzled against her and she found herself enjoying his closeness. He remained silent now, his attention once again focused on the ocean.

The flames from the fire danced wildly in the wind, offering little heat. But she didn't need any heat, did she? Especially with him sitting so close she could smell a trace of the soap he'd used in this morning's shower. The combination of the soap, his sweat and his unique male scent urged her to snuggle a little closer to his strong, lean body.

"Put your head on my shoulder and relax," he suggested. The tenderness in his voice unraveled the tension sifting through her at their conversation about her selling her lighthouse and settling for Skip.

Sighing, she put her head on his shoulder and felt that nice feeling of knowing she wasn't alone anymore. It had been so long since a man's scent had aroused her. So long since a man had kissed her as passionately as Chance had done yesterday.

"Emily?" His soft whisper snapped into her.

Oh God, he'd heard her sigh! Flames heated her cheeks as he looked at her with those gorgeous blue eyes. Eyes full of lust. Full of desire.

Suddenly he swore softly and then his head began to draw closer.

His eyes were no longer dark and dangerous, but tender, caring and full of desire. She felt herself melt under his gaze and her heart cracked against her chest as she realized he was going to kiss her.

Shit!

She shouldn't let him kiss her. Shouldn't— *Oh my!* He tasted so good, she thought as his hot mouth melted over her lips and chased away her doubts. His mouth devoured her lips. A wild fire exploded inside her abdomen. His tongue tasted, questioned and teased her lips with such urgency it frightened her.

And it excited her!

When his hands cupped both sides of her face, she could barely believe he touched her with such gentleness. Yet in direct contrast, his lips moved over hers like hot, demanding silk. He sipped her lower lip, unleashing such a powerful surge of need, she suddenly couldn't keep her hands off him.

As if he knew she wanted to touch him, he shifted himself so his body was facing hers. Reaching out, she ran her hands up underneath his arms and clutched the back of his broad shoulders, allowed herself to sink into the intoxicating kiss. His tongue stroked against her lips and she opened to him, allowing him inside.

Tingles dashed through her pussy as their tongues clashed. Mercy, he had such a powerful tongue, she thought numbly as he literally possessed her mouth with his force. All those sexual cravings she felt since meeting him rose from the depths and sensations lashed her.

Oh wow! This man knew how to kiss. She angled her head, desperate to kiss him harder. His tongue slammed against her tongue again, unleashing those delightful tingles in her pussy again.

He halted the kiss and she opened her eyes, noticing the flush of arousal flaring across his cheeks.

"You're so beautiful, Emily," he whispered, and for one split second she thought he *was* Steve. The feeling vanished as his hands dropped from her face. His fingers trailed down her throat, over her breasts, her tummy and to the hem of her sweater.

"I want to see you, Emily. All of you."

Oh God.

She found herself nodding and lifted her arms as he brought the hem up over her head. Beneath, she wore a flannel t-shirt and he had that off before she could blink. Lowering the bra straps down her arms, she held her breath as her breasts fell free.

Emotions she couldn't name careened through her as he gazed at her breasts. They felt full and tingly. Her nipples ached and peaked. Need for him to suck them skipped through her.

In front of them, the fire crackled and the waves crashed onto the nearby beach. The wind breathed against her hot flesh, but it didn't even feel cold. The wind caressed her body as Chance's hands stroked her breasts. He cupped her and moved the pads of his thumbs over her nipples until they ached so much.

When he began to lower his head, awareness stabbed into her belly and between her thighs. Her heart suspended in her chest as he swept one of her nipples into his moist mouth.

Oh! This feels so good, she thought. She moaned her appreciation. Loved the intimate way he sucked and she about came off the log from the arousal he caused. He seemed to know exactly how hard to suck to bring the sweet burst of pleasure-pain she always loved so much when Steve did this to her. She looked down and watched as his lips moved around her nipple.

Very nice full lips, she mused. Lips she wanted all over her body. His tongue lashed her flesh and she felt the tight bite of pain as his teeth nipped her. His eyes were closed, long, dark lashes framing his cheeks as he sucked. He looked as if he were asleep and she had to grin.

Slipping her arms from beneath his, she brought her hands up and touched her fingertips to those golden highlights in his hair. So much like Steve's hair, she pondered. Her fingers trailed down along the length of his corded, tanned neck to drop to his muscular shoulders.

He moved to her other breast, his eyes still closed, his hot mouth sucking her nipple until she was gasping at the sweet pain and shuddering. Slowly he pulled his head away to admire what he'd done to her nipples.

They were red and tight, like two succulent cherries.

"I'm not finished yet," he groaned as he stared into her eyes. "You taste too good. I want more of you."

His gaze dropped to the waistband of her jeans.

More? Like down between her legs?

In an instant his fingers were there and she swore she'd stopped breathing when he unbuttoned the clasp and unzipped her zipper.

"Shoes," he muttered as he started to slide her jeans over her hips.

It took her a moment to realize he meant she should remove her shoes. She did as he asked, quickly using her feet to press down the heels of her shoes and slid them off. He'd slipped her jeans down over her hips and the cold log she sat on bit into her butt. But he was ahead of her, taking the blanket, which miraculously was still on her shoulders, and shoving it under her.

For a few moments everything had felt so natural. His kiss. His suckling her breasts. Her touching his hair. Touching his neck, watching him suck her nipples. His removing her jeans and her now her panties.

But when he moved between her legs and sat there, his hands clasping her ankles, spreading her legs wide for him to see her pussy. This was different than she was used to. Sure, Steve had seen her down there, but Steve's face had never been down there!

And Chance's head was lowering, making it quite clear he would go down on her.

Disbelief rocked her. However, her disbelief vanished the instant his finger smoothed over her clit.

The firm pressure seared right through her, making her grab onto the log beneath her with both palms. She stilled, swallowed and watched him lick his lips as if her pussy were a delicious meal he was about to devour.

"So, fucking beautiful, Emily," he moaned, and then his head lowered more, and she was crying out as his finger increased the pressure on her clit, bringing her instantly to climax. And then his finger was gone, and his mouth consumed her orgasm.

His tongue slipped into her vaginal opening and he sucked. Oh! How he sucked her!

The pleasure gripped her mind and short-circuited all her thoughts. She felt her vagina tighten, gasped as erotic spasms washed through her. Rocking her hips, she cried out as he sucked harder, his tongue licking her clit and his hands holding her thighs apart so she couldn't bring them together. Her cream gushed and she heard him slurping and moaning as if he were thoroughly enjoying a meal.

Wow! She'd never known anything like this existed. Her mind and body continued to spiral out of control. Pleasure wave after pleasure wave consumed her and he just kept on sucking. When she swore, she could stand it no longer, he moved his mouth away and thrust his fingers into her.

"Oh my God!" she gasped as he began a fast pump that simply tore her apart again. Un-fucking-believable! she thought as she convulsed and gyrated and simply enjoyed what he did to her. She was barely aware of his heavy breathing. Barely aware of his rough voice whispering to her in soothing tones.

"That's it, Em. Let it go. Just let it go and enjoy."

She kept her eyes closed as he pumped. Kept herself in the pleasure for as long as she could. Enjoying it. Living it. Loving it.

When she finally came down from the high, he'd withdrawn his fingers.

Her knees were weak, and her thighs were trembling. Damned if she didn't feel embarrassed as he gazed at her with the most sparkling blue eyes while he licked her cream from his lips.

"I could tell it's been a long time," he said as he began to slip her panties on her again.

Oh? So he'd taken pity on her and decided to mouth and finger-fuck her? Great, just great. Now she was accepting sexual charity.

But she'd never felt so satisfied in her life. Bring on more charity please! Okay, so she wasn't too embarrassed to see the humor in the situation. What would he say if she asked to return the favor?

No! She couldn't do that! Could she?

Okay, now she really was getting embarrassed. Did he expect her to go oral on him?

"Someone's coming. I heard a boat engine. I think whoever is here saw *Sweet Lies* anchored and is coming in from the west side of the island. Better get dressed. Just in case."

Sweet heavens! She hadn't heard a thing. Had they been seen? Now *that* would be embarrassing.

As she struggled into her jeans, she scanned the surroundings. Because they were in a cove, she couldn't see too much, except the whitecapped waves out on the ocean. The tugboat was docked at the point. Scrubby twisted trees and bushes hid them from three sides, but they were wide open in front.

"I'd better go and take a look," Chance said, and stood.

Peering down at her, his hot gaze flicked across her naked breasts, making her wish they hadn't been interrupted. But maybe he was making up having heard a boat?

"We'll have to pick this up another time."

Oh dear! Definitely!

She nodded, her head feeling wobbly as she reached for her flannel tank and sweater.

Oh definitely, Chance Donovan.

Crazy. She was crazy. Crazy. Crazy. Crazy. Emily chastised as she waited for Chance to return. Crazy for letting him kiss her and do those naughty things to her. Oh, she had to call off the wedding to Skip. She'd disgraced him. How could she do this to him?

Guilt slammed into her. She was a slut. She'd humiliated him and herself for folding so easily to the first man who she truly felt sexually attracted to after all these years.

Yes, she was a slut. But a very satisfied one, Emily pondered as she huddled beneath the blanket and stared into the fire.

The orange flames licked greedily at the several pieces of driftwood she'd just placed there. Licking greedily like Chance had licked her. Her pussy moistened and throbbed in memory. She wanted him down there again. Boy oh boy, she wanted him down there.

We'll have to pick this up another time, he'd promised.

Wow. Hot stuff like this only happened in those erotic romances she downloaded to her electronic book reader.

Thank God! She'd read those stories and would have an idea of how to go down on Chance. Her breathing grew shallow at that thought. A man going down on her. Unbelievable.

Okay, calm down. You have to act experienced about this. Don't let him know this is the first time you have a man's head between your legs. He would probably laugh at her inexperience.

Mercy! How old was she? She giggled at that question. She was old enough that she should have had a handful of lovers. But she'd only had Steve. Chance didn't have to know anything. She would act normal. Casual, as if it were perfectly natural for her to have sex with a stranger.

Condoms. Okay, she needed condoms. Safe sex. No pregnancies.

Wait. Pregnant she could handle.

Emily frowned at the realization that she didn't need a man to have her family. Women had kids without the man hanging around these days. Why hadn't she contemplated that angle before?

Chance could be a donor. Her heart picked up speed at that thought. She could ask him. No, she couldn't. She had to think this through. She couldn't raise a baby out here on her own. Besides, she wanted several of them. Not just one. She wanted her kids to have siblings, not grow up alone as she had.

She definitely needed to think this idea through. She'd never been impulsive in her life. Well, except for sleeping with Steve on their first date. That had felt so right. Just as today felt so right.

Being with Chance excited her. Dammit! She hadn't had excitement in way too long. She deserved to be happy again.

Okay, slow down, Emily. He's not marrying you. Just pleasuring you. She had to remember that and keep her emotions out of it. Emotions only got her into trouble.

Suddenly she heard a crashing sound of someone coming through the nearby cluster of scraggly spruce trees from the west. Alarm snapped her to her feet, and before she could look for any kind of weapon, Chance erupted from behind the trees, dragging a skinny teenager along with him.

"Caught this fellow lurking around. Don't know how much he saw."

"Let me go!" The teen screeched as he tried to wriggle free from Chance's grip on his elbow.

"Chad Sullivan! What are you doing here?" Emily shouted at the panicked kid.

The teenager's face blushed a crimson red.

"You know this kid?" Chance asked.

"The baker's son."

Chance's eyes narrowed into dangerous slits as he gazed at the struggling teen.

"Who hired you to spy on us?"

Emily couldn't believe his accusation. "Chance! Stop it! He's just a curious boy!"

Chance shook his head and gave the kid a rough shake. "This curious boy is the one who was in the lighthouse the other night."

"How can you be so sure it's him?"

"His aftershave is the same smell."

Yes, Chance was right. There had been an overpowering smell when the person had swept past her. She'd forgotten all about it until just now. This was the same smell.

He threw Chad a scowl that made the boy shiver with fright. "The truth, kid. Or I'll stick your hand in that fire until you talk."

"It was her fiancé," Chad gasped and pointed to Emily.

"Skip?" Emily couldn't believe it.

"He wanted me to keep an eye on her. To tell him if she made it home okay and to keep an eye on her for the next few days."

"Cole wanted you to search the lighthouse, right?" Chance queried.

"Aw c'mon. No one hired me to steal anything or search Mrs. McCullen's place. Just to check if she made it safely home and to keep an eye on her."

"How'd you find the laptop?" Chance asked.

The boy's face flushed a deeper shade of red. "Aw man, I found the ancient thing when I was trying to pry the wall slat away so I could jimmy the door open easier and get inside the lamp room to see the view."

"The door to that platform was locked," Chance said. "That should have been your first clue to stay out."

"Chad Sullivan!" Emily shouted at the panicked kid.

The teenager shifted uncomfortably under her intense stare.

"I didn't break in. I promise. The main level door to the lighthouse was unlocked. Just the one up to the next level was locked. Besides taking a look at the view I wanted to see if you were coming back, like Skip asked me to do at the fair."

"Do you know you could have broken your neck going up there without proper supervision?" Chance said sternly. "And you can go to prison for what you did. Trespassing, attempted stealing and assault when you crashed into me. You're setting yourself and your parents up for some heavy-duty grief."

Emily's heart went out to Chad as he looked about to cry. But Chance was right. Chad could have fallen and hurt himself or even died.

Chance's voice turned soft and gentle. "Do you know what happens to a young man like yourself in prison?"

The teen's eyes widened into worrisome saucers and his Adam's apple bounced uncontrollably.

"You don't want to ever find out, kid. Believe me. If I ever hear you're in trouble again, Emily and I will come forward and report what happened at her lighthouse the other night. They'll slap ten to fifteen years on to your sentence. Hell, that's conservative, twenty years, and with any luck, you'll get out when you're an old man like me. Is that clear?"

Chad nodded slowly, his face showing all the fear a sixteen-year-old's imagination could conjure.

"Now I want you to apologize to Emily," Chance commanded.

"I'm sorry, Mrs. McCullen. I truly am."

"I wish I could say it's all right, Chad." Emily sighed.

"Yes, ma'am." The boy's face turned pale as a ghost. Obviously, it had sunk in how extremely lucky he was to be let off so easily.

"I will have to speak to your parents about this matter the next time I'm in town," Emily said.

The boy shook his head, his wide gray eyes pleading with her not to do that.

"That won't be necessary, Emily," Chance said. "He understands. Don't you, kid?"

"Yes."

"Next summer you'll work at seaweeding here with Emily. It'll keep you out of trouble," he commanded.

"She's selling her place, sir. She won't be here next year."

"She'll be here. She won't sell."

Emily started at Chance's words. How dare he say she wasn't selling the lighthouse.

"She'll be in touch next summer," Chance said.

"Yes, sir. Thank you, sir."

"Now tell Cole I want to speak with him at his earliest convenience."

"I can't," the boy cried.

"Why the hell not?"

"I don't know how to contact him, sir. He said he'd contact me tonight."

"Tell him when you hear from him then."

"Yes, sir."

Chance released the boy and Chad sped off like a bullet headlong through the nearby bushes.

"You let him off way too easy, Chance. If he were my kid..."

"He's almost a man, Emily. Do you know how humiliated he would have been if you'd told his parents?"

"As well he should be. What he did is serious. He could have fallen and been seriously injured or died."

"If you treat him like a criminal, then he'll turn into one. Just the threat of his parents ever being told about this should hold him in line."

"What if it doesn't?"

"Has he ever been in trouble with the law before?"

"No. Maybe he's never been caught. You could be encouraging him by letting him get away with it. He might try something again."

Chance sighed and remained silent for a moment. He seemed to be deep in thought then finally spoke.

"I think I'm a pretty good judge of character. He strikes me as the type of kid who's very sensitive to other peoples' opinions about him."

"Yes, he is. I've known him since he was about eight, but kids change."

"It's called growing up, Em. For a young man it's tough enough. It's kind of nice when someone cuts you some slack once in a while. Makes you think twice as hard."

"You're speaking from experience, aren't you?"

He laughed. "I was sixteen at one point."

"And...what about your jail speech? Is that from experience too?"

She noticed him stiffen at her accusation and her tummy hollowed in a warning. Okay jail time was definitely on his plate.

"Something bad happened to you in the past, didn't it?"

"Why don't we keep my past out of the present," he said curtly. "Let's get back to work."

He began piling the food containers into the empty cooler. Clearly, she had struck a nerve. And by the way his jaw was clenched, it was a very painful and raw nerve.

Chapter Eleven

"So, this is your factory?" Chance said as he scanned the run-down-looking warehouse dominating most of the nearby shoreline.

Emily smiled to herself. Thankfully he hadn't mentioned what had happened on the beach between them during lunchtime when they'd returned to seaweeding for the rest of the afternoon. She was still dealing with the excitement and the embarrassment of being mouth-fucked by a total stranger.

"Used to be the local fish-processing plant until it went belly-up. We bought it and the weed is dried inside before shipping it out to the separate factories to do with what they will. I know it doesn't look too impressive from the outside, but we're expanding slowly."

"That's the best way to go. Nice and slow. You don't make as many mistakes that way." He lifted his hand to wave to someone. "Who is that lady over there? She seems excited to see us."

Emily spied the tall, dark-haired woman who was waving wildly at them. "That's Jen, my partner. We went to high school together and then she moved to British Columbia to work in a greenhouse and nursery. She came back last year, and we hooked up as if the years hadn't slipped away between us."

"Hi, Emily!" Jen shouted from the wharf. "Slip 10 is open. Bring her in."

Emily waved back acknowledgment and steered *Sweet Lies* toward the end of the wharf. A few minutes later they climbed out of the tugboat and she made the introductions. "Chance Donovan this is Jen Crystal. Jen, this is Chance."

Chance extended his hand and they shook. "Pleased to meet you, ma'am."

"Ma'am?" Jen laughed. "Please, Chance, leave the ma'am out on the ocean for the boss lady. She'll appreciate it more than I ever will."

"Will do." Chance chuckled.

Jen placed her hands on her hips and shook her head as she stared curiously at Chance. "I heard about you. You're the one who outbid Emily's fiancé for a date with her." She didn't wait for an answer as she turned to Emily. "I got your wedding invitation in the mail a few days ago."

Emily's heart sank at the news.

"That's my cue to cut out," Chance said. "I've got a few errands to run unless you need help unloading?"

"The workers unload." Jen grinned. "I have a couple of workers inside waiting for this work. Pay is pretty good and that's what we pay them the big bucks for."

"Don't you want to come inside and take a look around? Get some more info about seaweeding?" Emily teased, knowing he probably had enough of seaweed for today.

He winked. "Thanks, but I'll take a rain check."

Emily nodded, remembering firsthand how she couldn't wait to be free of seaweeding on her first few days back on the job.

"One hour long enough?" she asked.

"Should do."

"Meet back here?"

"Sure thing," Chance replied, and turned to her friend. "Nice meeting you, Jen."

"Likewise," Jen said cheerfully.

Emily watched as he sauntered off down the pier.

"Nice buns!" Jen shouted after Chance.

He threw them a sheepish grin over his shoulder, and when he disappeared around the corner of the factory, Jen focused her

attention on Emily. She was giggling with excitement and her brown
eyes flashed with curiosity.

Oh God. If Jen only knew what had happened today, she would
be screaming with joy. Jen didn't think Skip was right for her and
she'd been quite vocal with her protests about the impending
wedding. For a split second she almost confessed to Jen that things
had gotten very complicated very fast with Chance and totally out
of control. But then Jen grabbed her by the hand and started tugging
her toward the back door of the factory.

"My God, Emily. Where did you fish him out from? He's
absolutely to die for." She cooed dreamily.

"He's an old friend of my husband's," Emily announced, hoping
this would be the end of her friend's curiosity.

"An old friend of Steve's, eh? He sure doesn't like the idea of you
getting married. He's got the hots for you."

"I brought a big load of seaweed, Jen," Emily said, trying to
change the subject. It didn't work.

"Girl! By the way you're blushing I'd say you're interested in him
too. What has been going on between you two?"

Here was her chance to spill the beans, but she just couldn't do
it. What had happened with Chance going down on her seemed
something too personal to share.

"Nothing." Emily avoided Jen's eager stare.

"Nothing, my behind." Jen grinned. "More like something. A
little la-de-da before the wedding? If you know what I mean?"

She wriggled her eyebrows up and down a few times before
throwing her arms around Emily to give her a comforting hug.

"I'm only teasing you, eh? You have been thinking on it, haven't
you?" She let Emily loose and winked at her.

Emily laughed. "Yes."

"Good. You wouldn't be normal if you didn't think about it," Jen
replied, and Emily found herself smiling at her friend's bold teasing.

Jen looked over Emily's shoulder and her eyes twinkled happily as she surveyed *Sweet Lies*.

"Looks like you hauled in a great catch. Especially for this late in the season. You two do good together. Now let's get this stuff unloaded. I've got our last two employees who are sitting on the edges of their seat waiting for a pink slip. Your haul will keep them employed for an extra day or so. You going to be bringing in more weed?"

"As long as the quality and weather hold."

Jen nodded her approval and pushed a red button on the side of the building. They heard the bell ring inside signaling to the employees that a load was here and needed to be taken care of.

"The workers will appreciate it. It's not easygoing this late in the season, what with the crazy weather around this time of the year. I have to warn you, there's a storm that might be heading up this way in a couple of days. A big one. They're saying it might turn into a hurricane. You might want to keep your ear on the radio."

"Heard about it."

"Good."

Jen headed for the boat and whistled at the fishing net bulging with seaweed as it swayed in the stiff evening breeze. "Did I say you two work great together?"

"Yes, you did," Emily laughed, suddenly feeling proud of the haul they'd gathered.

"Did I?" Jen grinned. "Well...let's get'er unloaded, eh?"

•• ❧ ••

CHANCE COULDN'T HELP but chuckle as he headed down the street. Emily's friend Jen seemed like a nice woman. Not too many women were so friendly and outspoken on a first meeting. Instincts told him she was a good friend to Emily.

In the past he remembered mention of Emily's school chum who, shortly after graduation, had hooked up with a guy out west. Apparently, the guy had been doing a cross-country stint, taking a year off college to travel Canada and the States. If he remembered right, the couple had met at Jake's Bar and a few days later Jen had gone with him, sending a postcard every now and then, keeping Emily updated on her whereabouts.

Last he heard, she'd settled out west with the guy and was working there. Now she was back home. Funny how old friends lost connections over the years and then suddenly picked up their friendships again. Just as he and Emily had suddenly reconnected again.

Fuck. He shouldn't have kissed her the other day or today. He should have had more sense. Should have known he wouldn't have been able to hold back. Sitting on that log, her hair windswept over her blushing cheeks, her legs spread wide, her pussy and soft, curvy breasts exposed to him. She was the most beautiful woman in the world.

He'd stared at her pussy, feasting on her with his eyes, breathing in her aroused scent and couldn't hold back for an instant longer, diving between her legs like a man possessed. He'd never gone down on her before. Had wanted to in the old days. Had held back because of her inexperience and shyness. But she didn't seem too shy anymore, Chance mused as he stepped into the local flower shop. Why had he ever thought she was shy in the old days anyway?

They'd slept together on their first date. He'd moved in with her shortly after. Maybe he'd been the one who'd been too shy?

His thoughts returned to Emily. He could still taste her in her mouth. Like spicy honey. Very intoxicating taste indeed. He couldn't wait to go down on her again. Couldn't wait to palm her breasts and take her succulent nipples into his mouth again. Or to listen to her aroused breaths as he tongue and finger-fucked her again.

The thoughts flashed away when the lady in the flower shop asked him if he needed any help. He was crazy getting involved with Emily and dragging her into his dangerous world.

That local kid Skip had sent to follow them today as well as the other night sure as hell wasn't the guy who'd been following him around yesterday. Why would Skip hire a kid to follow her around? Perhaps it would seem less conspicuous? So why send the other guy who'd followed him in town?

Chance shivered at Garrett's description of the man. If it was who he suspected, then he really should contact his brothers and tell them there could be trouble. He'd forgotten to do that yesterday, getting sidetracked with the wharf as well as the trip to town and everything else. Tonight. He would wait until Emily was asleep and then he'd put out the call.

• • ❧ • •

AFTER EMILY AND JEN helped the workers unload the seaweed into the warehouse, she left them to handle the drying-out process. She needed to attend to an errand before heading back to meet Chance.

First and foremost, she had to get to the drugstore before it closed. A box of condoms was in order. Just in case they did pick up where they'd left off on the beach today.

She still couldn't believe it had really happened, she thought as she crossed the street. Couldn't believe how fast everything was happening. With Skip she'd never had the urge to get condoms. Never had the urge to have sex with him. Maybe if she'd spent more time with him, she would have developed that wild attraction she had for Chance?

Oh boy, who was she kidding? She'd allowed herself to be steered into this marriage by Skip and Helena. What had she been thinking not to listen to Jen and Daniel? Emily bit her bottom lip and stepped into the drugstore.

If she was lucky, the owner wouldn't be working cash tonight. Sometimes Bill worked both his pharmacy and the cash if it wasn't busy. He probably wouldn't ask questions but one never knew with the locals. They enjoyed their harmless gossip, just as Emily did. As long as she wasn't the one being gossiped about. Her tummy hollowed as she spied Bill behind the counter.

Shit! Just her luck.

"Hi, Emily!" he waved. "Long time no see. How's it going?"

"Fine, Bill. How goes it with you?"

"Oh, you know the drill. Getting older. Heard some guy paid a thousand bucks for your pie."

Shit. Word sure got around.

"Yep, he did."

"Heard you hired him to help out at your place."

May as well not deny it or rumors would fly.

"Just for a few days, Bill."

"He must be crazy, or he must have really wanted a date with you, Emily," he chuckled.

Emily didn't want to encourage a conversation, so she said nothing and kept moving down the aisle.

"Let me know if you need some help with something. I'll be in the back room."

Yes. I need condoms. Which size would you suggest? she questioned silently.

Good grief! She hadn't bought condoms. Ever! Steve had always taken care of that. She blew out an anxious breath as the old floorboards creaked beneath her feet.

Heck, she didn't even know where the condoms were kept. Maybe she should just get out of here and hope Chance had protection on him?

Yeah right. She knew enough about safe sex to know she shouldn't be dependent on the guy to supply protection. She should be carrying a couple of condoms in her wallet at all times. Just in case. Acting as if she'd been having wild, passionate sex on the spur-of-the-moment over the past years. Not.

As she started up the next aisle in her quest, she found herself thinking about Chance. She could still feel how fabulous his mouth had melted over her pussy. Oh boy, that orgasm had been so hot! She'd exploded like a bomb.

Emily found herself giving out a little moan as her pussy spasmed in remembrance and quickly checked to make sure no one was around to have heard. No one was around.

Another thought occurred to her. Maybe she could steal the box of condoms? That would certainly save her the aggravation of plopping it down on the counter in front of Bill. They didn't have security features on these boxes, did they? As if she needed to get caught going through the security device at the front of the store and have all the bells and whistles screeching through the air, branding her a condom thief.

She could just imagine getting caught. That would really go over well with the locals. Really well. Talk about mortifyingly embarrassing.

Okay, so theft was out of the picture. Where the hell did he keep the condoms in this store, anyway?

She glanced back from where she'd just come down the aisle and realized she'd been so deep in thought she'd missed them.

Crud!

Walking back to the end, she glanced up at the round security mirror in the corner just above her. Okay, coast was clear. Bill was still in the back room and no one was in the store. No one was watching her admire all the colorful boxes on display.

God! She was being ridiculous, wasn't she? People bought condoms all the time. Bill wouldn't question her. They were both adults.

She saw a box that caught her eye. Made sure it was in the large size. What if Chance wasn't as big as she'd hoped? Emily thought as she tucked the package into her hand. What if he was bigger?

Oh dear. She had to stop fantasizing and get the box out of here and get back to the boat before Chance got there. She literally breathed a sigh of relief when she spied a teenage girl behind the counter. She didn't recognize her.

Plopping the box onto the counter, she ignored the girl's suddenly bright red cheeks. Okay so her own cheeks felt quite warm too. Was she pathetic or what? She was feeling as embarrassed as an inexperienced teenager.

Man, who knew this errand would be so stressful? Paying the girl, Emily grabbed the bag and couldn't get out of the pharmacy fast enough.

• • ❧ • •

CHANCE STARED DOWN at the tombstone and tried hard to remain emotionless, but it didn't work. Sadness enveloped him. The person lying beneath the sparkling gray stone had sacrificed his life to help him.

He'd been an inmate. On Death Row. With Chance.

He'd been a man who decided he didn't want to wait for a chemical injection or death by electrocution to die. Instead, he'd caused a fight that landed Chance in a hospital where his two brothers had found him.

Of course, it hadn't been as simple as that, but Chance preferred not to dwell on how many lucky breaks he'd gotten in order to get his freedom. He knew if he did think about his close call with death and never seeing Emily again, he would surely start screaming and never stop for the rest of his life.

Biting back that familiar panic that sometimes still swept over him whenever he thought about that period of time in his life, he focused on the errand he'd come to do. Exhaling a shuddering breath, he knelt onto the yellowing cold lawn beside the gravestone. With shaky hands he placed the bundle of purple lupine flowers intermingled with pink and blue bachelor buttons into the metal vase attached to the stone.

"I finally came to look you up, buddy, and to say thanks," he said to the stone.

Tears sparked the back of his eyes, and before he broke down into a washer of emotions, he quickly stood. On wobbly legs, he turned from the stone and walked away from that part of his past.

•• ⚬⚭ ••

EMILY WAITED UNTIL Chance left the cemetery before leaving her hiding spot behind the nearby giant pine tree. She stared down at the tombstone that he had visited. The mysterious grave had appeared late last fall. She'd wondered who he'd been and how he'd died. She'd never seen anyone visit or put flowers on the man's grave...until today.

She looked at the pretty bouquet of purple lupines and the dainty bachelor buttons. Why would Chance bring this man flowers? There was an inscription etched into the stone too. *A good friend. Free At Last. May you rest in peace.*

Her gaze wandered to the man's name, Michael... Was he a friend of Chance's? He'd been very emotional during the visit.

She removed a daisy from the bouquet she'd brought for her uncle Jeb and placed it into the vase on the stranger's grave. "I don't know who you are, mister, but whoever you are, you made some sort of impact on Chance's life."

Chapter Twelve

Emily sighed with relief when she spotted Chance turn the corner of the warehouse and stroll casually toward where she stood at the stern of *Sweet Lies*. There wasn't a hint of the emotional turmoil she'd seen brewing in him back at the cemetery. If anything, he seemed quite cheerful as he shifted a couple of paper grocery bags in his strong arms and those yummy biceps were surely bulging beneath his sweater, making her knees weaken. Oh boy, this guy was turning her world so upside down in the way he made her feel. And right now, just watching him strolling toward her was making her feel nice and hot. Not to mention ready to pick up where they'd left off this afternoon during their lunch break.

Sweet Pete! Even her pussy dripped with anticipation. Okay, she had to stop this. She had to call it off with Skip and cut herself loose with Chance. Or was she crazy?

Maybe she was making a mistake in following her feelings for this guy? He probably thought she was a little bit of fun and recreation during down time. Okay, pardon the pun about down time, but, boy oh boy, this confusion was eating her up alive.

"Glad you could make it back," she teased as he hopped onto the deck and she accepted the two bags from him. "Thought I'd have to sail without you."

"Made a couple of pit stops," he answered with a heart-thumping grin.

She stretched her neck to peek inside one of the bags, but his amused chuckle and stern warning stopped her cold.

"Don't look in there. It's a surprise. Just put them in one of the coolers and I'll cast off."

He turned away and began untying the lines while she fought the urge to stick her nose into the bags. His occasional knowing glances tempered her curiosity. She wouldn't give him the satisfaction of catching her snooping.

Dumping the bags into one of the fish coolers, she climbed the bridge ladder into the wheelhouse where she waited until he was safely onboard before turning the ignition key. The boat roared to life. Pushing the throttle, she eased *Sweet Lies* away from the slip.

They moved slowly past many other fishing boats, lobster boats and tugs motoring to town to sell their daily catch. Most boats were smaller than hers but just as rusty.

Working in the fishing industry was a tough way to make a living. For most of these people fishing, lobstering and seaweeding were the only work they knew. Their fathers, grandfathers and ancestors before them had worked the ocean. It was in their blood. Just as it was now in hers.

Rain or shine there was always a haul for her to chase. Especially when her workers had bills to pay and food to set on the table. No air-conditioned offices in this neck of the woods. Only the cool breeze off the ocean to keep her company.

Emily recognized many of the men and women in the boats. Most wore the traditional black wool caps to keep their heads warm from the chilly November winds and all waved to her. Even Chance waved cheerfully or shouted a hello from his perch on the bow.

Soon the town was left behind, and they were cruising swiftly over the long ocean swells. A stiff breeze had blown up while they were in town and the bow of the tugboat bounced hard over the waves, casting a white, blinding shower of ocean spray along the sides of the boat. If Emily hadn't spotted Chance sneaking down below earlier, she would have panicked thinking he'd fallen overboard.

The sun struggled slowly past the horizon and she felt the first throes of the cold night air slam into her. Pulling up the collar on the red and black hunting jacket she'd thrown on minutes earlier, she nestled in for the half-hour ride home.

"How does a mug of hot chocolate sound?" Chance's soft voice caressed her senses and she whirled around to find him standing behind her, an uncertain look glued to his face as he held a steaming mug in one hand and a giant platter of food in the other hand.

"Oh my God! You went to Bernie's." Emily laughed as she recognized the variety of homemade square crackers, cheeses, thick slices of fruit and wedges of vegetables as well as the lobster and cream cheese dip she absolutely loved.

"You approve?"

"Of course, I approve. Bernie's is absolutely my favorite restaurant. But it's so expensive, Chance. You shouldn't have."

That look of uncertainty deepened and she felt guilty at having said that last sentence.

"I'm so glad you did though. I'm absolutely starving."

He grinned and slid the platter onto the dash beside her.

"It's to help make up for eating all that food on the night I snuck in. I realized you made it for the fair the next day and I felt guilty."

"I like the way you feel guilty," Emily laughed.

"I'll take the helm. You enjoy the hot chocolate before it gets cold."

They switched places and she eagerly wrapped her hands around the hot mug he held. She inhaled the misty chocolate aroma and then gasped when she spied the miniature marshmallows dancing amidst the thick foam.

"Mr. Donovan, you are spoiling me," she said as she sipped the hot liquid. Sweetness sparked her taste buds. "Absolutely spoiling me."

"You deserve to be spoiled. Especially after the hard day you put in today."

"I did have lots of help. You deserve it just as much as I do." Impulsively she grabbed a baby Gouda cheese and held it up to his sexy lips. "Open."

He did and she slipped it between his teeth, watching him chew. His mouth looked so appetizing and she found herself anxiously awaiting another kiss like she'd experienced this afternoon.

When he turned from studying the ocean and saw her watching him, embarrassment rushed through her at the way her thoughts were headed, she quickly avoided his sharp blue gaze and focused her attention back on the giant platter. She didn't want him to know what she'd been thinking because if he did and they picked up where they'd left off at lunchtime, there sure wouldn't be any interruptions way out here. Thank God, she'd put a couple of those foiled packets into her pocket before stuffing the remainder of the box of condoms inside one of the drawers in the kitchenette of the tugboat.

Picking up a cracker, she dipped it into the lobster cream cheese and shoved it into her mouth.

Flavor seduced her taste buds.

"I think I've died and gone to heaven," she said between the delicious bites of the expensive delicacy.

He threw her an amused grin. A sexy grin that made her insides quiver with excitement. With suddenly shaky hands she lifted the mug to her lips and took a quick gulp of the sweet liquid.

"You make hot chocolate exactly the way my husband's mother used to make it. Smooth, sweet, a dash of whipping cream in the milk, tiny white marshmallows and a generous helping of wine. Absolutely fabulous."

He didn't say anything, but by the way his eyes crinkled slightly at the sides, she knew he loved her compliment. She slid another cracker into her mouth and turned to look at the increasingly dark sky. Suddenly a flash of light streaked across the sky.

"Quick! Falling star! Make a wish!" Emily shouted. Scrunching her eyes tight, she made a wish. When she opened them, she found Chance's dark blue gaze upon her face.

"What did you wish for?" he whispered, looking both amused as well as curious.

"I can't tell you. It won't come true."

"Oh, come on. Give me a hint."

Okay she could give him a hint. Maybe she could learn more about him too.

"True love," she admitted, and noted surprise wash through his eyes.

"True love?"

"Yes. True love."

He shrugged his shoulders, looked out across the dark sky and the rolling white-crested waves. "I thought you'd wish for something different."

"Oh? Like?"

"I don't know. Something more practical, I guess."

"What would be more practical than true love? Don't you believe in it?" She held her breath as she waited for his answer.

"I do. What's your interpretation of it?"

She shrugged, quite surprised he'd ask a question like that. She took a delicate sip of her hot chocolate and savored the tart sweetness for a moment. "I don't know. What do you think it should mean?"

"I never thought about it. I kind of figured if you fall in love, everything just kind of fits right."

"Well...I think a relationship should be based on honesty. Trust. No secrets. No sweet lies."

Chance nodded. "Sweet lies. Like the boat."

"That's right. My uncle Jeb named her *Sweet Lies* to remind him not to trust another woman. You want to hear the story?"

His lips twitched in obvious amusement.

"Sure."

"He fell deeply in love once. The woman was the sweetest most innocent creature he'd ever laid eyes on. She was perfect in every way. Too perfect it turned out. She told him she loved him and wanted to marry him. Apparently, there was a problem."

"She was already married." Chance grinned.

"Hey, I'm telling the story."

"Okay."

"She was already married."

"Told you," he chuckled.

"My uncle found out through a friend that the woman's husband worked on some oil rig in Alaska. He confronted her and she admitted it. She admitted she didn't have the heart to tell him the truth. Uncle Jeb cut off any further chance of relationship right then and there because he figured if she lied to him once, she'd do it again."

"Sometimes people tell lies to protect other people," he said quietly.

"And to protect themselves," Emily replied. "There's never any good in keeping secrets and telling lies because they eventually come into the open and hurt twice as much."

Chance remained silent for a long time. Maybe he was thinking over what she'd said? Maybe he had some secrets in his past? Lies that had caught up with him?

"The island is coming up," he said, his comment breaking into her thoughts.

He eased back the throttle to slow down *Sweet Lies*. A moment later he slid the boat expertly alongside the wharf and she quickly jumped out and secured the lines.

A few minutes later they'd gathered the food and were heading up the stairs when he pointed out to sea. "I don't want to scare you, but it looks like we've got company."

Emily immediately saw the dark silhouette of a boat anchored about a half mile offshore. An uneasiness slithered along the entire length of her spine. "It might simply be a fisherman or Chad."

"Or it could be someone else Skip hired to spy on us. Let's get inside."

She followed Chance as he cautiously strode through the semi-darkness up the steep rock staircase that led to her home perched at the top of the cliffs. Every few seconds he threw glances at the mysterious boat. She had half a mind to send Skip a scorching phone call, chastising him for not trusting her.

Emily frowned at the thought. She shouldn't be mad at him. She had to tell him she couldn't marry him. Although by now Chad might have already relayed that message if he'd seen what Chance had been doing to her on the beach.

Skip had every right to know she wasn't in love with him and probably never would be.

Any normal, sane woman would be lucky to get Skip. He truly was a nice guy. Just not the guy for her. She was an oddball. She'd proven it by giving up a lucrative career in journalism to come back home to eke out a modest living slinging seaweed, all alone most of the time, on a rusty old fishing boat in the middle of a dangerous ocean. She wouldn't give it up for the world.

That thought smashed into her brain like a bullet. Wasn't that exactly what she was doing? Giving up the way of life she loved to move to the city, get married and have babies with a man she did not love?

Chance had been right this afternoon. She wasn't pursuing a dream. She was settling. There was a heck of a big difference between the two. God, why had she been so stupid that she hadn't seen it herself?

Goodness. She had gotten herself into one heck of a pickle, hadn't she? Teenagers breaking into her home, spying on her and a sexy stranger who made her forget her fiancé. What in the world was going to happen next?

. . ⤳ . .

FROM HIS BEDROOM WINDOW Chance stared out at the mysterious boat as it drifted in and out of the white mist out on the ocean. The muscles around his mouth tightened from the frown he'd toted since the conversation about sweet lies.

He had told Emily his share of lies and up until tonight he'd thought they had been to protect her. Now he wondered if maybe he'd been protecting himself too. He didn't want her to know the hell he'd been through these past few years. He didn't want to see the guilt push aside the happiness gleaming in her eyes. Guilt because she hadn't been able to help him. The overwhelming anger she'd feel at the bastards who had ruined their life together. Telling her the truth would only shatter the tranquility she'd created for herself here on Shipwreck Island, and if he didn't get what he came for and soon, then all his lies just might bubble up to the surface as she had suggested and blow up in his face.

He listened to the croaking of the water pipes as Emily finished her shower and then allowed his thoughts to wander back to that boat which was still there. Wearily he pressed his fingers to massage away the throbbing pain in his temples. Once they'd gotten into the house, he'd quickly made his excuses, telling her that he was beat and wanted to turn in early.

He'd read the disappointment and surprise flare in her eyes and it had taken everything to keep himself from pulling her into his arms and picking up where they'd left on that beach, but her safety was now his top priority. He also figured the sooner he went to bed, the sooner she would too, allowing him to make that phone call to Daniel. Maybe his brother could put out feelers to check out the guy who Chance suspected might be following him yesterday. *And what about that kid, Chad?*

The kid appeared sincere. He'd told them Skip had asked him to make sure Emily got home safely the other night and to keep an eye on them today. Why had Skip hired a kid? Why not a professional? Someone who wouldn't be easily detected. Luckily the kid had shown up when he did because if he hadn't...

Chance inhaled softly at the memory of kissing Emily and going down on her. It had been years since he'd been with her. The softness of her body pressed against him had totally thrown him off balance. Flattened snugly against his chest, the softness of her breasts made him bold. For a little while today he'd held heaven in his arms and then that gangly teenager had puttered around in his boat.

Just like the other night. If the kid hadn't found the laptop, then Chance would have it by now and disappeared before giving Emily a memory of a stranger who stepped into her life and would probably wreck it if he wasn't careful.

Instead he sat on his bed, waiting. Waiting for her to go to bed so he could search her room. Once again he peered out the window at the boat that bobbed against the dark horizon. Who the hell was out there?

· · ༄ · ·

EMILY'S DREAM EXPLODED and her heart pounded frantically against her chest as she saw Chance standing naked in the bedroom doorway. He watched her with lust-filled eyes while he leisurely stroked the length of his long cock.

"I've wanted you from the minute I laid eyes on you," he whispered, his blue eyes drugging her as he walked toward her. The heat of his body

splashed around her like a seductive blanket as he lay down on the bed beside her.

"You're so beautiful."

She shivered at his words. Trembled as he reached for her, his hot hands settling against her upper arms, leaning in to kiss her. His mouth melted over hers like fire, the heat spreading through her like lightning, igniting every nerve and fiber, sparking all her senses into overload. His tongue parted her lips and plunged into her mouth, bringing a surge of sexual hunger thrashing into her brain. Her tongue pressed against his, boldly mating with him and the pleasure rocked her to her very core.

She cried out in protest as his mouth slipped away from her lips, and his kisses drifted down her neck like erotic butterfly wings, over her collar bone and along the outside curve of her left breast.

"Oh please, suck my nipples!" she hissed. Arching her body, she whimpered as his mouth touched her, drawing her aching nipple between his moist lips. She loved the way his powerful sucks destroyed her self-control. He moved to her other breast, taking her there until her breast felt swollen and hard. She whimpered as his hands moved between her legs, parting her thighs.

Oh yes. There. Right there. Touch me. Fuck me. *And then his body was coming down on top of hers. She gasped as his thick swollen cock head speared into her wet vagina and she welcomed the stretch, loved the way he groaned as he thrust into her.*

Emily came awake on a moan and fully alert as if she'd never been asleep. Her arousal vanished and her senses were picking up something in the air. Instantly she knew she wasn't alone. Someone was moving about in her bedroom. Fear forced her to tense as a dark shadow moved in front of her window. In a split second she recognized the silent profile of Chance.

"Good God, you scared me half to death! What are you doing here?"

The sound of her whisper brought him instantly to attention. He drew away from the window, strode to the foot of her bed and gazed down at her. In the moonlight she noticed he was grinning, but the laughter didn't reach his eyes. Eyes filled with lust.

"Caught again," his voice sounded dark and sensual.

She scanned his broad chest, wide shoulders and his lean hips, realizing he was still fully dressed.

"Haven't you gone to bed yet?"

"No," he said hoarsely. "Thought I heard a noise, so I decided to look for the mace."

"Do you think someone's here?"

Alarm slithered through her and she made an attempt to get out of bed, but his gruff voice stopped her.

"Don't get up! I'm sure it's nothing. Just the wind."

"The mace is over here." She pointed to the night table beside her bed.

Chance didn't reach for it. Instead he headed for the portrait on the wall. "So, this your wedding picture. Steve wasn't a bad-looking character when he wore a tuxedo, was he?"

"He was quite a dashing groom," she admitted.

Although they had eloped in Vegas, she'd insisted he wear a tuxedo and she buy a wedding dress at one of the local stores.

"The bride in this picture is absolutely breathtaking. I wonder who she could be?" he teased.

When he turned in the semi-darkness, his smile widened into that irresistible crooked grin and her breath backed up in her lungs. The realization hit her like a thunderbolt. Chance stood directly beside the portrait of Steve and had an almost identical smile to Steve's.

Could this be why she was so drawn to Chance? Because of his smile? Because sometimes he reminded her of Steve?

Something deep inside her suddenly screamed at her that she should know Chance Donovan. Yet all she had to go on were these *déjà vu* feelings that crept over her once in a while and the overwhelming feelings of attraction that sizzled between them.

"Why did you really sneak into my house the other night?" she found herself asking.

"I told you—"

"That was bullshit and you know it. My brother-in-law Daniel sent you, didn't he? You're here because he thinks I'm in some sort of danger and you were supposed to keep a close eye on me and that's why he told you where my emergency key was."

He shook his head. "I should let you get back to sleep."

"Why can't you just tell me?" Desperation made her whip her blankets aside and swing her legs out of bed. Suddenly she wanted answers and she wanted them very bad.

"I've been patient, Chance. God knows I've been patient."

"Are you referring to what happened on the beach today?"

Her cheeks flushed with heat. He was talking about going down on her.

"Don't try to change the subject."

"Then you'd better crawl right back under those sheets, Emily, and let me leave."

He drew his gaze from her face, down the length of her neck and lower. She followed his gaze and realized the first three buttons on her nightgown were open, revealing the top curves of her breasts. Plus her hem was hiked up around her hips, showing him her bare thighs and panties.

In the moonlight she saw him swallow. Felt his heated stare on her and her heart thundered. In a flash, her sexual instincts kicked in. Big-time.

He wanted her. Now. Tonight.

She wanted him too. Big-time.

"Why did you really come into my bedroom tonight, Chance? Guys don't usually go around looking for protection in a can of mace," she whispered, knowing full well her question was an invitation to him.

He shook his head as if denying her offer and made a move to the door.

"I should go."

"Don't go," she whispered. He just kept on walking and her hopes plummeted. Hopes of having him in bed with her. Of him making love to her.

"At least let me return the favor you did for me on the beach today."

He stopped and swore beneath his breath.

"I'm sure you must be throbbing," she prodded. "Needing relief. Just as I am."

She sounded desperate. Her voice thick and husky. She didn't want to appear desperate. Especially if he didn't want her.

"Don't push me, Emily. Just go back to bed." There was a warning underlying his rough voice. A warning she knew she should heed. But she couldn't.

He stepped through the doorway.

She tensed.

"No strings, Chance." Okay, now she was really being an idiot. She couldn't sleep with a man and have no emotions afterward, could she? No, not with this one.

She held her breath as he stopped.

He didn't turn around as he spoke.

"Be careful, Emily. I don't want to hurt you."

And there it was. Her out. He would hurt her. She knew it just as she knew he would turn around and come back into her room, and that's exactly what he did. Turned around, stepped back into her room and closed the door behind him.

"I won't ask any more questions," she promised. At least not tonight, she added silently.

He stood stiff for a moment. She could hear his uneven breathing as he stared at her. Could feel the way he was fighting his self-control. Could feel him losing the fight.

Reaching down, she lifted the hem of her nightgown. Lifted the garment over her head and off.

Chance inhaled roughly and swore.

"I don't have protection."

"I do," she answered.

He looked surprised.

"I bought a box. In town today."

Her body ached as he moved toward her and dark hunger swept through her as she inhaled his scent. He smelled lightly of the ocean air and sweat. He smelled so good. He always smelled so good.

"You won't be sorry in the morning?" he asked as one of his hands settled on her bare waist and he drew her against him.

"Sore, maybe, but sorry, never." *Oh my!* Had she just said that?

His warm breath breezed against her mouth as he tilted her chin up with his forefinger. In anticipation, she slid her hands beneath his arms, bringing them up to splay against his shoulders.

"Sore, can be easily arranged."

Oh God.

He lowered his head and took her mouth like a man possessed. She literally saw stars when he crushed her lips beneath his with such a bruising force. He thrust his tongue into her mouth and his moan of satisfaction curled through her as she moved hers against his.

Their tongues dueled, got reacquainted from their time on the beach, making her feel so wonderfully hot. Just like her dream. But was she still dreaming? She found herself wondering that as she melted into his hard length.

As he kissed her, her body shuddered. She could clearly feel his erection pressed against her lower abdomen. His mouth intoxicated her, and his erotic groans unleashed all her pent-up lust for him. While he kissed her, she forced her hands from his broad shoulders, dipping down to his waist and then to the front of his jeans. She worked the button there, her hands trembling as it popped open and she pulled on the zipper. Trembling at the sound of the zipper lowering, her fingers touched his hot skin, making him inhale sharply into her mouth.

She pried the material apart and he groaned. It was a hot, silky sound that purred over her nerve endings. His heart pounded against her chest as she pressed her breasts against him, but she drew her lower half away just enough to dip her fingers beneath the waistband of his underwear. She found his cock. His body jerked.

She swallowed.

Sweet mercy! He was so hard. And so big. Long and thick. Anticipation hummed through her as she grabbed his swollen shaft. Beneath her fingers, she could feel the pulsing power. She squeezed lightly, feeling the velvet skin and steel beneath. Just as big as Steve, her mind shouted with joy.

She wanted to see him!

She was about to reach for the light when his hands speared through her hair and he broke the kiss.

"Damn," he whispered, his strangled voice tore from his throat. It was hoarse and filled with lust.

"I want your lips around my cock, Emily. Wanted it for so long."

She felt his hands drop to her shoulders, his palms like fire as he gently pushed her to her knees.

"Take me into your mouth, Emily."

Hot lust pooled between her thighs at his words. In the moonlight she could see his cock erupting from his pants, angling toward his belly. Could see the swollen sac beneath. His fingers came down over hers, holding his staff steady.

"Hold tight here, even when I let go." His voice sounded harsh now. Desperate. "It'll prevent me from going too deep. I don't want to hurt you."

She gazed up at his face. In the moon glow he looked fierce, almost savage in his need. Fear and excitement mingled within her and excitement won out. She nodded, understanding. Sensed he was fighting to control himself and that he was quickly losing the battle.

Opening her mouth, she leaned forward. His strong, pulsing shaft seared her lips. Branded her, and all her thoughts were spiraling. Gripping his shaft tighter, she took more of him into her mouth. The silky feel of his flesh was unbelievable. He came in until her lips were stretched tightly over his mushroom-shaped cock head and then her hands stopped him from entering more.

Wow! Such power. It exuded from his penis in throbbing waves. Made her pussy clench in appreciation. And in want.

"Emily, I want you—"

She didn't understand what else he said because she was hollowing her cheeks and pulling her head away, allowing his shaft to withdraw before she angled her head toward him again, bringing his cock into her mouth again.

Boy, she loved the strong feel of his flesh in her mouth. So hard and masculine. So erotic. She really could get into this. She heard him curse and smiled to herself. He sure did swear a lot when he was aroused.

Suddenly his hands roughly sifted through her hair, grabbing her, holding her head steady. Pinpricks of painful sensations screamed through her scalp. She found herself liking the erotic feel.

Tightening her lips around his shaft, she suckled him. He had a hot, salty male taste. Very nice.

She took her time exploring his cock and listened to his grunts and groans. She enjoyed the sensual shape of his cock head. Steve had been shaped like this too, she mused. Big and strong. Regret pulsed through her at never having taken her late husband's cock into her mouth. She pushed the unwanted emotion aside. He was gone and Chance was here. And she liked that he was here.

He began fucking her mouth in slow, even and tightly constrained strokes. Awareness buzzed between her thighs with his every plunge. She needed him stroking his cock in and out of her pussy. Needed him fucking her there too. Maybe even fucking her ass.

At that last thought, pleasure scrambled through her. Deep and heavy it pooled inside her vagina and pounded with insistence. She moaned around his cock at the sensual feeling.

As if sensing her needs, he withdrew his cock from her mouth, leaving her feeling empty, disappointed and shaking.

"On the bed. On your hands and knees."

She was breathing so hard she could hardly hear what he'd said. Anticipation screamed through her and she did as he instructed. She could barely stand, her knees felt weak, her body so hot. So feverish.

Sweet heavens! She'd never felt so odd like this before. Head rush, probably, she mused as she climbed onto the bed.

Had he truly said hands and knees? As in doggie style?

Shock mixed with excitement. She'd never had sex like this before. The bed moved as he climbed on behind her. Her breath became suspended in her chest as she felt his long fingers lash on to his waistband of her panties. He slid them over her hips and legs, and she lifted one knee at a time so he could remove the garment.

She arched as his finger found her clit and began massaging, zinging exquisite sensations into her. His finger was wet, he must have moistened it with his saliva, she thought. And she swore she was already on the verge of an explosion but held herself back, wanting to orgasm with him inside her. She could barely think as the arousal whipped through her. He knew exactly how to make her soar. Knew exactly how much pressure and how fast to rub her clit. Within seconds she was gasping and whimpering.

His hands settled on her hips like two brands of fire and he dug in. Held her steady. She cried out as he came into her vagina in one solid thrust. Burying himself right up to his balls. She didn't even have time to appreciate how long and swollen he felt inside her before he was pulling out and plunging into her again.

Once, twice, three times. Harder and faster. Her mind disintegrated. Her body tightened as the sensations grabbed her. She shattered on a cry, the sexual tension exploding like a bomb.

She came hard and she came fast. Her vagina greedily clenched around his cock as he continued his thrusts. They were powerful plunges that sunk deep inside her pussy, unraveling all the sexual lust she'd been harboring for him.

She was flying. Melting into the pleasure. Mind, body and soul. From somewhere far away she heard him cry out. Felt the hot, pulsing liquid fill her and she numbly realized they'd forgotten to use a condom. Oddly enough, that didn't matter right now. Nothing mattered. Just the exquisite pleasure pulsing through her like a wild drug. That's all that mattered.

Chapter Thirteen

E mily knew he was awake. She could hear it in the quick, unrelaxed way he breathed. Could feel it in the way his body felt tense against her side. Sensed his regret of having sex with her. Felt it coil through her like a sharp blade.

But she didn't regret what happened. Not one bit. She'd needed the sex. It made her remember how it should be between a man and a woman. Passionate. Fulfilling. Raw with pleasure.

"I should leave," he said from beside her. But he made no move to get out from beneath the covers they'd crawled under after their respective orgasms.

She wanted to tell him to stay. Wanted to tell him to fuck her again. She didn't. She needed to think this through. She'd just had sex with a virtual stranger and without a condom.

"I'm safe from STD's. In case that's what's worrying you," he whispered.

There he went again. Reading her mind.

"I am too. I don't usually—"

"You don't have to explain. I know you don't go hopping into bed with every guy you meet."

How did he know she didn't? She wanted to ask him that question but decided against it. He was just being nice.

"If I made you pregnant—"

"I'm on the Pill," she lied, and then realized he probably was wondering why she'd bought condoms.

"But I still practice safe sex," she replied quickly in order to reinforce his thoughts she was a nice girl and didn't sleep around.

"I...have a low sperm count so the chances are remote that you are. But just in case I would stand by you. I'm not the kind of guy who cuts and runs."

Despite a momentary pang of regret at his admitting he had a low sperm count she smiled into the darkness. Felt her heart warm at his words. She wanted to reach out to him. To tell him she sensed he was a very caring man, but it was too soon in the relationship. That is if she could call this a relationship.

Her tummy did a weird hollowing feeling at the confusion of what had just happened. What could she call it? A roll in the hay? Release of many years' worth of sexual tension? Confusion about her upcoming marriage? Okay, scrap the marriage. There would not be one now. If she'd been harboring even an inkling of doubt that once Chance was out of the picture she would pick up with Skip again, that idea was totally dead.

Skip was out of the picture. She would have to do a trip to New York and tell him personally. She owed him a face-to-face meeting. And poor Helena would be devastated. She'd poured so much money into the planning, but Emily would pay her back. It was the least she could do.

Despite all the heartache she would create by backing out of a marriage that should never have been planned in the first place, Emily felt better. As if the weight of the world were off her shoulders.

Beside her Chance moved and she realized he was getting out of bed. Her heart fluttered as she spied his naked silhouette stand in the darkness. The man was built with perfection, she mused as she watched him bend over and grab his clothes, giving her a nice view of his perfectly shaped ass.

Yes, Jen had been right. Chance did have nice buns.

As he turned slightly, she caught a glimpse of his long, thick, semi-erect cock and thanked God it was dark enough in here that he couldn't see the way her face flushed at the erotic sight.

Oh, his cock had felt so right in her mouth. Firm and hard. A swollen velvety heat that screamed of power. She'd felt that awesome power as he'd pistoned in and out of her pussy.

"Did you want me to leave?" he asked as he sat on the bed and slipped into his underwear.

His question zapped into her like an explosion.

"I mean leave the island." Translation he was leaving her bed, but he wanted to know if she wanted to kick him out of her home.

"No, I don't want you to leave, Chance." *I want you to stay and make love to me all night.* She should just say it. But she said nothing as he stood. She didn't want him to think she was begging him for sex. It would have to come from him the next time around.

"I'll see you in the morning then."

"In the morning. Another day of seaweeding."

She saw him flinch and found herself laughing.

"That is if you're up to it," she teased, feeling her confidence suddenly come back again.

"I'll be up to it. Good night."

"Good night."

She watched him leave. Watched the sultry way the moonlight splashed over his well-made upper torso as he strolled to the door. In the darkness, she thought she made out some scars on his back but figured it was just a play of the moonlight. A moment later she heard the soft click of her bedroom door as he closed it behind him.

Confusion welled up inside like an untapped spring as she found herself once again alone in bed. For a little while tonight it had felt so natural to have a man back in her bed. Normal to have a man thrusting his cock deep into her.

She pondered if maybe her taking his cock into her mouth had really happened. Or if she'd somehow dreamed that Chance Donovan had taken her from behind on the bed, allowing her experience one of the best orgasms she'd ever had in her life.

No, he'd been real.

The gentle soreness between her legs was proof it had happened and the way her lips continued to tingle made it real.

She'd just had sex with a man for the first time in over eight years. And for the first time in a long time she felt sexually satisfied.

Very satisfied.

• • ❧ • •

CHANCE PEERED OUT HIS bedroom window at the white waves crashing against the wharf below and felt the jagged sting of confusion slash through him.

He'd made love to Emily. It had been fast and furious. Full of passion and it was over too quickly. It hadn't been anything like he'd wanted for her. What he wanted was a romantic candlelight dinner. Some foreplay in the form of feeding her chocolate-dipped strawberries, spraying whipped cream on her pussy and eating her there until she was ready for his cock. He wanted a night of tender lovemaking. An unforgettable night of orgasms for both of them.

Instead it had been a bing, bam, thank you, ma'am, kind of sex. But it had been good. Really good.

Hell. It had been fantastic.

Now he just wanted more of her. More and more and more. He also wished he could tell her the truth. Spill his guts about being alive. Tell her he loved her so much that sometimes he couldn't even think straight.

Like tonight. Seeing her standing there in her bedroom, he couldn't think. He could only feel the need pulsing through his every fiber. The need to be with her. To love her.

Oddly enough, he didn't feel regret at having made love to her. Just regret at how quickly it had happened and then the way he'd left her bed. If he hadn't, then he would have started fucking her right then and there, condoms or no condoms.

He'd told her the truth about being clean. He'd had many tests to make sure he hadn't picked up anything in that prison. It was best to be safe than sorry, so he'd taken the tests to make sure he didn't have HIV or AIDS or any other type of sexually transmitted disease. He'd tested clean over the years.

But he had lied to her about one thing. He hadn't come into her bedroom looking for the mace. He'd come looking for the laptop after placing a phone call to his brother Daniel. But no one had been home, so he'd left a message on their answering machine there was trouble and he would call them back.

He'd banked on Emily being a sound sleeper as she'd been in the past. Obviously, she wasn't anymore. Unless he'd been noisier than necessary, subconsciously hoping she'd wake him before he could grab the disc and the laptop and disappear on her.

His plan of leaving after he found the laptop was growing harder and harder to stick to with every passing hour. He sensed it wouldn't be long before he finally caved in and blew her world apart.

In her bedroom, when he'd turned away from the wedding portrait to look at her, he'd been shaken to the core. She'd been looking at him with that familiar warm sparkle of love shining in her eyes. The same way she'd looked at him in the past, when he was Steve.

His heart had leapt with joy and he'd wanted to tell her everything. Then the rush of denial crashed through her eyes as she realized he wasn't Steve.

Yes, she'd been thinking of Steve. Unfortunately, he was dead, and Chance was the leftovers.

Despite the danger of being with her, he ached to touch her sleep-tousled hair. Needed to feel her delicate lips brush against his mouth as they'd done during the picnic on the peninsula.

She'd always possessed absolute power over him. From the moment he'd spotted her at the White House press conference years earlier when she was a newly hired cub reporter with *The New York Times,* and she'd asked the president a question. She'd smiled at the president's satisfactory answer and the breathtaking hint of dimples in her cheeks had totally captured Steve's attention.

He'd made it a point to get into the same elevator with her. He must have been staring too hard because she'd turned around and smiled at him. At that moment he realized he had already fallen in love with Emily Montgomery and he still was in love her.

· · ⌁ · ·

THE NEXT MORNING AT breakfast they didn't speak about what happened between them last night. It was embarrassment on her part. She'd never been this bold with Steve as to hop out of bed and practically beg him to fuck her. But Chance just seemed to make her desperate for sex.

He kept quiet this morning too as he eagerly chowed down the bacon, eggs and toast laden with the sweet, homemade blueberry jam her sister-in-law Jo made from the blueberries she'd picked this past summer over in Maine where she lived with Daniel.

Emily figured Chance wasn't mentioning last night's sexcapade because he probably regretted it happening. Maybe he felt as if things had happened too fast between them? Whatever the reason for his silence, she kept herself busy by packing them a hearty lunch and listening to the news.

The radio revealed the hurricane was still forecast to hit the Nova Scotia coastline tomorrow and expected to be downgraded into a depression once it made landfall. But before then another storm was expected later this afternoon. If they played their cards right, they could get a good seaweed catch, dump the contents at the warehouse and get back home by the time the storm hit.

When they ventured outside, they were greeted by dark, gunmetal gray skies with rolling black clouds that threatened rain.

Quickly they made their way down the stairs, which hugged the cliffs to the wharf where *Sweet Lies* was anchored. Out on the ocean a brisk, cold wind slammed into them, making Emily catch her breath at its intensity.

This northwest breeze promised them a cold day. The dark, choppy water made it difficult to spot the seaweed, so she suggested they work the beaches where piles of fresh seaweed had washed ashore from the wind. Manually they scooped the weed into baskets and dragged the heavy baskets to the boat, tossing the weed onto the net in the middle of the deck. Basketing seaweed was a technique used in the pioneer days before the use of horses and modern machinery, and with such abundance of it here, they would have a full haul by lunchtime.

Yes, it was unusual to have so much fresh seaweed on the shores, but over the years it did occasionally happen, and Emily looked forward to those half days of work. Unfortunately, today wasn't one of them. Time off would only get her thinking on Chance. But the net eventually did fill to bursting and she could no longer hold off on calling it quits for the day, informing Chance that if he wanted, they could have lunch in town today and save today's lunch for tomorrow.

He readily agreed.

Asking Chance to hoist the anchor, she climbed the bridge ladder into the tugboat's wheelhouse, noting her muscles ached as if she'd put in a full day's work instead of half a day. Suddenly all she wanted to do was deliver today's catch of seaweed to her warehouse, grab a hot meal in town and maybe have a couple of hours of gabbing over at Jake's with some beers with the local fishermen, catching up on the gossip. Something normal. Something routine. Just as she'd been doing almost daily over the years.

It was better than being alone with Chance. Chance who made her feel anything but normal or routine.

Unfortunately, *Sweet Lies* had other plans.

She had just turned the ignition key, eased the throttle forward and inhaled a nauseating lungful of diesel fumes, which the wind blasted into her face, when the engine sputtered and promptly died. She groaned, not believing her luck, and turned the ignition key again. The boat merely coughed and began drifting away from the shoreline.

"Uh-oh. Sounds like we're out of diesel," Chance shouted from where he stood beside the near-to-bursting net of seaweed he'd just winched into the air.

"We can't be out of fuel," Emily called back to him. She always made sure she had enough fuel before heading out. But, dammit, since Chance had come into her life, she'd been too preoccupied to bother checking.

"I'll go down and see what's wrong," Chance said, and waved as he went around to the back end of the boat, lifted the hatch to the engine room and disappeared down the hull into the belly of her boat.

Her heart pounded as she waited impatiently for him to return. He didn't know anything about tugboats, did he? But what if it was something serious? The engine was so old anything could go wrong at this point in its life.

"You're out of diesel," Chance called out as moments later he came out of the hold, crossed the deck and stopped at the bottom of the bridge ladder, hands on his hips, looking up at her. His mouth twisted into a halfhearted smile.

She opened the window and looked down at him.

"What? Are you kidding me?" He had to be teasing her.

"If I didn't know better, I'd say you staged this whole thing so you could be alone with me."

Oh God. Did he seriously think she would do something like that? Irritation rammed into her. She was not that desperate to have sex with him again. Was she? Okay so she did want more of what they had last night. Maybe that's why she was getting pissed off. Because he could read her so damn well.

Yes! She wanted sex. Red-hot sex with Chance. Any way he could throw it at her, she wanted it. Oral, finger, vaginal and whatever else they could think of.

She'd take him. And she'd love it.

Son of a bitch. Why was she suddenly feeling so hot for him again? She'd managed to keep her mind off him all morning, but the minute work stopped she wanted to be all over him.

"Chance, this is not funny. Just use the backup diesel drum."

His smile dropped into a serious frown that sent shivers up her spine.

"What? Didn't you check it?" Her anger flared.

"There is no extra diesel drum."

Oh damn! It would be all her fault if they got stranded out here. Heck, they were already more than fifty feet offshore, and the fog seemed to be getting thicker by the minute. It would be a long, cold swim if they wanted to abandon ship and get to land. And it would be a lengthy chilly walk back to her lighthouse.

Shit! She should have told him to weigh anchor again before going down to check on the engine. Heck, she should have done it herself!

"It can't be gone. There should be two drums. I put a full one down there a few days ago and the other was still half full. We didn't use that much diesel."

"I'm serious, Emily. It is gone. And the one barrel is empty."

Her tummy hollowed as she studied his stern face and realized he wasn't kidding.

"There should be a full barrel there and the other one should be at least half full. I can't believe it! Someone stole my fuel?"

"Can you blame them? With the way prices are these days?"

She sensed an underlying tenseness in his voice. Noticed his frown. He was worried.

"You think it might have been someone from that mysterious boat we saw anchored offshore last night?" she asked.

"Thought crossed my mind." His frown deepened. "Where'd you put the laptop?"

"They won't find it."

"You sound confident."

"You're acting too spooky, Chance. You make it sound as if someone has deliberately stranded us here so they can get a hold of that laptop."

"You said it, I didn't."

"You're thinking it. Why else mention it?"

He shrugged his shoulders and turned away to look out across the mist-shrouded waters. That's when she noticed the wind had died down and the thick, white mist had rolled in.

Okay, Emily. Calm down. Your mind is whirling too much. This is not the time to panic. Not the time to argue with him. They were too far away from shore now to drop anchor. The wind was dying down. If they were lucky, they wouldn't get blown too far out. But she wasn't going to chance it. If the wind picked up again and changed directions the gust could push them so far out, they could be in serious trouble from that hurricane out in the ocean.

She refocused her attention on Chance. What was he looking for? she thought as he continued to stare into the fog. In this thick soup he'd be lucky to see anyone to flag down for help. His jaw was clenched so tight a muscle twitched in his cheek. *Déjà vu* spilled over her at the sight. When Steve had been worried, the muscles in his cheeks had jumped in a similar fashion.

Shaking the weird idea aside, she reached for the CB.

"Do you know how embarrassing this is? For an old pro like me to get caught without extra diesel on board? I'll never live it down."

"What do you care?" Chance said as he kept squinting out into the fog. "You won't be living here anymore. You're selling out, remember?"

His rude jab made Emily mad and she violently clicked her thumb on the talk button.

"Mayday. Mayday. Mayday. This is *Sweet Lies* looking for some assistance off the north shore of Shipwreck Island. Anyone in the vicinity? Over?"

"Emily! Stop!"

His angry shout startled her, and she removed her thumb from the button. "What is wrong?" she asked as she looked down to see him shaking his head in anger.

"Don't call for help!"

"Why not?"

"Just don't," he said tightly.

His anger frightened her, and she turned around to replace the CB on the hook. With full intention of confronting him as to why they shouldn't be calling for help, she whirled around and cursed. Chance was nowhere in sight. Why did he do that? Here one minute. Gone the next. Just like a darn ghost.

"Chance?"

"Down here," he shouted from the cabin.

She found him there, searching the kitchenette's cabinets. His shoulders were tense, his frown now so severe her stomach did a couple of really bad flips she didn't much care for.

"What are you looking for?"

He didn't say anything but continued to search behind the stash of canned goods she kept in the cupboards for just such an emergency as they were in now.

"Are you that hungry?" Her attempt at teasing made his shoulders tense even more.

Not good. He was upset and it made her feel the same way.

"No, I am not hungry," he snapped, his face slanting in a way she could read his features. His frantic look sent a sliver of fear shooting up her spine.

"What are you looking for? Or do I want to know?"

He didn't reply, but his search intensified and then suddenly his arms stopped moving and he inhaled sharply.

"It's happening again," he muttered beneath his breath.

"What's happening again?"

To her horror he withdrew a liter-sized clear plastic bag stuffed with a white powdery substance.

"Please tell me that's sugar," she begged, knowing full well the bag was definitely not hers and it was anything but sugar.

"It's sugar."

For a split-second relief splashed through her as her mind frantically clung to the fact he was telling the truth. But the relief was short-lived as his wobbly smirk told her he was only trying to humor her.

"How'd you know you'd find something?" she asked, swallowing at the terrible lump of anxiety clogging up her throat.

"Just a hunch. I was hoping I was wrong. If someone removed the diesel, they wanted us stranded for a reason."

Okay, he knew something, and he wasn't saying.

"What the hell do *they* want us stranded for? And who are *they*?"

To her irritation, he didn't answer. Instead he grabbed a knife from a drawer, sliced a small hole in the top of the clear plastic bag, licked his finger and then touched the white powder. The powder stuck to his finger and he brought it to his tongue. His reaction was violently quick.

He spit it out, cursed and raced toward the tiny porthole above the bed. Opening the window, he carefully stuffed the bag outside. With his other hand he used the knife to slice the bag all th way open. Then he dumped the contents into the ocean, dropping the bag out the porthole too. When he turned to her, she shivered at the raw fear shining in his eyes.

"It's heroin. Better go check the wheelhouse, engine room and the bow area, Emily. Check everything. Cans. Drums. Pails. Freezers. Look anywhere where they can hide one- or two-liter bags. I'll check the cabin, the back deck and the roof of the wheelhouse."

She nodded numbly.

"Take this knife." He handed her the knife he'd just used. "If you find something, get rid of it. Do it the same way I did. Pour it overboard. Don't get any of it on the side of the boat. Don't get anything on you. When you've covered everything then wipe the knife clean of your fingerprints and throw the knife and whatever you cleaned it with over too. Go!"

She whirled around and headed for the stairs.

"Emily!" His sharp voice made her halt halfway up.

"Move fast. We're probably going to have company soon and they'll be looking for these drugs."

Shit! A drug setup? But why her? It had to have something to do with that boat they'd seen anchored offshore last night. The bastards planted drugs on *Sweet Lies* for some reason and she had the feeling Chance knew why.

She nodded again and her limbs trembled as she frantically scrambled topside.

Damp air greeted her, and she quickly scanned the white mist hovering around the boat. She saw nothing. Heard nothing but the wind and the waves slapping against the sides. That didn't mean someone wasn't lurking nearby.

Move fast. Chance's words echoed through her brain, prompting her into action. She searched everywhere. Cans, pails, drums, coils of rope, ice chests. Everywhere she could think where someone might hide illegal drugs. When she finished with the obvious places around the deck, she climbed up the bridge ladder to the wheelhouse and checked any cubbyholes. Thankfully she found nothing.

Climbing back down from the wheelhouse, she headed toward the gunwale and the hatch that led to the engine room. Raising the lid, she descended the steep metal ladder into the dark and oily smelling hole. Flipping on the light, she did a thorough inspection of the room. Just when she thought she'd covered the whole area, she spied something white and out of place peeking from behind the propeller motor. Blood curdled in her veins and with shaky hands she picked up the evidence and headed topside. Leaning over the portside, she sliced open the bag and dumped the contents into the ocean. The plastic bag quickly followed.

She began to search the bow area of *Sweet Lies*, checking behind the life buoys and wondering if maybe someone had tossed a bag or two into the tires of the tire fender around her boat when she suddenly heard the low hum of a finely tuned engine.

As she listened, she swore it was getting closer to them by the second.

"Chance!" she yelled.

"I hear them," he said from behind her.

Whirling around she spotted Chance holding another liter plastic bag filled with the white powdery substance.

"Found it stuffed behind the main mast," he explained.

"Dear God! Get rid of it!" she screeched at him as a round of panic slammed into her.

He moved quickly. Grabbing the knife from her hand he threw it and the entire bag overboard.

"Shit! It's the Coast Guard," he groaned.

To her surprise he pulled her against his body. Without warning he crushed his lips over her mouth. Unfortunately, she was so terrified she could only hang on to his hard, muscular arms until he decided to come up for air.

Suddenly a flash of bright light slashed through the fog and slammed against them, blinding her. She clamped down on the overwhelming urge to dive into the ocean.

"This is the Canadian Coast Guard!" A mechanical voice erupted from a large gray boat that emerged from the mist and gently nudged the starboard side of *Sweet Lies*.

Chance drew away from her and lifted his arm to shield his eyes against the light.

"We are boarding your vessel," the mechanical voice blared.

Chance smiled and threw a friendly wave.

"Did you cover everything?" he asked from the corner of his mouth.

"Not the entire bow."

He cursed under his breath then said, "Stick close to me."

She nodded and followed him as he strolled toward the starboard side where two uniformed officers were climbing down a rope ladder onto her boat. The first one was tall and seemed friendly as he smiled at them. The second man, Emily instantly disliked. There was something wrong with his eyes, she noted. He smiled, but the smile didn't reach eyes that were a cold blue.

"Hi!" Chance greeted the first officer as he stepped onto the deck. "You must have heard our mayday."

"Yes, we heard your call for help over the radio but couldn't get a response."

"That was me, sir," Emily said. "The radio is old and it's on the blitz half the time."

"What's the problem?" the friendly man asked as he began surveying the area around her deck. He didn't seem to be looking for drugs, merely inspecting her boat. Probably making sure it was safe since it looked rusty and beaten from years of use.

"We ran out of diesel and it's all my fault, Officer," Chance said. He acted as if they hadn't just found a bunch of drugs on her boat.

"She told me to put an extra drum of diesel onboard this morning, but I forgot. Too many other things going on. Too much work as you can see by all this seaweed we need to get into town. It never ends, I tell you. It never ends." Chance shook his head slowly and heaved a sigh.

"Do you mind if I get a drink of water?" The second officer, the one who gave her the creeps, suddenly stepped forward. He stared at her with those beady blue eyes and she found herself shivering with revulsion.

She felt Chance stiffen at the man's request and sensed Chance's hostility.

"Sure. I can get you a glass," he replied. He sounded so cool and confident that for a split-second Emily thought she might have actually dreamed they'd found a stash of drugs moments earlier on her boat.

"Oh no. I can get it myself." The officer began walking past them toward the cabin.

"It's this way, right?"

Emily nodded, not believing the audacity of this fellow to invite himself into her cabin.

"I'll show you," Chance said coldly, and stepped in beside him.

"Oh, no need."

"I insist."

An icy sliver of fear crawled across Emily's back at Chance's cold command. His jaw was tense, his eyes dangerous slits as he passed her and followed the officer into the cabin.

"Ma'am, how much diesel do you need?" the remaining officer asked. He didn't seem the least bit disturbed at Chance's insistence at following the other officer.

"About five miles' worth. It'll be enough to get us home."

"I'll get it for you. Back in a minute."

When the officer turned and hopped onto the rope ladder that led up to his much higher craft, Emily sighed with relief. After he was out of sight, she held her breath and listened for any sounds from *Sweet Lies*' cabin. From where she stood, she couldn't see into the salt crusted cabin windows but she did hear a couple of creaks indicating someone was opening the cabinet doors where they'd just found one of the bags of drugs.

Had the second officer used the excuse he was thirsty so he could execute a search? Her breath caught at that thought. Oh God, please don't let him find anything.

When a shadow appeared in the open cabin doorway, she jumped. The creepy officer walked out onto the deck. Thankfully his hands were empty, but the scowl he threw her way made her cringe. When Chance, toting an equally fierce look on his face, came through the cabin doorway, Emily breathed a sigh of relief.

A clatter of footsteps behind them captured Emily's attention and she turned to find the other officer jumping off the transom onto the deck with a small plastic jerry can of diesel fuel.

"Ma'am, here's the diesel. Where can I put it?"

"I'll take it," the officer who'd gone down into the cabin with Chance said quickly. He made a move forward to take the jerry can, but Chance was quicker and accepted the can.

"I'll take care of it," Chance said.

The officer who'd given the drum to Chance suddenly frowned at his companion's behavior.

"You can go back to the ship, Northam. You're not needed here any longer," the friendly officer snapped at the nasty one, obviously not liking the guy's attitude.

"Yes, Sir." As Northam departed, he threw another dark scowl over his shoulder at Chance and Emily.

"How much do we owe you?" Chance asked.

"Since this is your first time, it's on the Canadian Coast Guard. Next time there will be a hefty price for the diesel as well as a fine. Best be careful and keep extra fuel onboard."

"We will. Thank you for coming to our rescue. We sure do appreciate your help," Chance said.

"Glad to be of assistance. I also need to warn you about the storm brewing. Should hit by tomorrow. It's been upgraded this morning to a category one hurricane and once it hits Nova Scotia it'll be downgraded again. But it will hit your area here with fierce winds, so you'll do good to stay on land over the next couple of days."

"Thanks for the update, Officer," Emily said, feeling her legs begin to shake at their close call and at their luck of not being caught with all those drugs onboard.

The officer nodded.

"I'll leave you to your business then. Have a good day."

Emily held her breath as she and Chance watched the man climb the rope ladder.

A few moments later the Coast Guard's cruiser roared to life and disappeared into the curls of mist. Emily slumped onto a nearby cooler, her heart crashing against her chest like a battering ram.

"My God, that was so close."

"You stay here," Chance ordered. "Keep watch. I'm going to get the diesel into the system and then we're getting out of here."

He hoisted the drum a little higher on his shoulder and headed to the engine hatch.

Emily found herself looking up toward the white mist-filled sky to thank God that today hadn't turned into a horrible catastrophe.

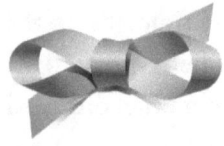

Chapter Fourteen

F ive miles later Emily shook from both frustration and anger as Chance helped her climb out of *Sweet Lies*. Quietly they tied the tugboat to the mooring, and he clutched her hand again before quickly leading her along the wharf through the thick mist up the rickety rock stairs toward her home. All the years she'd lived here she'd never been afraid of her lighthouse.

This afternoon, however, with the dark, menacing clouds looming overhead, it looked almost as if it were nighttime. Up ahead, at the end of the rock stairs on the cliff, the towering silhouette of her home appeared ghostly and foreign as the trails of mist hugged the octagonal white building. It looked down on her as if it might crash right on top of her. She shook her head at the silly thought.

She was tired from all the hard seaweeding this morning, weary from doing yet another check of the entire boat while Chance steered them back to Shipwreck Island and freaked because of the close call with the Coast Guard. As well, she was frustrated at being targeted in this way by someone putting heroin on her boat. On top of that, she was also angry at Chance for not trying to soothe her ruffled nerves.

He'd been totally silent on the ride back. After he'd taken charge of her boat and maneuvered them toward home, she'd checked around for more drugs, thankfully coming up with nothing more. She was nervous, jittery and ready to start crying as she imagined that maybe someone might even have stashed drugs inside the walls of her boat.

God! Was she being too paranoid? Or could someone have put drugs inside the walls? A drug-sniffing dog sure would find them and then they'd be in trouble. Anyone could be lurking around here in the foggy shadows. Any second a garrison of lawmen could appear from behind the scraggy pine trees lacing the rocky cliffs surround them and haul them off to jail.

She should have kept an extra container of diesel in the shed. Should have kept the shed locked so no one could get in. But she'd never locked that shed since coming here. Never had trouble with the diesel disappearing. However, since she was going to sell the lighthouse, she hadn't stocked up. She'd used it all except for the extra filled one she'd placed onboard *Sweet Lies*.

She should have asked for more diesel from the Coast Guard. She realized that now. What she'd asked for was enough to get them to her place but not enough to get to the main island and get some help. Even if they could get to town, to whom could they tell their story? The cops? They'd want to know what happened to the drugs. That is if they believed their story. With her luck, they'd execute a search of *Sweet Lies* and conveniently find more drugs.

She shivered at that thought.

"When we get inside, we'll hit the shower and crash for a while."

Chance's unexpected whisper almost unraveled her, making her jump in fright, and she pulled away from his grasp.

"How can you even think about sleeping?" she hissed to his broad back as he continued to climb the stairs.

"Any second the cops could storm this place and search for planted drugs. And with our luck they'll find them this time. Who knows who was in here today? There could be drugs all over my place just like on the boat."

"Emily, just relax. I'll check around."

"Not alone you won't. I'm sticking to you like glue."

Ignoring his concerned grin, she grabbed the back of his jacket, and as he unlocked the door, she braced herself, anticipating police in SWAT clothing jumping out at them.

Thankfully nothing happened and she followed him into her home. When he flicked on the lights, she scanned the kitchen. Everything seemed to be in place. Then again everything had seemed fine on *Sweet Lies* too until the extra diesel barrel was found missing and Chance discovered the drugs.

To her relief he reached around and took her by the hand. She followed him like a second skin while he checked the doors and windows. Everything was locked up tight.

"You'll feel better once you take a shower," Chance said as they entered the living room.

"Why do I get the feeling you want to get rid of me?"

He chuckled; the friendly sound of his voice made her feel just a bit relaxed.

"Go. Take a shower. Take as long as you need. I'll be right here when you get out. I'm sure the worst is over. Besides, I don't think anyone will be venturing outside in this weather."

He pointed to the windows where she noticed raindrops begin to splash against the panes. The wind was picking up too. She could hear the roar of the waves pounding the shores below.

"It looks like we made it back just in time," he commented.

Plopping himself onto the couch, he crossed his arms, kicked off his shoes and placed his stocking feet on the coffee table, appearing as if he didn't have a care in the world.

Looking over at her with that reassuring grin she truly loved, he winked.

"I promise you'll feel better when you come out."

Yeah, right, she thought as she headed into the hallway.

"Okay, but I don't think I'll ever feel relaxed again."

• • ◦◦◦ • •

CHANCE WAITED UNTIL he heard Emily turn on the shower taps before moving to recheck the windows and doors. He breathed a very small sigh of relief when he didn't find any evidence someone had jimmied the doors or windows. Not that it didn't mean someone hadn't gained entrance to the house. There were plenty of ways to get inside a building without being detected. So he took this opportunity to do a quick check around the place to make sure there weren't any drugs stashed here either. After doing a fast search of the first floor and coming up empty, he headed upstairs to his room and began to feel just a bit of the tension spill from his body when it passed inspection.

Someone was playing with them. Letting him know they knew he was back. Or warning him this time they were going to involve Emily and not just threaten to do it as they'd done over the years.

He inhaled deeply at the thought of Emily. She was exhausted. Strained to the max. He was surprised she'd even agreed to take a shower, but he'd figured it was the safest place for her to be while he checked around.

Visions of the movie *Psycho* suddenly danced around in his head. Wasn't there a creepy shower scene in that movie? A woman in the shower and a knife slashing through the shower curtains, stabbing her?

He gritted his teeth against the goose bumps racing up his spine and forced himself to shake those silly thoughts away. He needed to talk to someone who could calm him down. He'd call Daniel and tell him what happened today. Then he would tell Emily to call her friend Jen to come out and get them. Too bad Emily didn't have a backup boat out here. He hadn't seen one around, so he assumed she didn't. But he would ask her just to make sure when she got out of the shower.

Grabbing the phone, his stomach dropped in a gut-wrenching blow as he realized there was no dial tone.

• • ⚓ • •

"WHAT A DAY!" EMILY sighed into the hot shower spray, loving the way the wet liquid caressed her face as she tried to force herself to relax. Now she knew how Steve must have felt when the Coast Guard boarded *Sweet Lies* all those years ago. He must have been absolutely horrified at having them find drugs onboard and then stunned at being hauled off to jail.

She closed her eyes and felt the hot sting of tears crash against her eyelids. Thank God Chance had been around for her today. If she'd been alone, the Coast Guard would surely have found the drugs and she'd be in jail right now. Awaiting the same fate as Steve.

Thankfully Chance had known what to look for and what to do.

It's happening again. Chance's exact words while she watched him pull the white bag full of drugs from behind her *Sweet Lies'* kitchenette cabinet. He must have been thinking about Steve and how he'd been framed this same way. It looked like whoever had been behind Steve's frame-up had resurfaced. Why now? Why after all these years?

Questions with no answers. It was enough to throw her hands up in the air and scream in frustration.

• • ⚓ • •

"BEFORE YOU TAKE YOUR turn to hit the shower, I need to ask you some questions."

Emily's strong tone made Chance realize she wasn't going to let him let get out of not answering her questions this time around. This time she meant business. But when she noticed he'd placed a couple of blankets and a pillow on the couch he sat on, she frowned.

"What are you doing?"

"Thought I'd sleep down here."

She seemed to tense at the idea and a split second later she relaxed. He admired the warm flush of red in her cheeks from the shower and at how sexy she looked with tangled, wet hair.

She'd changed out of her work clothes and donned a cute violet-colored track suit that hugged her curves quite effectively. He tried hard to ignore the throb of appreciation his cock threw his way as he suddenly remembered last night. Of touching those curves, tasting her nipples and taking her from behind. Oh man, he ached to have her in his arms again tonight. Heck, right now too.

He swallowed at his suddenly dry mouth and cleared his throat.

"What is it you want to know?"

"How did you know it was the Coast Guard coming and not someone else?"

"Saw the emblem on its side as it pulled alongside."

"What if they weren't the authorities? What would you have done?"

"Grabbed you, dove overboard and then kissed you."

Emily's frown deepened. It appeared the shower didn't do as good a job in relaxing her as he'd hoped.

"Chance, be serious. How did you know those people weren't simply imitating the Coast Guard?"

"Emily, people don't go around imitating the Canadian Coast Guard. They infiltrate it. I was looking for a suspicious character. When the man asked for water, I suspected him and that's why I stuck to him like glue."

It wasn't the truth. Another sweet lie to protect them. The minute Chance had spotted the fellow, he'd recognized him as the same man who'd found the drugs on *Sweet Lies* years earlier. Whoever was behind this nightmare was using the same techniques and same people they'd used in the past.

They *knew* he was back.

"Someone tipped him off there would be drugs on my boat?" she said in disbelief.

He nodded.

"The Canadian Coast Guard is crooked?"

"No. Just one man. I think the next time we're in town I'll hit the library's internet and send my..." He was about to say his brothers and caught himself. "I'll send the McCullen brothers an email. Tell them what happened and to check into this guy's background. I'm sure they'll find something."

"You can use my internet. It runs on the phone line so it is quite slow or you can call them from here."

"Someone is probably monitoring your emails and maybe even listening in on the phone lines. It's better if I use a neutral computer."

He opted not to tell her about the phone not working and that meant her internet was down too. It would only add to her stress.

"Who are *they*? Why would someone tap my phone lines? Or monitor my emails? What the hell is going on?"

These were the questions he'd expected, and he already had his false story ready for her.

"I'm sure it has something to do with the transplant surgeon Steve was interviewing just before he died."

He noted the puzzlement cross Emily's face. He'd never told her how dangerous those interviews he'd done with the famous organ transplant surgeon had been. Had never explained he'd been doing undercover work for a top-secret government organization either. Interviewing the surgeon had been a ploy to draw the usually secluded man out into the open so the government agents could follow them.

It was time to tell her the truth about that secret part of Steve's life. He hoped that she wouldn't think too badly of him. But she had to know the danger they were in now.

"Steve wasn't working on anything that should have had someone frame him for drugs. I already asked his boss Helena, and she said there wasn't anything dangerous."

Emily frowned and sat down on the couch beside him.

"Helena didn't know. Steve was working undercover. He didn't want you to know how much danger he was in."

To his surprise, she held up her hands and shook her head. Anger flared in her eyes.

"Okay, just stop. How do you know all this?"

"His brothers told me."

He could tell by the tight twist of a smile that she was offended as well as frustrated at this new bit of news.

"And they didn't bother to tell me."

"They wanted to protect you. Steve promised you he had stopped doing dangerous assignments. What he didn't tell you was he had one left that he was working on. It had to do with a series of interviews he was doing."

"With that organ transplant surgeon you mentioned. I remember. Dr. Seth Martin. He's the same one Daniel was investigating undercover. Daniel killed him last year down in Florida. He had something to do with the illegal organ transplant trade and murdered a teenage friend of Daniel's wife and illegally harvested his organs."

"That's right," Chance agreed. Heck, she seemed to be taking this pretty well. He'd expected her to be angrier at being kept in the dark.

She flinched.

"Now things make sense. They were on to Steve. So, they planted drugs on the boat so they could get him to jail. But why go to all that trouble when they could have just killed him and tossed him overboard? Unless they were trying to ruin his reputation, and something went wrong in jail?"

"I'm sure they had their reasons for doing what they did." No use telling her how close to the truth she was. He was sure they were only looking to toss him into jail to scare him. The jail guards going ballistic and beating him half to death during the interrogation probably hadn't been planned.

He'd been cocky with the guards. Teasing them, provoking them. Hell, he'd been pissed off and scared shitless at having all those drugs found on the boat. Had thanked God over the years that he'd been the one on the boat that morning and not Emily.

If they hadn't covered up his beating with a suicide story, then the cops would have had a lawsuit up their asses and left no choice but to let him go. So, they'd given Emily his supposed ashes in the hopes she'd go away with her questions and his criminal defense brother Daniel would vanish too. Then they'd stuffed him in some prison infirmary until he was healthy enough to be questioned again and again over the years.

"What do we do now?" her soft voice cut into his thoughts.

"It's safer if you go and stay with Daniel and Jo."

She looked shocked at his suggestion. He hadn't expected anything different. She was an independent, strong woman who wasn't used to being ordered around.

"You've got to be kidding. I'm not leaving my home because of those assholes."

"Don't be stubborn about this, Em. This is serious. We'll take the laptop to their place and see if we can crack the password into it."

"So why do you think they want the laptop? They don't know about it. Chad was the one who found it..."

Her eyes widened with sudden understanding.

"No, you don't think Chad mentioned the laptop to Skip and that Skip is somehow involved in all this?"

Chance shrugged his shoulders. It was about time she knew Skip may not be such a great guy as they'd thought.

"The thought crossed my mind."

"But you're just speculating, right?"

"You mentioned someone had broken into your place right after Steve's death and his computer and other items were stolen. And then a second break-in shortly after. And now with the discovery of the laptop they realize we may have something important against them if Steve has something on that laptop..."

Emily frowned. "And if Chad did mention the appearance of the laptop to Skip and he is somehow involved in all this, then all this trouble with the siphoned diesel fuel and planted drugs is what? A message? That they are powerful enough to do whatever they want to me? So why not just break in and get the laptop? Why not just kidnap me and demand I tell them where it is?"

"For all I know they've already searched this place and found it. Have you checked if it's still where you put it?"

"I already checked before I went for my shower. The laptop is in the exact spot I left it."

A tinge of relief swung through Chance. Wherever she'd hidden it, it didn't mean they hadn't been here and possibly erased the contents of his hard drive and removed the disc then slipped the laptop back into its hiding place. The fact she'd been able to so quickly check led him to believe it was in the bedroom, probably in the wall safe behind their wedding portrait.

Cripes! Instead of checking the windows and doors and setting up a cozy bed for himself on the couch he should have seeing if that safe password was the same as the one they'd had all those years ago. He could have pretended they'd taken it and that would have been that. She would be in the clear. But even as he thought about it, he knew she was now in deep danger right along with him. They wouldn't believe her if she said she had no idea what was on the laptop, even if it did disappear. They would kill her just to make sure there weren't any loose ends.

And the two of them were big loose ends walking around. Unprotected.

He must be the biggest idiot for not thinking this entire thing through. He'd slipped away in the middle of the night from Daniel and his wife's protection without so much as hinting to them he was him coming here or telling them about the laptop. He should have confided in them that the possibility did exist his laptop might not have been stolen.

Ah hell, he'd screwed up royally. He had no excuses except to say he was selfish and was just thinking about seeing Emily again now that his new face had healed and the violent anger bursts he'd experienced since being freed had cooled with the help of counseling.

"I'm going to go and try to crack the password again. I think you were right earlier. I don't think anyone will be out in this weather," she said, and nodded to the nearest window.

He followed her gaze to where the rain ran in rivers down the panes. Man, he'd been so involved with checking the house he hadn't even noticed the weather having gotten worse. Once she went into her bedroom, he'd go for a shower then do a quick run to the adjoining lighthouse and check things in the lamp room and surrounding platform. Just in case he'd missed something.

He watched as she started toward her bedroom and then halted in the hallway, turning around.

His breath caught at her beauty.

"Give me twenty-four hours to crack this password. Then we call for help," she said, hope flashing in her eyes.

Twenty-four hours. Not that he had a choice with the phones out. Since Emily only had dial-up access to the internet, there was no internet service available either. He didn't have much choice but to agree to the twenty-four hours. In the meantime, when he got the chance, he would check to see if the phone lines had been cut or if the lack of communication was simply because of the storm. Truth was, anything could happen in twenty-four hours. If someone had cut the line, he would fix it and call for help.

"Twenty-four hours," Chance lied.

He noticed her shoulders relax slightly at his compliance. It sure felt good to know she trusted him and he felt better being closer to her tonight. Even if it meant sleeping on the couch.

"I'm going to try to break the code into Steve's laptop. I've put our lunch into the fridge. I'm not hungry, but go ahead and grab whatever you need," she said.

Chance nodded and stood.

"I'm going to take a shower then check around outside. Oh, and before I forget. Do you have an emergency boat out here somewhere?"

To his disappointment she shook her head. "I did have an old small motorboat until I gave it to Jen a couple of weeks ago since I thought—"

Her words trailed off and she grimaced.

He knew what she'd been about to say. She gave her extra boat away because she thought she would be getting married and wouldn't need it anymore.

"Just thought I'd ask. Go ahead. Take a nap if you need to too. You look tired. If you need something, come and get me."

"Thanks, Chance," she said softly. Instincts told him she wasn't saying thanks about him telling her she looked tired.

"For what?"

"For being there today. For knowing where to look for the drugs and for getting rid of them before the Coast Guard showed up...and thanks for being here. I feel much better knowing you're here."

Her words made him feel good. Too damn good, considering he'd just put doubts into her head about Skip as well as revealing he'd been working on one final dangerous assignment shortly before his supposed demise.

"You're welcome," he replied, resisting the urge to take her into his arms and tell her the truth about his identity. About how sorry he was for bringing all this shit down around her. But he kept quiet and watched her disappear into the bedroom.

Chapter Fifteen

Chance peered up at the living room's knotty pine ceiling and once again wondered if maybe he was dreaming being here on the island with Emily. For years he'd fantasized about it. Imagined himself back in this cozy little keeper's house, peering up at this ceiling while taking an afternoon nap or lying beside his wife after making love to her on the couch. For years he'd awakened and found himself staring at the round, black metal bars holding him prisoner, totally alone and feeling devastated that their lives had been so utterly torn apart.

However, over the past couple of days when thinking about his hellish past, trapped in prison, his thoughts didn't spark the usual raw anger. Something had changed inside of him by being here. Maybe it was partly due to the soothing salty smell of the fresh ocean air, the physically challenging work of lugging in the seaweed and the scenic rock-riddled and red sandy beaches that helped heal some of his inner turmoil.

Most of all though, it was Emily. Being near her, her letting him touch her and making love to her, gave him the confidence he needed to start living again. He owed her a lot of thanks. He owed her his life. Over the years of incarceration, just thinking about her had saved his sanity on many occasions.

He continued to stare up at the ceiling and lazily drifted in the soft buzz of warmth and feeling of belonging he found here. After his shower, he'd checked on Emily and found her fast asleep.

She'd looked ultra-sexy lying there on the bed. Curled into a fetal position, her hands tucked beneath her cheek. He couldn't get enough of studying the womanly curve of her hip, remembering how he'd held those hips last night. Held them tight while he'd fucked her from behind. Groaning at the way her pussy wrapped around his cock, welcoming him inside with his every plunge.

Nor had he been able to keep his gaze from drifting to her slightly parted lips and remembering how hard she'd sucked his cock.

While she'd slept he'd reached out and touched a silky damp strand of her hair, traced his finger featherlight down her cheek bone to her rose-colored lips. Lips both sweet and demanding. A lethal combination.

Slowly he'd lifted his finger from her face and held his breath as she nestled more snugly on the bed. She remained asleep.

He knew how she felt. He wanted to stay cuddled up, pretending that everything was all right. The truth was, if he didn't get her out of here, away from this danger, there would be no chance at a future for either of them. Covering her with a blanket, he'd tiptoed out of the bedroom, and finding a raincoat hanging on a peg near the side door, he put it on and went outside into the pouring rain to check the phone lines.

The slicker did wonders to protect him from the cold. He found the phone line easily enough, and thankfully it hadn't been cut so it was probably the impending storm that caused the problem.

He checked all around the base of the octagonal white lighthouse too, as well as the adjoining keeper house for anything out of the ordinary and found nothing. He also found no sign of anyone trying to gain entrance from any of the easily accessible windows. After a thorough search of the lighthouse, he came inside and discovered Emily was still fast asleep.

He ached to wake her. Craved to make love to her. But he held himself in check. She'd been through hell today and she needed as much rest as possible to keep herself grounded. In turn, he ate lunch in the kitchen and settled on the couch to grab a bit of rest.

.. ⌀ ..

TANTALIZING AROMAS of fresh-brewed coffee sifted through the thick layers of Emily's sleep and unleashed a memory of how Steve would start the coffee machine every morning. The peaceful vision made her wake up and reality crashed in around her.

Steve was dead.

And earlier today she and Chance had almost ended up in jail. She'd also fallen asleep while listening to Chance in the shower. Taking her mind off their close call, she'd begun to fantasize about the water splashing over his muscular body. Fantasized about stepping into the shower with him, taking his cock into her hand and guiding it inside her.

Emily moaned softly and tried to ignore the fluttery feeling sifting through her abdomen as she remembered Chance fucking her last night. God, it had felt so good. So right. But so wrong this morning in the bright of daylight. Yet so right again this afternoon after their narrow escape, and when she'd fantasized about him while he'd been in the shower.

Funny, after everything that had happened today, she'd been totally convinced she wouldn't sleep despite the weariness of hauling all that seaweed this morning. But she'd drifted off with Chance on her mind.

Blinking her eyes open, she glanced at the clock on the night table and started. It was way past lunchtime. She'd slept for a solid two hours and it would be dark in about three hours. She also realized Chance had thrown a blanket over her while she'd slept. That meant he'd been in here.

Erotic warmth curled through her at the thought. She wondered what she would have done had he kissed her awake and said he would make love to her. Heck, who was she kidding? She would have pulled him onto the bed right on top of her.

She smiled at that thought. Definitely would have kissed him hard and taken his cock out of his pants.

At the thought of Chance, she found herself wondering where he'd gone. The house was quiet. Yet the rich aroma of coffee hung in the air.

From the quietness she knew the rain and wind had subsided, but for how long? She felt so snug and warm here beneath the blanket, but the smell of coffee prodded her from her cocoon.

A few moments later she entered the kitchen and found the steaming glass pot set on the coffee machine heater and a note sitting on the counter. Picking up the piece of paper, she breathed a huge sigh of relief when she read the handwritten words, *Up in the lamp room.*

A strange feeling fluttered through her at the large, bold and confidently written words. They looked very similar to the way Steve used to write. Shoving aside the feeling, she headed to the freezer to look for something to whip up for supper.

•• ⤲ ••

CHANCE STOOD AT THE steel railing on the octagonal platform just outside the lamp room near the top of the lighthouse and peered out across darkening sky to the east. The rain had stopped, and over the past few minutes the wind had picked up again, whipping against him like a battering ram. He caught brief interludes of the decaying odor of seaweed washed ashore below as well as the foul odor of rotting fish. He could also smell the ocean salt as it intermingled with the sweet pine scent drifting up from the nearby stunted trees, which cradled the cliffs below the lighthouse.

In the eastern distance, out over the ocean, silver forks of lightning blazed from billowing black clouds, warning of the approaching hurricane. It had made landfall and would be here soon enough. Yet in direct contrast to the hurricane in the east, the western horizon was filled with color.

Puffy white clouds were streaked with pinks, powdery blues and pale violet as they drifted in front of the descending golden sun. The rays of sunshine illuminated the roaring ocean waves with sparkles of gold and light blue. The remarkable sight made him feel in awe of the beauty he was surrounded with out here on the tiny red-colored rocky island just half an hour north of Prince Edward Island.

After being away from here for so many years, he could now truly appreciate why Emily would want to raise kids here. Out here there were no snow-capped Montana mountains in the background like where he'd grown up, instead there were mighty clouds that looked like mountains. There were no endless green pastures filled with cows, or hundreds of acres of golden wheat fields shimmering beneath the hot sunshine as he'd experienced on the McCullen ranch-farm where he'd grown up, but this ocean scenery with exquisite sunsets gave him just as good a feeling of being home that the beautiful Montana sunsets and scenery had done when he'd been younger.

He was just about to ponder whether he should go down and wake Emily so she could get a look at this fantastic sunset when a sound behind him made him whirl around. Emily stood in the doorway with a tray of food in her hands.

"Here, let me get that," Chance offered. Before he could help her, she shook her head and set the tray on the wide windowsill of the lamp house.

"I might have slept through to breakfast if I hadn't smelled that coffee brewing in the kitchen," she laughed.

Heat scorched through him like a bolt of electricity as she smiled at him. Man, if he wasn't already head over heels in love with her, he would have fallen in love all over again just be seeing those cute dimples burst in her cheeks.

"Is supper out here okay with you? I have a couple of old lawn chairs inside the lamp room and we can watch the sunset out here over pizza and hot coffee."

"Sounds great. I'll get the chairs."

It only took him a moment and he had the lawn chairs set up in an area that was shielded by the wind and facing the glowing sunset. In moments they were seated, and he had a toasty plate warming his cold hands along with a huge slice of pepperoni pizza and a hot cup of steaming coffee.

"It's so beautiful, isn't it?" she whispered as she looked at the sunset. Her eyes sparkled with excitement and her cheeks and nose were already pink from the cold air. He was glad she'd donned a warm winter jacket and her black toque because he could feel it was getting colder by the minute out here.

He nodded as he wolfed down the hot pizza and groaned at the fantastic saltiness of the pepperoni exploding against his taste buds.

"Frozen pizza never tasted so good," he muttered between hearty bites and remembered that this type of pizza was one of her favorites.

"I wanted something fast so I could come up and watch the sunset. When we head back downstairs, we can have some fruit for dessert and I can toss us a nice seaweed salad."

He grimaced at the thought of eating seaweed salad and she laughed, her gaze sparkling with humor.

"I'll pass on the salad," he mumbled, and took another bite of the pizza.

"Oh, but you have to at least try it. I make a mean seaweed salad with croutons and Caesar's salad dressing."

He squirmed uneasily in his seat, not really wanting to see more seaweed let alone eat some.

"Really, seriously. I'll pass."

To his surprise she placed a warm hand on his knee and squeezed with reassurance before withdrawing her hand again.

"I'm only kidding about the seaweed, Chance. But I will whip up a regular Caesar's salad for us. You'll love it. I guarantee it."

I love you, Emily. Not your seaweed pie or your seaweed salad but you. God, he wished he could just blurt it out and tell her. Instead he chowed down more of the quickly cooling pizza and followed her gaze out to where the hurricane hovered.

"When the pizza was in the microwave I was listening to the radio. They say the hurricane has been downgraded to a tropical depression. It's over Nova Scotia now and it'll pack a punch sometime tonight. We'll probably be out of electricity by then and the generators will kick in automatically."

Unless whoever stole their diesel had helped themselves to the fuel for the generator as well, he mused to himself. He would have to go into the small generator shed on the back deck to make sure there was fuel available.

"I checked the phone. It is down. So no internet either. No telling how long the phone will be out. Could be days. I came up with an idea on how we can get some help," she said.

The sad sound of her voice made Chance stop chewing and he suddenly got the feeling he wasn't going to like what she was about to say.

She continued. "It's a long shot. But I'll tell you after we finish dinner. If I talk about it now, I'll lose my appetite."

He detected the tears glistening in her eyes and opted to do as she asked. He turned his attention to the sunset and things suddenly didn't seem as beautiful as they were a minute ago.

•• ⚓ ••

WITH SADNESS IN HER heart and thick emotion clogging her throat, Emily watched Chance untie the ropes holding her boat securely against her wharf.

Although there was still a couple hours' worth of good daylight left, she knew the chances were slim that someone would see anything wrong with her boat floating out on the ocean. Hopefully though, they might get suspicious that something might be wrong if they noticed it going out to sea instead of heading inland and that no one was in the pilothouse steering the tug.

"Are you sure you want to do this?" he shouted into the wind as he held the last of the lines in his hand and waited for her okay.

She swallowed back her tears and forced herself to nod.

He frowned and threw the lines into the boat. Her boat and the full cargo of seaweed they'd worked so hard to gather this morning caught in the stiff wind and quickly drifted away.

One foot. Three feet. Six feet. Nine feet. Her uncle's old tugboat was heading directly toward the rolling black clouds that might destroy it. But hopefully if everything went right it would save them and someone would recognize her, board her and alert the authorities that something was wrong.

"Do you think it'll work?" Chance asked.

"I don't know. The wind direction is almost right. I know a lot of true fishermen would have been out today looking for their catch like we were and they'll be heading back to the mainland about now. Hopefully *Sweet Lies* will get blown into the shipping lanes and someone will recognize she's going the wrong way before the main storm hits."

"What if she falls into the wrong hands? Are you sure you're prepared for that?"

Her breath caught at his words. Yes, she'd thought of that possibility. For all she knew, this would be the last time she'd ever see *Sweet Lies*. Anyone could find her and decide to lay claim to her. They would refit her, repaint her and take her for their own. Even worse, whoever had planted the drugs on her boat could find *Sweet*

Lies and come straight back here. That's why they'd opted not to leave a note of help inside.

As if sensing her sadness, Chance placed his strong hands on her shoulders and squeezed reassuringly.

"Even if no one recognizes her out there and the bad guys don't see her berthed here, they might think we aren't here and not come ashore. It's a good plan all the way around, Emily. You did good in thinking of it."

She nodded, feeling anything but good as she watched the boat drift toward the point.

"Or she'll get dragged out to sea, or capsize against the rocks and be lost forever," she whispered and watched *Sweet Lies* disappear around the point and felt as if the boat was disappearing from her life forever.

He didn't say anything. She knew he was thinking the same thing.

· · ᗡ᠊᠊ · ·

THE SADNESS AT THE loss of her boat still clutched painfully at Emily's heart. Even concentrating on trying to crack the password was useless as she kept casting glances at the bedroom windows and the looming grayness outside.

After releasing her tugboat to whatever fate it would encounter, they'd headed back into the house. Chance had asked her to delay making the Caesar salad as he wanted to head back up to the lamp house to keep an eye out for boats. Grabbing some fruit, he'd taken off.

More than an hour had passed, and it was getting gloomier by the minute. Soon it would be completely dark, and if no one came, they would be here for the duration of the storm, which according to the newscasts would last a good twenty-four hours with high winds being forecast for up to several days afterward.

She wondered if someone would spot her boat before it was pulled forever out to sea? Would someone come to the island and take them away? She'd told Chance she didn't want to leave her home, but now that she'd had time to think on it, she did want to get out of here. She was nervous and anxious, and she didn't like this feeling at all.

The wind was howling. Giant waves pounded the shores below her lighthouse with such ferocity she swore she could feel the bed where she sat cross-legged with the computer in her lap shaking ever so slightly. She didn't think there had ever been such a bad storm. But she knew she could be overreacting because of what happened today with the drug plant on her boat. She could also be feeling a bit uneasy because Chance wasn't nearby in case someone decided to break in. That's probably his real reason for being up in the tower. To make sure they didn't get any surprise visitors.

Refocusing her attention to the laptop, she sighed with annoyance at the *Access Denied* words. She'd tried every password she could think of and nothing worked. Now her eyes smarted from staring at the computer screen, yet her mind and hands ached to keep busy so she wouldn't concentrate on her anxiety.

It seemed an eternity since Chance had shown up at her place. A lifetime. As if he'd always lived here with her. As if...Steve had never left. She stopped herself. Her thoughts were going haywire. Chance Donovan and Steve McCullen were two totally different men with similar personalities. In this world it was quite possible two men could be similar, wasn't it?

He had a comparable grin to Steve. Almost identical color of hair with the same golden highlights. His chin had a cleft, whereas Steve didn't. His face was different. And his eyes were a different color. Yet the rest of his profile looked eerily the same to Steve.

A muscular build. Wide shoulders. Lean hips. Powerful thighs.

Although it had been dark last night when he'd come to her room and she'd taken him into her mouth, she knew his cock was the same size as Steve's. And the way he'd thrust into her pussy had a similar rhythm to Steve.

She moaned out loud at the thought of how hard and perfectly he'd plunged into her. Long, deep strokes that had her orgasming and exploding within moments. Her pussy throbbed and clenched in remembrance, making her want to start masturbate right here on the bed. It certainly would take her mind off things, wouldn't it? she mused.

But she couldn't masturbate. Not with Chance around. He could come in anytime and catch her.

She smiled to herself wondering what he would do if he found her lying naked on her bed, her legs spread wide and her fingers rubbing her clit and plucking her breasts.

Would he climb onto the bed and start fucking her? Or would he think her pathetic for displaying herself like that to him?

Okay. Stop! She needed to think of something else besides Chance.

Flicking off Steve's laptop, she got off the bed and headed for the wall safe behind her wedding portrait. She needed to do something else to keep her mind occupied and she knew just what to do.

·· ⚓ ··

EMILY SET ABOUT CLEANING her home with a vengeance. She'd vacuumed the first floor, lugged the vacuum cleaner up the narrow stairs to the loft, cleaned the rugs and then under the bed. She was about to turn and leave when she spotted a lip balm container sitting on the windowsill of his room.

She couldn't help but smile as she remembered Steve also needed lip protection from the fierce winds. Her gaze dropped to Chance's green duffel bag. It was still propped against the wall where she'd placed it the morning after he'd arrived. Apparently, he was one of those men who didn't like to unpack.

Looking down at it, she shook her head. Didn't he realize all his damp clothes needed to get dried? They would be smelly now, sitting in the damp bag. She'd have to wash them. Her gaze dropped to the chair where he'd draped the clothing he'd used belonging to Steve. With all the excitement she'd forgotten to tell him to bring down the clothes that needed washing or drying.

Opening the drawstring to the duffel bag, she lifted out two wrinkled shirts and a pair of heavy track pants then heard a strange rattle at the bottom of the bag. Digging past some underwear, she gasped when she spied three pill bottles.

A shiver of unease curled through her as she withdrew one. She didn't recognize the name of the drug being prescribed nor did she recognize the name Richard Call on the label. Reaching inside the bag again she took out the other two bottles.

One read Prednisone. The other said Cyclosporine.

A shiver of alarm ripped through her as she remembered why people took these types of medications. Both were anti-rejection drugs for organ transplant recipients.

Why would Chance Donovan have anti-rejection drugs for a man named Richard Call?

Looking into the bag, she saw a brown leather wallet. Digging it out, she flipped it open. Right there on one side of the wallet in a plastic window was a driver's license for a man named Richard Call. Her mouth dropped open in shock when she saw a very familiar man's picture on the license.

Why on earth wouldn't Chance Donovan tell her his real name was Richard Call?

• • ༄ • •

CHANCE SHIVERED AS he stepped into the lamp house from the outside terrace of the lighthouse. It was damn cold out there and getting colder. Blasts of rain shot against the windows like bullets and he jumped as a silver bolt of lightning zig-zagged out of the black sky about a third of a mile to the north. Thunder followed, crashing around him like an explosion.

He grimaced at the racket. That was too close for comfort, he mused as he flicked off the inside lights of the lamp house and headed into the cold, damp stairwell that would lead him down to the keeper house and to Emily.

At the thought of Emily, he picked up his pace. He hoped she wasn't fearful of the storm. In the past she hadn't been afraid. She'd grown up with violent ocean weather and was as tough as nails when it came to howling winds and pummeling rainstorms. He just hoped lightning wouldn't strike the tower and burn this place down and spread to the attached keeper house.

Okay, stop toying with these scaredy-cat thoughts, my man, or Emily will think you're a wimp, he pondered, and found himself grinning at that thought. Wimps wouldn't get far with his strong wife. So he'd better act just as tough as she was when he got down there or she'd have a field day teasing him.

He was halfway down the stairs when the several bare light bulbs, which illuminated the steep stairwell flickered to brown and then brightened into a yellow glow again. Another jolt of thunder exploded around him.

He stopped and held his breath as a sense of foreboding snapped through him. He'd forgotten to check the generator to make sure there was fuel. He should have done it earlier, but he'd forgotten with hanging out in the lamp house, waiting to see if anyone came as a result of the tugboat floating out there on the ocean.

But in the way the winds had picked up into a violent pitch over the past half an hour and now the darkness and the storm lashing the island, he doubted anyone would venture out here. Emily's tugboat was tough and seaworthy, but with no one at the helm aiming it in the right directions against the huge waves it had probably capsized in the increasing swells and was lying at the bottom of the ocean.

Visions of the movie *Perfect Storm* flipped through his head. He'd watched that movie on Daniel and Jo's DVD player just a couple days before he'd come here. It had been a good movie. The boat that the actor named Clooney had piloted reminded him of Emily's tugboat and the ocean scenes made him homesick for this island and, oh hell, he'd wanted to be with Emily.

Sadness swept through him as he thought how the loss of *Sweet Lies* would put a crimp into Emily's plans for expanding her seaweed business. On top of that, she'd worked so hard today raking the weed on the beach and hauling those filled baskets onto the boat. The thought of her losing the tug and the haul was probably making her feel like shit tonight. Just as it was making him feel bad.

Sighing, he pulled the collar of his jacket up around his neck. It was definitely getting colder. When he pushed open the lighthouse door, an icy blast of wind slammed into his tender face, making him wince.

And then he noticed something out of the ordinary. The lights in the keeper house were off.

Gazing back inside the stairwell he'd just come down, he only saw blackness. The electricity had just gone off. If the generator was in good working order it would kick in within seconds and the outside lights would come on.

He stood at the doorway and watched lightning streak out of the sky about a quarter of a mile away. Thunder crashed and shook the wooden deck beneath his feet.

But the lights didn't come back on.

Dammit!

Stumbling into the wild wind and pummeling rain, he shut the door behind him and waited for the next flash of lightning. It came quickly and he oriented himself. Luckily right in front of him the deck railing hovered into view and he grabbed a hold of it. The cold metal felt icy beneath his fingers and sent a volley of shivers coursing up his back. This time he didn't have the raincoat for protection, and he was drenched in cold wetness within seconds. Stumbling along the railing, he winced as the wind screamed in his ears and the precipitation stung his face like a bunch of bees.

Shit! This storm was certainly going to be a bitch. He couldn't see a thing as the rain and darkness virtually blinded him. Hopefully he was going in the right direction. If not, then he could most likely end up falling off the cliffs into the roaring surf below, his drowned body carried out to sea.

Okay, enough of those bullshit thoughts. Stay focused. The railing was solid and aside for the opening to the stairs down to the ocean, it would lead him to the generator shed.

Using his memory, and with the help of the silver flashes of lightning, he moved quickly. Glancing over the railing, he caught his breath as the giant white-capped waves pummeled the beach and huge dock below. For a second, he thought he saw a figure moving along the wharf toward the shed. But it was gone so quickly he had to believe it was just a figment of his imagination.

He picked up his pace, and a few moments later the guardrail stopped and his hand touched the wooden shed housing the generator. Ripping open the door, it was almost yanked out of his grasp due to the violent winds. Quickly he stepped inside the musty, damp room, welcoming the refuge from the wild wind and pouring rain.

Years ago, he'd placed a self-generating battery-less flashlight on the shelf just inside the door for such emergencies. He hoped it was still here. Running his fingers along the black wall, he found the shelf and sighed with relief as his numb fingers wrapped around the frosty handle of the metal flashlight.

He'd found it. But would it still work after all this time?

Feeling the small crank on the side of the flashlight, he grabbed it and turned it few times. Damn, but it worked! The yellow light flickered and burst to life.

He shone the light around the murky shed to the generator in the far corner. A second later he opted to yank on the starter rope instead of wasting precious moments checking the fuel, praying the generator would work. To his surprise the old relic wheezed and puffed to life. A long second later obscene gas fumes permeated the air.

Why the generator hadn't come on was something to worry about another time. The fact it was working, and the nearby jerry can was full made him grateful whoever had screwed around with the boat fuel hadn't been sabotaging the generator.

Opening the door, he smiled at the outside lights splashing through the silvery rain, illuminating everything in sight. Leaves and sand peppered his face as came out of the shed. Closing the door firmly behind him, he rushed across the deck and let himself into the lighthouse.

"Emily!" he called out as he tossed his wet jacket onto a peg just inside the door and removed his soaked shoes and socks. "That's one hell of a storm out there! I'm going to take a shower and get rid of this chill!" he called as he started unbuttoning his wet shirt.

He padded down the hallway and stuck his head inside her bedroom. The laptop sat on the bed but no Emily. And the house seemed awfully quiet.

"Emily!" he called out as a fringe of uneasiness snapped through him.

No answer.

Damn! Where was she?'

Maybe upstairs in his room? Had she been snooping through his things? A rush of urgency pushed him to head upstairs. But she wasn't here either. Back downstairs, he called out several times, but she was nowhere to be found.

Panic edged away his uneasiness. Had someone come and taken her. In this weather?

Is that what he'd seen down there on the wharf? Someone taking Emily? Or had it been Emily? He gazed at the pegs where she kept the raincoats and array of sweater on a string of pegs. Her raincoat and her rubber boots were missing.

Shit! Why in the world would she go down to the beach in this weather? She knew how dangerous it could be.

Okay chill! he admonished himself. He had to keep his head. Needed to get his shoes back on. Needed to get something dry to wear and go out and look for her.

Grabbing an old sweater off the peg, he struggled into it. It was small but warm and would help keep his body from going into hypothermia out there. Yanking the raincoat he'd used before off the hook, he grimaced at the soggy feel of his bare feet slipping back into the wet shoes.

He rushed outside and caught his breath at the fierceness of the storm. Rain and wind continued to lash against him, and despite the roar of the pounding surf below the cliffs and the crash of waves rolling onto the beach, he continued to call out her name as he made his way down the dangerously slippery rock steps, hoping to hell he'd made a mistake in thinking she was here and that he'd missed her when he'd gone into the generator shed and maybe she'd just gone up the tower to look for him. Instincts told him that wasn't the case. Now more than ever he believed he'd seen someone down on the beach earlier. That someone had to be Emily.

Fuck! He was going to give her so much shit for coming down here alone in this storm. All around him lightning danced a dangerous dance. Blades of silver forked through the sky, zapping into the ocean. Thankfully they'd installed lamps along the stairs as well as a couple of lamp posts down by the wharf. Despite the half-decent lighting he held tight to the flashlight. Just in case the generator died.

He shouted her name again as he stepped off the bottom step and started toward the wharf, squinting and cursing as the sand painfully peppered his face. Christ! She could be anywhere. She could even have...

Chance clamped his jaw shut. No, he wouldn't think about that. Emily was fine. She had to be.

And then, just as if he'd willed it, he saw Emily. Her bright yellow raincoat looked like a beacon of light. She sat on the picnic table in front of the debilitated wooden shack at the end of the wharf. She was hunched over as if in pain, cradling her face in her hands.

"Emily?" he called out, feeling both anxiety and relief rip at his guts to see she was okay. Taking care not to slide on the slippery wet wharf planks, he began to make his way toward her.

She turned at his voice, but her hands still covered her face.

"Chance! I've got something in my eyes!" she screamed.

"Give me your hands!" he shouted.

She didn't move and he figured maybe she hadn't heard him above the drone of thunder. Beneath his feet the wooden planks trembled with every crash of the waves and he hoped to hell the wooden structure he'd braced the other day would hold on until they were back on land.

Impatience raced through him as he watched her continue to cradle her face with her hands. Dammit! He couldn't check her eyes now. It was too dangerous out here.

Grabbing her elbow, he hauled her off the picnic table. Ignoring her surprised screech, he swept her into his arms. She seemed as light as a feather as he carried her quickly along the pier, bracing himself against the pummeling gusts of wind that threatened to blow them into the churning waters nearby.

The harder the wind blew, the angrier he got. How the hell had she been able to get this far without being tossed into the ocean? She should know better than to come out here in this kind of weather. What was wrong with her?

Overhead, the buttery yellow string of metal lamps shone fiercely through the silver downpour and he was able to gaze down at her face. The hood from her raincoat had blown down and her hair was wet and matted. He could tell her skin looked red from being beaten by the cold wind and her eyes were scrunched tight due to whatever had gotten into them. Her lips were slightly parted and he noticed her teeth were chattering. Her body trembled against him from the cold, or maybe it was from fear at her close call. Despite his concern about her eyes, he couldn't help but notice how nice she felt cuddled against him as he carried her up the steep stairs and across the deck.

Yanking the door open, he pushed-carried her inside and placed her on her feet.

He froze when he noticed how truly red her face was.

"You look like a damn lobster!"

She flinched at his shout but then smiled as if enjoying his anger.

"At this moment I wish I were one dangling over a pot of boiling water. I'm so cold and my eyes are stinging like mad. Sand from the beach got into them."

Her eyes remained closed, tears mingling with the rain.

He jumped into action. Prying open her left eyelid, he gazed into her bloodshot eye and then quickly checked the other.

He sighed with relief, "You're right. It's sand."

The clicking of her teeth chattering together made him burst into action. Prying off her raincoat, he began to lead her down the hall.

"We can clean your eyes out in the shower. What the hell were you doing out there?" he asked as once again anger brushed through him like a red-hot torch.

"I forgot to shut the shutters on the shed down by the wharf. I knew if I didn't shut them the wind would blow out the windows and probably shove the old shed out to sea too. I guess I shouldn't care so much about the building. But my uncle built it and it has sentimental value. Oh boy, listen to me moan about this place and here I was all ready to sell."

She inhaled and continued talking despite her chattering teeth. He wondered if maybe her chattiness was due to shock.

"I didn't think it would get this bad this fast. I'd just finished closing the shutters when a blast of wind blew the sand up from the beach and hit me square in the face. I managed to get to the picnic table and thought I'd better stay there until I could get the sand out. But then the lights went out and no matter how hard I tried to get the sand out of my eyes I couldn't see..."

Her voice lowered to a lusty whisper that made Chance's breath catch.

"And I knew you'd come to my rescue again."

Come to her rescue. Like a fucking hero. He was far from being a hero by bringing danger into her life. Anger sparked his already short fuse and he ushered her quicker down the hall toward the bathroom.

Flicking on the lights, he suddenly realized how shaky his legs felt as he led her into the room. Man, she'd scared the shit out of him disappearing like that.

"Stay right here," he instructed, trying to ignore the crisp edge to his voice. Making sure she stood still, he turned on the hot and cold faucets until he had the right mix of heat for her.

"Okay, I can leave you here and you can get off your clothes..."

"I think I need you to stay," she whispered, and smiled. His stomach did a rather interesting flip that he really like when she smiled at him this way.

Sultry. Sexy.

Oh fuck. If he stayed here and helped her undress, he couldn't be responsible for what happened between them. Could he?

"I mean, I can't see, so how can I get undressed?"

There, she was smiling and it wasn't a friendly thank-you smile. The cute way her lips were curved made his cock harden in remembrance at how fantastic she'd done oral on him.

Man, didn't she know what a lethal smile she had?

Suddenly he was unable to speak. Unable to think as he got her message loud and clear.

She wanted sex. Shower sex.

Oh boy.

Chapter Sixteen

C hance's erotic male scent invaded Emily's nostrils like a jolt of intoxicating fire and she reacted. Boy! Did she ever react!

Sensations sizzled into her abdomen. Wild heat melted through her breasts and she swore she could feel them tighten against her clothing. She suddenly wanted him so bad her cold skin turned warm and burned for the caress of his fingers.

She wanted him.

Under her. Around her. On her. Inside her.

Oh God. What in the world was wrong with her? Wanting an almost total stranger in the same way she'd always wanted her late husband?

Instinctively she knew he sensed her desires. It was in the way he touched her. The way his fingers gently wiped her wet hair from her chilled face. The sultry way his fingers trailed along her neck, moving downward, meeting his other hand as they settled on the lapels of her wet raincoat.

"If I help you out of your clothes, I can't be held responsible for what I do to you," he whispered in a hoarse voice that suddenly sounded so much like Steve's.

Oh, she had to stop thinking of Steve. She wanted this man. Richard or Chance or whatever the hell his name was. She would ask questions about his name later. Right now she wanted him to warm her and make her blood boil, but first, she needed to get the sand out of her burning eyes!

"Lean forward over the tub so we can get the sand out of your eyes with the water."

She felt his hands release the raincoat. Heard him quickly turn on the water taps and then a moment later she felt an arm cradle her belly while he leaned her over the tub with his other hand.

"Turn your face upward."

She did as he asked and she heard him withdraw the shower hose from the hanger.

"Here it comes."

A few seconds later, warm water slashed into her cold face like little jolts of fire, and she forced herself to squint her eyes open. Letting the soothing water pool into her eyes, she blinked and felt the burn begin to subside.

"Better?" he asked after a few moments.

She nodded, and he eased her away from the tub, replacing the shower hose on the handle.

Slowly, erotically, he unzipped her raincoat and moved the garment over her shoulders, letting it fall into a dripping heap on the floor.

Suddenly she wanted to touch him and surprise flashed in his eyes as she reached up and gently traced her fingertips over the water droplets dangling along the gentle raise of his right cheekbone and the sensual shape of his slightly bristled jaw.

He inhaled sharply as her index finger wandered into the deep cleft of his chin. The pulse throbbed there in his neck.

"Emily..." he whispered with softness in his voice.

"You like that do you?"

"Like isn't quite the word I had in mind."

His large hands cupped the sides of her hips and he pulled her against him. She relished the powerful pressure of his body. Absolutely loved the fascinating way his eyes sparkled with desire as he looked into her eyes. His exotic look only encouraged another round of intense heat to uncurl into her very core.

A flash of lightning lit the bathroom window and thunder cracked violently rattling the soap dish on the nearby counter.

Chance didn't so much as blink as he gazed into her eyes.

"You seem to be getting used to loud noises," she said, referring to the night he'd first arrived and been so jumpy when she'd settled the plate of food on the railing for him.

"You seem to have a calming effect on me."

"I don't think calm is quite the word I had in mind for it," she teased as she boldly pressed her lower abdomen against his exquisite hard bulge. A sexy groan escaped his lips and in a flash his mouth lowered to claim hers.

With his hands tightening on her hips, she felt the eager pressure of his hot lips as it seared a path straight into her pussy. Parting her mouth, she tasted his erotic power as his tongue entered and explored, probed and stroked. She arched her back and pressed harder into his erection, and her fingers trembled with a mind of their own as they quickly worked at unzipping his raincoat. The zipper caught a couple of times, and with a sudden burst of impatience, she yanked at it until it loosened and she was able to slip the coat over his broad shoulders. His invigorating body heat washed against her and she kissed him harder.

Abruptly he broke the magical kiss and impatiently shrugged off his shirt.

In the light, she could see the scars lacing his chest and wondered what they were from. Small round ones that looked like burns and others were fine, thin lines lashed across his chest.

Now, however, was not the time to question him about his name or his scars. For if she did, she knew it would break the mood. He was a man of secrets. A mystery. She had the feeling he would always hide a part of him from her. She didn't know how she knew this or why she knew it. She just did.

It was stormy outside and no one would be coming for hours if not days. She had time for her questions. At this moment, she just wanted to be with him. Wanted to be loved and fucked and to forget how much she missed Steve.

He began to unbutton her blouse, his fingers trembling with apparent disuse at such an intimate task. Impatience urged her to help him, and in a moment her blouse and bra joined his clothing on the floor. Her swollen breasts spilled free and he inhaled as he looked at her.

His eyes were darkening into pools of brilliant blue and his Adam's apple bobbed as he swallowed.

Masculine fingers trailed a scorching blaze along the outside curves of her breasts downward to cup the undersides of her breasts. His large thumbs arced up to provocatively caress her sensitive nipples, which instantly hardened into sweetly painful rosebuds.

She knew this ecstasy. Had experienced it under Steve's confident hands. Chance's lips caressed hers in tender, whispered strokes and his touches evoked such a raging heat in her breasts she couldn't help but moan.

She touched his warm hairy chest. Smoothed her palms over his taut muscles and explored the thin raised scars that crisscrossed his chest. At first, he tensed beneath her touches, and for a split second she thought he didn't wish to continue. She felt so hot at this moment; she swore if he decided he didn't want her she would scream bloody murder.

But then he relaxed, his searing hands lowering from her tight breasts to slip beneath the waistband of her pants. Then he got down onto his knees, peeling her pants and underwear over her hips, down her legs until she quickly stepped out of them.

She moaned as his warm hands dipped between her thighs and widened her legs. She cried out as his head moved between her legs and a hot tongue lashed her labia and licked her clit.

The muscles of her lower abdomen tightened, and sweet moistness smoothed down her pussy, readying her for penetration. She was breathing hard as his tongue teased her clit. Touching her, poking her, licking her until her legs trembled and she was gasping at the erotic intensity of pleasure. Her pussy felt as if it were on fire, burning with need. Yearning to be filled by his cock.

Oh God! Every nerve fiber inside of her was suddenly needing him to be inside her.

"Chance?" she called out his name, and she could barely hear her cry above the gush of the shower water. Called out his name maybe to make sure this was actually happening and not a dream.

She gasped as two fingers suddenly slipped into her vagina. He felt thick and so perfect as he began to thrust. He did it effortlessly, bringing her right to the edge of a climax she knew would have her screaming.

And then he backed off.

"No," she moaned, grabbing for his shoulders, ready to press her pussy into the top of his head and start gyrating herself to climax.

But he was pulling away, standing up, and when she looked down between them, she could see the huge bulge pressing against his jeans.

Sweet mercy! She needed him so bad. He was like a drug and she needed a fix of him. Needed him now!

His eyes were heated and so full of desire as he looked at her. His look had her shivering in its fierce intensity. How could he want her so much? How could this attraction have happened so quickly between them?

Questions for later.

"Shower sex," he croaked, and then quickly asked. "Condoms?"

Yes, condoms. Thank God, at least he was clearheaded this time. Somewhere at the back of her mind she remembered him saying he had a low sperm count as well as he was clean.

Who needed condoms? Safe sex be damned.

No, she had to play safe. Had to.

Turning on trembling legs, she reached out, thrust open the nearby cabinet door, grabbed the box and plopped it down on the counter. In the wall mirror, across from the shower, she caught him sliding off his jeans and underwear. Her heart cracked against her ribs as she watched his cock spring free.

Oh, such a wonderfully shaped cock. Long and thick and so much like Steve's.

Her breath caught at the sheer size of him. This was the first time she'd seen him in the light and he was definitely as big as he'd felt sliding into her the other night.

Just like Steve.

The teasing whisper slipped from that cavern where she'd chased all her thoughts of her late husband.

Looking away from the mirror, she turned and stared down at his erection, watching in stunned fascination as his cock continued to lengthen and swell. His cockhead slid from its sheath and she grew hotter at the thought of having him plunging into her.

He reached down and grabbed the base of his penis, and for a minute she wanted to go down on him, but he shook his head, instructing her to step further into the shower.

The hot water cascaded over her shoulder muscles as she did his bidding. When she looked around, eagerly expecting him to join her, she noticed he had stepped out of the shower and now held a long slender box in his hand, and it wasn't the condoms.

Letting go of his swollen cock, he slid the box beside the condoms and then flipped it open and lifted out a plastic-wrapped item.

Oh my God! A vibrator!

Her pussy creamed as it had never creamed before. She felt the sticky wetness slide down the insides of her legs and she inhaled at the excitement slicing through her like a torch.

He lifted his head and he caught her watching him. His eyes were so dark, she wondered how she'd never noticed how carnal the color of blue could truly be. There was a question in his eyes.

Did she want this?

Yes, oh yes, she wanted this.

She nodded and bit her lower lip.

"I was able to read a couple of your erotic romances while you were sleeping. It gave me some ideas. I bought this the last time we were in town," he whispered.

"Naughty man," she said with a giggle.

"About to get very naughty," he growled.

She swallowed when he slid open the drawer and withdrew a tube of lube.

Oh dear. Lube? Her heart began to hammer as she got his meaning.

Anal with the vibrator.

Moments later he had the plastic wrapping off and the vibrator cleaned with soap rand rinsed. Then when he stepped into the shower to rejoin her, she thought she would go wild with need. She was suddenly feeling so spicy hot she could barely stand it.

She swallowed back both the fear of the unknown and her curiosity as he handed her the tube of lube and the vibrator.

"You do the honors," he said. His voice sounded strangled and she could feel his excitement crackling like lightning between them.

Holding her breath, she squirted a substantial amount of lube onto the shaft of the vibrator. In the erotic books she'd read they always squirted a generous amount for anal. And she suddenly felt weird thinking that her sex life over the last years had been so nonexistent that she'd masturbated while reading those types of books and now she was actually acting out what she'd read. How awesome was that!

When she finished lubing the vibrator, she handed it back to him.

He placed the vibrator onto the soap holder and then began to squirt lube over his index finger.

Emily swallowed as he said nothing and motioned for her to turn around so he would have access to her ass.

Grabbing the showerhead from the stand, she bent over and aimed the water at her breasts. The harsh, warm jet of water splashing against her tender nipples made her cry out at the intense pleasure sensations.

The touch of his lubed finger prodding against her sphincter arched shock through her and the feeling of awe at what was about to happen shook her to the foundation of her very soul. No one had ever touched her there and yet here was Chance, a man she barely knew, touching her so intimately, so perfectly that she found herself widening her legs, wanting his fingers prodding into her.

The lube felt cool, and heated sensations gripped her as her anus stretched at his inserting finger.

"Tight. So tight," he moaned.

Inside her, the yearning exploded, and a fear of the unknown screamed through her.

Gently he moved a finger around until her muscles began to relax beneath his probing. As if sensitive to her diminishing fear, he began a slow, erotic stroke into her ass, and he had her panting in no time flat. Needing more stimulation on her breasts, she quickly adjusted the water jets to a more powerful setting.

He added a second lubed finger, the cool gel soothing the bite of pain as the finger stretched her oh-so perfectly that she couldn't stop the strangled cry as an erotic bite of pain zipped through her.

Instinctively she knew she needed to relax. She heard him murmur approval as she inhaled a few deep calming breaths. Heard slurping sounds and felt the lube slip and slide as he stroked his two fingers into her like a cock.

His other hand came to her hip, branding her there, holding her while he plunged gently. Her legs were trembling. Her pussy weeping with need.

Using her fingers from her free hand she plucked and tweaked each of her nipples and darted the showerhead to between her legs, allowing the pulse of the water to hit her plump, hot clitoris. She moaned as the water powered into her clit creating instant pleasure waves.

Soon he removed his fingers and then slowly inserted the vibrator into her ass. The slender shaft of the toy vibrated against her sensitive anal muscles and she gasped as he began to erotically stroke the toy in and out of her. With the pulsing water against her clit and the thrusting vibrator, she was quickly brought to the edge of bliss. She drove two of her fingers into her vagina, sucking breaths as the climax took over.

Somewhere at the back of her mind she knew being double penetrated by two men would be like this but on a much larger scale. Yes, she'd fantasized about a ménage with two men but knew in her heart she could never do it. This would be the closest she would come.

Pleasure screamed through her and she rode the waves. Rode them nice and hard. Bucked and gyrated until she felt nothing but exquisite happiness and extreme satisfaction.

In the throes of ecstasy, she hadn't even realized he'd withdrawn the vibrator. Her dazed mind quickly tried to catch up to what had happened while her body had been in explosive pleasure mode.

"Easy," Chance murmured.

A warm hand smoothed over her left ass cheek and she concentrated on how wonderful that felt.

But then an idea hit her. Turning, she aimed the showerhead at his swollen erection and laughed at the way he gasped and then reached for her wrists.

"Shit, woman. Easy on the family jewels."

"Tender are we?" Emily giggled as she tried to fight his overwhelming strength. But he won out, grabbing the showerhead from her grip and adjusting the jet to a gentle level before aiming it as his large sac.

"You would be too if you've had a hard-on for the boss since first laying eyes on her."

The hot gleam in his eyes erotically stroked her nerve endings, the deep baritone sound of his voice made her shiver with delight and his words made her fight for control. But she lost the fight, feeling like a starstruck gushy teenager again.

"Since you met me?" Happiness melted through her. Chance was attracted to her.

He nodded and lifted the showerhead to aim between her legs. She danced and squirmed at the splashing water hitting her pussy.

"The instant I saw you, Emily," he reassured with a crooked grin that had her heart racing. That's what Steve had said to her too. That he'd fallen in love with her at first sight.

Suddenly Chance came closer. Excitement flared.

Reaching up, she curled her hands against the back of his head, bringing him closer. She could hear his ragged breathing and his lips touched hers in such a possessive manner she could feel nothing but the desperate throb of need exploding inside her.

God, he knew how to kiss. Oh baby, he kissed so good.

In a split second his mouth dominated her. His sensual lips melted over hers in such an exotic way she fought to get air into her lungs.

"I love you."

His words were such a low whisper amidst the snapping sound of rain at the bathroom window, the thrumming of water erupting from the shower jets and the crackle of the thunder, Emily wasn't sure if she'd wished he'd said those magical words or if he'd actually truly said them.

When his lips covered hers again, his tongue pushing into her mouth, her thoughts vanished and need overtook her. The showerhead came up against her pussy and she found herself moaning and her body arching, wanting him.

She was about to reach down, to palm his heavy length in her hands and bring his thick flesh inside her when the showerhead fell away. She moaned in disappointment, her body flushing with heat as he palmed her breasts, plucking her nipples, igniting the burn of pleasure-pain she loved so much.

Still kissing her, Chance's lips ground against hers in such a savage erotic way he had her truly intoxicated and she could barely breathe through the fire of arousal as he drove his thick cock into her. Dropping her hands from the back of his head, she clutched at his strong shoulders, her fingers curling over the muscles and her fingernails digging into his flesh. She twisted against him, urging him to start thrusting.

He didn't.

Instead he prolonged her anticipation and stopped kissing her.

Their eyes met and she gasped at his flushed face and at the striking way his pupils dilated as he looked at her.

Gosh, the sensual way he gazed at her was so intense she almost allowed herself to come.

"You're the most beautiful woman in the world, Emmy" he whispered. His breaths were ragged as he spoke. Confusion zipped through her at his words as she hadn't heard similar words spoken to her since before her late husband died. But deep inside the confusion her heart sang and raced with a happiness she'd feared long dead.

"I've fallen hard for you, Emily. Hard and fast."

He continued to tweak and pinch her nipples, and he nuzzled his lips against her ear, biting her earlobe sharply, creating the sweetest bite of pain there.

"I've wanted you too, Chance. Needed you," she confessed.

She felt his lips twist in what she assumed was a grin and felt all bubbly with wooziness to think there might be second chance at happiness for her.

He released her breasts, gripped her hips, withdrew and thrust into her again.

Oh Lord! She almost came apart but held herself tight.

Gritting her teeth, she moaned and gasped as he came into her again. And again. Pressure built inside her as he moved harder against her, stroked into her until she couldn't hold back the needs any longer.

Intense pleasure seared through her as she suddenly felt as if she were coming home again. With welcome, she cried out her release and he quickly captured her cries with his mouth.

The pleasure overtook her, and beautiful spasms zipped through her over and over again until she knew in her heart that sexually she would never be the same again.

• • ᘛ • •

CHANCE BREATHED ROUGHLY as lust raced through his body. He caught Emily's aroused cries in his mouth and breathed them in as if they were a life force for him. She was exploding. Her body had been tight with arousal moments earlier and was now freefalling into the pleasure he'd created.

It did his heart good to know she still enjoyed sex with him. Last night, God, had it only been last night? It had been fast. Tonight, he would make it last.

Holding back his own release, which tortured the heck out of him, he continued to thrust until she exploded a second time. And then a third.

Until they were both perspiring in the warmth of the bathroom and she began calling out his name between his kisses. Until she begged him to join her.

And that's when he did.

He allowed himself to go free. Let himself spiral.

Plunging into her, he shuddered from the desire. Pleasure whirled through him like the storm outside, splintering his mind and shocking his body so much he thought he just might die from it.

When he came down from the intense climax, he felt dazed and satiated and feeling so weak, he wasn't sure he could lift his legs to step out of the shower. But he did. And he swept Emily up into his arms.

She whimpered as he did, her warm curves melting into him like exquisite honey. She nudged her face into his shoulder and he noticed her brown eyes were closing. She looked just as weak as he felt from the intensity of the lovemaking.

Yes, lovemaking, not just sex, he thought as flicked off the light and carried her into her dark bedroom. He smiled. Correct that. Their bedroom.

Holding her with one arm, he quickly pulled back the blankets and sheets and lay her down. He didn't cover her. In the increasing flashes of silver lightning spilling into the room, he couldn't get enough of gazing upon her perfectness while making himself believe she truly was here. He realized he'd been doing that often since getting here. Making sure she really was here.

Reaching out, he fingered a wet strand of her hair. That's when her eyes opened and she reached out, her sweet, warm fingers wrapping around his wrist like a love cuff.

"Come to bed with me," she whispered with pleading eyes.

He swallowed at the intensity of the desire flashing across her face for him. She wanted more sex when she woke up. He could tell in the way she looked at him. All sleepy-eyed and happy.

If he climbed into bed with her, it would be just like old times. As if there had been no incarceration. No prison. No dead husband.

He noticed the chill in the air and grabbed the sheets and blankets, bringing them up over her and tucked them under her chin.

"Get in," she pleaded, and beneath the covers she moved over to her side of the bed.

Jesus. He'd forgotten she preferred the other side of the bed. How had he forgotten something like that?

What else had he forgotten? What else would he remember if he climbed into bed with her and stayed there?

"The generator needs to be checked."

Lame excuse. The generator was huge. It had enough fuel in it to take them to the morning without a problem.

"Don't worry about it. Leave the other lights on. It'll remind the storm that we're here."

Okay, she was getting groggy with a comment like that. It had been a hell of a day.

All morning doing heavy labor with the seaweed. The afternoon filled with tension regarding the drug plant and losing *Sweet Lies*. And then the fiery, intense sex that had followed.

It was as if she were thinking just what he was thinking, and she smiled that beautiful smile that popped out those cute dimples in her cheeks. Suddenly his mind was made up.

Tossing the blankets aside he climbed in and inhaled sharply at how quickly she burrowed against him. Grabbing his wrist, she stretched his arm out and beneath her head, used his arm like a pillow, just like in the old days. That was something else he'd forgotten.

He stiffened as she suddenly wrapped her hand around his shaft.

"Is it okay if I hold you like this?" she murmured, and squeezed his cock ever so gently, making his breath catch in his lungs.

Lightning flashed at the windows and he noticed her eyes were sparkling. Was she crying? Or remembering that it had been like this with Steve? Holding his cock until she fell asleep. Or until he fell asleep.

His heart clenched in remembrance.

Wow, sleeping in his old bed was going to do a number on him. Despite that, he nodded.

Fuck, how nice it felt to have her hand wrapped around his cock again, her palm burning his shaft like a velvet brand. Beneath her touch he hardened again. He knew now that she was sexually satisfied, she would just want to snuggle until they both fell asleep and pick up again in the middle of the night when one or the other awoke. Just like the old days.

Oh man. It was going to be a long night.

$$\bullet \bullet \text{ \reflectbox{o}o } \bullet \bullet$$

CONTENTMENT AND BLISS sizzled through Emily and she snuggled closer to Chance, relishing the intoxicating way his body heat curled against her skin. Loving his powerful masculine scent as she laid her cheek against his muscular arm. She couldn't get over how nice and hard yet also velvety his muscles felt beneath her face.

He just seemed so perfect.

Waiting for another flash of lightning, she peered at his chest and found herself wondering about those scars she'd seen there. They were questions she could ask another time. It wasn't important now. Nothing was important except exploring their feelings for each other and getting out of here alive so she could avenge Steve's death. Hopefully something on his laptop would lead her in the right direction.

Reaching out, she laid her hand upon Chance's heart, feeling the steady tapping of his heart beating against her fingertips, indicating he had finally fallen asleep. Truth was, she thought he never would fall asleep. She'd removed her hand from his cock, thinking that's why he was still awake, and it hadn't been too long after that she sensed he'd fallen asleep.

Yet she remained awake thinking about him.

The sex between them was awesome. It was so intense she'd literally felt drained afterward. Her pussy throbbed in a way it hadn't in years. Her breasts still felt swollen and her nipples were aching from his tweaking. She really should be trying to fall asleep, recharge her batteries. Yet she couldn't close her eyes.

A strange fear hovered at the back of her mind. An eerie premonition that if she fell asleep Chance would be gone just like Steve, and she'd awaken with reality crashing in all around her once again.

So, she lay awake, her eyes wide, listening to his soft breathing as it intermingled with the sounds of rain peppering the windows, the cracking thunder and the powerful roar of the waves crashing against the cliffs.

Eventually she turned into a more comfortable position and found herself relaxing as she stared at the rear wall and the area where her wedding portrait should be hanging. For some reason it wasn't there.

Oh yeah, now she remembered. When she'd put the laptop into the fireproof safe, she'd forgotten to put the wedding portrait back up. Relief splashed through her at having forgotten. She would have felt very guilty to have known Steve's green eyes had been watching her in their bed with another man.

She wouldn't put the picture back up. It was time to move on.

Her eyelids drooped with heaviness and she fell asleep with a smile on her face.

．．ᪧ．．

CHANCE SIGHED WITH frustration as he sat at the kitchen table and stared at the laptop he'd stolen from Emily's safe. The password into the safe had been the first number he'd tried. His birthday. Too easy. He'd have to warn her about using personal information for a password.

With shaky fingers he slid the disc out of the computer's drive and examined it carefully. It had been years since he'd held this disc in his hands. And this disc had destroyed their lives. What little information he'd read while downloading the contents and making a copy had literally blown him away.

He should be reading the rest of it. Should be committing everything to memory.

So? Why was he hesitating? Why wasn't he inputting the passwords he'd created and read the rest of the information? Years ago, he hadn't wanted to get involved. Had wanted nothing to interfere with their dream of living here and raising a family. But those dreams had been killed.

Anger rushed through him in one solid blow and he realized exactly how much he had lost by not immediately handing this disc over to the agency he'd been working undercover for.

Fuck! Instead of doing what would have freed him, he'd seen the explosive stories that could come out of this information and decided to let the newspaper he worked for have the scoop. That decision had cost him Emily, his life and so much more.

From what little he'd read off the disc, it implicated Dr. Seth Martin, a world-renowned organ transplant specialist who researched anti-rejection drugs with less side-effects and the underground organ transplant organization he ran through his private hospitals. It named names, implicating top cops, officials, foster homes, adoption agencies, prisons and more.

Impatiently he tapped the disc on the table and tried to ignore the wind slashing against the windows. The storm was still raging, but thankfully not as bad as before. Despite the storm, uneasiness slithered up his naked back. Once the weather got better, he was sure they would have company. He looked at the gun he'd brought down from where he kept it under the bed in his room. If someone came, he'd be ready.

Oddly enough, after making love to Emily he'd slept a few hours without so much as stirring. It had been a deep, restful sleep and he'd woken to find her snuggled up against him. Her hot curves and sweet scent had intoxicated him. Aroused him to the point where he wanted to reach out for her. Wake her and make love to her again and again. Burying himself inside her sweet, hot pussy and give her the pleasure she'd been missing over the years. But she'd looked so peaceful he'd opted to let her sleep.

Easing out of the bed, he'd tapped the password into the safe and removed the laptop.

As he held the disc in his hand, the memory of when he'd handed a copy of this original to Skip sliced through his thoughts. He'd walked into Helena's office and found Skip searching through Helena's desk drawers...

"Glad I caught you, buddy," Steve said as he dumped his resignation onto Helena's desk.

Skip's head snapped up and he cursed a round of blue words that had Steve laughing at the paleness seeping into his best friend and coworker Skip's otherwise tanned face.

"You better ease up on that coffee, Skip. It's getting too easy to scare the shit out of you."

Skip shook his head, cursed some more and slid the drawer he'd been sniffing through closed. Coming around to sit on the edge of Helena's desk, he threw Steve a shaky smile that had Steve wondering what was up with the guy. Usually he had nerves of steel. At the moment though, he didn't want to ask questions. He just wanted to dump the disc and get back to Emily and their new island home.

"Helena's not here. Gone to lunch. I was trying to find a pen. You know me, always losing my pen," Skip replied. His brown eyes darted over Steve's shoulder toward the door. Obviously, he needed to speak to Helena and was using the pen thing as an excuse.

"You should get yourself a laptop, Skip. No need for pens," Steve teased.

"Pens are cheaper." Skip chuckled. "So, what kind of business you got with Helena? Trying to get another deadline extended? Hey! I've been hinting to her to team us together again so we can work on another war story overseas."

Steve swallowed at the hopeful look on his friend's face. He didn't want to drop this bombshell on him right here and now. He would have preferred to do it over lunch with the guy but maybe it would be best to tell him right now. That would cut down his time by a couple of hours and he could get back home sooner.

Home. He really liked the sound of that.

"Sorry, Skip. You were my next stop."

"By the tone of your voice I take it I'm not going to like what you're going to say."

"I've quit."

Skip's mouth dropped open in shock and guilt slammed into Steve. Yeah, he should have bought the guy lunch and done it then. He owed the guy so much. They'd saved each other's asses many times during their assignments, and now Steve felt as if he were bailing on the guy. Could see that realization flash across Skip's face as well.

"But why? I thought you loved investigative work? Is it the money? 'Cause if it's money, I can beg Helena to give you more. She'll understand with you being newly married. You're going to want wee ones in the future. I know how much Emily wants kids."

"Nothing to do with money, Skip. I just don't want to be away from my wife anymore."

Skip frowned and then nodded.

"Well, I guess that makes sense. I knew this was going to happen when bachelorhood abandoned you."

"You'll feel the same way when the right woman comes along."

"I think not!" Skip threw Steve a horrified look. "I'm not a one-woman man. Never have been. Never will be. You bloody well know that, my man."

"Never say never, buddy. I said the exact same thing not too long ago and look what happened to me."

Skip's eyes widened at the realization of the truthfulness in his words.

"Yeah, you're right. I'd better watch out. So, what kind of work are you going to do? Maybe Helena can get you a desk job? We can still hang out."

"We've already moved our things into the little lighthouse Emily's uncle left her. I'm heading back there tonight. Going to surprise her. She is expecting to be alone tonight."

"You've quit as of today?" Skip asked. Disbelief etched his words and he truly looked stunned.

"Resignation's right here."

Steve snaked his arm around Skip and tossed the sealed envelope onto Helena's desk.

"When she comes back, I hope she doesn't blow her stack."

"She will. You're moving too fast," Skip stated.

"I know, but we're going to get started on the family right away."

"Hence your rush to get out of here today," Skip laughed.

"Oh! I almost forgot. Here, I got this disc anonymously. Thought you might like to take a look at it. It's going to be one hell of a story. Since I've resigned, I'll have to leave it in your capable hands." He tried to contain the wild thrill flooding through him. Tried to appear as if the stuff he'd read on the disc weren't that important. If Skip got wind of his excitement, he'd be shooting questions at Steve left right and center and he'd never get out of here. But it sure was hard to ignore this kind of damaging evidence and hard to not hang around and watch Skip's face when he read the contents.

"I'll give you twenty-four hours to verify whatever you can before I hand it over to the cops," Steve said.

Skip accepted the disc without even glancing at it and focused his attention to Steve. Another round of guilt slammed through him for leaving Skip in this way.

"Are you going to come back and visit?" he asked.

"You can count on it. You know you're welcome out to Shipwreck Island any time. Emily enjoys your jokes."

Skip frowned.

"Just my jokes?"

"Your company...I think."

Skip smirked. "Ha! Ha! You know what? You've picked an exceptional woman in Emily. I'm proud of you."

His friend eased off Helena's desk and held out his hand to Steve. Emotions, thick and raw welled inside him as he took Skip's hand and they shook.

"Prouder even when Uncle Skip can bounce babies on his knees," Skip said with a smile.

"You'll be the first to know when we succeed," he replied, fighting the intense emotion sweeping over him whenever he thought of his wife.

"Emily's a gem, Skip. So sweet and innocent. I don't want her involved in this kind of investigative work."

"I can understand, bud. But she's a writer too. She knows the risks. In this line of work, you never know whose toes you're stepping on until it's too late."

"No more close calls. It'll be a big relief for Emily. I'd better get going. I still have to clean out my desk."

"I'll come out to your island soon and see how it's going," Skip said as Steve headed for the door that would take him out to the main area where the journalists had their desks.

"Sounds like a plan. We'll leave it at that then. Come on over anytime. Go on and get back to looking for your pens before Helena gets back. You know how huffy she gets when someone's in her office alone."

Steve smiled as he heard Skip grumble and open yet another drawer. He left the office, cleaned out his desk and it was the last time he saw Skip...until the fair.

That evening, Steve made it back to Prince Edward Island. He stepped onto Sweet Lies *where he'd had the tug anchored at the town near North Cape. He hadn't even started the engine when he'd been swarmed by the Coast Guard and other authorities who'd quickly arrested and taken him into custody after finding drugs on the boat. Life had never been the same.*

The raw anger raced through him like an abscess and Chance slid the disc into his laptop. He may as well check if the information was still here and on the hard drive.

Besides, someone had to pay for ruining his and Emily's chance at a normal life, so he may as well read all of it. With that thought squarely in his mind, he flipped on the computer.

Chapter Seventeen

E mily awoke to coolness where Chance had lain beside her. Immediately she noted the gray light of dawn splashing into the bedroom window. It was still raining, and the wind sounded like a battering ram on the panes. The alarm clock read a little after six a.m.

She wondered how long he'd been up and where he'd gotten off to. She smiled when she spied the splash of light shining in from the hallway to the bedroom. He was probably hungry and in the kitchen making himself some breakfast.

She was hungry too. They'd had only pizza last night. He was probably making something to eat. Gathering strength so they could pick up where they'd left off.

Excitement swirled at that thought and she hugged herself tight beneath the warm blankets. She really didn't understand why this wonderful attraction existed between them. Or why she already cared so deeply about him. Sexy Chance Donovan made such good love to her she wouldn't be able to sleep with another man after this guy. No way.

It had all happened so unbelievably fast. In a matter of days. This connection seemed too good to be true and before she started getting all freaked out like she used to get in the past when things were too good to be true, she decided to get out of bed and find that hunk of a man and get back to where they'd left off.

Pushing the blankets aside she got out of bed, reached for her robe hanging on the bedpost and wrapped herself in its snugness. But before she went to find Chance she needed to go to the bathroom. Slipping her feet into her snug slippers, she plodded to the door that adjoined her bedroom with the bathroom. Flicking on the lights, she smiled at the mess they'd left in here. Clothing was strewn all over the floor. It looked as if they'd been in one heck of a hurry. Or like a hurricane had blasted through in here as well as outside.

She started picking up her clothing and then noticed Chance's clothes were soaked.

Huh. In their haste to get undressed, she hadn't noticed that.

Bending, she picked up his wet jeans and blinked in surprise when a gold glittery item fell out of his pocket and onto the ceramic tiled floor. A Saint Christopher medallion sparkled up at her.

Wow. She'd forgotten he'd been wearing a necklace that first night he'd broken into her place. Talk about more similarities between Steve and Chance. Unreal. And the medallion looked just as scratched up as the one she'd given to Steve a long time ago.

Scooping it up into her hand, she was about to place it onto the counter when she inadvertently turned it over.

Her heart skidded to a halt.

Shock slammed into her to the point she couldn't even form a thought. It was unmistakable. This belonged to Steve! The inscription on the back was the one she'd had engraved for Steve!

She clutched the necklace in the palm of her hand and rushed from the bathroom into the hallway.

What was Chance doing with her husband's necklace? She knew Steve had been wearing it the day he left here. Knew she hadn't gotten the necklace back when the jail he'd been killed in had sent her his personal effects. She'd assumed someone had stolen it.

As she stood in the kitchen doorway, she spotted Chance. He wore nothing but a green towel slung over his hips as he sat at the intimate table for two. Cool, gray early morning light seeped into the room, giving it a surreal appearance. She could scarcely breathe as she watched him. His broad naked back was turned to her and she noted the tenseness bunching his shoulders. Shoulders that looked strangely familiar.

There was that oddly familiar slight tilt to his head. The one Steve used to do too when he was studying something. She noted those golden highlights so much like Steve's sprinkled with a dash of white in his sandy hair.

Those spooky *déjà vu* feelings grabbed a hold of her again and she didn't like it. She didn't like it one bit. Suddenly she didn't appreciate this man and his secrets and suddenly she didn't like the similarities between the only two men in her life who made her feel so alive and full of love.

Dammit! Who was this guy?

With heart hammering insanely in her ears she eased behind him and peeked over his shoulder. Surprise rammed through her as she spotted Steve's laptop computer lying wide open in front of Chance. The screen was lit up and full of data.

Chance had cracked the password.

How had he done it so quickly?

"What's going on?" she asked.

At the sound of her voice, he whirled around. There was an instant of panic in his blue eyes as their gazes met. Then her stomach clenched in a terrible sickening way as she watched the color drain from his face when he spied the gold medallion in her outstretched hand. He looked as if he might collapse right there in front of her.

Quickly he stood and blocked her view of the contents on the computer screen.

"Go back to bed, Emily," he commanded.

His momentary shock of discovering she was in the room had clearly vanished and she saw the anger rage through him. Could see it in the way his knuckles were white as he held his hands into fists and in the way the muscles twitched in his clenched jaw. She noticed he was trembling too.

What in the world had gotten him so pissed off? She's the one who should be mad. He broke into the safe after he'd screwed her! What an interesting diversion, she thought, and unexpectedly began to feel as if she might have been used.

Pushing aside her concern, she met his anger with her own. He would answer her questions and he would answer them now. Whether he liked it or not, she would find out what the fuck was going on.

"Why do you have my husband's medallion?" she asked. To her surprise her voice sounded a hell of a lot stronger than she felt.

"I found it. In the generator shed."

She didn't know how, but she knew he was lying.

"I want the truth."

His eyes widened.

"I read the initials scratched in over top. C.D. for Chance Donovan. And TX? I'm assuming it means Texas since you mentioned during the Timber Sports competition you were from Texas. Who are you? Why didn't you tell me your real name is Richard Call?"

He flinched and swore softly beneath his breath. She realized he was trying to hold on to his anger, but she wasn't afraid of it or of him. It seemed as if she knew he needed to release it. He needed to tell her something very important. About the medallion? Or the contents of Steve's laptop?

"Please, just go back to bed," he said, starting to turn away from her.

For a heart-stopping moment she wanted to do exactly what he said because something in his face told her she was better off not knowing what he'd found in Steve's computer files. Whatever it was, it had gotten her husband killed. But she fought the urge to do as he said. Fought it like a she-cat.

Grabbing his biceps, she tried to pull him away from the table so she could look at the computer screen. He remained as solid as a tree.

Son of a bitch!

"Chance Donovan! Move aside!"

"I'm warning you, Emily. You don't want to see what's on the screen."

"Like hell I don't!"

She made a move to go around him, but he stopped her cold by twisting away from her grasp. Grabbing her by the shoulders, he prevented her from moving around him.

"Don't, Emily," he hissed as he stared her down. There was an underlying warning tone in his voice and it just made her madder. Made her want to see what he was hiding from her on that damn screen.

"Get out of my way, Donovan. I need to avenge my husband!"

"I don't want your help!" he snapped.

She gasped at his words and felt as if she'd just been slapped.

I don't want your help. What did he mean by that?

She tried to clutch at the meaning. Tried to figure out what he was saying. As she did finally start to understand, horrific icy fingers tapped a violent forewarning along her spine and her knees threatened to buckle.

I have to avenge my husband, she'd said.

I don't want your help, he'd said.

Déjà vu slammed through her like an explosion. She remembered the slight tilt to Chance's head just moments ago. The familiarity of it. The golden highlights in his hair. The wide shoulders. The freckles and moles spattered lightly across his chest as she stared at him now. Freckles and moles, she refused to acknowledge as looking the same as Steve's. But they certainly did appear to be in the same areas.

But about the fair? The way he'd held her while they'd danced to her wedding song. He'd set up the song for them? She remembered how he seemed to know where to steer the boat. As if he knew where they were going.

There were other little things. How he liked his coffee. The same way as Steve did. The sizzling attraction between them from almost the minute they'd met. Yet he didn't look like Steve...but there was always plastic surgery. The rest of him though...she shook her head in denial.

No. Stuff like that only happened on the soap operas or in the movies. Didn't they?

Oh God. She couldn't even think about that angle. It would be too good to be true. Something else must be going on here. Something sinister.

"Why did you break into my husband's laptop?"

He said nothing. Just stood there shaking his head. His breathing was ragged. Tension smashed his handsome face. A face she should know. Shouldn't she?

"Who are you?" she asked, realizing she knew the answer. But it wasn't a possible answer.

He continued to hold her shoulders tightly. Continued that damn shaking of the head.

"Leave it alone, Emily."

"What's the password?" she breathed. She was still breathing, wasn't she?

He stiffened at her question and finally loosened his tight grip on her shoulders.

Her thoughts were whirling so badly she truly didn't think she could talk but somehow, she managed.

"I'm the only person close to Steve who could possibly crack the password. Here you walk into my life, a complete stranger and just like that," she snapped her fingers, "you're in my husband's computer. Where's my husband? Is he the one who told you the password?"

The other alternative couldn't be true. It just couldn't. God, help her if it was.

She watched him closely. There was something about him. Something in his eyes. The color of his eyes *were* different. Contacts maybe? She didn't think so. The rest of his face was different, but if she really looked hard... No, she couldn't go there. Wouldn't go there.

But the only person the information on the laptop would be important to would be...

"Steve..." she whispered, feeling the strangeness of his name in her ears. Feeling the disconnected dots suddenly start to connect. The pieces of the puzzle that had been floating aimlessly around her head since she'd met him suddenly seemed to fit.

At Steve's name on her lips, Chance let go of her shoulders and staggered backward as if he'd been shot.

Why wasn't he denying he was Steve? Why did she suddenly believe, no matter how hard she didn't want to believe, that the man standing in front of her, this virtual stranger who called himself Chance Donovan or Richard Call or whoever the hell he was, could actually be her dead husband?

Questions exploded in her head. How could it be possible? He didn't look like Steve. No, don't go there again.

Except the night she'd found him in her bedroom looking for the can of mace. He'd stood beside the wedding portrait. Their smiles had been so similar. What about the intense *déjà vu* warnings she tried to ignore? The Halloween romance formula that night only moments before she'd found him with his head stuck in her fridge. And their sexual chemistry...

The man so near and dear to her heart looked so different. Yet eerily familiar too.

He had a stranger's face. A stranger's eyes. Yet she recognized the love in those eyes now. Should have recognized it right from the instant she'd looked into them.

"How is it possible?" she asked, suddenly feeling as if she were floating, disjointed. She barely heard the Saint Christopher medal hit the wood floor with a tingle and realized it had slipped from her suddenly numb fingers.

"Emmie, please." His rough voice had a desperate edge to it. But now she recognized it. It was raspy and damaged, but if she really listened hard, she could hear Steve's voice. Couldn't she?

How could this be possible? It couldn't be.

"Where have you been?" she asked.

She reached up and she saw him flinch as with a horribly trembling hand she brushed the tips of her fingers across the warm, seductive curves of his lips and then brought a finger down to dip into the deep cleft in his chin. A cleft that hadn't been there years earlier.

"You always said you loved men with clefts in their chin. You had the hots for Michael Douglas for a while there. Remember?" he asked, and a strangled chuckle escaped his voice.

She dropped her hand as if it were burned and clutched it to her heart.

Yes, she did have the hots for that movie star.

Shock reeled through her as he eased his unsteady fingers to his hairline by his left temple and pushed back his hair. He traced a long finger along the faint scar she'd never noticed. Traced it until it disappeared behind his ear.

Oh my God.

"Miracles of reconstructive surgery." He shrugged.

At that split-second Emily thought she'd somehow gone insane, or maybe this was a nightmare.

She closed her eyes as a wave of lightheadedness whirled around her. She barely felt his firm embrace as he led her to a kitchen chair. She practically fell into it.

There was the oddest buzzing in her ears. The strangest sensation that for a moment she wasn't even here. That Steve wasn't here. That she truly had to be dreaming.

Crouching in front of her, he took her hands into his. They were trembling and warm and so gentle.

Oh, sweet Jesus, his touch felt so good.

"Close your mouth and breathe through your nose. Deep," he instructed.

She took a deep breath. The room began to swirl.

Oh shit.

"Dizzy," she muttered, feeling a knot of nausea grab at her tummy. Feeling the sharp swirls of panic as the room moved.

"Come on, Emmie. Close your mouth and breathe through your nose."

She concentrated on his voice. Strong and so beautiful. She breathed in nice and slow. Did it again.

"That's it. Hold it. One. Two. Three. Four. Let it go. It's just like having a baby."

Just like having a baby.

She exhaled on a chuckle and caught his grin but only felt nausea uncoil into her stomach.

"I think I'm going to be sick."

"You'll be fine. Inhale. That's it. Hold it in... Let it go."

She followed his soothing voice for what seemed an eternity and finally the sickness clawing at her belly resided, only to be replaced by an intense uneasiness.

"Better?" he asked as he watched her with concern.

She nodded and bravely held back the dam of sharp tears threatening to unravel her.

"I guess I can't drop big news without expecting some sort of fallout," Steve said.

Worry lurked in his blue eyes. Blue eyes not green.

She shook her head in denial.

"This is unbelievable. A bad joke. A nightmare."

Steve smiled and squeezed her hands in reassurance.

"The nightmare is over, Emily. I'm home."

Heart pounding against her chest, she found herself asking questions she wasn't sure she wanted to hear. Surely, he had some sort of good excuse for pretending to be dead all these years?

"What happened to you? Where have you been?"

"I think maybe you need some time to digest everything."

Indecision lurked in his eyes and she suddenly got the feeling if he didn't start answering her questions right now, he'd disappear. He made a move to usher her out of the chair, but she gripped his hands, refusing to let him go.

"Tell me everything. Tell me now," she begged, feeling despair creep deep into her bones. What had happened to have him do this to her? To pretend to be dead all these years.

"Emily, there's things you shouldn't know."

"I want to know the truth. All of it." Her mind was screaming. This can't be true. She had to be dreaming.

He frowned and his eyes narrowed.

"Do you really want to know?"

"Yes," she lied. Maybe later. No. Now. Before he leaves. Or before she woke up from this dream.

"I need to know. So, I can somehow hold on to my sanity."

Her heart clenched as she recognized the intense pain, the haunted sadness in his eyes. His mouth was unsmiling now. Serious. Deadly serious.

He stared into her eyes a long time before he finally spoke.

"What do you want to know?"

"What happened to you? Your face. Your voice. All those scars. Your eyes are different... Where have you been?"

Her voice trailed off as she looked into those stranger's eyes and saw pain. Hurt. Anger. Other emotions she couldn't put a name to swirled like a brewing storm.

"Death row," he whispered it so low she wasn't sure she'd heard right.

"Death row?"

Was he crazy? Was she?

He nodded and she shook her head in disbelief as the two words resounded in her head like a maddening echo. Leaning over, he picked up the medallion and accompanying necklace from the floor. The gold item glittered in his hands as he pulled up a chair and sat down beside her.

With trembling fingers, he lay the medallion out in front of them on the table as if it were a piece of precious jewelry. Then he leaned his elbows on the table and scrubbed his trembling hands over his face in apparent frustration. A moment later he bowed his head, tucked his hands beneath his chin and clasped them tight as if in prayer.

It took several breathtaking moments before he dropped his hands to the table in apparent defeat. That's when she knew he would tell her what had happened all those years ago.

"That day...when it happened. I was in a hurry to get back home to you. I resigned just like I said I would. I decided not to stay the night in New York."

His voice cracked and he cleared his throat.

"It was late when I'd just stepped onto *Sweet Lies* where I had her berthed on the main island when the authorities swarmed the boat. They found drugs. They were planted."

"I never believed they belonged to you. Not for a minute." He had to know she trusted him regarding that.

Steve nodded. His lips were twisted in grim distaste.

"They used the drug charges as a lever against me. A prosecutor presented me with a deal. He'd drop the drug charges if I told him what he wanted to know."

"What did you know?"

His gaze drew to the laptop then swung back to catch her again.

"I knew enough to know I was set up and that they wanted information about the disc someone had dropped off anonymously that morning. I'm sorry I didn't tell you about it, but I wanted to just get on with our lives. I told him I didn't know anything and that deals should be made with my lawyer present. He left and came back after a while with some guards."

He winced. She wished he wouldn't say any more. She didn't want to know what happened. Didn't want to dwell on the fact she hadn't been able to help him.

"Let's just say I didn't talk, and they got carried away. I ended up in a coma. Lost my eyes and there was extensive damage to my kidneys, so they gave me a kidney transplant when I was in the coma. They told me I was in it for six months. When I woke up, I had a new kidney, new eyes and a new identity."

Oh my God. This isn't happening.

He emitted a strangled sort of laugh, and the sound felt like the sharp tip of a knife piercing her heart as she pictured him lying in a hospital bed all alone God knew where without any family around.

"I thought I'd gone mad. I tried to tell people I wasn't Chance Donovan. They quickly transferred me to a prison infirmary in the States via I believe private plane. When I got better, they sent me to solitary. I think for a while I did go mad. I wouldn't answer any of their questions. They kept asking me where is it? Where is it?"

"Where is the disc."

"Yes. The disc. The one I found on our doorstep. Someone put it there. That morning I had inserted it into the laptop and read a couple of pages and knew this was dangerous shit. I knew I had to turn it over to..."

"To those people who you were working undercover for?"

He nodded and then suddenly it was as if a dam was bursting within him. He started talking and didn't stop.

"I also knew that there was a hell of a story on that disc. I wanted to stay out of it. Wanted us to start our family. I couldn't do that if I stayed on this case. I also know how governments work. They can make things disappear if they want. They can make people disappear too. So, I wanted the word to get out via newspaper about the stuff on the disc. It was my best chance of coming out of this whole thing in one piece. Or at least that's what I thought. I made a copy and also downloaded it to the hard drive. Then I put the laptop in my hiding place in the lighthouse. I figured if I handed it over to Helena and Skip there wouldn't be any trouble coming our way. With the disc I went to New York to give it to Skip and Helena. I found Skip in her office, but Helena wasn't around. So, I left my resignation on her desk and gave Skip the disc. I cleared out my desk and came back. I wanted so badly to get home to you. But the minute I stepped on *Sweet Lies* I was surrounded."

His words chilled her, and she wanted to ask him to stop, but she sensed he needed to spill all the hurt so he could begin to heal. He picked up the Saint Christopher medallion from the table and rubbed it gently between his thumb and forefinger.

A tiny smile lit up his lips.

"When I was in prison, they finally they gave me back the medallion and I began to have hope. I was who I said I was. I started to look for a way out."

She pressed a hand to her heart, trying to calm the intense pounding as she tried to absorb what Steve was telling her. She couldn't make sense of it. Couldn't concentrate. Couldn't grab a hold of it. He was alive. He'd been held against his will in a prison?

How can something like this happen? It didn't make sense. Nothing made sense. She swallowed back the bitter bile climbing up her throat and tried to maintain eye contact with him.

Eye contact with her man who had stranger's eyes. Her husband who was also her intimate stranger.

"After a couple of years, they started letting me out into the exercise yard. I managed to get a few convicts to believe me. It seemed everyone who tried to help me ended up dead."

She shook her head in denial. Could he be crazy? Could she be crazy? Prisoners ended up dead if they tried to help Steve?

"Dead?" she whispered as she tried to get her head around everything he was saying.

Steve nodded.

"I couldn't believe it myself. The private prison I'd been locked in had many eyes on me and it was obvious they weren't going to let me go until I told them what information I knew and where I got it. And my gut told me if I told them, I still would end up dead. You would end up dead."

"But you got out."

"With the help of Michael..."

"The man in the grave you visited the other day?"

Steve nodded. His Adam's apple bobbed as he swallowed back emotions that she could read clearly on his face.

Guilt. Pain. Sadness.

He looked away and shook his head. He continued speaking. Continued telling her things she didn't want to hear.

"It took me another couple of years to gain his trust. I had to be careful. It was like something out of a conspiracy movie. I was a nervous wreck. Didn't know who I could trust. Didn't know if I wanted another death on my head. Finally, I managed to get to Michael. He was the top man. If you wanted something done like having another inmate killed, he was the man to arrange it. For a price. Said he'd take on my problem if I agreed to bury him over on Prince Edward Island. Wanted bachelor buttons and lupines on his grave. Wanted to know if I could arrange it when I got out."

Steve emitted a strangled laugh and his eyes were piercing as he gazed at her again.

"When I got out? Can you believe it? The man had confidence in himself in getting me out."

Emily shivered and pulled her robe tighter around her neck. Her husband had been held captive in a prison and she hadn't known a thing. All these years he'd been suffering, and she'd gone on with her life.

She was going to be sick over this whole thing. She wanted to beg Steve to stop talking. But she knew he needed to say these things. To tell her what had happened.

"I told him my problem. He said he'd heard about me. Rumors mostly. He didn't take the rumors seriously because he didn't believe in rumors. Only cold, hard facts. He eventually believed me that I was Steve McCullen, the journalist."

Steve smiled.

"To him, I was not Chance Donovan, convicted inmate. I warned him not to tell anyone we were talking, or he'd end up dead. He said he'd heard those rumors too. About people ending up dead who spoke to me. Since he didn't believe in rumors—"

"He decided to help you."

Steve nodded and frowned.

"Big-time. In that prison on death row every visitor is monitored. He didn't want to put any of the people who came to visit him into possible harm's way, so he never spoke about me to them. Instead we spoke in the exercise yards and extremely briefly every time. He did manage to smuggle out a note through the channels, telling my whereabouts, but the note must have got lost somewhere. No one came to help."

Steve lifted the Saint Christopher medal from the table and turned it over.

"I scratched my convict initials and TX meaning Texas into the back of the medallion. I knew it was a long shot that anyone would even figure out what it meant. Michael managed to smuggle it out and had it delivered to Daniel. We waited for weeks but no one came. By then my kidney was starting to reject. Surprisingly the eyes didn't do too badly. I got a little cocky with the guards when I lost the medallion. They put me back into solitary again."

"Oh Steve."

He cracked another grin.

"I wasn't a model prisoner. I had a defiance problem."

Then his face fell into a severe frown.

"Michael probably thought I didn't have much time. I think he somehow fixed it so we were in the same exercise yard again on that final day. He picked a fight with an inmate who was three times his size. I think he wanted me to rush the wall and I was about to, but the guards started shooting. I saw him get killed and then I got shot."

In all the excitement she had forgotten his scars. In the darkness she hadn't seen them. In the shower she'd been too aroused to pay much attention.

Emily touched the bullet hole above his heart.

"That's how you got this scar."

He inhaled a shuddering breath, and she noted something flicker in his eyes. Something that resembled fear. Why was he suddenly afraid?

"The prison officials transferred me to a private hospital...in another state. Someone needed a new pair of lungs. I was a perfect match. Anyway, the hospital was under investigation at the time. I was in the private hospital in Florida where Daniel shot and killed the organ transplant surgeon Seth Martin last year."

Emily finally understood his fear. Betrayal swamped her as she became painfully aware of the timing. Last year. Steve had been free for a year and hadn't contacted her.

"They were using that private hospital to harvest organs from prisoners and other kidnapped people from across the country."

"It happened a year ago, Steve. Obviously, you were found and everyone neglected to tell me."

"Why should I have contacted you?"

His cold question sent her reeling.

"How can you say that? You don't think I would want to know my husband is still alive?"

"So, you could see what they had done to my face? To my mind? So, you could feel sorry for me?"

He shook his head.

"Thanks, but no thanks. Over the past year I've been in the hospital more times than out. The kidney they forced into me rejected. Daniel was a perfect match and so he donated one of his to me. My face needed numerous surgeries and my temper...I was so angry, Emily. I was sick of life—I'm surprised my brothers and dad stuck with me through it."

A swarm of emotions slammed into her and her anger overflowed.

"In sickness and in health, Steve. Those words were in our wedding vows. I guess you didn't take them as seriously as I did."

"'Til death do us part, Emily. You thought I was dead. I didn't want to interfere—"

Emily let out a strangled laugh. How in the world could he think this shit?

"Oh my God. Are you for real? Didn't want to interfere? What do you think you're doing now?"

"I want you safe. I want you safe and happy."

"Happy? Do I look happy? Didn't you think I'd be glad to know my husband was alive? All these years I'd lie awake in our bed thinking about you. I used to dream about the things we'd planned for. My heart would break every time I thought about you."

He grimaced at her words.

Good. She wanted him to hurt. Hurt as badly as she was hurt by his actions of not letting her know he was alive.

"There has to be a better reason why you didn't tell me you were alive, Steve. There has to be. I mean, come on. Your face? Whoopee shit about a face. What's the real reason? Like maybe you didn't love me enough?"

Her heart clutched at the shocked look slashing across his face. Okay, that was a low blow but she was pissed off.

"I can't give you the kids you want, Emily."

Each of his words punched her like a physical blow. But she remained steadfast. She had to.

"I see. One of the side effects of anti-rejection drugs could be sterility. There are other ways to have children. Adoption. Sperm donation."

He turned his face away from her and she felt a spear of shame shoot directly into her heart at hounding him like this. But she didn't care. He should know he was more than just a sperm donor to her.

"That's why you didn't tell me you were alive? Because you can't give me kids?"

"That's one of the reasons."

"Why did you come back to me now? Is it because I'm marrying Skip?"

"Yes. He might be behind what happened to me."

Okay she could understand that angle of why he'd come back.

"Why are you pretending to be someone else? Were you ever planning on telling me who you really are?"

Steve shook his head. "I don't know."

You don't know? The shock of his answer screamed along her nerves.

"So, I don't mean a thing to you. This attraction. The sex. Us. It all means nothing to you."

He cursed and slammed a fist onto the table in anger. His eyes flashed with annoyance.

"Dammit! How can you say that? All I want to do is wake up every morning next to you. All I want is to see your beautiful smile every day. I've never stopped loving you. You are the reason I'm alive today. Just you. So, don't go putting bullshit into your head. I love you like I haven't loved anyone in my life."

"You sure have a funny way of showing it. I've never stopped loving you either, but I can't let you walk into my life and rip my heart apart again."

His eyes narrowed and he scowled. He didn't like the implications of what she was saying.

"What do you mean?"

"I'm saying you just can't show up here and expect to come into my bedroom and make love to me and then decide you have to leave because you don't want me to get hurt."

"I can't stay, Emily. It's too dangerous. I'll take you to my brother's place. Daniel and Jo will keep you safe while I take care of the fallout over this information."

"And after that?"

He shook his head.

"I can't say."

Damn him! She couldn't believe she was having this conversation with Steve. It was insane. Her husband was alive? He was neck-deep in bad stuff and he wasn't even going to tell her who he really was. How could she even go on with her life knowing what he'd gone through? Knowing he was somewhere out there in the world without her by his side.

"The past is in the past, Emily. Things can't be the same."

His words dripped with iciness and she could feel her insides ripping apart at the finality in the tone of his voice. He didn't even want to try to get back together? She knew if she said anything she would start crying. She needed to take some time away from him. Time to digest this insanity.

Fighting the burn of tears that welled in her eyes she forced herself to stand and look at him. To her annoyance, he avoided her gaze. His head was once again bowed. He didn't look up. Didn't say anything else.

She drew the robe tighter around her body, using it as if it were a security blanket of armor against his sudden coldness toward her. With as much dignity as she could muster, she walked out of her kitchen.

Chapter Eighteen

The swirling sickness in Emily's stomach had settled to a somewhat tolerable sensation but mass confusion still hovered around her. Chance Donovan was Steve McCullen. Her dead husband was alive.

To make matters worse, everyone in the family knew except her. The old saying was so true. The wife was always the last to know.

Betrayal and hurt ran a rampant gantlet through her as with violently trembling fingers she frantically tried to make some headway knitting the booty with the baby wool she'd found in one of her drawers. She'd hoped knitting booties for both Jo and Sara's babies would keep her mind off of Steve. Unfortunately, her thoughts kept straying to the Saint Christopher medallion and to what might have happened had she not found it.

She shook her head in disgust. If she hadn't picked up the medallion and examined it, or if she hadn't caught him breaking into the laptop, she'd still be in the dark.

The delicate job of knitting just didn't hold up under her anger and she whipped the knitting needles and tiny booty across the bedroom. The items landed square against Steve's bare chest and he managed to grab them before they fell to the floor.

"I guess I deserved that."

His gentle voice carried no hint of the anger that had been so evident between them when they'd fought several hours earlier. To her surprise, he smiled. It was a soft smile that just irritated her more.

"Ever hear of knocking?" she snapped.

"I did. I guess you were otherwise occupied."

"Oh."

She ripped her gaze away from his amused look and clenched her hands tightly together so he wouldn't be able to see how much they were shaking.

"You okay?"

"Aren't I always? What did you expect? A raging lunatic throwing pots and pans at your head?"

"Just knitting needles. Can I come in?"

God no. Please just go away! She couldn't deal with him now.

"It's your bedroom too. Oh sorry, let me rephrase that. It used to be your bedroom. Seems to me you don't want it or me anymore."

His sweet smile drifted away, replaced by an angry frown. Good! He deserved to be unhappy after everything he'd put her through. He walked into the room and held out a steaming mug.

"Chamomile. It'll help settle your stomach."

"Thanks."

She accepted the mug, careful not to touch his fingers. But the sight of his lean fingers evoked a fiery memory of how his gentle touch had traced seductively along the curves of her breasts and touched intimate parts of her body. She closed her eyes and chased away the images. This was not the time to be thinking about sex. Or love.

It was time for war.

Steve walked over to the window and peered out. She couldn't help but to stare at his partially nude body as she sipped the warm chamomile tea. He'd had several hours to change, yet he still wore that towel wrapped low over his hips.

"I added more fuel to the generator. We have enough for a couple of days."

She nodded and took another sip.

He'd gone outside wearing just the towel? Was he crazy?

Emily shook that thought away. No, he wasn't. He was alive. Maybe damaged but alive.

Now that she knew the truth about him, she noted again how heart-stoppingly familiar he really looked and acted. She didn't know how she hadn't guessed his true identity on her own.

Sure, his face was different. His voice altered. His eyes were the wrong color. The rest of his body should have clued her in. She'd known Steve's body intimately. Touched him everywhere. Kissed him everywhere. Why hadn't she *known*? It wasn't as if she hadn't had many clues.

The sizzling connection between them. What about his large hands? The shape of them. The way they'd gently cupped her waist when they'd danced together. It was now obvious he had requested *their* song that night at the fair. She'd melted in his arms just as she'd done in the past. What about the night she'd captured him in her room supposedly looking for the mace? That night she'd first realized Chance's smile was so similar to Steve's.

"You must have had a good laugh. Get me into bed and when I'm sleeping, you have access to my safe and your laptop."

He frowned yet kept gazing out the window. It was gray out there in the early afternoon. The wind and rain still pounded against the panes. But the thunder and lightning were gone.

"It's nothing like that."

"Then how is it?"

"I love you, Emily but I can't give you any children, so I don't want anything to do with you."

"As if you not being able to give me kids would make me love you any less."

"Emily, please. Don't do this."

"Why not? I'm on a roll. Do you know how insulting it is for my husband not to want to see me after he's been through whatever horrors he's endured?"

She emitted a strangled laugh that made him flinch.

"I'm sorry you're still upset."

He turned to leave, but she dropped her cup on the bed, not caring that it would make a mess and scrambled off. She was burning mad and she wanted him to know it.

"Don't you dare walk away from me Chance Donovan or Steve McCullen or whatever you're calling yourself these days."

He stopped and turned to her. His eyes filled with tormented anguish and all she wanted to do was forget her anger, take him in her arms and tell him she loved him. Yet she couldn't bring herself to give in. Not this easily.

"I realize I may have been too hasty walking away from our earlier conversation. You're absolutely right when you said the past is in the past. You're right when you said things can't be the same," Emily said.

A chill scrambled up her spine as raw fear suddenly flared in his eyes. He was afraid she was dumping him. Turning him loose without a fight. The man needed his confidence boosted when it came to her love for him. Pushing aside her raw anger, she raised her hand to touch his face. He inhaled as she parted the fluffy hair covering his hairline. Electricity shot through her fingers as she lightly traced the faint white surgical line until it disappeared behind his ear.

"A stranger's face..." she whispered thoughtfully. "Yet beneath these physical changes, these scars, you're still the same man I fell in love with. All over again."

He went completely still at her admission and she allowed her shaky fingers to lightly move down across his brow, his cheek then his stubbled jaw to rest in the dent in his chin.

"You obviously were holding out some sort of hope for us getting back together or you wouldn't have had them install a cleft in your chin."

She could see the pulse hammer in his throat, the uncertainty glowing in his eyes. Uncertainty about what? She'd just told him she loved him. What else was wrong?

"I think we need to talk some more before you say anything else." His voice sounded hoarse. She detected an underlying warning that made her believe he still hadn't told her everything.

Dizziness rocked her. *My God!* What else was there?

"When I was in prison, they did things to me no human being should have to endure, let alone explain to his wife."

He watched her carefully, obviously expecting her to protest. She clamped down on the torrents of helplessness washing over her.

"Okay. I understand. You need space."

"Someday I might be able to share, but not now. Maybe not ever."

What was he saying? Had he been raped? Tortured?

Her heart began to thump wildly as she realized he was obviously setting down some ground rules. Ground rules for their marriage. It meant he was still interested in staying together.

"I have nightmares. They come with the package, meaning me. Sometimes they can be violent. I haven't had any bad ones since coming here, but if you can't handle them, just say so and I'll walk."

"I can handle it." She could handle anything as long as he didn't walk out on her without them at least trying.

"There's something else."

He held her gaze and she knew instinctively she had to agree to this next rule or else he'd walk, as he so eloquently put it.

"Go ahead."

"My two brothers and their wives begged me to allow them to tell you I was alive. I just couldn't let them. I see I was wrong. I'm sorry for not telling you. Please don't hold my mistake against them."

"Of course I won't. They're my family too."

"And I'm broke."

"You look to be in fine shape to me." But she knew what he meant. Financially broke.

"I'm serious. I don't have any money. My operations...there are debts."

"We'll manage. Don't worry. All married couples work off debts together."

"There's something else I need to tell you. As I said on the beach the other day, I'm clean. The first thing I had done was tests for diseases. I'm not carrying anything."

Oh, sweet Lord. He must have been raped. Once again Emily clamped down on the fears at the horrible visions of what might have happened to him behind bars.

"One more thing. That is if you're up to the challenge?"

"Name it."

"I'm going to need lots of this to help me heal..."

He cupped her chin with his left hand and her breath backed up in her lungs at his potent look.

His eyes were fired up with raw hunger. A hunger that made her warm and tingly and excited with an achingly sweet need.

"I'm going to need the love of a good woman," he breathed.

She could smell the faint scent of chamomile tea on his breath. Obviously, he had needed some of the calming tea too after revealing to her that he was her husband. He tilted her face up and stared straight into her soul.

"A good woman. With strong muscles to keep me in line and to challenge me at next year's Timber Sports contest at the fall fair."

Strong muscles? Okay, humor was good. They would be okay. She knew that now. It would take time, but they would make it.

"I don't know if I can agree to that. My muscles need daily workouts so they can stay strong and limber."

"These workouts..." His ragged breath caressed her lips and a delicious golden need uncurled deep inside her pussy.

"Are these workouts a part of your set of ground rules?" he asked.

"Yes."

Her fingers slipped off his chin and both her hands reached up to curl around to the back of his neck. The solid wall of his hot body pressed against her, firing her blood. She wanted his mouth on hers. Wanted his mouth, his fingers, his cock. She wanted all of him.

He grinned and a wave of love shot straight into her heart.

"What are your other needs, Emily?"

"This."

She pulled his head down to her and brushed her mouth against his lips with a butterfly kiss.

"And this."

She uncurled her hands from around his warm neck, ran her palms down the front of his muscular chest and stopped over his nipples. Then she pushed against him with all her might.

Suddenly he was falling. Right onto her bed. He bounced there and the look of momentary shock on his face made her laugh with wicked intent. The towel around his waist suddenly loosened and flapped slightly open.

Oh my, she thought as she spied the partial length of his swollen cock peeking from beneath the towel. Before he could move, she stepped in between his parted legs. Long legs that dangled seductively over the mattress.

She grinned and pushed everything out of her mind. Pushed aside the fact Steve was alive. Steve was Chance.

The reality that she still had so many questions but wouldn't ask them yet made her think that maybe she was running away from what he'd endured over the past few years. But she knew when he was ready to talk, he would tell her, and they would deal with what had happened to him together.

Until that happened, she would focus on the warmth filling her heart at the way he looked at her. He had a stranger's eyes, yet they were so familiar to her now. His eyes were blazing with lust and love, and for a moment she was overwhelmed that he loved her so much. That he needed her so much.

Needed her not only sexually but emotionally and spiritually.

"Your towel seems to be too small for you. We're going to have to get you out of it..." she said, feeling that his immediate needs were of a sexual nature.

He blinked up at her. His eyes were wide with passion, his sexy mouth upturned into a gorgeous smile as she slid both ends of the towel apart and onto the bed, revealing his muscular thighs and swollen erection.

Just looking at his rock-hard cock sent a furnace blast of heat through her. Feeling the desire of touching him and ignoring the raised scar on his side from the kidney transplant and the raised scar tissue from his bullet wound, she reached out and splayed her hands over his chest. Hot, sleek bands of muscles rippled erotically beneath her fingers. As she touched him, his breathing became louder and raspier.

Obviously he was enjoying her playful mood, and she had every right to be playful. Her husband was back and she wasn't going to waste another minute making war with him.

"While I'm getting reacquainted with your body, I'm going to have to lay down some ground rules," she whispered.

Peeling the towel away from his hips, she felt her eyes widen at his size.

Oh my! What a nice cock he had. So long and thick and hard as steel. So much longer and thicker than she remembered. She found herself visually inspecting his cock and balls for scars down there too. Found herself wondering if they'd touched him here.

Oh, don't go there, Emily, she chastised herself.

Steve is back. Just accept him. Live inside him until it's time to go back to reality, a voice whispered inside her head.

Yes, live inside him. They had so much time to make up for and she didn't want to waste any time feeling sorry for him or for herself at what they'd lost.

"Maybe you should drink some more of that chamomile tea to calm yourself down," she teased as his cock seemed to just keep on growing the longer she studied him.

"Only you can calm me down, Emmie."

Emmie. He was using his nickname for her. He'd used it a few times already. How had she forgotten that nickname? What else had she forgotten?

Desperation and a wicked anticipation of making love to her husband had her trembling with such a fierce need she wasn't sure if it was too soon to have sex with him. She'd only known the truth for a few hours. She was still reeling from the impact. Hadn't even been able to process things. Would it be a mistake to follow her instincts and get physical with him without having her emotions under control?

Doubts swirled. She didn't know him. Not really. All this time she'd thought he was Chance, a friend of Steve's. And now he was her husband. How could she jump into bed so quickly with him? Was it normal to be so aroused over a man she had thought long dead?

Suddenly he reached out, curling his fingers around her biceps. She could feel the power in his hands as he tugged her down on top of him. Could feel the barely restrained control of his naked flesh as his heat seared straight through her clothing and fondled her skin. Molten heat rushed into her pussy where his bold arousal pushed against her body. The thought of him fucking her sent a jolt of adrenaline shooting like lightning through her bloodstream.

Oh man. It felt so good. So damn good.

"This is crazy," she found herself saying as the lust for him burned through her strong and bright.

"Workout time," he murmured.

She noticed his voice, drenched with such gorgeous huskiness, it made her breath catch, made the ache inside her pussy explode for him. Looking down at his face, she found it roughened with desire and she'd never seen such a wild intense look in his eyes.

He let go of her arms and slid his hands beneath her top, splaying his palms against her stomach. His fingers were like beautiful sparks of love upon her skin and he moved them upward until he cupped her breasts.

She wasn't wearing a bra. Had been too upset earlier to do much except just step into a pair of track pants and a track top.

His hands squeezed her breasts gently and she inhaled at the erotic way he pinched her nipples.

"You like?" he whispered. His eyes were such an intoxicating blue that she felt herself drowning in them. It was a good feeling. Very good to just let herself go and sink into him. Sink into this minute. This moment.

"No fair. I'm still laying down my ground rules," she protested, and positioned herself so that she straddled his bare thighs and his cock pressed against her clothed pussy.

Despite her pants being between them she could feel the heat of him scorching her flesh. Could feel his cock pulsing beneath her as she began to gyrate her hips, using the material from her pants and letting the bulge of his cock provide just the right amount of friction against her clit.

"Ground rules, which are?" he ground out between his teeth, obviously enjoying the rasp of the material against his cock and the sultry rhythm from her gyrating.

"Breakfast in bed every weekend," she stated, feeling the surging sensations of arousal take hold.

"Sounds reasonable."

Reaching down she lifted her top and quickly took it off.

His eyes blazed as he looked at her bared breasts. He let go of her nipples and uncupped her, his fingers now searing fire against the sides of her breasts. With deliberate strokes, he touched her there making her inhale sharply as fiery nerve endings sizzled to life.

"What else?" he asked.

"Candlelight dinners every night."

"Who's cooking?"

"We'll take turns."

"I'm a lousy cook."

"Who said anything about cooking dinner?"

He chuckled as he got her meaning. His laugh was an awesome sound. Light and true and straight from his heart.

Sensually moving her hips, she leaned over him, bringing her mouth to his left nipple. Taking the rock-hard bead of heat into her mouth, she bit his flesh gently and heard him moan. Licking him with her tongue, she soothed the hurt and took him again. Sucking his nipple into her mouth.

He shuddered.

"Jesus, woman."

She took her time tending to his nipples. First one and then the other. She bit and tongued him and sucked until he was panting. Until his hands came up and seized each side of her waist like two searing brands of power. He held her steady and she found him pushing his hips upward, trying to get a harder pressure from her gyrations. His movements increased the delightful friction on her clit. Pleasure mounted and the erotic sensations made her suddenly impatient to have his hard length inside her again.

"Oh damn. I'll tell you the rest later."

"Thought you'd see it my way," he muttered thickly.

Letting go of her waist, he allowed her to lift herself off him. She ditched her pants and in an instant, she climbed back into position. This time no clothes prevented their flesh from touching and his cock scorched her, making her pussy clench with eager anticipation of having him. Rubbing her clit over his fat cock head, she felt the moist heat gush down her vagina, and she moaned at the killing pleasure lashing through her like a storm.

She was losing control fast. Could feel the tension building in her. Rubbing herself harder against his cock head, she yearned to bring herself higher. She was quickly becoming lost in the pleasure. Panting and moaning and—

From somewhere far away she heard him groan and call out her name. Suddenly she remembered Steve. Remembered his needs too. With one quick movement she sheathed herself on him. They both moaned as his cock slid into her like velvet-encased steel.

His hands curled around her shoulders, pulling her down on top of him. Her breasts flattened against his solid chest and her mouth fastened over his. His lips were moist and firm and demanding. Just the way she liked him.

She felt his hands find hers and their fingers intertwined. They held tight to each other and he kissed her with a hunger that made her blood boil. Opening her mouth, she felt her senses spiral as their tongues touched and mated.

She rode him with erotic thrusts of her hips. Kissing him with hot, desperate kisses that sent her spiraling out of control. Her climax exploded.

Convulsing, she cried into the wet, heated kisses and quickly went to the place where pleasure and love sparkled stars and beauty. Beneath her, his body tightened and jackknifed. His muscles taut as he neared climax.

And then they were rolling on the bed and she was on her back and he was on top. The new position made her body and emotions splinter as he thrust into her. Deep and fast and utterly uncontrollable. The wildness broke down all barriers and they became one. Mind, body and soul.

Welcome home, Steve, she whispered in her mind.
Welcome home.

• • ❧ • •

"COME ON, TELL ME THE password. I promise I won't go into the laptop without your permission," Emily said, smoothing a hot palm against his chest as she snuggled against him.

Ever since their last bout of sex, Steve held her cradled her in his arms, not wanting to ever let her go. She smelled so good. Of sex and her own sultry, sweet female scent. The damn good combo made him want to inhale her all the way into his lungs and live inside her smell and just ignore the fact that he'd eventually have to come back to reality.

Even from their perch in the bed he sensed the storm was a little less extreme. The howling winds didn't shriek as much against the windowpanes and the angry gray skies had lightened just a bit. When the weather returned to normal, he'd have to return to being a practical man. That it would be too dangerous here on the island for them.

But he didn't want to give in to it. He wanted to stay here in bed. Wanted to give in to this awesome peace of being home. Feel her soft body next to his, her fingers intertwined with his as they lay together after an afternoon of loving.

"Steve?"

He inhaled deeply at the curiosity in her voice. He knew Emily wouldn't stop bugging him until he caved.

"Okay, you promise not to even look at the computer or the disc without my being there?"

"I promise. I promise."

He grinned at the excitement in her voice.

"Okay. There is more than one password."

She blinked at him in puzzlement and he chuckled.

"I encrypted one password on top of another."

"You mean I type in one password hit enter and then type in the second one and hit enter?"

"If there were only two passwords."

"There's more than two?"

He shrugged, chuckled again and held her closer. She looked so cute when she was curious.

"Why make it easy when you can make it hard?"

"I can see that. How many? What are the words?"

He lifted his hand to the Saint Christopher necklace he now wore around his neck. Turning the medallion over, he held it up so she could see the engraved inscription.

"No way! My inscription is the password? But how? I gave you this medallion the morning you left?"

"I saw the medallion a few days before you gave it to me. You shouldn't have left it in the drawer with our socks."

"And you call me a snoop." She slapped his arm playfully.

"I learned from the best."

She lifted the medallion from his fingers and read the back.

"To Steve. Your endearment always. Love, Emily."

She turned her attention back to him and he smiled at the surprise flash in her eyes.

"Seven words? Seven passwords?"

"Actually, three passwords. Each one is a sentence. You happy now?"

She shook her head and snuggled her face into the crook of his neck. It felt good having her warm breath splash against his flesh. It made him secure in the knowledge that he wasn't dreaming. That he truly was here in bed with his wife.

Cripes, he hoped this feeling of disbelief that shot out of the blue every once in a while that he was actually dreaming he was here instead of being here with Emily would eventually stay away.

"No. I won't be happy until you tell me what you found on the disc."

"Emily, you promised," he groaned.

"I promised I wouldn't break into the computer. I didn't promise anything about not annoying you to tell me what's inside."

"Hmm. That's true."

"And I'll keep bugging you until I get what I want," she whispered. To his surprise he felt the tip of her hot, moist tongue melt against his earlobe. Erotic sensations zipped through him straight down to the tips of his toes. Suddenly he understood what she wanted and it had nothing to do with talking about the laptop and passwords.

"I like this kind of bugging," he admitted, loving her scent. Loving the sweet way she sucked his earlobe into her hot mouth.

"Thought you might."

He moved closer to her, his hand reaching beneath the blankets. He found her legs already spread. Found her pussy. She was wet. Soaked with her warm cream. Dipping into her vagina, he collected some moisture and then found her clit. Rubbing her firmly, it wasn't long before she began rocking her hips against him. His cock reacted, thickening into a hard rod of steel it literally ached.

"I love you so much, Steve," she whispered against his neck.

"I love you too, Emmie."

"Keep doing what you're doing," she breathed, and she pushed the blankets off them. He kept up his firm rhythm as she climbed on top of him, impaling herself upon his shaft. Her lashes closed as he sank inside her. Then she started gyrating her hips, moaning softly as she brought herself to climax. Reaching up, he cupped her breasts. Brushing his thumb over her erect nipples, he watched her pretty lips part as she began to pant. His body tightened as she gyrated harder. Her pussy was tight and hot and so wet and creamy.

God, he needed her so much. Needed her love, her companionship, her understanding. Her pussy convulsed around him, her satiny muscles hugging him so tightly he felt a groan rumble through his chest at the shards of arousal shifting through him.

She was keening now. Her pussy tightening more and he greedily took the pleasure wrapping around him. She shuddered and came on a cry, her hips bucking so wildly that the combinations of her rough gyrations and sweet convulsing pussy tore a fantastic explosion through him.

He bucked against her movements, grabbing more pleasure. He felt his release, strong and long, spilling into her and pooling out of her.

Afterward, she lay on top of him, his cock buried deep inside, he found himself hoping against all hope he would make her pregnant. Tonight. Now. Before they could have a chance to think of what the consequences would mean of having a baby. Before they were forced to face reality. That the side effects from the anti-rejection drugs gave him a low sperm count or possibly made him sterile.

Before they would face reality though, they would have to get off this island alive.

Chapter Nineteen

"Oh my God, Steve." Emily raised her surprised gaze from the computer screen and stared up at him.

Her full mouth turned down into a severe frown and his gut clenched at the sight. He wished he'd followed his instincts and thrown the disc into the ocean that day he'd found it on their front doorstep. Wished he had never given the disc to Skip. Wished he'd never agreed to go undercover and interview that son-of-a-bitch transplant surgeon for the government's Cops' Angels Network.

Most of all he yearned that Emily wasn't so curious about the contents on his laptop. After making love to her, she'd started in again on him. Insisted on seeing what had kept him imprisoned for so many years. He could certainly understand why she'd want to know, so against his better judgment, he caved like an avalanche.

"You've got doctors, prison systems, police precincts, homeless shelters, foster care homes, lawyers and even charities. All linked to the underground transplant system in the States and Canada. Where did you get this information?"

"Like I said, a little birdie dropped it on the doorstep."

She exhaled sharply and shook her head in apparent anger.

"This isn't funny. We're sitting on a powder keg. Why didn't you turn it over to the police or those people you were working undercover for?"

Translation, if he had turned it over to the cops like a good little boy when it had arrived on his doorstep, then none of this would have happened.

"Because I don't want it exploding in our faces."

"What do you mean?"

God, was she so damn innocent? Or just blind.

"This information will slip me right back into the justice system."

"You'll be on the right side this time."

"Will I? Once the police figure out who I am, I'll be back behind bars so fast our heads will still be spinning twenty years from now when I'm still on the inside. I still have those drug charges hanging over my head. Remember? The drugs they planted years ago on the boat. More than the few bags we found this time around. Enough to hold me for questioning again. And I sure as hell am not looking forward to seeing the other side of a jail cell again."

"It's all circumstantial evidence. No one saw you bring the drugs onboard. No one saw you buy it. No one saw anything. Besides, the boat was registered in my name. I'm the one they should have questioned and arrested. Not you."

"There's no way in hell I will let you take the rap for this. No way are you going for questioning. I don't give a fucking shit who the boat is registered to. You will not get involved in this."

"We can't do anything with this information. We have to give it to someone who can blow the lid open and get some action going. Someone we can trust."

Fuck! She still was an innocent journalist, he thought and fought against the raw, poisonous anger threatening to overwhelm him. Talk like hers could get her into serious shit. He took a few calming breaths before answering.

"I trusted Skip and look were that got us. Besides, the information has been doing nothing for the last eight years. Why be in a hurry now?"

A pretty, puzzled little wrinkle appeared between her eyebrows.

"What's happened to you? Where's your spirit? Your drive to help others?"

He frowned. "Died. Like your husband."

"I'm beginning to think you're right." She shook her head in apparent disgust and returned her attention to the screen.

The disappointment in her voice and face left him reeling. She thought he was a spineless coward. Dammit, he wanted her safe. Wanted all this shit gone. If she thought he was a coward, then so be it.

Suddenly he noticed Emily lift her hand and she pointed to a familiar name on the screen.

"Oh my God. How can this be?"

His throat knotted up as he read the person's name. He hadn't realized she'd already gone this far into the files. He'd wanted to tell her about what he'd found earlier when he'd been exploring but hadn't had the heart to do it. He placed his hand on top of her fingers and squeezed gently.

"I know, Emily. I know."

•• ⌘ ••

THE NEXT MORNING THE hurricane had vanished, leaving Steve and Emily on edge. While she kept herself busy in the kitchen preparing an early lunch, he resumed lookout in the lamp room of the lighthouse tower. He squinted at the November sunrays as he kept a sharp eye out for any movement while his thoughts whirled around him. Thoughts about how easily she had accepted him back into his life. How much he loved her and about the danger they were in...

He stiffened as he detected movement in the water just off the point. A boat! It was zeroing in on Shipwreck Island. Heading straight for the lighthouse.

Grabbing his gun off the lamp room windowsill where he'd placed it earlier he slipped it inside the waistband of his jeans. The gun's cold metal hugged the small of his back, giving him little reassurance that he could handle trouble.

When he returned his attention to the ocean, his mouth fell open in surprise. The boat bouncing along the large swells around twenty feet from the wharf was none other than *Sweet Lies*.

•• ⌘ ••

WHEN STEVE BARRELED into the kitchen, Emily almost dropped the pot of spaghetti she'd removed from the stove. By the tense expression on his face she knew someone was coming. Her heart picked up a panicked thump and suddenly she couldn't think straight as the adrenaline zipped through her system.

"Who is it?"

"Didn't hang around to find out."

Shit.

Ripping the pot from her grasp, he stuffed it back onto the stove, grabbed her by the hand and led her into the living room just as a light noise came from the other side of the kitchen door.

Someone was already in here?

"Behind the couch," he ordered.

A wave of lightheadedness swooped over her as he pushed her into the tight confines behind the couch. He shoved the can of mace into her hand and a knife. Then he pressed her head down.

"Keep out of sight. No matter what."

With a horrible sinking feeling in the pit of her tummy, she watched Steve as he raced to the other end of the room and hugged the living room wall beside the kitchen door.

Holding her breath, she listened to the click of the kitchen door opening. Whoever was here wasn't a friend or they would have knocked. Dread draped over her like an icy blanket. From her vantage point behind the couch, she shivered at the quietly paced footsteps sounded in her kitchen. When the steps stopped, another jolt of adrenaline squirted into her veins, bringing another wave of lightheadedness.

Who could it be? How many of them were there?

She watched Steve as he kept his eyes glued to the open doorway. She prayed he would glance her way and throw her a reassuring smile just so she would feel a bit better.

He didn't.

Tenseness held him still like a statue. He raised his gun and she hoped he'd released the safety catch on that thing. Sure, he had. God, she hoped he had.

Suddenly she could understand why he carried a gun. Wished she had one too.

The footsteps moved again. Slowly.

She could picture the intruder moving in front of the stove, staring down at the pot of spaghetti. Noticing the steam wafting into the air. Dead giveaway they were still here.

A tiny click from the kitchen area sent a volley of shivers screaming up her spine. It almost sounded like the person had shut off the stove. Then again, it also sounded like someone had released the safety catch of their gun.

Oh God.

.. ❦ ..

A GUN POKED ITS HEAD through the living room doorway and Steve didn't hesitate. With icy smoothness he kissed his weapon against the intruder's temple.

Skip Cole froze.

"I could pull the trigger right now, Cole. Might save me a lot of trouble," Steve said, feeling the familiar acrid hatred seething through his veins.

"Shit, Steve. I can see you still aren't an early morning person."

Red-hot rage made him want to shoot Skip. That he'd immediately recognized him as Steve and not questioned him as to his identity, just confirmed that he was behind this nightmare. But something in Skip's soft brown eyes stopped him from pulling the trigger. He'd expected to see fear in those brown depths. Fear that he would get killed, but Steve saw only the familiar mischievous twinkle. It gave him the uneasy feeling he might be misreading this whole situation.

"Easy, buddy. I got your message from the boy. You wanted to see me," Skip said.

"I want to kill you," he ground out, hoping by saying it, he would do it. He couldn't. At least not yet.

"Just relax."

"Hiring a kid to do your dirty work. That's low, Skip. Real low and to come back here in *Sweet Lies*. Talk about putting salt into the wound."

"I needed some help keeping an eye on Emily, so the kid was the fastest help available. As to the tug, well, a local fisherman recognized the boat as Emily's. It was drifting out to sea. The storm was heading in fast. The fisherman thought there might be a problem and boarded. No one was there so he called in a mayday and brought the boat in. You did good leaving the keys in the ignition. It saved your boat so the fisherman could drive it in. The Coast Guard is quite busy with the fallout from the storm this morning. Several missing people. They couldn't get out a search party to look for you, so I volunteered to come out. I was worried about you two."

"I bet you were," Steve sneered.

"I'm disarming. Can I put my gun down on the floor?"

God, it wounded him to keep eye to eye contact with Skip. The burn of betrayal hurt so much. Skip was acting so casually as if he'd never done anything to Emily and himself. He wanted to believe Skip was a good guy. But the guy could simply be toying with him. Gaining his trust so he could kill them.

"Move slowly, Skip. Or you're dead. No second chances."

Skip nodded and gingerly removed his finger from the trigger on his gun then cautiously began to squat. Steve tensed, fully expecting Skip to try for his gun and when it didn't happen and Skip placed the gun on the wood floor, Steve found himself letting out a slow, calming breath.

"Okay, step into the living room and away from the gun. Get your hands up in the air and keep your back to me," Steve ordered.

Skip did as Steve asked and moved into the living room. As Steve swooped over and grabbed the gun, he noted Skip scanning the living room.

"Okay, so now I'm unarmed. Where is Emily? Is she all right?"

"Such sweet concern from someone who has brought her so much grief," he snapped angrily as he checked Skip's gun. The safety catch was off and the clip was loaded with bullets. The man meant business.

"Hey, I don't know what you're talking about. Why not clue me in."

Skip made a move to turn around.

"Don't turn around. Keep moving into the living room and have a seat."

He needed to get back into the kitchen and make sure no one else was around, but first he'd peek out the windows.

"You got it all wrong, Steve. I work for the U.S. Marshals Service."

Yeah, right.

"Nice try, Skip. Sit your ass down on this couch and stay put."

Skip did as Steve asked.

"Okay, Emily. It's safe," Steve said.

When he looked over to her hiding place, he noticed she'd already risen and with knife in hand came around the couch to stand about ten feet from Skip. She looked pissed off. Her cheeks were flushed and her dark brown eyes blazed with anger.

"Prove what you said, Skip. Prove to us you are a marshall. And even when you do, we still won't believe you. Not after what we know," she stated as Steve handed her his own gun.

Shit. She'd said too much. He wanted to throw her a warning look, but he doubted she would listen to him anyway.

"Keep it on him at all times, Emily. I need to see if he's alone."

He turned his attention to Skip again.

"Don't say a word to her and don't make a move. If you do, she'll shoot you and I'm not kidding," he said, giving Emily the hint that he was serious.

He noted Emily and Skip both nodded.

As fast as possible he slipped to the nearest window which gave him a good view of the wharf. *Sweet Lies* was docked and he didn't detect any other movement along the steps to the house nor any movement along this side of the keeper house. But that didn't mean Skip had come alone. Checking the other windows, he saw nothing.

He'd hoped that the sign of no one else being here would calm him. It didn't. Unless Skip Cole had taken lessons over the years Steve had been incarcerated, he didn't know how to operate a tugboat. That meant they had company out there somewhere.

He joined Emily and trained his gun onto Skip again, keeping himself alert for any suspicious movements as his ex-friend smiled and focused his gaze on Steve.

"May I go for my ID now?"

"Like Emily said, I'll need more convincing than a possible forged ID."

"No problems."

Steve tensed as Skip carefully drew aside his suit coat. His eyes remained steady, confident...maybe even friendly?

A glimmer of hope began gnawing against his rage and betrayal at seeing the familiar twinkle of friendship in Skip's face. Once again Steve clamped down on it.

Hard.

He couldn't afford the least bit of wishful thinking at this point. One mistake and Emily and he would be dead. He watched Skip produce a laminated ID folder from an inside pocket. He held it up for Steve and Emily to read.

It looked legitimate enough, but it could be a fake. As he said earlier, he would need more proof.

"I had no idea," Emily gasped.

Then Skip held up a marshal's badge. Steve had seen a few of them in his line of work and this really looked real, but he wasn't quite ready to believe.

"Anyone can get an ID like that made up. How do I know it's for real?"

"You don't. You'll just have to trust me."

"I don't think so," Steve said tightly.

"After everything you've been through, I'd be surprised if you could trust someone. It's okay, you keep the gun. Just don't shoot try to them because they'd have to protect themselves."

Shoot them? What the hell was he talking about?

Steve watched Skip's gaze shift to the other door in the corner of the living room. He heard Emily gasp and felt his stomach drop in a sickening lurch as he spotted two men dressed in black. Guns drawn. Pointed at both Emily and him.

They'd come in through the other door.

"Everything's fine here. Both of you can wait in the boat," Skip said.

The two men nodded, shoved their guns into shoulder holsters and quietly disappeared.

Jesus. That was too close.

"I almost blew your goddamn head off," Steve whispered as the anger against Skip began to crumble like an avalanche.

"You wouldn't have. You don't have the murderous gleam in your eye. Why don't you both have a seat with me in the kitchen? I'll explain everything. But first if you don't mind, I'll just help myself to some of that spaghetti you have in the pot. It smells good and I'm starved."

• • ⌦ • •

"YOU'VE BEEN WORKING undercover spying on Helena all these years?" Steve still couldn't quite believe what Skip had told them, and he couldn't quite allow himself to lower the gun he still held in his hand as the three of them sat at the kitchen table.

"Yep," Skip said as he swallowed his final forkful of spaghetti.

"A disgruntled employee of hers who got fingered for extortion in a separate case tipped the Feds off that Helena was a shady character. He told us Helena was using her newspaper journalists as a cover for smuggling drugs in from other countries."

"Is that why you stuck to me like glue when we worked together? Pretended to be friends with me? To see if I was one of her goons?"

"At first, yes."

Steve frowned as that familiar feeling of betrayal reared its ugly head again.

"But I have pretty good instincts about people," Skip continued. "I knew early on you weren't involved in her shady dealings. Hey! Cheer up! I wouldn't waste my great sense of humor on just anybody."

"I thought you were behind everything."

"Don't look so down, man. You give me too much credit, Steve. I'm not that powerful, but apparently Helena is."

"Who the hell sent me that anonymous disc I gave to you?"

Skip frowned and a blank look crossed his face. "What disc?"

"The one I gave to you the day I resigned? When you were in her office? Looking for a pen? I snuck up on you and scared the shit out of you."

Skip's blank look continued then suddenly he swore.

"Oh man. I remember. You said it was a big story. I put it on Helena's desk right on top of your resignation letter. Then I went back to searching her office. When I left, I forgot the disc."

He forgot the fucking disc? On Helena's desk? How could he forget the fucking disc?

"You forgot the disc on her desk?" Emily whispered in a strangled voice.

Skip turned to Emily.

"Well, at the time I assumed it was just a big story. Journalism stuff. My workload was already heavy so I really didn't think much about it. And I was in the process of searching Helena's office. I had that on my mind. I'm hoping you can tell me if you have another disc around? Maybe that's why they didn't kill you because they didn't know if you had one?"

Emily made eye contact with Steve and he wondered if she was thinking the same thing he was. Skip could be setting this whole thing up so he could have them hand over the disc and laptop. It would save them looking for it. He shook his head in warning to her and she remained silent.

"Still don't trust me." Skip nodded slowly. "I can understand that. So, shoot. Er, okay bad choice of words with you holding a gun on me. Fire away. I mean with the questions. What do I need to do to prove myself?"

Skip grinned and another round of irritation gripped Steve. How could Skip be so easygoing with all the shit he and Emily had been through?

"How did you know it was me when you walked into my gun earlier?" Steve found himself asking.

Skip pushed away his plate and rubbed his hands with amused anticipation.

"Okay, test questions. That's a good start. It means you are at least willing to give me the benefit of the doubt. Okay, well, I hope I don't shock the shit out of you, but I've known about you for months."

Steve's finger found the trigger of his gun. If Skip already knew who he was, then he had knowledge of his kidnapping.

"Easy, my man. I've known because your brothers contacted me."

"Bullshit. They would never trust you after what I told them I suspected."

"Aside from their busy married lives they did have undercover jobs, Steve. I was first contacted by your brother Matt. Whoever he hangs around with has quite a few connections. He came to me with knowledge that I was working undercover investigating Helena and told me about you being alive. At least your brothers trust me."

Skip let the sentence dangle in the air.

"They would have told me. I know they would have." He knew that without a doubt. If his brothers knew Skip was one of the good guys they would have told him. He knew that deep in his heart.

Skip shook his head.

"Unfortunately, with all the shit hanging over your head, your anger issues and my not knowing how extensively damaged you were mentally, I asked your brothers to not mention me at all. I couldn't take the chance of you blowing my cover. You understand that, don't you?"

Steve could read the desperation in his friend's eyes. The hope that yes, he could understand. That maybe he could forgive him for leaving that damn disc on Helena's desk. Yes, he could forgive Skip. It was his own fault for being in a hurry that day and for not explaining to him what the disc contained.

"I need to talk to my brothers to verify your story. I hope you understand that."

"No problem. I'll get them on my cell."

He made a move for his jacket pocket and Steve stiffened. Obviously Skip noticed his reaction and stopped.

"It's just my cell phone. You can dial."

"Okay, you go ahead."

"I don't get cell reception out here. You know that, Skip," Emily burst in. She was frowning and not trusting Skip. He sensed she was thinking this was some kind of a trick, just like he was suspecting.

Skip nodded and winked at Emily.

"Well, regular folks don't around these secluded parts, but us sneaky undercover government employees don't have dead zones on our cells."

Steve watched Emily's mouth drop open in surprise.

Well, here was Skip's chance to prove he spoke the truth. If his cell phone worked and Skip could get his brothers' to confirm his story, then Steve had been wrong about the man.

He wasn't sure if he should be disappointed or happy.

Keeping his finger on the trigger, he watched Skip dig out a cell phone. He tapped in a password and then he placed the cell onto the table and pushed it over toward Steve.

"Keep him covered," Steve instructed Emily as he dialed Daniel's number. His brother picked up on the second ring.

"Hello," came his brother's easygoing voice.

"I have one question," Steve said tightly. "Can I trust Skip Cole with Emily and my lives?"

"Steve? What's going on? What's wrong?" His brother suddenly sounded frantic.

"Answer my question. Can I trust Skip with our lives?"

Daniel swore. "Is he there?"

"He's here."

"Can I speak to him?"

Steve held out the phone and Skip accepted it with a frown. He listened for a moment then said yes. That one word carved a hole right through Steve's gut and his hands shook as he accepted the cell and listened to his brother.

"Yes, you can trust him, Steve. I'm sorry I couldn't tell you."

"I have to go now," he said, burying his feelings of betrayal deep inside. Without waiting for Daniel to reply, he disconnected. He would have to deal with his brothers at another time. Right now, they needed to get this shit fixed.

"We have the disc and people are still looking for it," Emily blurted, and Steve suddenly felt relieved that at least Emily could still trust someone.

Skip cocked an inquiring eyebrow at her.

"Trouble?" he asked.

It was as if a dam burst. Suddenly Emily was revealing everything from the night in the tower when she found the laptop, to when they discovered the empty fuel on *Sweet Lies*, the drugs planted on the boat and to what she'd seen on the computer screen.

Steve remained quiet as he watched the two interact. Skip grilled her for every piece of information and she so easily gave it.

Fuck. He swore he felt jealous at how easy they were able to talk to one another. He, on the other hand, was reeling. His brothers knew Skip was a good guy and had never told him. They could have saved him a year of aggravation with the shrink.

"I'm going to need that disc and your laptop, Steve."

"What happens if I hand them over to you?" If he did, he would have no bargaining chips to work with.

"Before we hand it over, we need guarantees," Emily stated. Steve found himself grinning. Was she was thinking the same thing he was?

"What happens to Steve? He still has the drug charges hanging over his head. When the police find out he's not dead, they'll put him right back in jail."

"We can make a deal with the Feds. I won't hand over the disc and laptop until I have their guarantees you are pardoned. How's that?"

"You get it in writing, and we have a deal," Emily stated.

"She's quite the lawyer, Steve," Skip chuckled, and Steve found himself grinning at her.

"She's quite a woman too."

He enjoyed the way Emily's cheeks flushed pink at his comment and loved the frown on Skip's face at the comment. Obviously, Skip must have had some feelings for Emily, or he wouldn't be reacting, would he?

"It'll only take an hour to get it in writing. I'll have them fax it to your brother and I can tell him to call me and verify it. Is that good for you?"

He looked at Emily and awaited her answer.

She nodded and Skip turned to Steve again. This time there was no sign of humor in his friend's face. Just a grim smile.

"Good. After I make the call, I need you to do some work on your own. But it will be dangerous as hell. You up to it?"

Before Emily could answer, Steve nodded.

"Let's hear it."

. . ᦔᦱ . .

THE GENTLE SWAY OF *Sweet Lies* rocking against the ocean swells did nothing to comfort Emily as she stood at the helm, peering down to the bow area where Steve and Skip were engaged in an intense discussion on how to bring down Helena and her empire.

She felt sick to her tummy at the thought that Skip wanted Steve to help him. And she felt even sicker that Steve dared considering putting his life into danger once again in an effort to get Helena who just happened to be involved in this underground transplant organization.

Sure, Skip said Steve would have plenty of backup but, God, if something went wrong and something happened to him... Emily shivered at the memory of the magnitude of emptiness she'd experienced when she'd been told Steve was dead. Now he was home and she was whole again. They were together. Why did he want to casually throw what they have away?

A tear betrayed her as she tried to remain strong. It streamed down her cheek and she angrily swiped it away. To top everything off, the woman she had trusted all these years was the one behind this whole nightmare of Steve being kidnapped, hurt and held in prison. Helena had found the disc on top of Steve's resignation and must have believed Steve had been the one who'd dropped it there. It was too much to take. She felt like screaming, or better yet, having it out with Helena. One on one.

She didn't hear Skip come up behind her until he spoke.

"I'll take the helm, Emily. You go and be with Steve."

"For how long?" she snapped, suddenly losing her grip on control. "Until Helena kills him?"

"We've gone over the plan numerous times, Emily. Chances of something going wrong are small."

"There is a chance. That's already too big a risk for me to take." Another tear betrayed her, and she angrily swiped at it.

"It's up to Steve, Emily. He's the one who's been sitting helpless in a prison. I know him. He'll want to avenge what the two of you have been through. He's going to want to take down Helena. And then maybe he can live with his demons."

"He won't live if he fails, Skip. I'd rather have him alive and with his demons."

Skip smiled. There was a really sweet tenderness in his eyes as he reached out and gently wiped away another stray tear from her cheek.

"Maybe you should tell Steve how you feel?"

"Apparently he doesn't care. He made the decision on his own. Didn't even bother to ask me, did he?"

"I guess we got caught up in the excitement. You know us adrenaline junkies."

"Just like old times. Right, Skip? Chasing adrenaline rush after rush."

He avoided her gaze and her heart plummeted with guilt.

"I'm sorry. I didn't mean to snap at you. It's Steve I'm mad at, not you."

"No harm done. Now go and talk to him. I'll take the helm."

"I'll talk to him later. I don't want to put you or your men through all the yelling when we come to blows."

"Or the making-up part?" Amusement etched his voice.

She didn't reply. As far as she was concerned, there would be no making up if Steve decided to go through with this.

A moment later, she heard Skip's footsteps echo down the steps to the deck. Squinting against the white glare of sunshine reflecting off the surrounding ocean waves, she returned her attention to the looming silhouette of Prince Edward Island in front of her.

There would be no making up after this fight. Not if Steve went ahead with his plans to go after Helena tomorrow.

Because if he did, she'd leave him, for good.

• • ❧ • •

AFTER CATCHING A CHARTER plane from Prince Edward Island to New York, Skip secured two motel rooms for the three of them and Steve had left Emily in the other room with a couple of Skip's men standing guard outside the door.

Skip was as good as his word. He'd gotten the drug charges dropped and sent a fax to that effect to Daniel's place. In turn, Daniel, a lawyer, had checked it over and called Steve, saying he was in the clear.

Emily had been quiet on the trip over to the States and Steve figured she was tired and scared and probably still very confused. She'd had a lot to digest in a very short time and he was amazed at how well she'd adjusted. She'd taken the news he was alive better than he could ever hope for. Had been devastated by Helena's part in all this, yet she'd accepted it easily enough and hadn't fought him on his decision to go after Helena.

He ached to go back to their hotel room to reassure her everything would work out, yet at the moment getting Helena was his top priority.

Skip grilled Steve until his nerves were frayed and then Skip grilled him some more. When Skip was finished, he nodded approval, leaned back against the chair on the opposite side of the small hotel table they were using, and with a severe frown on his face, proceeded to thoughtfully rub his thumb up and down the moist film on the tequila bottle he'd retrieved from the small fridge in the room.

Instinctively Steve knew Skip wanted to say something he wouldn't like and was figuring out a delicate way of saying it.

"Just come out with it, Skip. What's up?"

"Are you sure about tomorrow?"

"What do you mean? Am I sure? Of course I'm sure. Unless...you changed your mind and chickened out?" Steve toyed. He doubted Skip was chicken. But something was bugging him.

"It's not me I'm worried about."

"Don't worry about me. I'm in. All the way."

"What about Emily?" Skip asked quietly.

Confusion rocked Steve.

"What about Emily?"

"Do you still love her?"

Shock at his friend's questions made Steve frown. Did Skip have more feelings about his wife than he was letting on? If that was the case, he needed to tell Skip the flat-out truth that he better dissolve any feelings his friend might harbor for his wife.

"I can't go five feet away from her without missing her. Does that answer your question?"

"I don't mean that. Have you asked her what she thinks about you going up against Helena tomorrow?"

"She understands."

Skip quirked an eyebrow at him.

"Does she?"

"What do you mean? Of course, she understands."

"She's pretty upset about this whole thing," Skip said softly.

"She told you this?"

"On the boat."

She was confiding in Skip and not him? What the hell was going on?

"How come she didn't tell me?"

"Probably because you didn't ask her how she felt."

"I figured she understood my need to get Helena for what she's done to us."

"Maybe she just needs your reassurance you'll be around for her in the future, buddy."

"We both know there aren't any guarantees." Even as he said it, he suddenly realized why Emily had been so quiet on the trip over. Man, he was a bloody idiot. With his need for revenge he'd totally ignored her feelings. Shit, he needed to make things right between them.

"Which brings me back to my question. Are you sure you want to do this? If not, then tell me now. I'll go in myself and try it."

"This is my fight, Skip. Besides, Helena might get suspicious if you show up and carry out the plan. You might blow your cover. You're going to need it if something happens to me."

"It's your call."

Skip leaned forward, placed his elbows on the table and clasped his bottle with both hands. His eyes narrowed into serious slits.

"Before I forget. The man you mentioned you suspect as being crooked in the Canadian Coast Guard was found dead in his car outside his home last night."

Shit.

"Make sure the same doesn't happen to you, Steve."

"I'll try my best."

"You do better than your best. Is there anything else we need to go over?"

"Not unless you want to. I just want to get some sleep."

Skip smiled. "Go on. Get out of here. Besides, I saw a cute redhead checking in when we registered. She looked as if she might be up for some fun. I saw her heading into the motel bar when I brought in the suitcases earlier. If I'm lucky she might still be there."

"Haven't changed, have you?" Steve chuckled as he pushed out his chair.

"I'm still a sucker for redheads," he admitted.

"I'd better let you get on with your business then."

"Not business, my dear boy. Pleasure. Pure. Sweet. Pleasure."

"My mistake. I'll let you get on with your...pleasure. Good night."

"Nighty-night. See you in the a.m."

As he let himself out of Skip's room, he couldn't help but notice a redhead coming up the hall. A couple of quick raps on the door and Skip answered. When he saw the woman, he threw Steve a quick wink of thanks and headed on down the hallway after her.

As Steve headed down the hallway, he glanced over his shoulder and watched his friend in action. The redhead was a curvy one and quite pretty. And she didn't appear to have a problem laughing at something Skip said. A moment later she was nodding her head and Skip was heading back to Steve.

"She agreed to meet me at the bar for drinks in a few minutes," Skip replied, seemingly happier than a pig in shit.

"Haven't lost your touch, buddy," Steve laughed. Skip had always managed to easily woo a woman into his bed with his sense of humor and gentlemanly manners.

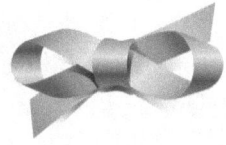

Chapter Twenty

S teve nodded to the two bodyguards standing in front of their room and then quietly swiped the electronic key into the lock, opened the door and slipped inside the hotel room. It was dark. And quiet. Thank God. He was way too tired to argue with Emily tonight.

Checking first to make sure the door was locked, he turned around and froze. Through the semidarkness of the room he spotted movement on the queen-sized bed and immediately smelled her sexy scent. A light flicked on and he saw her sitting on their bed, blankets nestled around her waist and her arms folded around the stuffed red lobster he'd won for her at the fair.

How in the heck had she smuggled that into their suitcases, he mused. He almost smiled at how cute she looked, but then his heart began to pound in his ears at the grim determined frown plastered on her face.

Yep, now that Skip had mentioned it, he realized she'd been pissed off the whole way over and he'd been too high on a rush of their plans in getting Helena that he hadn't paid the attention he'd needed to pay to her.

"Thought you'd be asleep by now," he said as he dropped the card onto the table beside the television set.

"So, you could avoid a fight with me? Not a chance," she said tightly as her eyes flashed with anger.

"I don't want to fight with you, Emily," he reassured, and started undressing. All he wanted to do was climb into bed and just sleep.

"Then we won't fight. You tell me you won't go through with your plans to get Helena tomorrow and we won't fight. Let Skip do it. Let him bring down Helena and her empire. It's his job."

Irritation slammed through him.

"You know I can't do that, Emmie. She's the one who fucked us over. I want my revenge. She deserves to get her ass nailed to the wall."

Emily's angry frown cracked, and he caught a glimpse of the devastating fear she'd been hiding. For the first time he knew exactly how frightened she was for his safety. The truth left him reeling, and he ached to comfort her.

In a couple of quick strides, he was on the bed beside her, wanting to draw her into his arms and comfort her, but she threw the lobster at his head and jumped away from him like a hyper jack-in-the-box. The lobster bounced off his left temple and dropped to the ground.

"If you run off tomorrow chasing after another one of your adrenaline rushes like you did in the old days, you can forget about me being here if you come back."

If. Damn.

He inhaled a steadying breath. She was dead serious.

"I didn't know you felt this strongly."

"If you'd bothered to ask, maybe you would have saved us a lot of anguish."

"If I don't go tomorrow, we won't be able to live at the lighthouse. We'll have to go into Witness Protection and that's not the life I want for us."

"I don't care. I just want you safe."

"I want you safe too, sweetheart."

"You sure have a strange way of showing it. Especially if you don't come back."

At the tinge of a tremble in her otherwise tough voice, he felt his resolve slip away. No matter how strongly he felt about getting Helena, he didn't want to hurt Emily by going against her wishes.

"Okay, you win. If you don't want me to go, I won't. You're the best thing that's ever happened to me and I don't want to lose you."

At his reassurance, relief sparkled in her eyes and her shoulders slumped. However, seeing her relieved did nothing to dispel the disappointment slithering through him. Disappointment that he'd been so close to finally getting a chance to put some sort of closure to this whole thing. To be able to lead a somewhat normal life with the woman he loved.

"I'll go and tell Skip. I'll tell him everything's off. I'll be right back."

He stood, and on shaky legs, he turned and headed for the door. He'd been so close. So damn close and to not even have a chance at trying to get Helena...

He exhaled wearily. Emily was right. He might not make it back to her and their future would go up in smoke. Again.

He'd been crazy to put his life on the line. To put their love on the line just so he could exact some sort of vengeance. He was about to slip out the door when her hand curled over his right shoulder and she pulled him back inside the room.

When he turned to face her, he blinked in surprise as her strong façade crumbled. Her lower lip trembled, and tears bubbled up in her eyes. Thick lashes lowered as she lifted his hand and placed it directly upon her warm nightgown, directly over her heart. Judging by the way her heart pounded against his palm she was terrified. She threw him a wobbly smile he figured was meant to cheer him up. It didn't.

"What kind of a woman am I? Instead of supporting my husband when he needs me the most, I'm thinking only about myself. I know you're scared too. I can see it in your eyes."

He inhaled sharply at her tender touch as she then placed her other hand over his heart.

"I can feel it here too. We're both scared. Terrified. I have to tell you that every minute that goes by I feel as if I'm going to wake up and you'll just have been a beautiful dream."

At her admission a hard knot formed in his throat.

"I'm letting my fears control me, control us," she continued, and her voice lowered to a soft whisper.

"You do what you need to do tomorrow. Just make sure you come back because I'll be waiting."

Emotions, thick and raw, welled inside him. He couldn't believe she was going to support him with his decision to go after Helena. Drawing her into his arms, and before she could say anything else, he lowered his head and kissed her.

Her warm lips trembled against his and then suddenly that familiar obsession swooped over him. The same uneasiness he'd felt that afternoon on the beach years ago when she told him not to go to New York that day because she'd had a bad feeling. But he'd ignored both their feelings and their world had fallen apart.

Was this feeling a premonition?

Suddenly he realized he tasted chocolate on her lips and his thoughts drew back to Emily.

He chuckled. She always nibbled on chocolate or drank hot chocolate when she was nervous.

Abruptly she broke the kiss. "Why are you laughing?"

"You taste good."

She smiled and brushed her passion-swelled lips urgently against his.

"This makes you happy?" she asked.

"Extremely. You smell good too. Clean and fresh."

"Took a long, hot shower while you were out."

"Mmm, sounds heavenly."

Her eyes twinkled with mischief and her smile turned secretive. The sensual sight sent his heart to pounding and heated blood raced straight south.

"Okay, you're up to something. What is it?"

"You'll find out."

Fresh urgency zipped along every nerve ending as she took his hand in hers and led him into the bathroom. Warm mist greeted him.

"I want you to make love to me in the shower," she breathed.

"You're going to turn into a prune," he joked, and curled his arms around her waist.

To his surprise she grabbed him by his biceps and tenderly pushed him away.

"Before we start, let me take care of something first."

He inhaled sharply as her hot hands slipped beneath his sweater and T-shirt. Her fingers skimmed along his naked waist around to his back.

"We won't need this," she whispered.

In one quick move she slid his gun from its resting place against the small of his back and lowered it to the restroom seat. Her sultry gaze showed both love and bits of fear as she stared into his eyes.

"Or needing this."

Her hands popped the brass button on his jeans, and he heard the zipper lowering. His heart thundered in his ears as she yanked both his jeans and underwear past his hips and below, allowing his full arousal to spring free and he knew he was in for one hell of a good night.

•• ❧ ••

THE LIGHT KNOCK AT the door came very early the next morning when Steve was in the shower and Emily paced a path into the hotel carpet as she worriedly nibbled on her knuckles. At the intruding sound adrenaline seared like a bolt of lightning through her veins. She didn't make a move to answer it. She could only stare at the door and wish Skip would just go away. Maybe he would leave if he thought they weren't here? Maybe her husband would change his mind if he thought Skip had left without him?

"Maybe you should get that?" Steve's strangled whisper erupted from the open doorway of the bathroom. Mist flowed out and he wore nothing but a skimpy towel slung low over his hips.

God, he looked so good. She wanted him to stay so bad. Wanted them to just forget everything and just love each other.

"I can't."

"If you don't want me to go, I won't."

Emily could see the disappointment flicker in his eyes again just like it had last night when she demanded he not go after Helena. She felt the devastation of surrender roll through like a giant punch. Despite her fear, she realized he needed to do this. For himself and for them. She knew it would tear him up inside if he didn't at least get a chance.

God help her, but she was going to crack up permanently this time if he died.

"Go, get ready. I'll let him in," she found herself saying.

"Are you sure?"

No. She was not sure. What had she been thinking in changing her mind last night and letting him go?

Emily jumped as another round of taps echoed through the room. Steve didn't move. His eyes were stormy and her heart thundered against her ribs as she debated whether to beg him not to go. For a moment he looked as if he might not go and then the confidence spilled back into his face.

Her tummy dropped like a stone as he nodded and then he disappeared into the bathroom.

As she slowly headed toward the door, she became very aware that her legs were about to give out, but she forced herself to keep moving. She peeked through the security hole and then answered the door.

Skip stood in the hallway, his hand poised to knock again. He seemed startled to see her.

"Thought you might have changed your minds," he said softly.

"Come on in. He'll be right out."

"It's okay. I'll stay out here and wait. Give you two time to say a proper goodbye."

"There won't be any goodbyes," Steve said from behind her as he struggled into his T-shirt. "Because I'm coming back."

Her heart fluttered at the intense confidence in his voice and a sharp sting of tears spiraled into her eyes. She turned to face Skip, who suddenly looked very uncomfortable.

"Skip, you have to take care of him. Please. Make sure he comes back to me."

"I'll make sure he stays safe," he said, and threw her a wobbly smile that made her feel worse.

Behind her, she heard a sharp click as Steve checked the clip in his gun.

"I got a hold of your brothers. We'll meet them there. Jo and Sara should be here any minute. I'd wait here a bit longer until they do, but we need to get going. I'm taking my men and Emily will be alone for about five minutes. Ten, tops, before they show."

"I don't want her here alone," Steve said coolly.

"I'll be fine. I need a few minutes anyway," she admitted as she tried to digest this newest bit of news. Sara and Jo were coming, just in case.

For her sake...in case she needed them. In case something happened to Steve. Oh God, help her. Please keep him safe.

When Steve's warm hands curled over her shoulder, she just about jumped out of her skin. He turned her around to face him. His hair was still wet, but he'd combed it straight back off his forehead. He looked good this way. Real good. And he smelled real good too. A delicious scent of strawberries curled around her and she realized he'd used the shampoo she'd brought from home. Perhaps it was a way to keep her with him? She started to shake at the thought that he might not be coming back and this might be their final goodbye.

Horrific sadness welled in her and she forced herself to blink back the hot tears and made herself meet his intense gaze. His warm breath caressed her face as he spoke.

"I'd rather stay, Emily."

"I'm fine, really."

The last thing he needed was to see her start crying like a blubbering idiot. And she would too, if he didn't leave right this instant.

"Okay but don't open the door to anyone but Skip or my brothers or Sara and Jo. Okay?"

She nodded weakly, noting instantly he hadn't mentioned himself.

His head lowered. The instant his warm, gentle lips touched hers, her brain shorted out and her fears vanished as every pleasure center in her body sizzled to life. If she hadn't wrapped her arms around his neck, she was sure she would have fallen. And then too soon he was easing away from her.

His eyes were dark, full of passion as he studied her for a long moment. Again, she silently prayed he would change his mind. Prayed as she'd never prayed before.

"I'll be back," he whispered, his voice full of promise.

Then he was gone. Leaving her with the sound of the door locking behind him and an intense fear uncoiling like a cobra inside her. She bit her bottom lip to prevent herself from crying, but it didn't work. The tears fell like two hot springs down her cheeks.

She let herself cry. Let herself just give in to her emotions. She didn't know how long she did, but it couldn't have been more than a few moments when a knock erupted at the door and her heart soared. Steve had changed his mind! He'd come back!

Wiping away her tears, she rushed to the door, quickly unlocked it and flung it open. Her heart stopped. It wasn't Steve at all.

She managed a quick smile. This was the last person on earth she'd expected to be here in New York.

"Hi! What are you doing here?"

Her smile vanished and a finger of ice stroked a frigid warning through her a split second before her unexpected visitor pulled out a gun and aimed it straight at her heart.

•• ⌀ ••

WHEN HE HEARD THE FAMILIAR high heels clicking toward Helena's office, Steve straightened in her plush office chair and forced himself to inhale a steady breath. The door swung inward. If Helena was surprised to see him sitting behind her desk, she didn't show it. She merely breezed inside as if she knew all along she had company.

Dropping her purse onto the desk in front of him, she smiled. A creepy shiver of what Steve could only figure out was fear slithered a chill warning up his spine.

"Why, Mister Donovan. What an unexpected pleasure," she said cheerfully.

"Cut the crap, Helena."

"Oh dear. Something's upset you," she said, seemingly unoffended by his bold reply.

"I hope you aren't too upset because I had to leave early the other day after Emily's fitting. I had an appointment. How about we get together today? For lunch? We can discuss plans for your future."

"How about we discuss plans for your future, Helena? Like how are you going to match your hair color with the orange overalls you'll be wearing in prison?"

She blinked rapidly for a second at his statement and then recovered quickly.

"My, you certainly are touchy. What is it that I can do for you, darling?"

"More like what I can do for you, Helena. I'm going to give you a couple of metal bracelets and crucify you. And that's just for starters."

She let out a chuckle of amusement. Man, he had to commend her for her good acting that's for sure. She didn't seem the least bit fazed at his threat.

"Dear boy, what are you babbling about?"

"I have evidence against you, Helena," he said. He wanted to shake her up, but nothing changed in her demeanor. The woman was unshakable. She seemed like a goddamn rock.

"Information that is being leaked to the press as we speak."

"Ah, I see. You want money. I'll write you a check."

She reached for her purse, but he grabbed it out of her hand and placed it back on the desk, closer to him and out of her reach.

"Aren't you afraid your security cameras will catch you bribing me?" he asked.

"Darling," she said gently. "My people mind their own business. Something you should have done years ago."

"Oh, sweet heavens, Helena. Don't tell me you're the one who planted those drugs on my boat? Oh wait! I already figured that out, didn't I? I had plenty of time in prison to figure things out."

She didn't say anything, but Steve didn't miss her quick glance at the purse.

"Dead giveaway, Helena."

In a flash he reached out and snapped up the purse. Keeping an eye on her, he used his touch senses to sift through the contents.

"Lipstick, compact, appointment book..."

"Please, there is no need for you pawing through my personal belongings, Mr. Donovan. You are being entirely too rude."

He ignored her snappy remark when his fingers brushed against cold metal. He threw her an amused grin.

"Oh look! A gun?"

He withdrew the deadly weapon from its hiding place in a side pocket and relieved it of all the bullets before placing it back into her purse.

"Shame on you, Helena."

"A woman can't be too careful these days, dear boy. It isn't like the old days when you could trust someone with a mere handshake or by their word."

"Funny you should mention that, Helena. Didn't you give me your word over the phone years ago when I used my one telephone call to ask you to send me a lawyer? Didn't you give me your word you'd get me out of there?"

Her smile wavered ever so slightly, and she reached up to brush away an imaginary stray strand of her neatly coiffured hair.

"Ouch, a sore spot?" he said coolly.

"You can't prove anything, Steve."

Steve. She knew exactly who he was.

"We have some things to discuss, Helena. Top of the list is something rather...personal."

Her eyes narrowed and he detected a crack in her otherwise cool demeanor.

"What are you insinuating, Mr. Donovan?"

"Revenge," he said coldly.

"How enticing," she replied. It surprised him to see how she seemed to cheer right up.

"And exactly how do you propose to exact your revenge?" she purred, seeming quite amused.

"Why don't you grab yourself a fresh cup of coffee over there? Stay a while. I'll explain everything in detail."

"Well, if I must stay and be entertained. Would you like a cup?"

Steve nodded. "Please."

He watched anxiously as she headed over to the bar where he'd prepared the pot of coffee and left it warming on the hot plate.

"As I remember correctly you prefer cream and three teaspoons of sugar?" she asked.

"You flatter me with your memory," Steve said dryly as she poured their coffee.

A moment later she walked toward him with both steaming cups in hands. She threw him another cheerful smile.

"Don't even think about throwing it in my face, Helena."

She chuckled and he suspected that thought had crossed her mind.

"You insult me, Mr. McCullen. I would never do such a hideous thing to a guest."

Instead of calling him Steve, she'd turned her tone to the formal of Mr. McCullen. She did that when she was pissed off at someone. He must be getting to her.

When she placed his mug down in front of him on the desk, he relaxed. She continued to stand as she sipped her coffee. He didn't touch his.

"Now what do you have in mind?" she said sweetly. "Torture? A knife to the heart?"

"Something a little different, but I'll tell you in a bit. First, we need to have a heart-to-heart."

"How pleasant. Would you mind if I have a seat?"

She waited for his answer; her well-coiffured eyebrows raised with inquisition.

"Please do. Only keep your hands where I can see them."

"You don't trust me? How insulting."

"Cut the act, Helena. I have the disc. The original of the copy that you found on your desk. I've seen it all."

A curiously satisfied smile slipped across Helena's red painted lips.

"I knew you had it. No matter how much you denied it. I knew you had it."

Steve leaned forward in the chair and placed his hands on the desk, watching her closely. She seemed quite smug now that he'd revealed he had the disc. Too smug for comfort.

"I expected you to be more loyal, Steven. Unlike my secretary Summer Robbins. She's the one who sent you that disc. She was upset with me and threatened me when her husband died on the table during his heart transplant operation. Unfortunately, she wasn't as loyal as I'd hoped. She knew the risks of using an illegal donor heart, but she still became upset. It happens more than you think. I wasn't able to remove her as quickly as I'd hoped, so she was able to get a disc to you. I gather you brought the original along with you this morning?"

Steve remembered Summer. Remembered her husband had been gravely ill and that he'd died. She'd committed suicide shortly after his death. Or was it supposed to have been suicide, like they had done to him? Apparently, it was just another murder in Helena's routine.

God! How could she keep such a tight handle on so many people without this underground transplant organization coming to the surface earlier?

But he knew the answer. There were a lot of desperate people out there who wanted to keep their loved ones alive. Many of them would do illegal things in order to get what they wanted. Helena and her people used their desperation and vulnerability. It was so insane that he could barely believe it. But he knew if he was in a similar situation and Emily needed a body part in order to live, he could see himself thinking about going down that avenue too.

"And if I said I did have the disc on me?"

"Then I would tell you I might be interested in taking a look at it."

"You already know what's on it. Unless...there's something on the disc you haven't been able to cover up? What's the problem, Helena? Too many people to kill? Too many angles to cover? There must be something you weren't able to cover. Someone you couldn't pay off for their silence."

Her face paled.

Bingo.

If her reaction was an indication, then something on that disc was still good. Still active.

"How much money do you want for it?"

"For the last and very incriminating copy? It might take me some time to think up a proper sum."

When she frowned, he allowed himself a smug smile.

"You were my best journalist, Steven. And a very dear friend as Emily is a very dear friend also. I assure you, what happened to you wasn't personal."

What a fucking bitch.

"Purely business? Is that right? You planted the drugs on my boat using a man in the Canadian Coast Guard who conveniently knew where the drugs would be. Not once but twice. This time around your guy failed to get me and you killed him."

"I did no such thing!"

"Okay so someone you hired did the job."

She remained silent.

"You used the planted drugs to get me into jail," he continued. "That's when another one of your hired goons, a prosecutor, no less, could try to work out a deal with me, right?"

"It was a brilliant plan on such short notice," she admitted with a self-righteous smile that nibbled away at his concentration.

"So your plan was for me to spill my guts and reveal what I know and where the original disc was and the drug charges would be dropped. Unfortunately for you, I didn't cave. I knew what I had and if I so much as gave an inkling of where it was, then Emily and I would be dead. So I kept my mouth shut. It must have pissed you off to no end, right, Helena?"

She kept quiet, her eyes drilling into him like swords. The intense look unnerved him a little and he found himself remembering the pain the guards inflicted, the smacking sounds of their fists upon his body.

He took a steadying breath and continued.

"Your goons beat me up. Too bad they lost control. They certainly weren't neat and tidy on this job. Very messy. When they were through with me, I couldn't talk for some time. I ended up almost dead."

"You would have died, had I not intervened, Steven."

Her hushed response brought an uncomfortable uneasiness shooting through him. Immediately he spied a gleam of excitement in her eyes and he straightened to attention. She was up to something. The touch of nervousness had vanished from her, replaced by pure confidence.

"Unfortunately, I needed you alive so I could question you about the disc's whereabouts. In order to save your life and allow you to see again, a youngster had to be sacrificed."

A youngster had to be sacrificed? What the hell did she mean by that?

"Let's get back on track, Helena," he warned. His insides began to tremble, and he knew she held information he didn't want to hear.

She must have noticed his uneasiness as immense delight snapped across her face.

"You don't know the identity of your donor, do you, dear?"

"Let's get on with what's going to happen to you."

"A young teenager. A dear sweet, innocent, young teenager who had just turned his life around. A lad who wanted to grow up to be a doctor. Oh, my, didn't your brother tell you? The young man was a friend of his wife."

Her voice was soft, gentle, and he found it extremely difficult to tune her out. He knew he should ignore her, but if she was behind the murder of a kid, he needed to dig up that information. She would need to pay for that crime as well.

"You're lying," he taunted.

"Oh, Daniel and Jocelyn didn't tell you about Johnny. Perhaps I should tell you."

No! He didn't want to hear it. If Daniel and Jo had kept silent, there had to be a reason.

But Helena ploughed right ahead.

"When you were beaten, your kidneys were severely damaged and your eyes were unsalvageable—"

"More like they were popped out like grapes by your personal goon squad," he said, trying to quell the nausea of remembering how easily he'd lost his eyes to a group of overzealous jail guards.

"Nonetheless, I felt you would be more...cooperative if you had a new set of eyes, along with a new kidney."

"So, you did what? Kill a kid for parts?"

"Must you be so indelicate, Steven? That was a job for an acquaintance of mine."

"And that made it okay?"

"You are living a virtually normal life, aren't you? And you do have a pair of eyes and kidneys that will keep you alive so you and Emily can be together again. Thanks to my genius acquaintance and his state-of-the-art techniques. Nonetheless, I don't hear you complaining."

"The kidneys rejected. My brother gave me one of his."

"How nice of him. Such brotherly love. But you still have little Johnny's eyes. He had such lovely blue eyes."

Shut up, bitch! He had the sudden urge to rip his eyes out of his sockets. No, not his eyes. They belonged to kid!

Shit! She was fucking with his head. Distracting him.

"Helena!" a familiar voice said from the doorway.

Immediately Steve recognized the voice of the man he'd met at the fair. His head snapped up and he spotted Dr. Baker standing in the doorway. And someone stood beside him.

His gut twisted in fear.

Emily stood there with the doctor. When Steve spotted the gun jabbed into her side, adrenaline squirted like wildfire through his veins. His mind urged him to scramble from his chair and knock the deadly weapon from Baker's fingers, yet he remained seated. Any movement from him would encourage Baker to pull the trigger.

"Brought you a special present, Helena," the doctor smirked.

Helena's confident gaze swung to Doc Baker.

"Well! Looks like we have company. What a delight! Please, do come in. Join the party."

Baker gave Emily a rough shove into the room.

"Mr. Donovan, we meet again," Doc Baker said as he came into the room and closed the door.

Steve held his breath as Baker cocked his gun and aimed it at Emily's head. Choking back a sob, Emily threw Steve a look that said she was sorry.

"Did you find it?" Helena ambled over to Baker.

"Got it."

Steve frowned. What were they talking about?

Baker withdrew the gun from Emily's head and Steve sighed a breath of relief. His relief was short-lived when Baker held up the briefcase containing his laptop.

Damn! Skip had placed it into the safe in his room. The safe was supposed to be secure.

"It was in Cole's hotel room. Good thing I know someone in housekeeping. She had access to the area where the safe fobs are kept. The original disc is inside the A drive," Dr. Baker said. "Damn computer sure is heavy. Thankfully they don't make them like this anymore."

"Helena! You are a horrid person. I trusted you," Emily screamed.

"Oh Emily, stop your melodramatics." Helena retrieved the case from Dr. Baker and lifted it onto the desk. She flipped the case open and a moment later lifted out the disc. She stared at it in awe.

"Just as I suspected. Same brand of disc my once trusted secretary used. She was a foolish woman. Very foolish."

He should go for his gun stashed inside his boot, Steve thought as he watched Helena examine the disc and Dr. Baker watching her. All he needed to do was cross his legs to get at it, but first he needed to call in the reinforcements.

"Helena, dear. Haven't you forgotten something?"

Her head snapped up and she threw him a bewildered look.

"Our little discussion we had earlier?"

Her perfectly manicured eyebrows crinkled into a puzzled frown.

"The matter about revenge?" he said smoothly.

She visibly relaxed. "My dear boy, you simply have no opportunity for revenge. I have the laptop, the disc, Emily and yourself. This is all I need."

Steve smiled.

"Ah, yes I do have an opportunity for revenge," he said in the coolest, calmest voice he swore he'd ever used.

Leaning back in his chair, he casually propped his elbows behind his head and tried hard to portray he didn't have a care in the world.

"You see, Helena. I told you my revenge is purely for selfish reasons. I want to watch you die in person."

"What's he talking about?" Doc Baker broke in.

"Not to worry, Steven is only toying with us."

"Am I? There was a nice batch of rat poison in your office kitchen. In the cupboard, way up top. Behind the paper plates."

Helena smiled shakily.

"By chance did you find the coffee tasting a bit...different?"

That was one of the phrase's Skip and he had agreed upon when Steve decided it was time to pull out. He braced himself for Skip's appearance. Nothing happened.

"What are you saying, Steven? You poisoned my coffee? You honestly think I'd believe you would poison me?"

"Prison changes a man."

Where the hell was his backup? Had the doctor taken them out?

"Does it?" There wasn't an ounce of softness left in her voice. Her gaze drifted to her half-full coffee mug.

"About now you should be experiencing the beginning of mild abdominal cramping."

Steve crossed his legs and slowly dropped his hands onto the table. Where the hell was Skip?

"Helena," Doc Baker said, "if what he's saying is true, we have to get you to the hospital, immediately."

She studied Steve with her icy stare, and he stopped moving his hands.

"Do you seriously think I would come here without a plan, Helena? By the way, is that a dusting of perspiration beading your brows?"

He fastened his gaze on Doc Baker. "Doc, don't you think she's getting a little pale?"

Doc Baker licked his lips nervously. The gun pressing against Emily's temple moved away an inch.

"Helena? How are you feeling?"

"Oh, for heaven's sake. I feel fine. Doctor, please check and see if Steven is armed."

Dammit! He needed to stall Baker.

"So, how'd you hook up with Helena, Doc? Did she blackmail you into helping her kill people? Or are you in it for the money?"

"A doctor's salary isn't what it used to be," the doctor replied. He held tight to Emily's elbow and made her move toward Steve. Emily looked terrified and Steve wished he could do or say something to calm her.

Shit. Don't think about Emily, he chastised himself. If he did, he'd lose focus on getting them out of here alive.

"So what? Do you kill people to earn your salary? Kill them for their body parts?"

"Gotta make a living."

Steve tensed as the doctor removed the gun from Emily's temple and jabbed it into her ribs.

"I assume you didn't come unarmed. Place your weapon on the table or else she dies right here and now—"

The doctor was cut off by a loud crash as the office door swung inward. Skip Cole stood in the doorway, his legs spread wide, gun in hand pointed directly at Dr. Baker.

The doctor, stunned by the sudden appearance of Skip, lifted his gun from Emily just as gunshots rang out.

He heard Emily scream and his gut twisted in anguish.

He didn't hesitate a moment longer. Digging into his boot, he snatched up the cold, deadly weapon and launched himself off his chair firing at Dr. Baker. He managed to get off a couple of shots before landing heavily on his side, his breath knocked painfully from his lungs.

For a split second a deadly silence and the acrid smell of gunpowder hung in the air. Steve managed to aim his gun at Doc Baker who stood clutching his wounded arm. Emily, bless her heart, had somehow managed to grab Baker's gun and held it on him, her eyes wide with fright.

Quickly, Steve swung his weapon on Skip, who had his arms wrapped around the waist of a struggling Helena.

"Easy, man! I'm on your side!" Skip shouted when he spotted Steve aiming at him.

"What the hell took you so long?" Steve shouted back, feeling red-hot anger push aside his fear now that he could clearly see Emily was safe.

"We didn't take into consideration the doctor would show up with Emily. We had to make sure she was out of the line of fire before making the move!"

Skip was still shouting.

"What's all the yelling about?" Daniel chuckled from the doorway.

Both of Steve's brothers stood there, their guns drawn.

"It's over, Helena," his oldest brother, Matt, said. "The only party you're going to is going to last a lifetime."

"We got everything on the security cameras," Daniel said. His eyes sparkled with excitement as he approached Helena, who now stood huffing and puffing beside Skip. He'd already cuffed her hands behind her back. She looked quite the pissed-off lady.

"And since you admitted you knew you were being filmed and that your security staff was on your payroll, your confessions will hold up in court," Daniel informed the woman.

"You really don't look too good, Helena." Skip chuckled as he held her by the elbow. "Don't you think you would have preferred the rat poison?"

"You're fired!" Helena snapped at Skip.

He grinned, withdrew his identification from his vest pocket and flashed it in front of her pale face.

"Looks like the joke is on you, Helena. You can't fire me. I don't even work for you. I work for Uncle Sam. Take them away, guys."

He cast a smile at Steve and Emily and then winked as he headed toward the door with the others.

"We'll read them their rights outside. Let's leave these two to get reacquainted. Although I do believe they've already gotten to that point."

Suddenly he and Emily were alone.

From across the room, she looked over at him.

"You okay?" she asked. She looked pale and shaky, but oh so beautiful.

"Better than okay."

He couldn't seem to stop himself from grinning. Emily was safe and Helena was under arrest. This whole shit was coming to an end. He felt really good about it and rolled onto his stomach, getting up on one knee.

"You're not hurt, are you?" she said as she came over and crouched down in front of him. Intense worry marred her pretty face.

"I'm fine."

"Here, let me help you up."

"No." He waved her hand away. "Just stand up."

She frowned and reluctantly stood.

Reaching into his back pocket he pulled out the item he needed, lifted the lid and held out a tiny velvet black box so she could see the sparkling diamond engagement ring. He'd bought it yesterday after Skip agreed to loan him some money for a ring. Then he'd dragged his friend to a nearby jewelry store where Steve picked out a delicate diamond that wasn't too expensive and something so pretty, he knew Emily would love it.

He had told Skip he was going to propose to Emily the instant Helena was arrested.

His heart burst with love as he watched her. She was smiling and those cute dimples that always took away his breath were there on her face, caving in her cheeks. Man, he loved her so much he literally ached.

Taking a deep breath, he said, "Will you marry me?"

She gasped, looking properly stunned.

"But we're already married," she said.

"That's not quite the answer I'm looking for."

"You're serious?"

"I can always take the ring back."

He made a move to close the lid on the box and she grabbed his wrist, stopping him.

"No!"

"No, you don't want to marry me?" he teased.

"Don't take the ring back. It's so beautiful," she said as she examined the sparkling diamond.

"Beautiful, just like you, Emmie." With suddenly trembling fingers, he managed to get the ring out of the much-too-tiny velvet box. Holding her left hand in his, he slipped the ring onto the appropriate ring finger.

"Perfect fit," she said softly. Tears crystalled in her eyes as she held her hand up and admired the ring.

He climbed to his feet and he was nearly bowled over when she literally threw herself at him. Curling her arms around his neck, she hoisted her legs around his waist. Automatically his hands cupped her rounded butt in an effort to hold her in place.

Her sexy scent just about drove him insane with desire for her. One by one his muscles contracted with need as her warm curves pressed against him.

"A perfect fit," she said again.

"Just like us." Steve stared into her glittering eyes and saw hope and love and tiny bits of fear. She reached out and smoothed a finger over the face of the medallion peeking out from between his open shirt collar.

"Saint Christopher gives safety to travelers," she said softly. "It worked for you."

"Took a while, but yes, it worked."

"And what about Helena? Do you think she'll leave us alone now?"

"Hey! You're forgetting I have two big brothers who'll look out for us."

Emily laughed and Steve caught his breath at the sight of those gorgeous dimples popping out once again in her flushed cheeks. He swore he fell in love with her all over again at that moment.

"Don't worry. Daniel's a good lawyer. He'll find ways to keep her wrapped in the court system for a few years. She won't have any time for us. Besides, I know the owner of this cozy little lighthouse on a secluded island tucked away in Canada. It's a great place for kids to run around on. There's only one problem."

"What?"

"We can't start anything until you answer my question. Will you marry me?"

His heart soared as she cupped her warm hands to both sides of his face.

"Yes, I'll marry you."

Before he could shout a happy howl, she captured his mouth in an erotic kiss that left him totally breathless. Suddenly he was the happiest man on the face of the planet.

Epilogue

Three months later

A t approximately ten minutes after one o'clock in the afternoon Steve stood at the altar anxiously waiting for his bride to walk down the aisle. On one side of him his dad stood as best man. On the other side the preacher continued to throw nervous glances at his watch.

The wedding was supposed to have started ten minutes ago, but it appeared something was holding up the women. They were probably putting the last-minute touches on their hair. It was quite windy outside, and with yesterday's major snowstorm, Steve had worried the wedding might have to be postponed. The snowplows, however, had managed to plow a path directly to the quaint, white church they'd picked just outside of Charlottetown, Prince Edward Island.

Here they were. All the people he loved so dearly.

Emily and his sisters-in-law had worked hard organizing the big event. The church looked fantastic. The sanctuary was decorated in breathtaking bunches of sweetheart pink and delicate purple lilacs. At the end of each pew huge garlands of sharp purple lupines were intermingled with a scattering of light powder blue bachelor buttons and one yellow rose. Their fragrance filled the air with a heady perfume he found extremely pleasant.

Matt and Daniel and Skip stood in the vestibule of the church. All were decked out in light grey tuxedos with black bow ties, hair slicked in place. They sure looked dapper.

All the men were casting quick nervous glances his way. Then back down to the end of the aisle where he spotted his sister-in-law Jo, casting her own nervous glances toward the side of the church where the bridesmaids and bride were supposed to have emerged from ten minutes ago.

He hadn't questioned Daniel or Jo about the boy Helena had mentioned had been killed to save him. They had kept it a secret for a reason and he would honor that. If they wanted to tell him in the future, he would have to deal with it then.

Right now, he just wanted to get on with his life.

He had to admit; Jo glowed in the lovely pale yellow matron-of-honor's dress. She held an overflowing bouquet of sharp purple lilacs over her abdomen, but it couldn't hide her rounded pregnancy.

Both Sara's and Jo's dresses had to be taken out several times over the past few weeks. Through it all, Emily had remained calm. Just like she'd remained calm and cool-headed as she'd leafed through all those dozens of wedding brochures, magazines and tons of other bridal items strewn around the lighthouse.

When Jo walked up the carpeted aisle alone, his nervousness picked up big-time. She threw him what he figured was a reassuring smile, but by the way Daniel was frowning as she whispered in his ear, Steve knew something was wrong.

• • ❧ • •

"STEVE! IT'S BAD LUCK for the groom to see the bride before the wedding," Sara's insistent voice shouted from out in the hall.

"We're already married. It doesn't count."

Emily cringed as Steve's loud voice returned fire a little closer now. Steve was in a rampage. He must have found out she wasn't feeling well and instead of walking down the aisle to marry him she'd raced for a bathroom stall instead.

"Emily? Where are you?"

A split second later, the door to her stall creaked open and she looked up to into his worried face. She couldn't help but throw him a wobbly smile from her perch on the floor in front of the toilet.

"My God! You look pale! You've picked up the flu, haven't you? I knew it. You've been looking green around the gills for the past week."

Green around the gills? Obviously, he'd been hanging around with the fishermen too much over at Jake's Bar. He was using their language. She couldn't help but laugh at the comment around the nausea that clutched her tummy.

"Steve, what are you doing here?"

"I'm taking you home. You need to get into bed and get lots of fluids into you and some proper food."

Her stomach heaved gently.

"Please, don't mention food."

She thought he'd get the hint. He didn't. Typical man.

He kneeled beside her, not caring that he was stepping on the hem of her pretty lace wedding dress with his shoes. Touching his hand to her forehead, he let it rest there for a moment before sighing in relief and brushing a stray curl of hair out of her eyes.

"Good. No fever. That's a good sign, right?"

"Yes, it's a good sign," she admitted.

"You look so sexy with your head in the toilet."

"I'm not sick," she snapped at his teasing remark.

"Okay. The flu. In a few days you'll feel better. We can have the wedding in the summer. A June wedding. Like our first one. We can have it in that vegetable garden I promised you."

A wedding in the vegetable garden? Oh dear, wouldn't that be a sight. Despite his humor, Emily's tummy heaved gently with another knot of nausea reminding her that a June wedding would be out of the picture. She wanted to get married now. Today. Just as they'd planned.

She wanted to be Mrs. Steve McCullen. Wanted to show her friends and family that she and her husband were in love now more than ever, despite what had happened to him. Despite their being apart for years.

"This dress won't fit in June, Steve."

"Sure, it will."

A gorgeous grin splashed across his face and she had the sudden urge to run her fingers through his smooth hair, ruffle it, and make it look messy as if he'd just climbed out of bed.

She liked him that way. Unshaven, mussed hair and so hot-looking that sometimes she just couldn't wait to get him into bed so they made love wherever they felt like it. On the intimate table for two. Up against the shed wall down on the wharf. Once they'd even had sex on top of the washing machine, with the machine on. That had been quite the erotic experience.

"Remember our workouts? They'll keep you in shape," he said with lusty softness in his voice.

"Well, those workouts worked."

She waited for recognition to light up his face. Nothing happened.

"Of course, they worked. That's why you look so damn good in the wedding dress. You have good-looking muscles too. Here let me help you up."

Emily sighed in frustration. He still wasn't getting it! The man was impossible!

He helped her up and led her out of the bathroom stall. She wanted to tell him about her pregnancy on their honeymoon in Hawaii. Over a romantic dinner set for three. By golly if the man didn't pick up the hint with the extra plate on the table, she was going to leave him.

Just then Sara popped her head into the room.

"Can we come in? The baby needs to have his diaper changed."

Steve brushed past Emily and reached out to take the squirming, pudgy angel.

"Hi, J.D." He held the baby high in the air. J.D. giggled furiously as he looked down at Steve with huge emerald green eyes.

"You're getting so big, little fellow."

"Are you feeling better?" Sara asked as she slid the baby's diaper bag onto the counter beside Emily.

"Much, thanks."

In the background, Steve made loud engine noises as with outstretched arms he whirled J.D. around as if he were a lightweight plane. After a moment of play, Steve returned the giggling baby to his mother.

Then he looked over at Emily, and she noticed something different in the depths of his blue eyes. She wasn't sure what it was, but it brought tears into her own eyes.

Hormones. She'd heard pregnant women got very emotional over nothing.

Steve rubbed a hand over his face and cursed lightly under his breath.

"I wanted to tell you something during our honeymoon, but I think I'd better tell you now," he said, and reached into J.D.'s diaper bag and dragged out a diaper.

"Here."

He handed the diaper to her and thumbed a tear from her cheek.

"Perhaps you should practice on J.D. before summer comes."

Shit! What was he saying?

"You already know?" she asked, suddenly realizing he'd been toying with her when she'd been dropping hints in the stall.

"I found the baby name book under your pillow, and I peeked over your shoulder a few times when you were on the internet. Saw the baby furniture sites you were on and..."

His face was now only inches away from hers and she could see the glitter of tears in his eyes.

"I found the early pregnancy test wrapper when it conveniently fell out of the garbage bag the other day. Like I said you've been looking green around the gills too."

"So much for the healthy glow a pregnant woman is supposed to have," Emily said.

"You're always beautiful to me," he whispered softly.

She raised her gaze to his and finally recognized the look in his eyes. Disbelief.

"I never thought I could love you any more than I already do, but I do. You've made me the happiest man, Emmie. Beyond my wildest dreams."

Tears streamed down her cheeks. God, he was making her cry like a blubbering idiot. It was going to ruin all the pretty makeup her sisters-in-law had taken such great care to put on her this morning.

"Do you think you two can get married now?" Mathew chuckled from behind her. She peered over Steve's shoulder to see Steve's two brothers Mathew and Daniel standing there.

"You can show her how much you love her on the honeymoon." Daniel's amused voice echoed through the bathroom. A chorus of voices agreed.

Emily and Steve turned around to find Mathew, Daniel, Jo and a whole flood of faces with huge smiles peeking through the now wide-open bathroom doorway.

Steve gently kissed her on the cheek and brushed away more of the tears.

"Duty calls. Do you think you can handle getting married today?" he whispered.

Emily nodded, suddenly feeling a whole hell of a lot better again.

"Okay let's get this show on the road, sweet baby."

He winked at her and then threw both hands in the air and headed for his brothers.

"Give me high-five, bros. I'm joining the ranks of fatherhood."

Cheers and slaps reverberated throughout the bathroom and Emily knew she was the happiest woman in the world.

The End

Mini Catalog

Jan Springer ~ Erotic Romance ~

Intimate Lover
Intimate Secrets Book One
Jan Springer
One stormy night an injured fugitive with amnesia forces his way into Sara Clarke's wilderness home...
SARA LIVES ALONE IN the isolated wilderness of Canada...until one stormy night when an injured fugitive forces his way into her home. He's dangerous, sexy-as-sin and unleashes lusty cravings she

never knew she had. Although there can be no future with a man on the run, she's willing to do whatever it takes to keep him in her life and in her bed.

She smells of sweet peppermint and makes him burn with hot desires. He wants her, needs her and yearns to forget the terror-filled flashbacks that haunt him. Crooked cops hold the key to his mysterious past, and if he's ever going to give Sara a future they both crave, he'll have to prove his innocence, and that means facing his dangerous past head on.

Includes a yummy Peppermint Cheesecake with Whipped Cream Recipe!

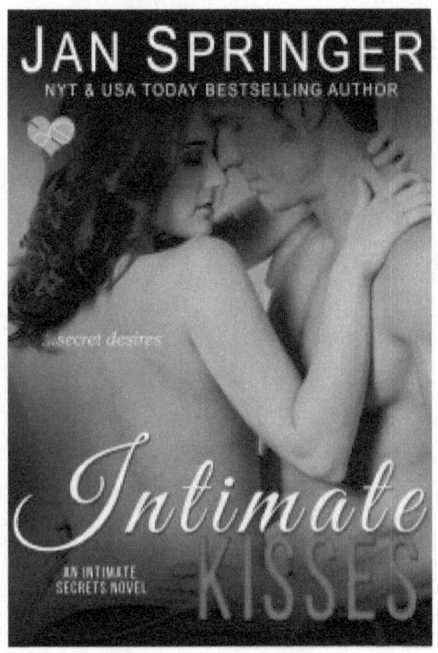

Intimate Kisses
Intimate Secrets Book 2
Jan Springer
Betrayed by her one-night stand...

MIND-BLOWING PLEASURE during a one-night stand makes Jo Brady fall hard for a sexy stranger she meets in a bar. But when he turns out to be the defense lawyer who helps free the murderer of a friend, Jo is devastated and vows her revenge.

Years later, private detective Jo Brady is hired to locate the same lawyer who, to her horror, will soon be her brother-in-law. Reluctantly she rescues the future best man from kidnappers and they're thrown together in a fight for their lives.

Being near his sexy rescuer fills Daniel McCullen with seductive visions of the one unforgettable night they shared. On the run from crooked cops and an evil transplant surgeon who wants them dead,

Jo and Daniel spend their days evading danger and their nights fighting their attraction for each other.

When Daniel discovers Jo is hiding secrets, he's suddenly not sure if she is friend...or foe.

Cowboys For Christmas
Cowboys Online 1 ~ Moose Ranch
Jan Springer
A Canadian Contemporary Ménage Romance m/f/m/m Series

• • ⚬⌘⚬ • •

Jennifer Jane (JJ) Watson has spent the past ten Christmases in a
maximum-security prison.
The last thing she expects is to get early parole, along with a job on a
remote Canadian cattle ranch serving Christmas holiday dinners to
three of the sexiest cowboys she's ever met!

Rafe, Brady and Dan thought they were getting a couple of male ex-cons to help out around their secluded ranch, but instead they get an attractive and very appealing female.

In the snowbound wilds of Northern Ontario, female companionship is rare.

It's a good thing the three men like to share...

They're dominating, sexy-as-sin and they fill JJ with the hottest ménage fantasies she's ever had. Suddenly she's craving cowboys for Christmas and wishing for something she knows she can never have...a happily ever after.

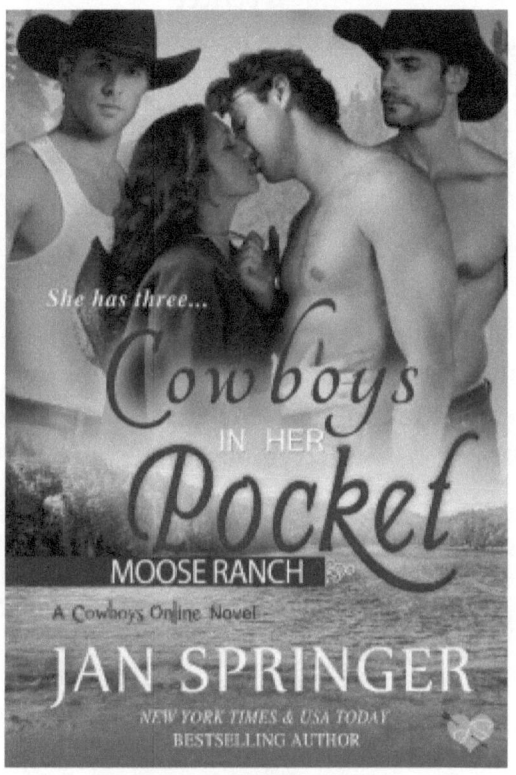

Cowboys In Her Pocket
Cowboys Online 2 ~ Moose Ranch
Jan Springer

After spending ten years in a maximum-security prison Jennifer Jane (JJ) Watson got early parole and a job on a remote Canadian cattle ranch playing housekeeper to three of the sexiest cowboys she's ever met...

Spring has finally arrived at Moose Ranch, and a single woman fresh out of prison shouldn't be experiencing scorching ménages with her three sexy-as-sin cowboys. But JJ's love for her men continues to grow as she gives into the fevered heat and scorching passions she feels for each of them.

Life is perfect.

Until her new life is tested when mysterious happenings occur on the ranch and then one of her cowboys is viciously attacked and injured. Will JJ's newfound freedom and happiness be ripped away?

Rafe, Brady and Dan never expected to find an attractive and very appealing female to help them out at their secluded ranch. But in the wilds of Northern Ontario, female companionship is rare. It's a good thing the three men like to share...

Brady, Dan and Rafe have never been happier. Their cattle ranch is flourishing and their continued desire to share the sexy woman who cares for them makes their life complete. Until danger threatens to rip everything apart...

Loving Her Cowboys
Cowboys Online 3 ~ Moose Ranch
Jan Springer

AFTER SPENDING TEN years in a maximum-security prison Jennifer Jane (JJ) Watson got early parole and a job on a remote Canadian cattle ranch playing housekeeper to three of the sexiest cowboys she's ever met...

Her love for her cowboys continues to grow as she gives into fevered heat. But JJ's simmering restlessness explodes and she's seriously making up for lost time by pursuing her dreams. There's only one little problem. She hasn't revealed to her bosses what she's been up to while they're away tending to the cattle. She knows when they discover her secret, there will be hell to pay.

Ranchers Rafe, Dan and Brady have found the woman who completes them. She makes their secluded ranch a home-sweet-home. She's vulnerable, sweet and willing to share her bed with all three of them. But when JJ's secret is unwittingly revealed, they're stunned and angry. They figure it's time to dole out some fiery punishment in some mighty naughty ways...

• • ❧ • •

Cowboys In Her Heart
Cowboys Online #4

• • ❧ • •

AFTER SPENDING TEN years in a maximum-security prison, JJ gets unexpected parole and a job on a Canadian ranch serving up scrumptious dinners and lots of hot love to three of the sexiest cowboys she's ever met.

Jennifer Jane "JJ" Watson has never been happier. She's going to have a baby!

Thankfully their wilderness ranch is a nice distraction for her three sexy cowboys while she's away flying her plane. But when she's home, her dominant hunks are tending to her naughty pregnant cravings and that includes plenty of sizzling ménages.

Rafe, Brady and Dan don't much like the idea of their woman flying the Canadian skies and being at the mercy of the unpredictable Northern Ontario weather. They would prefer having her warming their beds twenty-four seven. But she has a way of getting what she wants and right now she needs her new-found freedom.

Worst fears are realized when JJ, her friend and JJ's plane suddenly go missing and she doesn't come back home to them.

Always Her Cowboys
Cowboys Online 5 ~ Moose Ranch

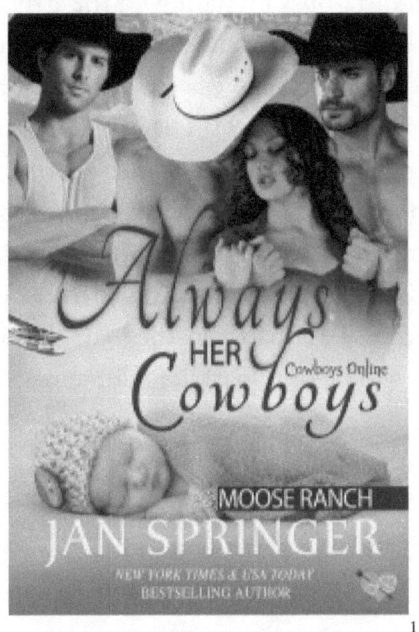

Reader Advisory: Best to read JJ's story in order. 1. Cowboys for Christmas, 2. Cowboys in Her Pocket, 3. Loving Her Cowboys, 4.Cowboys in Her Heart, 5. Always Her Cowboys. Enjoy!

A Canadian Contemporary Ménage Romance m/f/m/m

JENNIFER JANE (JJ) Watson has spent ten Christmases in a maximum-security prison. The last thing she expected was to get early parole, along with a job on a remote Canadian cattle ranch serving Christmas holiday dinners to three of the sexiest cowboys she's ever met!

Rafe, Brady and Dan thought they were getting male ex-cons to help out around their secluded ranch, but instead they got an attractive and very appealing female. In the snowbound wilds of Northern Ontario, female companionship is rare. It's a good thing the three men like to share...

---

1. https://janspringerauthor.files.wordpress.com/2017/11/alwayshercowboys_ebook-1new.jpg

Christmas is coming once again to Moose Ranch and with JJ's due date approaching, she's distracting herself from anxiety attacks by keeping herself ultra-busy preparing for the arrival of her baby and planning Moose Ranch's first annual Christmas party!

In having a wee baby on the way, there's a lot of stress for Brady, Rafe and Dan. Especially due to JJ's decision on having a wilderness mid-wife deliver the baby *at their secluded ranch* - with *all* of them present for the birth! But their concerns don't stop the men from showing JJ how much they love her...out of bed and in!

With wicked snowstorms, a grounded bush plane, a cheerful holiday party and a sweet baby on the way, the owners of Moose Ranch know this will be one sparkling Christmas season they won't soon forget...

Risqué Girl Delights Boxed Set
(Contemporary Erotic Romance)

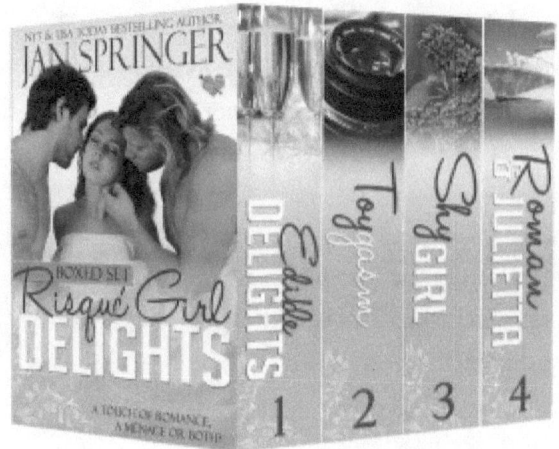

...a touch of romance, a ménage or both?

Edible Delights

YEARS AGO ALLIE MASTERS lost herself in the scorching passion of a ménage a trois relationship with her two bosses. In order to regain her independence, she walked away.

Max and Nick were very fulfilled with their gorgeous assistant. The lovemaking was breathtaking and both men willingly shared the woman they wanted to spend the rest of their lives with. Then she left.

Now Max and Nick have decided it's time to seduce Allie back into their lives.

• • ⚓ • •

Toygasm

---

2. https://janspringerauthor.files.wordpress.com/2015/02/
rgdelights_box_js_3d_noshadow-1.jpg

IT'S A CASE OF MISTAKEN identity when the two owners of Sexy Toys, show up for an erotic several day photo shoot of their toys with famous nude model Cammie Creek.

Cammie believes the two hunks are the male models she's supposed to work with. Usually she doesn't mix business with pleasure, but when they're seducing her right there in front of the camera, she can't resist turning them into her own personal naughty toys.

Josh and Jode are enjoying the perks of being male models; hot lust, sizzling toys and the best pleasure they've ever had. But how will Cammie react when she discovers they're actually her bosses and not just male models?

• • ❧ • •

Shy Girl

FINALLY FREE OF AN abusive relationship, "Shy Girl" Emma McCall sheds her inhibitions and explores her sensual side at Club Rendezvous, a club specializing in the Alternate Lifestyle.

At the club she's surprised to find Logan Masters, a sexy hunk she's secretly fantasized about since college. With Logan's help, Emma will experience her ultimate fantasy - a scorching ménage a trois.

• • ❧ • •

Roman and Julietta

HER PERFECT LOVER...

Modern day pirate Julietta Black's life has always been immersed in the violent and traditional ways of piracy. When her family's arch enemy puts a hit out on her family, Julietta knows there's only one way to lift the hit; she must kidnap the enemy's sexy grandson and force a union between the two warring families. Night after night, wrapped in Roman's strong arms, she can't deny the searing attraction blazing between them. Nor can she deny he now holds her heart as well as her life in his hands.

His dream angel...

When Roman Prince's mysterious captor offers him a luscious woman to bed, fierce desire ignites, melting his usually tight self-control. Lust quickly turns to love as he enjoys their naughty trysts more than he should. How will he react when he discovers he's been kidnapped, not for a ransom, but captured for his sperm?

Alpha Outlaws Boxed Set (Books 1-5 Outlaw Lovers)
5 Books!!

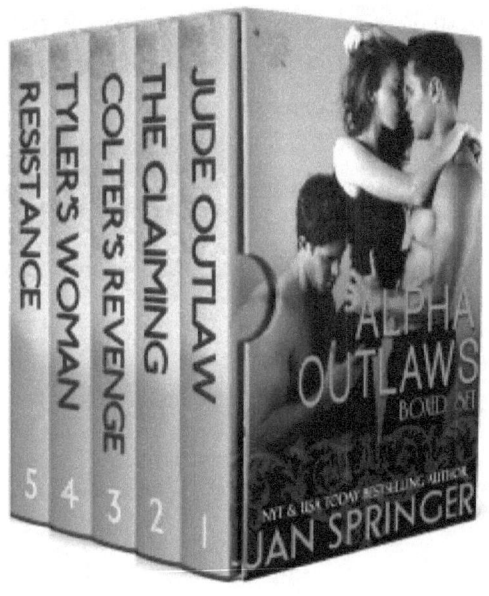

3

IN A WORLD GONE MAD...

A fast-acting virus has killed a majority of the world's female population. With the creation of The Claiming Law, groups of men suddenly have the right to claim a female as their sensual property and the sexy Outlaw brothers are going to declare ownership of the women they love...any way they can.

Jude Outlaw

When Cate Callahan learns Jude is coming home from the Terrorist Wars and is ready to claim her under the new law—with the help of his four brothers—she steals their boat and escapes to the high seas. Unfortunately, her runaway bid for freedom doesn't last long.

Quickly capturing his lover, Jude rekindles the flames and seduces Cate back into his bed.

But Jude holds a secret that could make him lose Cate forever...

PLUS

The Claiming

Seeking refuge from the Claiming Law, Callie Callahan hides in a deserted cabin in the Maine woods and is shocked when her ex-flame finds her. She's always craved being in Luke Outlaw's arms. Tasting him. Touching him. Taking him deeply within her. So, what's a girl to do but to delve into the sinful delights he offers.

Luke has finally reunited with the love of his life. He knows there is only one way to keep Callie safe and with him forever. He'll do it with the help of his three brothers and an assortment of naughty toys. Rekindling the flames between them, he unleashes Callie's sensual side, taking her in ways she never dreamed possible, all with the ultimate goal of introducing her to the Outlaw Lovers and The Claiming.

Colter's Revenge

Revenge belongs to Dr. Colter Outlaw when he unexpectedly reunites with the beautiful woman who broke his heart during the Terrorist Wars. Capturing her, collaring her and holding her against her will, he seduces her, fills her with wicked desires and naughty cravings for a delicious ménage. Fully intent on breaking her heart and walking away, Colter's plans unravel when he submits to the carnal pleasures Ashley gives him so freely.

Colter had told her he loved her. He'd whispered promises of rescue from her life as a slave, but when he'd suddenly disappeared, she'd been devastated. Infected with a version of the X-virus that leaves Ashley Blakely sexually excited on a daily basis, she has come to Pleasure Palace to bid on a cure for her illness. She never expected her Outlaw Lover to be there and screw her plans. Nor did she expect to give him her heart and body so easily...

Tyler's Woman

For years Tyler Outlaw and his best friend, Hunter Brown, endured brutal torture and worse in an overseas terrorist prison. Finally, free of their hell, they return home intent on seducing Laurie into their erotic-filled fantasies.

Laurie Callahan has always experienced red-hot pleasure and passionate love in Tyler Outlaw's arms. But when he's pronounced MIA, presumed dead in the Terrorist Wars, Laurie's world is shattered, and her heart is broken.

Shocked to discover Tyler is alive and he's taken a male lover, Laurie is thrust into a sensual world of sizzling seductions, scorching ménages and the carnal desires that both scarred men crave. But she fears Tyler won't want her when he discovers she's not the same woman he left behind...

****READER CAUTION IS ADVISED (m/m forced scenes) ****

Resistance

In the near future, a virus has been unleashed, killing a majority of the world's female population, forcing the introduction of the Claiming Law. A law that states men have all the rights and women are sexual property claimable by groups of men.

Fugitive female...

Renegade Resistance leader Reena "Red" Wilde is in for the fight of her life when she experiences an erotic attraction to the two most dangerous men she's ever met.

Black ops assassin...

Months ago, Will "Blade" Smith spent one sizzling evening in the arms of a red-haired seductress. Now she's his next assignment. One look into her gorgeous eyes and he's wrestling his heated cravings for her all over again.

Bounty Hunter...

When Cade Outlaw nabs his bounty, sexy-as-sin Reena Wilde, his profession dictates she's hands-off. But he can't ignore the magnetic sparks between them...or that she is the biggest temptation of his life.

Resistance is futile...

After Reena escapes Cade and Will and falls prey to a band of evil hunters, she's grateful her sexy hunks come to her rescue...and in return, saves their lives. Trapped in a solitary cabin during a wicked snowstorm, she can't resist her two, well-hung studs, nor can she deny they've claimed her heart.

Jasmine Black ~Erotica~

Here are some more Jasmine Black ebooks...

Taken by Two Cowboys

• • ◦∞◦ • •

Sierra Allan works hard at her late-father's horse ranch. When her step-brother adds her handy girl services to a private auction to help raise money for the failing ranch, she figures there's no harm...but she's stunned when her services are sold to two sexy cowboys who give her an erotic way to save the ranch—submitting to their dark desires..

Taken by Three Billionaires

• • ❧ • •

Billionaire friends, Liam, Theo and Elijah have just won Princess Isabella in a billionaire card game. Isabella knows exactly what the three men will want from her...she just hadn't expected to have all three of them at once!

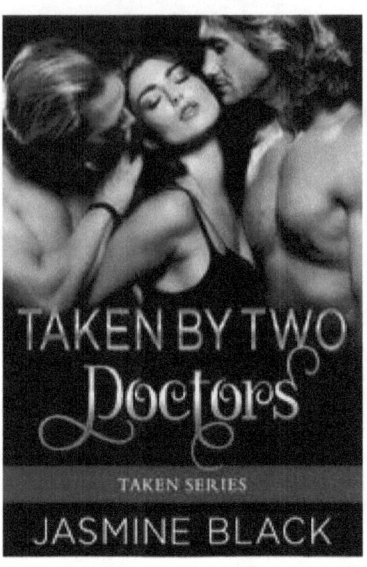

Taken by Two Doctors
A BDSM Medical Fetish Erotica Quickie MFM

• • ⧯ • •

Waitress Jean Spelling visits her controversial doctor once a month for some much-needed...stress relief. She looks forward to putting her feet up in the stirrups and enjoys Dr. Ball's naughty unconventional treatments. This time when she arrives, she's surprised to discover that she'll be physically examined by two doctors and they'll prescribe her some much-needed release right there on the examination table!

eBooks in the Ménage series
Taken by Three Bikers
Taken by Three Billionaires
Taken by Three Doctors
Taken by Three Cowboys

•• ➷ ••

eBooks in the Taken series
Taken by Two Doctors
Taken by Two Firefighters
Taken by Two Bikers
Taken by Two Billionaires
Taken by Two Bosses
Taken by Two Cowboys
Taken by Two Personal Trainers
Taken by Two Carpenters

•• ➷ ••

Jasmine Black Website ~ http://www.jasmine-black.com
Twitter ~ @blackerotica1

More from Jan Springer

~

Many more Jasmine Black and Jan Springer ebooks, print books,
audiobooks plus translated ebooks and print books can be found at
http://www.janspringer.com

Here are ways we can connect:

Jasmine Black Website at http://janspringerauthor.wordpress.com/jasmine-black/

Jan Springer Website at http://www.janspringer.com[1]

Instagram – http://www.instagram.com/janspringerauthor

Facebook - https://www.facebook.com/janspringereroticromance

Twitter Jan Springer- https://twitter.com/janspringer @janspringer

Twitter Jasmine Black - https://twitter.com/blackerotica1 @blackerotica1

Pinterest - http://www.pinterest.com/janspringer1/

Jan's Blog - http://janspringerauthor.wordpress.com/blog-2/

Happy Reading,

Jasmine Black / Jan Springer

---

1.   http://www.janspringer.com/

Don't miss out!

Visit the website below and you can sign up to receive emails whenever Jan Springer publishes a new book. There's no charge and no obligation.

https://books2read.com/r/B-A-WGQ-JKSBB

BOOKS 2 READ

Connecting independent readers to independent writers.

www.ingramcontent.com/pod-product-compliance
Lightning Source LLC
Chambersburg PA
CBHW051548250626
47157CB00001B/225